AIR FORCE TWO WAS MISSING!

When last contacted, Air Force Two, with the Vice-President of the United States aboard, was flying high over the Philippine jungle.

On board was not only the Vice-President, but the "football" that gave him the power to initiate nuclear war. For in Washington, D.C., the U.S. President lay dying.

At Clark Air Force Base, the orders went out. Air Force Two, aloft or downed, had to be found. The Vice-President, alive or dead, had to be brought back.

The hunt was on. The race against time and the ultimate terror had begun . . . in an action-packed military thriller of supersonic suspense and explosive excitement—

STRIKE EAGLE

Buckle yourself in and hang on tight!

STRIKE EAGLE

Doug Beason

A SIGNET BOOK

To those that have lived in the Philippines

Published by the Penguin Group
Penguin Books USA Inc., 375 Hudson Street,
New York, New York 10014, U.S.A.
Penguin Books Ltd, 27 Wrights Lane,
London W8 5TZ, England
Penguin Books Australia Ltd, Ringwood,
Victoria, Australia
Penguin Books Canada Ltd, 10 Alcorn Avenue,
Toronto, Ontario, Canada M4V 3B2
Penguin Books (N.Z.) Ltd, 182–190 Wairau Road,
Auckland 10, New Zealand

Penguin Books Ltd, Registered Offices:
Harmondsworth, Middlesex, England

First published by Signet, an imprint of New American Library,
a division of Penguin Books USA Inc.

First Printing, October, 1991
10 9 8 7 6 5 4 3 2 1

PUBLISHER'S NOTE
This is a work of fiction. Names, characters, places, and incidents
either are the product of the author's imagination or are used ficti-
tiously, and any resemblance to actual persons, living or dead, events,
or locales is entirely coincidental.

Acknowledgments

To Kevin J. Anderson and Michael Berch, Esq. for their editorial insight and suggestions; Colonel Terry "Moose" Millard, Lieutenant Colonel "Mongo" Monahan, Major Dave Harris and the 1550th Combat Crew Training Wing, Major Wayne Crist and the 3rd TFW, Captain Jim Beason, and Alan Gould for their technical details; Richard Curtis and John Sibersack for making this happen; Billy Joel's "Storm Front," for inspiration; and Tamara, Amanda and Cindy—as always—for being there and putting up with me.

Principal Characters

The Family

First Lieutenant (1Lt) Bruce Steele, USAF (ASSASSIN)

Ashley Woodman—Bruce's ex-wife

Joe Steele—Bruce's father

Cheryl Steele—his mother

Fred Steele—his (deceased) younger brother

The Boys

Captain Charlie Fargassamo (FOGGY)—Bruce's backseater

CATMAN (1Lt Ed Holstrom)—F-15E pilot, Maddog 3

ROBIN (2Lt Steve Garcioni)—CATMAN's backseater

SKIPPER (Capt Thorin A. Olsen)—"Maddog" Flight Commander, Maddog 1

COUGAR (Capt Emmanuel Y. Bonita)—SKIPPER's backseater

RHINO (Capt Harley Rheinquist)—F-15E pilot, Maddog 2

DIGGER (1Lt Lucius Brown)—RHINO's backseater

Clark Air Base

Lt Col McConnell—Squadron Commander, 3rd Tac Fighter Squadron

Ms. Hosteader—Housing counselor

Capt Richard Head—MH-60G helicopter pilot (FOX 1)

Capt Bob Gould—MH-60G co-pilot

Tech Sgt Noresteader—Bruce's crew chief

Capt Uberlang—F-15C pilot, Kadena AFB, Okinawa

CMSGT Grune—Instructor, Jungle Survival School

Abuj Qyantrolo—Negrito jungle survival instructor

SSgt Zazbrewski—MH-60G flight engineer

SSgt Hank McCormack—MH-60G gunner

SSgt Sal Flores—MH-60G gunner

Maj Gen Peter Simone—Commander, Thirteenth Air Force

Major Steve Hendhold—his aide

Col William F. Bolte (LIGHTNING)—Commander, 3rd TAC Fighter Wing

Michele Bolte—his wife

Nanette Bolte—his daughter

SSgt Evette Whiltee—Air Traffic Controller

CMSGT Figarno—her supervisor

Major Brad Dubois—3rd TFW Flight Scheduler

TSgt Merkowitz—Gate Guard

Col Ben Lutler—Commander, 353d Special Operations Wing

Juanita Sanchez—Major General Simone's secretary

Other Locations

Major Kathy Yulok—SR-71 pilot, Kadena AFB, Okinawa

Major Ed Prsybalwyki—SR-71 co-pilot, Kadena AFB, Okinawa

Admiral Greshan, USN—Fleet Admiral 7th Fleet, Subic Bay, P.I.

Gen Westschloe—Commander, Pacific Air Forces, Hickam AFB, HI

Chaplain (Commander) White, USN—Base Chaplain, Subic Bay

Taco Charlie—Okinawan restaurant owner

Oniksuki—Taco Charlie's grandson

Soloette Arquine—Agency operative, South Korea

Roger Epstein—Agency Station Chief, South Korea

Yan Kawnleno—North Korean terrorist

Minister Ieyasu—Japanese Minister of Trade

Col Alan Merke—Division Vice-Commander, Kadena AFB

President Rizular—President of the P.I.

Col Pat Wingate—Aircraft Commander, Air Force Two

Colonel Rader—Deputy for Operations, 313th Air Division, Kadena AFB, Okinawa

Angeles City

Yolanda Sicat

Pompano Sicat—her father

Lucila Sicat—his deceased wife

Ceravant Escindo—New People's Army (NPA) cell leader

Barguyo—NPA terrorist

Edgar—NPA terrorist

Julio—NPA terrorist

Tanila—Bruce's father's girlfriend

Emil Oloner—black market runner

Washington, D.C.

Lucius K. Longmire—President of the U.S.

Robert E. Adleman—Vice-President of the U.S. (LONESTAR)

LtCol Merke, USAF—VP Adleman's aide

Harley Dubois—Secret Service agent

Cyndi Fount—Director, CIA

Francis Woodrow Acht—Secretary of State

Jerry Weinstein—Chairman, National Demoractic Party

Ensign Julia Clounch—President's nurse

Captain (Dr.) Barnett—Commanding Officer, Bethesda Hospital

Ebert Zering—Secretary of Defense

General David Newman, USAF—Chief of Staff, Joint Chiefs of Staff

Juan Salaguiz—White House Press Secretary

Mr. Kelt—State Department Philippine Specialist

PROLOGUE

Fifteen miles south of Bagio City,
Philippine Islands

Ceravant watched the road, waiting for the convoy, and wondered what it felt like to die.

Lying on a tightly braided grass mat, he had wedged himself far enough back from the crest to make himself invisible from below. Propped in front of him, between the roots of a towering tree, his M-16 had a direct line of shot to any point on the road. It was the only direction that Ceravant could see for more than two feet without being smothered by the dense jungle.

A fine mist filled the air, pushing the humidity up so high he thought he would have to pull out a machete and chop his way through it. Broad leaves collected the mist, pooling the liquid into thimble-sized drops before the weight of the water became too great for the leaf to hold. Thousands of such leaves filled the jungle; together, they produced a symphony of random drips. Birds chattered high up in the trees, adding to the cacophony. Ceravant couldn't hear any other sounds as he waited for the convoy.

He shifted his weight on the mat. An array of grenades hanging from his belt poked him in the thigh; he wiggled to push them out of the way, and soon was comfortable again.

Water drenched Ceravant, but he had grown used

to it as he waited for the precise moment to strike, as if he were the feared *habu*, the stealthy jungle snake that struck without warning.

A faint sound caught his attention. It came from below, channeled down the foliage-canopied road like a whistle blast through a pipe. Ceravant grew alert. The birds stopped chirping, leaving only the eerie sound of splashing water.

He crept forward by pulling himself on his elbows. As he gripped the M-16, he swung the rifle back and forth across the road, ensuring latitude in his view. The sound grew louder: the unmistakable roar of trucks, the groaning of diesel engines as they chugged up the mountain road. The road narrowed to one lane just around the bend. He knew the drivers would be using parabolic mirrors, set by the curve, to see if any vehicles would be approaching from the opposite direction.

Ceravant could not hear his compatriots, but he knew that around him three dozen men were preparing for the attack. The fine wires that led to patches on the road, plastique, were the sole signs of the men's presence.

Ceravant wished he had situated himself closer to the young man Barguyo—a boy no older than fourteen—who would throw the switch and detonate the explosives when the armored personnel carrier appeared; but Ceravant had too many items to take care of, and not enough of himself to go around.

It was the hardest lesson he had to learn: assigning responsibilities to the Huks and allowing them to work alone. It was a far cry from the way things used to be, but their ability to strike bigger targets, penetrate deeper into the establishment, had increased tremendously.

Ceravant was no longer a one-man operation, and the lessons pounded into him in the training camps north of the South Korean border would meet its first big test today. If the Huks were going to survive and turn things around, it had to start now. They had to strike the Philippine Constabulary at the very heart of its operation and steal the weapons that had been tapped to ferret out the Huks.

Ceravant could now make out the sounds of individual vehicles. The engine running at high gear had to be the jeep that preceded the convoy. It would be well ahead of the main body, and it should soon pass. The deeper roar came from troop and supply trucks, belching black smoke and grinding their gears in an attempt to climb the four-thousand-foot rise to Bagio City. Ceravant wiggled to his side and pulled up five grenades. He left three hanging on his belt, in case the group had to flee back into the jungle and use the explosives for a makeshift booby trap.

Seconds passed. Ceravant wet his lips. It sounded as if the jeep were right on top of them. . . .

The vehicle pulled around the bend. Five men sat in the overloaded jeep, rifles held loosely. All but the driver smoked cigarettes. The jeep took the corner recklessly, eliciting wild laughter from the passengers. The soldiers knew they were near their base. It was just the state of mind Ceravant had hoped for: If the convoy's commanding officers were jocular, then the troops would be in a similar vein.

When the jeep disappeared from view, Ceravant's grip on his rifle tightened. The humidity continued to bear down on him; sweat rolled off his nose, but aside from an occasional wipe to remove the perspiration, Ceravant focused on the road. Waiting.

A puff of black smoke gave the first troop truck away. As it rounded the curve, the driver honked its horn to warn approaching vehicles of its presence. The truck lurched; a grinding sound came from the vehicle as the driver shifted to a lower gear. There would be more trucks, and Ceravant had to wait for the precise one—too soon, and the convoy would combine forces and flush the Huks out; too late, and the convoy would speed up to outrun the ambush.

Another truck passed, full of PC—the Filipino Philippine Constabulary troops, heading for their home base.

Ceravant counted the tenth truck before he decided. The driver had just put his cigarette back in his mouth and expelled a cloud of smoke when Ceravant pulled the trigger.

The windshield shattered into a thousand pieces. Gunfire erupted everywhere, enveloping the once peaceful jungle in a barrage of white noise.

The truck veered wildly and flipped off the side of the road. It barreled through the brush and disappeared. Screams came from all around. The next truck did not have a chance to slow down. Blasts of gunfire peppered the air. The truck somehow managed to weave along the narrow road, then drove into the side of the mountain.

Ceravant rammed a new cartridge of bullets into the M-16, throwing the spent package to the side. He continued to pump bullets at the next truck. Soldiers leapt from the truck and scurried down the hillside; those who stopped to take aim at Ceravant's unseen companions were mowed down in a barrage.

Nothing came from up the road—the small PC contingent that had turned back to assist had encountered gunfire from the Huks stationed on the hill.

Ceravant waited for a full ten heartbeats before yelling the order to search the vehicle, but an armored personnel carrier crept around the bend. Bullets ricocheted off the vehicle. Ceravant wet his lips. He hoped that the boy Barguyo would not hurry, would wait until the precise moment. . . .

The APC stayed in its lowest gear, grinding up the steep roadway, and firing bursts from an exterior gun mount. As the vehicle crept over the wires in the road, the plastique exploded. The APC lifted slightly off the ground, then stopped moving.

Ceravant struggled to his feet, pulling the M-16 up with him. He flung himself down the slope and raced to the APC. Smoke billowed from underneath the vehicle. Muffled screams came from the APC's interior. As Ceravant moved to the vehicle, Huks started pouring out from the jungle. The men clutched various types of rifles, and ranged in age from preteen to late middle-aged.

Ceravant pulled a grenade from his side. He snapped at the men still coming from the jungle. "Quickly, the supply truck!" He pointed with the grenade to the truck that had careened into the side of the hill.

Dropping his rifle, Ceravant scrambled on top of the armored vehicle. He tried to open the APC hatch, but when the access did not give, he pushed his foot against the lever and kicked; the hatch barely creaked open. He pulled the grenade pin with his teeth.

A voice wailed from the vehicle in Tagalog: "Mother Maria, please help me!"

Ceravant tossed the grenade into the APC, then leaped to the ground, running. When he was thirty feet from the APC, a muffled explosion rocked the area; the screaming inside the vehicle stopped.

A horn beeped down the road.

Seconds later a truck driven by a Huk sympathizer roared into view. The old man driving the truck slammed on his brakes at the sight of the smoking armored personnel carrier. Ceravant motioned at the man.

"Pompano! Get as close to the truck as you can."

As Pompano crept forward, Ceravant huffed up to the supply vehicle.

Two Huks threw wooden crates from the truck. Some cracked open, spilling bullets and rifles. Pompano positioned his truck, and a line of men quickly filled it with crates.

Ceravant pulled himself inside the PC supply truck and made a quick scan for anything they should take. Several large crates caught his eye. He felt his pulse quicken at the prospect of finding some missiles. As he scrambled over the jumble of crates, he made out stenciled lettering written in English:

United States Army
Battlefield High-Power Microwave Weapon
Caution: Capacitors May Carry High Voltage!

The boy Barguyo stuck his head in the back of the truck: "Hurry, we are ready!"

Ceravant pulled himself up. The gunshots grew louder. The Huks had taken nearly all the supplies . . . yet this "high-power microwave" device intrigued him. He snapped out, "Quickly, get me some help— we must take this with us."

Moments later, Ceravant was sitting in the rear with his comrades. Their spirits were high, and understandably so: bullets, rifles, and enough supplies to last the band of Huks six months. The truck bounced as it sped down the winding mountain road.

Ceravant rummaged through the crates. Every new find heightened his elation: ammunition, food packets, medical supplies.

Finally, he pulled out a thick manual. Written in English with large print, the title read:

User's manual for United States Army Battlefield
High-Power Microwave

Situation Room, White House

The Cabinet stood as President Longmire hobbled in, escorted by his nurse. The President entered with his head bent. Clear tubes emanated from his nostril and a bottle of oxygen trailed behind him.

Vice-President Adleman watched from the oval table, reaching out a hand as the President approached. Once strong hands grasped the Vice-President's. Adleman spoke in a low voice. "Are you all right?"

President Longmire waved Adleman aside as he sat. "Let's get on with it." Then, wearily, "Take it, will you, Cyndi? Why don't you start."

A tall, dark-haired woman nodded to the President as she pushed back her chair and stood. Wearing a dark suit, skirt, and subdued jewelry, Cyndi Fount strode to the front of the chamber and waited in front of a large TV screen. She seemed to command respect, with a no-nonsense presence and an unsmiling face. As Director of the CIA, Cyndi had ruled the Agency with an iron fist, turning the Ivy League Mafia into one of the most efficiently run government organizations.

Vice-President Robert Adleman leaned back in his chair and tapped his fingers, waiting for the President to return Cyndi's glance. He studied the CIA Director: quiet, efficient, slim—no, *lithe* was the word. The word seemed to convey a willowiness, an exotic character.

The President waved a feeble hand. "Go on, Cyndi."

A slide appeared in the TV monitor; a drawing of an eagle's head with the words CENTRAL INTELLI-GENCE AGENCY blocked in blue filled the screen.

"Mr. President, no changes in status since yesterday." The screen behind her flashed with locations, numbers, and mnemonics, listing local operations and operatives. She ran through a quick update of the usual hot spots of activity.

Adleman continued to tap his fingers as Cyndi spoke in clipped sentences.

There were no surprises here. He had seen a "talking paper" on the briefings just a half hour earlier, and skimmed through the presentations to be given by Intelligence, Defense, and State. He made a point of staying on top of everything. But he strived to anticipate the direction that events would take and have a contingency ready just in case. His enthusiasm was infectious, and his staff was ready to follow him off a cliff if necessary—and not because of his good looks or his longish blond hair. Rather, he radiated charisma, fueled by a seemingly boundless supply of energy.

He quickly reviewed the events scheduled for that day. Church socials, supermarket openings, and press interviews weren't the most exciting activities, but he was grooming an image, one of competence and élan to get the job done. Everything would fall into place with sufficient exuberance. It was a sure mark of presidential material to look beyond the mundane duties of the Vice-Presidency, and strive to *excel* in those same mundane responsibilities.

Adleman almost missed Cyndi's concluding remarks, but her inflection pulled him out of his thoughts.

"Although the last item isn't part of the Agency's agenda, I feel that it has a propensity to affect our operatives and thus deserves your attention."

President Longmire coughed violently, expelling fluid. His nurse hastily wiped up the majority of the spittle. He wheezed and motioned for the CIA Director to continue.

Adleman raised his eyebrows at the exchange. The President's health had worsened lately, contrary to the glowing reports given to the press. Adleman pressed his lips together as Cyndi concluded her briefing.

"The lease extension to cover our military bases in the Philippines runs out at the end of the next calender year. The extension was originally granted in 1991, but there has been no progress since then on a permanent treaty. The administration has being going round and round on this for years, and—"

"Mr. President, Ms. Fount is correct. This is a matter for State," interrupted Francis Acht, "and not the CIA."

Adleman bit his lip at the exchange. Like everyone else in the room, he thought that Secretary Acht was an egotistical boor—but the man knew his stuff, and would win any altercation. Many despised his demeanor, yet respected his insight.

Longmire spoke quietly, plunging the room into silence so his words could be understood. "*Please* continue, Cyndi."

Acht promptly shut his mouth. The CIA Director continued without breaking stride.

"The United States has been debating the Philippine question for several years now, Mr. President. We have reason to believe that the leases will not be extended. The Filipinos will play hardball. I don't have to go into the implications of the importance of the lease—losing the Philippines as a staging area will not only result in degrading our ability to project naval and air power, but will adversely affect our intelligence operations in the Far East. *That* is my concern."

Acht tapped a pencil on the table. The sound echoed around the chamber and focused attention on the Secretary of State. "It more than threatens our military options in the Far East, Mr. President. After all, we've nearly lost Clark. It affects the entire Pacific Rim, the security of a hemisphere. If something happens in the Philippines, it's not a sure bet that we will come out on top. Maintaining our bases there is a critical necessity—the threat to the U.S. would probably not be an immediate military one, but something far more drastic, and probably not even geopolitical: economic.

"The Pacific Rim is following Japan's lead, jockeying to dominate world economy," said Acht warily. "Malaysia, Korea, Taiwan, Hong Kong, New Guinea, and even Australia have all jumped on the bandwagon. Without a strong U.S. presence in the Philippine Islands, we would loose our *economic* foothold and become a mere player—and an outsider." He paused. "I concur with Ms. Fount's concern, but for a farther-reaching reason. As to how to do it," he shrugged, "I haven't a clue. We can't even keep our fighter aircraft there now for more than a few months at a time."

Silence; then, over wheezing, "What do you propose, Cyndi?"

"Immediate high-level negotiations. Negotiations in good faith and at a high level, to let the Filipinos know that we take them seriously."

Vice-President Adleman interrupted. "She's got a good point, Mr. President. The usual channels have been stalled for years. We've tried shipping more military aid to the Philippine forces—the PC, or Philippine Constabulary, they call it—in an attempt to free the log jam. Fifty million dollars over the last year."

Another voice spoke up, that of General Newman, Chairman of the Joint Chiefs. "That's an increase of twenty million, if you remember, Mr. President—the House upped the ante."

Secretary Acht swung his attention to the General. "Was that for new weapons, Dave?"

General Newman shook his head. "No, sir. Mostly supplies—ammunition, rifles, that sort of thing. The only new item we sent them was an HPM weapon—high-power microwave."

Adleman's eyebrows rose. "Why did we give them an HPM device?"

"We've had them in the field for years now. Besides, HPMs are only good against a certain class of targets—electronics, mines. And they're relatively short-ranged; the type we sent them isn't effective past five hundred yards. The Philippine Constabulary will only be able to use them to detonate land mines, but it still impresses the hell out of the Filipinos. It's a psychological coup: They are convinced we're giving them our state-of-the-art equipment, and in return they've given us leeway on extending the leases of our bases."

Acht nodded. "Good move, if it works."

President Longmire paused. "Cyndi, you said the negotiations should proceed at a high level. . . ." He moved his head and squinted at Adleman. "Bob, what do you think?"

Adleman straightened; his mind clicked into high gear, assimilating events from the past few days. "She's right, Mr. President. Decisive negotiations— and I'm probably the one that should sign the deal. We should push this now, take the bull by the horns and come straight to the point with the Philippine government. Regardless of what we've said in public, the bases are too important to lose. Sending anyone below me to open the talks would be a slap in their face."

The Secretary of State placed his elbows on the table and extended his hands. "No high-level emissary has negotiated with the Philippines since Madame Aquino's visit, years ago. Properly briefed, Mr. Adleman could use his position to tilt the scales in our favor, wrap up a new treaty, and ensure our foothold in the Far East for the next three decades."

Longmire coughed again. He motioned with his hand to Adleman. "Bob, have Francis' people get you up to speed on the lease arrangements. Let's get you out there within three weeks."

He turned to General Newman, weakly. "How does that fit with the aid the Philippine Constabulary is getting, Dave?"

"They've got more than enough to last them, sir." He cracked a grin. "Bullets, rifles, blankets—you name it. And like I said, there's nothing for them to use the HPM weapon against, anyway."

Camp John Hay
Bagio, Philippine Islands

The Philippine Constabulary officer tapped a pencil on his desk. *The damned Huks*, he thought. *How do they keep doing this?* But he knew the answer—information was the most abundant commodity on the black market.

They had stolen one truck—ten percent of the total

convoy. And from only one convoy out of ten. Which meant the Huks now had one percent of the military aid given by the U.S. government.

The amount was miniscule, and a greater percentage of the aid would be missing during the next year from pilfering. The only missing item that disturbed the officer was the high-power microwave weapon. It was one out of five that the U.S. had sent.

The officer knew the percentages. And he also knew what had happened to the last officer who had commanded a unit that the Huks had raided.

He didn't want to be a scapegoat.

He stopped tapping his pencil. The PC Commandant would never learn of the missing truck. Men were constantly being kill during PC exercises, so that could be explained . . . even though seventeen dead men was an unusually high number. What the PC commander didn't know wouldn't hurt him.

CHAPTER 1

Friday, 1 June

Clark Air Base
Republic of The Philippine Islands

Clear and minus thirty degrees outside the cockpit window, thirty-five thousand feet above the ocean. Blue sky diffused into a mottled green where the jungle lay on the horizon. Five miles below them the Pacific Ocean looked like tiny ripples on a broad landscape of blue-green flatness, the clouds fluffy wisps. Strung out over a three-mile line flew five aircraft, four of them fighters, following a lumbering KC-10.

First Lieutenant Bruce Steele craned his neck around the cockpit of his F-15E Strike Eagle. Miniature color TV monitors were inlaid next to switches, buttons, and other instruments on the crowded cockpit panel. A heads-up display jutted up directly in front of him. Cockpit gray clashed against the rest of the color-filled outside world. He felt like he was flying a high-tech video game.

Bruce spotted the other aircraft by their contrails, dense white plumes of water vapor spewed from the engines. Just visible two hundred miles in front of him rose a volcanic hill, protruding thousands of feet above the surrounding jungle but still miles beneath the fighters. A voice came over his headphones.

"Maddog, Lead. Estimate 'feet dry' in twenty miles. Prepare to descend. Remain in loose route."

Bruce squinted out the cockpit to where the ocean ended. The "feet dry" warning confirmed Bruce's estimate that they'd soon fly over land. His helmet filled with the sounds of the other fighters confirming his orders. One after another the clipped replies came:

"Two."

"Three."

Bruce clicked his mike. "Four."

The lead aircraft kicked off a message to the Air Force version of the giant DC-10, the KC-10 tanker that had escorted them across the "pond," as the Pacific ocean was affectionately called. The dual-seated F-15E had a cruising range of more than twenty-eight hundred miles and could certainly make the hop over part of the pond—from Anderson AFB in Guam, where they had left some eight hours ago.

But Murphy's Law reigned supreme in the Air Force: If something was going to go wrong, then it usually did. So rather than have the fighters cross the long stretch of deep water alone, a KC-10 tanker accompanied the crafts and kept them refueled.

As the flight began to descend from its cruising altitude, Bruce heard the voice of his navigator and backseater, Charlie Fargassamo.

"I got a lock on the TACAN, 'sass-in." Charlie pronounced Bruce's call sign, "Assassin," in two syllables.

Bruce went "hot-mike": He flipped the mike to transmit within the fighter only. "That's a rog. Ready to stretch those legs?"

"You said it. I could piss for a week."

Bruce grinned. For the last eight hours he had been forced to use a "piddle pack" to urinate. Besides being inconvenient and uncomfortable, the device made Bruce nervous—he didn't like the possibility of loose liquid in the cockpit.

Charlie was another matter. The older man—by all of six years—refused to use the piddle pack, and instead opted to grit his teeth and bear it. When the

Wing Commander back at Luke Air Force Base had made the equipment mandatory, Charlie steadfastly refused to be "plugged in."

Charlie needed a little needling, just to drive the point home. "Twenty more minutes. Can you handle it, Foggy?"

Again, silence. Then weakly, "That's a rog, Assassin."

Bruce nearly gagged trying not to laugh. It felt good to be heading into a new place, a new environment. Damn good.

Bruce was on top of the world. And passing through thirty thousand feet, that was literally true.

He absently rubbed his left ring finger, feeling the absence of his wedding band. Wearing rings was strictly against regulations, and good common sense. If Bruce had to start rummaging through the cockpit, or suddenly flip switches, there was a chance his ring would catch on a protrusion, or allow electrical arcing. If he was lucky, he'd only tear some skin away. For the unlucky, entire fingers could be lost.

But it wasn't merely the missing wedding ring that felt strange; it was knowing that he would never put it back on.

The divorce had been finalized the day before he left Luke for the trip to Clark. *Ashley.* The memory still hurt—the times they had together and the promise of what was to come. You would think that after ten years together, including two years of marriage, you would learn something about the other person. No surprises, nothing major, but just pleasant, gentle discoveries . . .

The day he last saw her she looked just like she had ten years before, in high school. She had followed him to the Air Force Academy, waiting those long four years until he graduated and even through their wedding during June Week. . . . *Can you ever know anyone completely?*

The memory still tore at him. Even the uncontested

divorce, an Arizona "quickie" designed to numb the pain. He hadn't seen her since that night. . . .

Bruce pulled himself out of his memories, for he knew that they could become a fixation causing him to tune everything else out. And that was a cardinal sin when flying.

There were too many new things to experience, new relationships to build. A fleeting thought of his father crossed his mind. It had been years since he had really spoken with him, and now he was going to be so close; maybe this was the opportunity to start over. *Subic wasn't too far away.* . . .

Now over land, the fighters were left on their own. The KC-10 had peeled off when they had started to descend, winging its way up to Kadena AFB in Okinawa. The officers on the tanker had several more hours of flight time left, but at least they could get up and stretch—you could nearly play football inside the giant, wide-body aircraft. Cots for sleeping, a small kitchen—all the comforts of home. And a real toilet to boot.

Shaking his right hand to relieve cramping, Bruce grasped the throttle and clicked the mike switch.

"Foggy, you still awake?"

"Who do you think is minding the store when you're off on Mars?"

"What are you talking about?"

Charlie snorted. "Check altimeter, Assassin."

Bruce scanned the multi-display console. He was surprised to see that the flight had descended to less than twenty thousand feet. The descent had been that smooth.

Bruce normally allowed Charlie to fly the fighter whenever times were slow. Takeoffs, landings, and dogfights didn't qualify as slow, but then again Charlie had a pretty good feel for the craft. Besides, he could never tell when Charlie might have to come through for him and fly the airplane back home.

It had happened before; it would happen again.

"Sorry, Foggy. Guess I wasn't paying attention."

"S'all right, keeps my mind off the bathroom."

They were interrupted by the radio.

"Let's tighten it up, Maddog. Move in to fingertip."

"Twenty miles, Skipper. We've been cleared to break on initial to an overhead pattern."

"Roger that. Welcome to Clark, boys."

Charlie read the checklist over the intercom, checking off items as they prepared for landing. The words came as clipped, short sentences, checking over the range of items in the craft.

"Fuel."

"Ten thousand pounds."

"Altimeter."

"Passing nine thousand."

The minutes passed quickly. They came in from the south, heading straight for the sprawling complex. A single volcanic mountain jutted up from the jungle floor to the west. A checkerboard pattern of fields dotted the surrounding area. From a mile above ground the area look peaceful, lush. The day was hazy, barely affording a view of mountains. Bruce knew that Subic Naval Station, where his father was now stationed, lay to the southwest, some fifty miles away. He couldn't make out the Navy base through the clouds.

"Maddog, echelon right."

Maddog flight moved from a full, V-shaped fingertip formation to a half V. Two thousand feet to the right lay a town—dingy streets and tin-covered buildings. All around were the remnants of half-built buildings and a morass of people; the tops of brightly colored jeeps and a confusion of activity. Then suddenly, they popped over a wire fence. The fence seemed to delineate a different world, a different universe. Bright green grass, razor-straight streets, and a permeating sense of orderliness.

"Fifteen hundred," warned Charlie.

Bruce still followed in a tight wing, flying three feet

behind Maddog Three's wing tip and three feet to the left. They continued to fly over the expanse of Clark Air Base. The runway came up fast—even throttling back, they were on the landing strip almost before they knew it.

"Maddog, break to an overhead pattern on my command: one *break*!" Skipper's fighter tore off and down to the right, turning hard to come in for a landing. The rest of Maddog continued on.

The feeling hit Bruce like a sledgehammer, the suddenness of it.

The months pushing through the divorce, the rut he had fallen into . . . and now he was starting a new life, away from Ashley, but with the promise of a wide-open beginning. And with his Dad not fifty miles away, it had to be an omen.

"Two's in break."

He felt better than he had in his life—even including throwing the hat at June Week, or his interception in the Liberty Bowl. There was a crescendo lifting him up, pumping him into excitement.

"Three's in break."

When Maddog Three's F-15E Strike Eagle broke right, leaving him alone in the air, Bruce went nonlinear.

"Four—*break*."

He jammed the stick hard to his front and right. His fighter flipped over and executed the "break right" upside down. The gear warning horn blared throughout the cockpit.

"Yahoo!" Charlie's voice ricocheted over the intercom. "Go for it!"

They continued the tight turn upside down until the F-15 pointed at the runway. Buildings and cars whizzed by below them; Bruce didn't look, but he could imagine the open-mouthed stares as people gaped at the upside-down fighter. Now five hundred feet above ground level, Bruce continued to burn in toward the runway, still upside down.

Charlie's whoops added to the cacophony. Descending through three hundred feet, Bruce flipped the aircraft right side up and brought the aircraft on in. The airways were filled with excited voices—Bruce ignored them and greased his craft onto runway 02.

The fighter didn't even bounce as it glided in. Bruce automatically started the rundown sequence, disarmed the ejection seat, and switched to the runway frequency.

"Taxiway Alpha to Joliet Ramp, Maddog. Parking assigned after a maintenance check—you are cleared for crossover."

"Roger, tower."

"Rog, rog, Assassin!" said Charlie. "You really know how to bring them in. Let's hope nobody saw that, otherwise you're going to be one hurting mo'fro."

Bruce clicked his mike. He concentrated on taxiing the fighter.

By the time they arrived Bruce was too exhausted, too exhilarated to say anything. Charlie had kept quiet since landing, and the usual friendly banter was missing between the craft. Everyone was tired and ready to rest up for the next phase of the show—the start of the actual day-to-day flight operations.

When Bruce revved down his engines, the enlisted engineer popped him off a friendly salute and ran back to where a gaggle of people waited. She motioned to the group. They pushed aluminum stairs to the F-15 and she climbed up. As the cockpit opened, Bruce unbuckled and struggled out of his seat.

Long arms reached down to help him out. "Welcome to Clark, sir." The female crew chief smiled down at him. She wasn't a knockout, but she was pretty—and very female. It took a second before Bruce grinned. With his divorce, he had to keep reminding himself that it was all right to start looking again.

"Thanks." He decided he was going to like it here.

As he pushed out of the craft a blue-and-white staff car slid up to the fighter. A panel on the front of the car displayed an eagle—the symbol for a full Colonel—with the words 3rd TFW COMMANDER stenciled below the bird. Bruce's eyes widened.

Bruce nudged Charlie. "Think he's coming to personally welcome us to Clark?"

Charlie looked deadpan. "What you mean 'us,' Assassin? You're the pilot. And since that upside-down stunt broke every safety reg in the book, I'm not expecting the natives to be too friendly."

A blond, lanky officer pulled himself from the staff car. On his light blue shirt, command pilot wings were positioned over a shiny pair of Army "Jump Wings." The Jump Wings showed that the Colonel had completed the arduous parachute school at Fort Benning.

He wasn't smiling, and he looked straight at Bruce.

"Welcome to Clark, sir," whispered Charlie, mimicking the female airman.

Angeles City, Philippine Islands

The street smelled of urine, week-old garbage, and the odor of heavy cooking oil. Two- and three-story buildings enclosed the street in shadows. There was a danger of being hit by dirty water, or buckets of rotting vegetables thrown from the upper two stories. The noise was overwhelming. A half a block away, an open-air market spilled out into the street.

Ceravant Escindo had never gotten used to the backwardness, the cramped and crowded living style of this city. Manila to the south, or even Bagio to the north, was nothing like this, so backward and yet pulsating at the same time. People from the barrios, small villages that dotted the majority of the Philippines, found it difficult to adjust here. To Ceravant, it seemed inconceivable that such a state of affairs persisted.

But Ceravant Escindo knew why. And that was why he was here.

Fifty miles to the southwest lay a similar city, one

that could pass for Angeles if you shut your eyes and felt the pain weaving through the city—the pain of a people being raped. For Angeles' sister city Olongapo lay outside of the Subic Bay Naval Base, just as Angeles lay outside of Clark.

If it hadn't been for Clark and the thousands of Americans stationed at the sprawling military base, Angeles would have been nothing more than another dot on the map, a barrio peopled by a few hundred Filipinos. But the growth of Clark Field after World War Two, after the American "liberation" of the Filipinos from the Japanese, had caused Angeles City's population to skyrocket.

With the population increase came an exponential growth in prostitution, immorality, and other vices. Thousands of Americans filled the streets of Angeles every night—no wonder Angeles had turned out the way it had.

General MacArthur may have had good intentions, but the Philippines might never recover.

Ceravant waited outside a small sari-sari store. The same Americans who pumped millions of dollars into the Filipino economy were also responsible for the city's backwardness. It was unacceptable.

Tired of waiting for the old man, Ceravant ground out the cigarette he smoked, salvaged the remaining tobacco and filter, and entered the store.

A long counter ran the length of the store, about two thirds of the way into the building. A door in the rear opened to a back room. Shelves covered every inch of the walls, and items were crammed into every space: food cans, diapers, soap, nails, magazines. Electronic equipment—Japanese televisions, radios, CD players, Korean stereos—lined the bottom shelf. A refrigerator guarded the back corner; two cartons of cigarettes were split open.

As Ceravant entered, a young woman came from the back. She entered singing along with the latest pop song blasting from the radio. On the counter lay one of the digest-sized weekly magazines, printed in English, that listed the words of all the Top One Hundred songs. No music, just words. Most of the songs were American.

The girl spotted Ceravant and stopped singing. She lowered her eyes.

Ceravant asked tightly. "Where is Pompano?"

"Father . . . is not here."

The young woman was a master of the obvious. "Do you know when he will return?"

She shook her head and kept silent.

Ceravant studied her. Yolanda was almost too tall and light-skinned to pass for a native Filipino. At five feet seven, she towered a good half foot above her peers. Yolanda's high cheekbones, soft dark hair, and long legs distinguished her from other Filipinos.

Ceravant turned away from the young woman. Pompano was lucky that the sari-sari store was deep within the city, far enough away from "B-street"—the ubiquitous bar girl district—that Americans would not frequent it. Otherwise, Yolanda was pretty enough to draw the military men like bees to honey. And that would never do.

Ceravant had started to leave a message for Pompano when Yolanda placed her hands on the counter.

"Father!"

A short, graying man hobbled in. He dragged one foot slightly behind the other but carried himself with dignity. His eyes lit up. "Hello, little one." They both laughed at his greeting. Ceravant kept quiet at the obvious absurdity.

Before they said anything else, Yolanda gestured with her eyes towards Ceravant. Pompano swung around. He nodded tightly, then without looking to his daughter said, "Yolanda, San Miguel and water."

As she turned toward the refrigerator, Pompano took Ceravant's arm and led the younger man outside. Pompano leaned heavily on Ceravant as they made their way to a table just outside the door.

"I wish I could have stayed to see what you seized during the raid. Have you appropriated enough supplies?"

Ceravant nodded slightly. "Yes, and more."

Pompano raised his eyebrows. Ceravant leaned closer, and was about to speak when Yolanda came out of the store. She carried a San Miguel beer, her hand grasping the brown bottle with one hand and a glass of water with the other. She set the drinks on the table.

"Salamat po," smiled her father. He waved her away. "Go rest in the back, Yolanda—I will watch the front. Go on, we are just speaking man-talk."

"Thank you, father." When she left she ignored Ceravant.

Which was fine with Ceravant. Pompano Sicat was a good man and had his roots firmly entrenched in the movement. As long as Pompano kept his daughter separated from the Huks, Ceravant had no qualms. It had been an integral part of his intensive training: a strong delineation between pleasure and business.

Ceravant took a sip of his water.

"We have appropriated more than enough supplies to accomplish our goals. We can change the way we operate, expand our activities, and increase our power. There are several plantations in the mountains that will serve well as a base camp, a permanent place to extend the revolution."

Pompano looked tired. "Ceravant, is not my store good enough? From here we can ship people and supplies to any place on Luzon, without attracting attention. I am a clearinghouse, a way station for the Huks—not just your New People's Army faction." He waved his hand around, motioning to the street. "I have served this way for years and no one even suspects I am involved with the Huks—not even my very daughter! The store provides the perfect alibi."

Ceravant's eyes narrowed. "Yes, but in the shadow of the Americans. We have to watch everything we do. In the mountains we can build a true base, where we will not have to fear the damn Americans and PC everywhere we turn."

"What about the Huks in Angeles? You want to reorient our entire focus?"

"That is right! We can either stay small, forever nipping at the government's heels, or we can seize the opportunity to grow, to make an impact."

Pompano held up a hand. "I agree, Ceravant. It appears that we have an opportunity to grow, but that may be a *bad* thing." He smiled. "We will not decide today. This needs discussion, time to evolve, so we may grow and proceed carefully."

"And if we take too much time, the opportunity will pass us by." Ceravant felt his face grow hot.

Pompano spoke softly. "We must seize the proper opportunity. Take me to the supply cache and we will discuss the options."

Ceravant started to retort, but a group of children, all dressed in their school uniform of white shirts and dark pants, crossed the busy street and entered the store. They called out to Yolanda as they entered.

Ceravant kept his mouth shut, angry at Pompano's cool reception of his news. *That is what happens when the founding member of a Huk cell grows old*, he thought. Too set in his ways, he spurns change. He had been immersed in the details for so long that he has forgotten what the overall goal of the Huks entails.

First established as rebel activists after World War Two, the Huks had fought against the cruel plantation owners who dotted the Luzon jungles, trying to topple the system oppressing the people. The Huks gained a wide range of notoriety, and were even applauded for their democratic goals. But after the plantation owners had capitulated and the major Huk officers had surrendered to the PC, there still remained a dedicated core, a cadre of Huks that wanted reform.

The most famous, and most touted since it supported the Marcos government's anti-socialist move-ment, was the radical pro-Communist file that had emerged within the Huks—the New People's Army. Living in the mountains and striking fear into people's hearts, this group received most of the press. And it was this group that was the most hated and sought after, since the free world had been programmed to react with a knee-jerk, froth-at-the-mouth reaction at even the mention of Communism.

Pompano had been instrumental in starting the first Huk cell in Angeles City. No other cell was close to an American military base. It was this closeness that had attracted Ceravant to this particular cell. But Pompano was an old man, using old ideas to pursue old goals—he was content to steal from the Ameri-cans, support the vast black market that infected Clark.

As Ceravant studied the man, Yolanda walked out with the group of children. She bid the children fare-well, laughing at their joking, then brushed back her hair before heading back inside. Ceravant caught Pompano's attention and nodded to the store.

"Are you worried about your daughter, taking her up to the mountains?"

"Yolanda? She will attend the university in Quezon City later this year. She will not get involved in this. She knows nothing and suspects nothing." He set his bottle down. "As far as she is concerned, you and I are members of the Friends of Bataan, sharing a com-mon link in our country's history by building war memorials in the countryside."

Ceravant picked up his glass and swirled it around before draining it. "That is good. Very good. I must travel—" He hesitated, wondering briefly if he should let the old man know where he was going, but decided against it. The meeting with Kawnleno must remain secret.

"I must travel, but I will be back Sunday. When

can we meet next? I will know then when I can take you to the mountains."

Silence, then: "Monday, after the weekend."

Ceravant stood. "Good. Meet me in front of the Skyline Hotel—eight o'clock at night." He looked toward the door and saw the shadow of Yolanda's lithe figure.

Some time would elapse before his return.

CHAPTER 2

Friday, 1 June

Clark Air Base

Sweat rolled off Bruce's forehead. The humidity was as high as in a sauna.

Jet engines roared behind him. From the deep pitch it sounded like a C-5, one of the giant transports that flew into Clark. Without any wind, the heat was even more unbearable. He could see the Colonel, waiting by the staff car, hands on hips—ready to have Bruce's butt for flying upside down on final approach.

Bruce felt a gentle push against his back. Charlie spoke urgently. "Let's move, I gotta go."

Charlie squeezed around him at the top of the stairs, holding his helmet with one hand and his flight bag with the other. Unfastened from the helmet, Charlie's mask bounced against the stairs, looking like a miniature elephant's trunk as it dangled free.

Bruce swung his flight bag up and followed. As he climbed down the stairs he noticed that a small crowd had gathered around Skipper's fighter, Maddog One. They stood watching Bruce's aircraft.

Oh well, thought Bruce. *It's not like I haven't been chewed out before*. He braced himself for the tirade, the blast to come. It was something he had learned to endure at the Air Force Academy—thank God he had gotten something out of the arduous training. He had a dim memory of his fourth-class, or freshman year. *Doolies*, they had called them, meaning *slaves*, in Greek. The first year had been bad enough, but the worst was Hell Week—a seventy-two-hour period that made every Doolie wish he were dead. It had begun with a special ceremony. The Doolies had been ordered to wear their sharpest dress uniforms and line up in a row in the hall with their noses to the wall. After what seemed to be an hour, the strains of *Also Sprach Zarathustra*—the *2001* theme—rumbled down the hall, accompanied by the sound of marching upperclassmen.

The command was given—"Fourthclassmen, about face!"—and the screaming started. Each Doolie had been assigned a special "mentor"—an upperclassman who's sole purpose in life was to ensure that the Doolie's life was made as miserable as possible during Hell Week.

Except that Bruce's mentor was nowhere to be seen. Still looking straight ahead, and oblivious of the shouting around him, Bruce momentarily thought that they had forgotten him. After all, as a starting defensive back for the varsity football team, Bruce had not seen much of the usually unavoidable hazing.

Then Bruce remembered that the meanest upperclassman had also been the shortest.

Bruce looked down—right into the eyes of Cadet First Class Ping. Standing barely five feet tall, Cadet Ping glared up at Bruce. "Well, Steele, it is about time you look down. Now you are really going to eat shit!"

The experience had been a coda to an already formidable year, but it had prepared him for the blastings to come. To be indifferent, not to take it personally, and not to crack. No matter how bad this Colonel was, Bruce knew that the sun was going to rise tomorrow morning.

Really.

Charlie was waiting for him at the bottom of the stairs. As Bruce turned he kept a stony face, then started for the Colonel, fifty feet away. Bruce was taller than Charlie by a good six inches, but they soon fell into step as they left the plane. It was something every military man naturally dropped into, even if they tried to stay out of step—phase-locking, the phenomenon was called, just as pendulum clocks located across a room would start beating together.

"Afternoon, sir," saluted Charlie. His voice sounded pleasant, masking any emotion he might have felt.

The Colonel let them stand at attention, holding the salute. His name tag was now visible—BOLTE, read Bruce.

Slowly he removed his glasses. His blond hair fit the rest of the man perfectly: blue eyes, a deep tan, and a wry build. He had a fighter pilot's look about him, decided Bruce—cautious, almost catlike.

"Just . . . what . . . in . . . the . . . *hell* are you trying to do, young man? Buy the farm . . . before you even land?"

The question was rhetorical. Bruce and Charlie still held their salute.

Colonel Bolte dropped his hands, then whipped up a quick salute. Bruce and Charlie's hands hit the side of their flight suits at the same time as they brought their hands down.

Bolte glanced at their name tags. "Captain Fargassamo, you listen to what I have to say to your aircraft commander, *Lieutenant* Steele. This upside-down crap on final will cease as of *now*. Next time he tries one of those stupid-ass maneuvers, just remember that it's your butt on the line. He dies, you die too. Got that?"

"Yes, sir."

Bolte paused, then turned his attention to Bruce.

Bruce's face was emotionless. He stared straight ahead, unblinking. Bolte set his mouth.

"Well, well. The famous Lieutenant Steele. Your reputation precedes you, son. And to think Clark Air Base just about didn't get to see you. Flying in the jungle is unlike anywhere else. Winds come out of nowhere, thermals pop up, clear-air microbursts—this isn't Luke Air Force Base, Lieutenant. You aren't flying your bird above the desert, keeping the commies out of Phoenix. If the weather doesn't get you, then some Huk sitting in a tree might decide to take a potshot at your jet. And if he's lucky he just might hit you—go through your canopy and ruin some poor girl's day.

"Clark has seen your type, Steele, and I tell you, we don't want you. *I* don't need you. With the new treaty, we have to rotate our fighters in and out of here—we can't afford mistakes. You might be the best stick coming out of the F-15E program, but there's one thing I want to make perfectly clear: *Dead . . . pilots . . . don't . . . win . . . wars.* Got that? If you die, you aren't any good to me. Not only would you have wasted over a million dollars of good taxpayers' money spent training you, you would have destroyed America's top-line fighter. And that's the only reason I'm in this job, to win one if the balloon goes up. None of my boys died in the Gulf, and none are going to die here. Understand?"

"Yes, sir." Bruce's reply was quick, curt. *Smooth sailing*, thought Bruce. *This isn't bad at all.* And that crack about his reputation preceding him—did the wing commander know about Bruce's winning the Robbie Risner award, given to the top graduate of the Fighter Weapons School?

"Next time you think about doing anything foolish, remember your reputation. You still piss off every grad who watched that Notre Dame game. You're marked as a hot dog." Bolte pulled back. "Welcome to Clark, gentlemen." He turned for the staff car.

Charlie whispered, "Got off easy there, Assassin. I was expecting him to bite down on our butts and get lockjaw. But we got away with no teeth marks, much less blood loss. Now lets get going—I'm up to my eyeballs in piss."

Sweat ran down Bruce's face, and he was tired as

hell. Why did it seem so friggin' hard to breathe? It
had to be the humidity. They walked toward the bus.

As they approached, a short, overweight captain
dressed in a Nomex flight suit stepped from the bus.
He nodded as Charlie pushed past him.

"Foggy."

"Hey, Skipper. Nice to be on the ground."

"Yeah. We'll get you to a can as soon as Assassin
gets his ass in gear."

Charlie smiled weakly. "Thanks."

Skipper turned to Bruce. "Just a minute, Assassin."
He steered the younger man by the elbow away from
the bus.

Skipper was Captain Thorin Olsen's call sign, given
to the man the year he was in pilot training at Vance
AFB. Olsen was a dead-ringer for "Skipper" on the
old TV program *Gilligan's Island*: paunchy, a gleam
in his eye, and good-natured. But at that moment
Skipper's face wore an expression of pain.

"I guess he spoke to you about your stunt."

"Yeah."

"Do you know who he is?"

"Colonel Bolte—the Wing Commander, I guess."

"Yeah, the Wing Commander. For crying out loud,
that's the one guy who could have your ass in a sling,
Assassin. Don't screw around with him."

A redheaded man leaned out the bus window.
"Hey, Skipper, Assassin—either crap or get off the
pot. Foggy's about to pop."

Skipper slapped Bruce on the shoulder. "Let's
move. I don't want Foggy to hose down the crew
bus."

Bruce followed Skipper onto the bus. As soon as
they were on board the vehicle started off.

Skipper stood in the aisle and read out loud from a
sheet of paper given to him by the bus driver. He held
on to a rail that ran the length of the bus.

"All right, listen up. After Foggy relieves himself,
we've been booked into the Q for the next few

nights." "Q" was short for VOQ, or the Visiting Officer's Quarters. "The Housing Office has arranged appointments for us tomorrow, and you married guys will attend some additional briefings." He stopped reading as the bus rounded a corner—on two wheels, it seemed, from the Filipino driver's speed. "And congratulations on a safe trip. Beers are on me tonight. I'll show you the sights downtown."

The boys roared their approval—except for Charlie, who sat at the edge of his seat with a grim look on his face.

Angeles City

Ceravant sat alone in his apartment, smoking a cigarette and staring at a blank wall. He didn't know the time, or how long he had been sitting, thinking. His ashtray was spilling over and an empty pack of cigarettes lay at his feet.

He looked past the bare apartment wall, and remembered . . . the cold Korean nights; sloughing through the mud on a training mission; holding his hands over a fire and smelling the burning flesh, yet denying the pain. . . .

And all the time his master, Yan Kawnleno, silently watching the training. Observing as Ceravant grew wise in the ways of a true terrorist.

Ceravant had trained with the best. And now he was preparing to return for the final time, to gather the wisdom of his master.

He crushed out his cigarette. Tomorrow he would fly out from Manila, and within a week he would be ready to move against the Americans.

Clark AB

Two taxis pulled up to the Visiting Officers' Quarters and honked their horns. Half of Maddog Flight spilled out of the VOQ and made for the cars.

"They dragged me along," Charlie mumbled.

"Designated driver," said Skipper as he raced by.

"With taxis?" But Charlie's protests went unheard. Bruce waited for his backseater before heading to the cars.

"I thought you were staying home tonight."

Charlie nodded. "You heard him. I guess they need someone to keep them out of trouble."

"Good luck."

"I've been there before."

"You bring anything to keep you busy?"

Charlie pulled a paperback book out of his back pocket. "I don't plan on getting much read if I have to ride herd on you guys."

Bruce squinted at the title. It was written by some guy named Toynbee. Oh, well—to each his own. One thing though: It was nice to have Charlie around when the Flight got ripped. One cool head in the midst of an alcohol-induced fog was well worth it.

As they approached the Skipper's taxi a shock of red hair whizzed by. "Dibs on the front seat!" Ed Holstrom—Catman, by his call sign, ostensibly because he was such a smooth operator—slid in the front seat next to the driver. His red hair and freckled face made him look more like a teenager than a fighter pilot.

Bruce moved in the back with Skipper.

The Filipino driver slapped the wheel with both of his hands, enjoying the exchange. He was making money just sitting still.

After Charlie squeezed in the back, a face appeared by Charlie's window. Steve Garcioni—Robin, Catman's backseater and right-hand man—pushed his face up against the glass, squashing his nose and cheeks while keeping his mouth open; his tongue made crazy patterns.

Skipper called out, "Where are the rest of the guys?"

Robin rolled his eyes. "The married ones? Probably writing letters home."

"Come on, let's go," urged Catman. Robin squeezed in and pushed Catman next to the driver.

"Okay. Tell that other driver he's not needed."

Soon, all five officers and the driver were barreling down Mitchell Highway toward Friendship Gate.

The group hadn't even begun to drink, but from the yelling and laughing it sounded as if all the passengers had been soused for a week.

When they stopped, the taxi driver bowed several times at the waist, grinning as he collected his fare and tip. The men were deposited at the gate, the portal to Angeles City, since the American-owned taxis were forbidden to leave the base. And for a very good reason. More often than not, the taxi would keep heading out into the country after the party had been dropped off, only to wind up in some barrio or have its parts stripped in Manila.

Bruce followed Skipper to the pedestrian gate. Cars streamed in and out of the base through the four-lane road next to them. It sounded like a carnival outside the gate—laughing, children jabbering. Skipper turned to the group and held up his wallet.

"First lesson, gentlemen, is to keep your wallet in your front pocket at all times. You're going to be bumped every which way but loose out here."

As they entered Angeles City they were swarmed by a sea of brown bodies. Bruce was put off at first—something was missing, and he couldn't quite tell what it was. The five plowed through the crowd toward a string of gayly painted jeeps. They moved like ice-breakers, pushing aside the floes of people.

And then it hit Bruce what was wrong.

All five of the officers stood a good six inches to a full foot above the crowd. And the crowd were men and women, *not* children for the most part, all clamoring for their attention: "Say, Joe—my sister a virgin, short time, no?" "Ten pesos will blow you away, Joe!" "Blue Seal Special, you sell, Joe?" "Here down the street—long time, short time, just what you need!"

No one grabbed at his wallet, but there was a constant pushing that crowded the bodies against him. Skipper reached the jeeps first. The one he picked was elongated, painted in wild Day-glo colors. The back was open and had long seats running down both sides. Skipper bartered with the driver.

"Fire Empire—two peso?"

The Filipino held up five fingers. Skipper started off for the next jeep. The Filipino called out, "Wait, Joe—four peso."

"Three. No more." A second passed.

The driver motioned with his head to climb in. "Ziggy now."

Skipper turned to the group. "Let's go, gang. Get ready for the ride of your life." The men scrambled aboard and hung on for dear life.

The jeep started off through the crowd before all were seated. It shot across the traffic, causing several cars to squeal their tires. The streets were brightly lit and crowded. It reminded Bruce of New Orleans, a constant party.

Skipper called out over the noise, "Lesson number two: What we're in is called a jeepney. Never set foot inside one until you've bartered the price and exact destination. Otherwise you'll be driving around the city for the rest of the night and owe a hundred bucks. The PCs—that's short for the Philippine Constabulary, their local police and military—will back the driver up and throw you in jail." He handed out a wad of bills to each man. "The exchange rate changes daily, so I can't tell you what the peso is worth, but it's in our favor now. I got twenty bucks apiece for everyone at the club—pay me back later."

Catman let out a laugh. "Where you taking us, Skipper?"

"Don't ask. You are going to see the most amazing floor show this side of Paris. The last time I went to the Empire, there was this girl who smoked a cigarette in the damnedest way. . . ."

Washington D.C.

Throughout the last twenty years, Robert E. Lee Adleman had lived in many places, many climates, but the one thing he could not get used to was the sopping wet Washington, D.C., heat.

Adleman rocked back in his chair and steepled his fingers. "Ninety-five percent humidity, you say?"

"Yes, sir, that's right," the young project officer from the State Department confirmed. "The Philippines stays that high. Will that affect your plans?"

Adleman shook his head. A sudden vision raced through his mind of a summer he had spent in Mississippi, traipsing through the swamps. "No, that's fine."

"Any more questions, sir?"

"No thank you, Mr. Kelt."

The man nodded and left the room, leaving Adleman alone with Jerry Weinstein. The National Democratic Party Chairman had been silent throughout the briefing on the Philippine Islands. Weinstein had insisted on speaking to the Vice-President before the next Cabinet meeting, and this had been the only time that Adleman had not been fully committed.

Weinstein leaned forward, his elbows on his knees. This looked ridiculous, because the former NBA basketball star's kneecaps were at least a foot higher than the chair seat. Coming from a poverty-stricken background, Weinstein's exposure to opulence as a high six-figure basketball player had made him appreciate the inequities of the American dream.

"Robert . . . Ah, Bob . . ."

"Umm?" Adleman turned his attention away from the upcoming trip and focused on Weinstein.

"I wanted to spend some time with you, before the next meeting between the President and his Cabinet."

"Okay, what's up? We've got a half hour."

"This trip." Weinstein nodded with his head to all the information the State Department had left—briefing booklets, statistics, analyses of trends.

"It's critical for your political future. In fact, it might be the nail that drives in the lid on your election."

Adleman looked puzzled. "I missed something. Run that past me again."

Weinstein sat up. "Bob—Mr. Vice-President. We both know you are the unspoken leader for the next election. You've got Longmire's backing, you've got the experience and background, no skeletons in the closest. . . ."

You said it, thought Adleman. The FBI special investigation background check had been nothing compared to the scrutiny of the Democratic party. The Democrats hadn't had a viable Presidential contender for the last thirty years—including Carter, who Adleman was convinced had been a fluke, a backlash against the Nixon era. So they were going to make sure their candidates were squeaky-clean.

Weinstein had personally examined Adleman's record: As a Magna Cum Laude Princeton grad with his sights set on Congress, and armed with a law degree from Berkeley, Adleman hadn't made the same mistake as the last Vice-President: he had put in his time on active duty with the Army for a four-year-stint, serving as a staff judge advocate. The generals he had impressed were also the ones who introduced him to their congressional liaisons.

After leaving the Army Adleman served on several congressional staffs, making a name for himself as a hard-charging fact-finder, turning out policy prose in a coherent fashion. Senator Longmire had fingered the young blond staffer as an up-and-coming force, and helped him to rise through the ranks of various governmental positions.

Finally deciding to try his hand at political office, Adleman won his district in Albuquerque by a landslide. And then as a mere second-term Congressman, at forty, Robert E. Lee Adleman was chosen to run for Vice-President of the United States.

". . . but you need to show that you can pull off an international agreement, something that could affect the security of an entire hemisphere."

Adleman nodded to himself. "Sounds like what Francis Acht was pushing. Except that he had the economic security, not necessarily our defensive security, in mind."

"I'm sure he was speaking about both," said Weinstein softly. "Francis knows that without one, you can't have the other."

"So you think this can do it for me?"

Weinstein spread his hands. "That's why I wanted to catch you before the meeting—just in case someone tries to throw a wrench in the idea. Longmire's health is on pretty shaky grounds, and if something happens it would be better for you to go into office as a hero, who's been tested in international negotiations. This treaty could boost confidence in you and ensure the next election, if Longmire lasts that long. You should view this trip as more than a service to the country. It's a springboard for you as well."

Adleman kept eye contact with Weinstein. *Boost confidence and ensure the next election.* Suddenly he felt uneasy about his actions, about being calculating and anticipating President Longmire's demise.

His first lesson as an Army officer was that when things go wrong, the most important thing is to do something—it doesn't matter what. Reacting was better than sitting still and allowing events to pass him by, which was like striking out by watching the balls go by instead of swinging.

CHAPTER 3

Friday, 1 June

Angeles City, P.I.

Bruce watched the floor show for as long as he could stomach it. Without Ashley to go back to, he should have been enjoying it, if for no other reason than because of his freedom.

His gum grew stale; tired of popping it, he slipped it into an empty beer bottle that littered the table top.

Set in a smoky, low-ceilinged bar, the show oozed sleaze. Tables were pushed up around an elevated runway. On the bed in the middle of the stage a naked Filipino woman gyrated her hips to music. Bruce couldn't tell how old she was—it was difficult, since the Filipinos looked so much younger than he.

Disco sounds, driven by a throbbing bass and incessant drum, blared throughout the bar. The songs were old, from a different era than the one in which Bruce had grown up—not hard rock, but something more commercial, like the soundtrack to a cheap porno movie. It added to Bruce's discomfort. He pushed his chair back. There must have been twenty beer bottles on the table in front of him.

"Hey, where you going, Assassin?"

"Fresh air."

"You don't look too good. Too much to drink?"

Bruce paused. "Yeah."

Catman turned back to watch the act; he spoke loud

enough so everyone could hear him. "Don't wimp out on us."

Right, thought Bruce. *Talk about a wimp.* He remembered when Catman had finally soloed in the F-15—or rather he remembered the party afterward. They had stumbled into a bar during happy hour, and within a short time they were all drunk as skunks. Catman made a pass at the waitress, only to get sick and toss his cookies all over the table. Catman promptly passed out and slumped head-first into his vomit. Thrown out of the bar, the boys had had to push Catman around in a shopping cart until they found their car.

TAC solo. Catman's first solo flight in a Tactical Air Command fighter . . . a bonding experience known to only a few. Bruce's thoughts drifted to his own first solo, high above the desert, outside of Luke AFB in Arizona. . . .

"Heads up, Assassin."

"Rog." Bruce craned his neck around the cockpit. At eighteen thousand feet the view was breathtaking: cloudless blue sky above him, rugged red-brown terrain below. He felt one with the ancient F-15A fighter. He rocked the wings. The craft responded instantly.

What the hell, he thought. He slammed the stick to the right, and the fighter instantly rolled around. He saw brown-blue brown-blue as he spun. He jerked the stick to the neutral position and immediately flew level. "Holy shit."

"Say again, Assassin." His instructor pilot's voice from back at the training squadron on the ground came over his headphones.

"Ah, getting good response," paraphrased Bruce. "This bird is pretty agile." He had forgotten that his mike was "hot," the transmitter left on an open channel during this first solo.

"Copy that," came back his instructor, dryly. "You've got ten minutes before heading back. Go ahead and wring it out."

"Roger that." Bruce squinted out of the cockpit. Luke lay off the horizon to his left; directly below were mountains; on the other side a long fissure wound its way through the Arizona desert. "Request permission to descend through two thousand."

"Affirmative—but watch those mountains. We won't be able to paint you on the scope."

"Rog," said Bruce. *That's the whole idea*, he thought to himself. He pushed the stick forward and to the right. The F-15 broke out of its level flight and began to descend. Bruce flicked his eyes from the altimeter to the airspeed indicator to his radar.

The fissure lay before him. The walls seemed far enough apart to safely bring the craft. He spotted the rugged cliffs that opened up like a yawning mouth. A thin ribbon of water lay at the bottom of the fissure. It must have taken hundreds of thousands of years for the river to create the fissure.

"Five minutes, Assassin. Time to head back."

"Rog." *But not before I take a look-see*. Bruce shoved the stick forward; the craft screamed to the ground. The numbers on the altimeter dropped like a rock.

Bruce's whole attention was outside the aircraft. The F-15 descended into the fissure. Rocky cliff walls rose up on either side. As on the desert floor, the fissure showed no sign of vegetation, only red-brown earth of a gravel-like texture. The sharp edges of slanted geological zones, painting the walls in weird striped patterns, zoomed by. The walls were treeless. He inched the craft even lower.

The cliff walls closed to within a hundred feet of the wing tips. He lost radio contact in the canyon. As he grew closer to the water he slowed the craft by pulling back on the throttles. The F-15 bounced slightly from the the the thermals.

Bruce drew in a breath—the feeling was unfathomable: boulders as big as a house dashed by, a ripple of water below . . . it was almost a psychic experience, like that scene in *Star Wars*.

A fuzzy dot ahead, just over the water, caught his attention. As he grew closer, he could make out *two* dots—two red balloons that hovered in the middle of the fissure. His eyes widened.

Yanking back on the stick, Bruce hit full afterburners. The F-15 jerked up and stood on its tail, accelerating upward while still moving forward. "Come on," muttered Bruce. Sweat formed at his brow and ran into eyes. The craft seemed to claw upward as the acceleration pushed him back into his seat. He forced his head to the right and tried to find the balloons.

As the F-15 shot up from the fissure he spotted them below him. A thick strand of wire ran across the canyon, holding the balloons in place. The balloons warned low-flying planes that power lines crossed the fissure. If he had not pulled up when he did, his F-15 might have smashed into the rocky walls; a smoking pyre in testimony to his low-flying antics. . . .

". . . can you read? I say again, Assassin. Can you read?"

Bruce tried to keep his voice steady as he kicked off the afterburners and nosed the F-15 back to Luke. "Rog. I . . . I was pulling out of a roll. I've got a vector back home."

"Roger that."

Minutes later, after the F-15 Eagle had rolled to a stop, Bruce climbed out of the cockpit. Buckets of cold water doused him, chilling the sweat that still covered his body. He held up a hand to his classmates, who were enthusiastically participating in the ritual: After a first solo, the pilot was drenched in water. Catman threw the last bucket on him. "Congrats, Assassin. With your reputation as a hot dog, we all thought you'd try something spectacular."

Bruce only flashed a wan smile. . . .

The others kept watching the act. The woman lifted her hips high, arching her back and giving the audience an unobstructed view. From behind a set of curtains a man sauntered on stage to the music, also unclothed, carrying an assortment of items. "Holy shit, look at the size of *that!*"

Bruce left the table.

"Make sure Foggy goes with you, Assassin," called out Skipper. "You don't want to be caught out in this area alone."

Bruce wove his way around tables, mostly packed with young Americans. A few tables held Filipino men, quietly smoking their cigarettes, but the place obviously catered to foreigners such as himself. When he reached the lobby the air was clear of smoke; more importantly, the low music now enabled him to think.

Charlie sat at the end of a long red bench, opposite the door, reading his book. Two bouncers chatted quietly just outside, ignoring what was going on. Charlie looked up; he folded the top right-hand corner of the page to mark his place.

"You guys through?"

"*I* am."

Charlie raised an eyebrow. "What's up?"

"Nothing. Just ready to go." Bruce pushed his way out the door. The heat and humidity hit him as he left the air-conditioned building. At least there was no smoke, but the heavy air made up for it. It was just getting dark, with a little less than a half hour until night. The street outside the Fire Empire was still crazy with traffic, honking horns, and the cacophony of unfamiliar words. Charlie followed him outside. His paperback book bulged in his rear pocket.

A jeepney spotted the two and pulled a U-turn. The driver motioned with his head to climb in. "Back to base?"

Bruce remembered Skipper's lesson. "How much?"

"Four peso."

Charlie started to climb in the vehicle. "How much to take the long way?"

"Long way?" The driver looked puzzled.

Charlie swept his arm in a circle. "Yeah, the long way—show us some of the city."

"Ah, yes. A tour." The driver nodded. "For you, forty peso each. I show you Angeles."

Charlie snorted. "Ten peso."

The driver shook his head. "Thirty, special for you."

"Twenty-five." Charlie wasn't about to lose a centavo.

The man thought for a moment, then brightened. "Okay, twenty-five peso. Hop in, Joe."

Charlie climbed in and waved Bruce on board. They roared off. The Filipino driver turned in his seat to half face the two Americans. He kept a lazy hand on the wheel while darting in between cars. "You see something and want to stop, tell me loudly."

"Right, right." Charlie waved for the man to turn around.

Bruce watched the exchange without emotion. A short time ago he had been looking forward to a new locale, a new beginning, but now, in-country only six hours, he already felt like going home. The noise, heat, humidity, and strange smells all overloaded his senses. There was nothing in the Islands to anchor to, nothing familiar. And what he had just seen in the bar was beyond exotic—it bordered on the clinical.

They passed one place that seemed to provide a reminder of home—the sign was of a fried chicken fast-food place. But then Bruce saw carcasses hanging from the ceiling—the bodies of skinned dogs—with a sign "Dog-On-A-Log" displayed in English.

He felt a tap on his arm.

"Okay Bruce, what's eating you? You haven't talked since we landed." Charlie paused, then added, "What did Colonel Bolte tell you?"

"Uh?" Bruce shook his head and switched gears. He had almost forgotten about what Colonel Bolte had said, the crack about his reputation preceding him. "That? Nothing."

"Yeah. Think I believe it? Come on—he must have jabbed you pretty well."

"That's a rog." Compared with everything else going on, Colonel Bolte's remarks did seem ludicrous. "You know, when Bolte was going on about my reputation, I was sure he was alluding to the Risner Trophy we'd won."

"*You* won. That was for being the best stick, not a team effort."

Bruce shrugged Charlie's observation off. "We did it; it wasn't just me. Anyway, that's not the point." He looked away. *Ashley*, thought Bruce. *That's the real reason I'm down, isn't it? But Charlie would never understand.* . . . They expect you to bounce right back, act as if divorce were no big deal.

Charlie let the matter be.

Bruce tapped a finger on the railing that ran the length of the jeepney. Cloth decorated in psychedelic patterns covered the jeepney's top. Little cloth balls hung from the sides, running along the entire top. Large linked chains made up the steering wheel; in place of the rearview mirror there sat a black velvet painting of Jesus, which looked back at the passenger compartment and down on the driver.

The traffic thinned. The houses and stores were still packed together, but the crowds and noise had abated. Charlie finally spoke, as if he had been thinking.

"When will you try to see your father?"

"Dad?" It was Bruce's turn to be quiet. He nodded slowly. "He knows I'm here—or at least that I'll be coming soon. My mom spoke with him last week and he's expecting me. I guess I'll wait until I'm settled a little more before I give him a call."

"He lives in Subic?"

"Olongapo." Bruce looked around the dingy streets as they sped through the city. "It's right outside Subic."

"We all have some adjusting to do, Bruce. This has been a big change. Skipper's family won't be able to get over here for at least six months; Catman left a fiancée behind."

Bruce snorted.

"Okay," said Charlie, backing off. "So Catman has three or four fiancées. But look at it this way—you're a new man now: single, on flight pay, no kids, no alimony, and you've got your health. What more could you ask for?"

"Right." The "no alimony" pierced him. Divorced . . . He thought it would never happen to him—but no use dwelling on it. Charlie was right, they all had adjustments to make.

Bruce leaned to the front of the jeepney; he tried to speak over the onrushing air so that the driver could hear him. "Excuse me."

"Aih?" Again the driver turned, smiling back at Bruce.

"Are there any stores that sell gum?"

"Cigarettes? You want Blue Seal?"

"No, *gum*. You know chewing gum?" Bruce pantomimed putting a stick of gum in his mouth and chewing.

"Aih, gum! Yes, yes, the market! One minute."

The man turned back to the front and gunned the jeepney. He pulled off the main street and slid between long rows of buildings. As they slowed, they passed what appeared to be an open market. It was a cross between an outdoor and indoor shopping center: Merchants spilled out into the street hawking animals, complete meals, fabrics, stereo equipment, books, plants, furniture, fresh vegetables, mounds of rice three feet tall, chickens—anything imaginable. The selling extended far into a tin-covered, single-story building. Buildings in the neighborhood resembled warehouses more than offices.

The driver stopped in front of the market. An incoherent jabber of foreign language surrounded the jeepney. The driver nodded happily. "Here, you find gum."

Bruce turned to Charlie. "What do you think?"

"Whatever."

Now Bruce concentrated on the time. "Skipper cautioned us to stay together, and it's getting late. What do you say we skip it this time and head back to the Club—for dinner."

"That's a rog, Assassin."

Bruce waved the driver on. "Thanks, but we'll pass."

"No market?" The driver looked disappointed.

"It will take too long. We'll try another time."

The driver suddenly brightened. "Okay. Maybe I help you."

The jeepney shot off down the street, and had not had much time to accelerate before it screeched to a halt. It stopped before a low-slung building.

"Here—sari-sari store. Run in fast. Ziggy now." The driver tried to shoo Bruce into the tiny building.

"Uh?" Bruce looked bewildered. "What's going on?"

"He wants you to go in there."

"Master of the obvious. Maybe it's their equivalent of a 7-11." Bruce hopped out of the jeepney and started for the store. "Stay with this guy. I don't want to have to walk back."

"If we can even find our way back," muttered Charlie.

Six tiny tables were pushed to the side of the store, making it look like an Asian version of a Paris café. The screen door had a tiny bell attached to it. Inside, a long counter ran the entire length of one wall. Music came from an open door to the back; someone was singing "Obla-dee, obla-da" along with the Beatles.

The singing stopped as a girl walked into the room from the back. All Bruce could see was dark hair that extended halfway to the floor. When she swung her hair around and looked up, Bruce was floored, unable to talk. She was the most beautiful woman he'd seen in his life.

The girl lowered her eyes. She spoke in halting English. "May I . . . help you?"

Bruce stuttered, trying to talk coherently. "Uh, yeah. Do you have any gum?"

"Gun?" The girl looked up, puzzled.

"No, *gum*. You know, chewing gum? Chew, chew." Bruce pantomimed putting a stick of gum in his mouth and chewing. He felt suddenly foolish at his pidgin English.

She still avoided his eyes. "Gum, yes we have." The girl turned and stretched, reaching to the top shelf, and brought down several packs of Wrigley's gum, some of them open. She held them out to Bruce. "How many sticks?"

The girl finally looked at him, and he felt lost in her deep brown eyes. Her skin was flawless; she looked so innocent he couldn't tell her age. It took Bruce a moment to figure out what she was asking.

"How many sticks? Oh, you mean I can buy just a stick of gum, rather than a pack?"

"Yes." The girl seemed amused now.

"Well, then . . . here." Bruce dug into his pocket and pulled out a wad of pesos. He shoved the money to the girl. "I'll take all the gum. Is this enough money?" The foreign currency seemed more like play money—Monopoly bills—than hard cash.

The girl carefully counted out the money and held out the remainder to Bruce. As she counted, her long black hair fell over her shoulder, giving it the appearance of a waterfall. She pushed eleven packs of gum across the counter to him, then swung her hair back over her shoulder and lowered her eyes.

Bruce backed out of the tiny store. The screen door swung shut, cutting off his view of the young woman. He didn't know how long he stood there, but Charlie's voice seemed to pierce through a fog that enveloped him.

"Hey, *Bruce*! Would you get back in here? The O'Club is going to close."

Bruce turned and headed for the jeepney. Reaching out to grab the railing, he realized that he still tightly held the packs of gum. He shoved them into a pocket.

Charlie eyed his frontseater as the jeepney started off. "Get enough gum?"

"Umm? Yeah . . . sure." Bruce turned back to watch the traffic. He kept to himself the rest of the trip.

Headquarters, Thirteenth Air Force
Clark AB

The Commander of the Thirteenth Air Force reported directly to the Commander of the Pacific Air Forces, which was headquartered at Hickam AFB, Hawaii. Pacific Air Forces were responsible for the security of an area nearly four times the breadth of the United States—twelve thousand miles—a region that spanned seventeen time zones including the Philippine Islands.

As such, Major General Peter Simone, Commander of the Thirteenth Air Force, was literally on his own. With the exception of a three-star general at Yokota AFB, Japan and another one at Osan AFB, Korea, Simone was the highest-ranking officer for a thousand miles.

Discounting fleet operations at Subic Naval Base, just fifty miles down the road.

But that was Navy, and therefore didn't matter.

Simone had short, wirelike hair, dark ebony features, a solid build, and he always had a gleam in his eye and something up his sleeve. As long as you told him the truth and kept him informed, he would support you to the hilt. And that was the secret of his success. His hell-raising instinct was tempered by his charisma. The other generals regarded Simone as their alter ego, the person whom they'd like to be—let down their hair and go crazy. He was the stereotypical fighter pilot, and he played it for all he could.

Major General Simone reveled in his autonomy. He ran the base with an iron fist and didn't put up with anyone's crap. There was a base commander on Clark, a Colonel who served more as a housekeeper than anything else, but he didn't slow Simone's stride. Everyone knew who ran the base, who was the most important person on Clark, and everyone knew that if it weren't for his fighters—his *boys* out there who strapped themselves into screaming tons of metal— Clark would not have a purpose.

It was a perfect match. Simone's last assignment had been as Commandant of Cadets at the Air Force Academy. He had served the shortest time of any Commandant in history—five months—when the usual tour was two years; the impression he had made on the cadets had gotten him booted upstairs to where he couldn't influence such naive, pliable minds.

It wasn't an isolated incident that had led to his "promotion." It was a combination of events. One time he had gotten rip-roaring drunk with the senior class and puked at their graduation Dining-In—a formal dinner that was celebrated Air Force-wide; another time he had flown his F-15C over the Academy the day he was supposed to report in—and somehow the afterburners had kicked in and he'd passed Mach 1, sending a sonic boom thundering across the aluminum-and-glass campus, knocking out half the windows. Rather than blame Simone, they had taken the F-15 apart three times before finding a faulty wire to blame for the incident.

But the final straw was the food fight he had started in Mitchell Hall, the cadet mess hall. The scene had made the papers, and Simone was reassigned to Clark the very next week. With the addition of another star.

He'd like to think he'd gotten booted upstairs because of his competence and not because of his race, but he didn't dare question General Newman's decision on that one.

So Major General Peter Simone was having his last hurrah, and Clark vibrated with his presence, his aura.

When a visiting general came, the base straightened up and performed like clockwork. After the general left, the partying went on as before.

He kept an eye on his boys, just to make sure they didn't take things too far: His concept of "too far" was activated when the boys had to fly—there were no compromises in the air. But if the boys wanted to raise a little hell, drink a little beer, and didn't hurt anyone—well, Simone knew that it would be best in the long run. A happy crew would follow him to hell and back.

In his headquarters office, Simone rocked back and studied the memo given him by his aide, Major Steve Hendhold, who waited outside the door.

"Steve?"

"Yes, sir?" Hendhold appeared at the door.

"Has anybody else seen this?"

"Not that I know of, General. Colonel Bolte delivered it to me himself."

Simone nodded. "What about the flight line? Did anyone else report this, or see what the hell happened?"

"Nothing, sir. In fact, Colonel Bolte would not have seen it himself if he hadn't been waiting for the flight. He wanted to greet every new pilot that ferried in the planes. He was out by the flight line, watching the '15s do an overhead when he spotted Maddog Four." Hendhold shrugged. "Some people on the ground may have spotted it, but there was no way for them to know that it wasn't an approved pattern."

"Approved pattern! Flying a 'break-in' upside down?" Simone snorted, then slowly broke into a smile. He squinted at the memo. His eyes had been slowly getting worse for the past few years, but pride prevented him from getting glasses. Especially the black model prescribed by Air Force doctors—"B.C."

glasses, his cadets had called them, for "birth control" glasses: A girl wouldn't come within a hundred feet of you with them on. A true fighter pilot, Simone classed wire-rimmed flight glasses in the same category.

Major General Simone made out the pilot's name. "Bruce Steele. Bring his record . . . and his backseater's, too, Charles Fargassamo. I want to know something about these clowns before I meet them."

"Very well, sir."

As Major Hendhold turned to leave, Simone called out, "And knock off after you get them, Steve. It's too late for a young Major to be hanging around here."

"Thanks, sir."

Simone rocked back in his chair when his aide had left. *Inverted overhead*, he thought. *These young guys must have brass for balls*. He hadn't seen this much esprit since the Gulf.

He wasn't going to intervene at this time—"Lightning" Bolte had done the right thing by disciplining the kid on the spot, and not drawing it out. But it was refreshing to know that there was some untamed spunk out there. As long as it was nurtured, hope remained.

Major Hendhold laid the personnel folders on his boss's desk.

Simone scanned the document. "Steele . . . So he's a Zoomie, call sign 'Assassin.' " He looked up. "Do you know this guy?"

Hendhold narrowed his eyes. The young Major was also a Zoomie—an Air Force Academy graduate— and usually had the scuttle on other grads in the area. "Yes, sir. Football player, and one of the better defensive backs the Academy's ever seen. He has a reputation for being a killer—he put more than one receiver into the hospital—but he's a hot dog too. Some say Air Force lost that big Notre Dame game three years ago because Steele was trying to beat the all-time interception record."

"Would you have him as your wing man?"

Hendhold didn't hesitate. "Give me five minutes with him and I'll let you know, sir."

"Okay, thanks, Steve." He dismissed him with a wave. "Get lost, and have fun."

"Good night, General."

Simone glanced through the record: Risner Trophy, Top Stick out of Willie, recommend upgrade to Stan Eval—the prestigious Standardization and Evaluation crew, the cream of the crop. He nodded to himself.

As a general officer Simone was forbidden from flying the F-15E by himself—he needed an instructor pilot to accompany him. So far he'd flown the pants off the instructor pilots who went up with him. But now there just might be someone who could handle him.

He thought he was going to like this Bruce Steele.

Saturday, 2 June

Bangkok International Airport

Ceravant waited for Kawnleno to speak. The student did not interrupt the teacher, as a journeyman does not hurry a master.

They had met twice since Ceravant's initial training—each time in a crowded airport to avoid drawing attention.

They sat in a small coffee shop, just outside of security. With his small stature, sparse hair, and black glasses, Kawnleno looked far from formidable. He looked to be in his late sixties and seemed quite frail, not at all a dangerous terrorist. His fingernails were stylishly long—stylish for a Korean—extending out and curling up and over, at least ten centimeters if they could be stretched unbroken. He carefully smoked a filterless cigarette, allowing the smoke to corkscrew up into his nostrils as he inhaled.

The airport was jammed with people, all chattering

away; dogs barked in the background—it seemed as if an outdoor market had been rolled up and stuffed into the building. Ceravant glanced at his watch. Ten minutes until check-in for his flight back to Manila. He had only been with Kawnleno for half an hour, and once Ceravant had related the details of the latest Huk raid the older man had simply grown quiet, as if he were deep in thought.

Ceravant ground out his own cigarette as Kawnleno finally spoke.

"This high-power microwave weapon is very interesting." Kawnleno spoke low so that Ceravant had to strain to hear him.

Ceravant leaned forward and said, "But from the manuals I do not see much use for it. Clearing mine fields, disrupting communications—the only reason I can think the Americans gave the device to the Philippine Constabulary was that its uses are limited. The Americans are even stingy to their own allies," he said bitterly. "At least the extra supplies will enable us to equip more men. The resistance in the countryside will grow."

Kawnleno drew in a lungful of smoke. "Sometimes the obvious answer is the hardest to see." He stared straight at Ceravant.

Ceravant glanced at his watch. Eight minutes. The next flight to Manila was not until tomorrow. He began to grow irritated. "Teacher, you speak the truth, but I do not have the time for games. Is there something I must take back to my people? Are you not pleased with the way I am running the resistance movement?"

"I am very pleased. You have excelled as a student, and you are ahead of your goals in helping the New People's Army establish a foothold throughout the countryside." He nodded. "Yes, you have made considerable progress and have fared well after your training. But the obvious point is what you should do next. There is a time to reconsider your goals, the purpose in what you set out to do. And if the goals change, then you must grasp the moment—seize the day." He smiled slightly, as if bemused.

Ceravant shivered, thinking of the cold training camp Kawnleno had headed up. "So I must reconsider my goals? Freeing the Filipino people from their shackles to the rich, the government—am I not succeeding?"

"But now you have the chance to leap ahead. The ammunition and supplies you captured: Instead of enlisting more people, more children to randomly attack your Constabulary, why not use what assets you have? Now you are like angry bees attacking a lumbering elephant. This high-power microwave weapon can make you a tiger.

"Use the supplies to fortify yourself, and use the microwave device to directly attack the Satan that fuels your hatred."

"The Americans . . . ?"

Kawnleno stood. "I am sure that you can think of the appropriate measures to take. Doing so will elevate the stakes, and you must determine if it is worth it." He smiled. "A teacher can only point the way— it is the student who must climb the mountain."

Ceravant followed him out of the coffee shop. They were immediately swept along with the crowd. Just before reaching security they stopped.

"Six months from this day. Singapore."

Ceravant nodded as Kawnleno turned away. Ceravant trailed behind him, pushing toward security.

As Ceravant followed Kawnleno through the metal-detector, he ignored the bank of video cameras that scanned the crowd.

CHAPTER 4

Monday, 4 June

Clark AB

Zero-dark early: two hours before wheels up.

Bruce blew on his coffee and took another small sip, trying to keep awake. Maps covered the walls of the 3rd TAC Fighter Wing briefing room. Lines and circles made the charts look like a jumble of confusion; the air routes, bombing ranges, restricted areas, and flight patterns were all displayed in a fashion coherent only to an experienced pilot.

The eight pilots and backseaters comprising Maddog Flight surrounded a table, marking out their strategy for the day's bombing run. A bombing run without bombs, that is—the mission was merely to familiarize the crews with the idiosyncracies of Crow Valley, the bombing range fifteen miles to the west of Clark.

Once an area dotted with rice paddies, Crow Valley was part of the land thrown in when the Philippine government leased Clark and Subic back to the United States. The valley was now a restricted area, for use by Air Force and Navy pilots to practice laying down their weapons.

Before they flew their F-15s "hot"—loaded down with weapons—Maddog Flight would have to undergo Jungle Survival School. The thought was in the back of Bruce's mind but he didn't let it worry him. Getting back from today's flight was his first priority. That and staying awake.

"Time hack on my count," Skipper's voice broke in. "Five, four, three, two, one—*hack*."

Bruce zeroed his watch to coincide with the time Skipper had announced. The entire flight was now calibrated to the Flight Commander's clock.

The hour-long flight brief was over. The crews headed out to take a final leak before suiting up. Charlie loitered in the briefing room, making sure he was the last to empty his bladder.

Light banter filled the personal equipment room— PE room, as the pilots called it—as the men struggled into their equipment. Webbed netting made up survival vests, parachute harness, and jungle gear. Lockers and wooden benches packed the PE room. Posters on the wall displayed Soviet aircraft.

Bruce finished snapping on his survival vest and slammed his locker shut. Patting his pockets, he pulled out a stick of gum and popped it in his mouth. He stuffed his helmet in his flight bag. "Foggy, you ready?"

"Yo."

They pushed through the locker room and down the hall to the Squadron Duty Desk. Just outside the door and to the right, a dark blue crew bus waited to take the officers to their jets. Charlie peeled off for the bathroom.

"Meet you on the bus."

Bruce grunted, then turned left into the Squadron Duty Area.

At the end of the hall Major Brad Dubois sat behind an empty desk. Built like a fireplug but not quite as pretty, the major was completely bald. A long whiteboard, filled with grease-penciled names, times, and dates, took up the wall behind him; the board matched aircraft numbers with pilots' names, dates, and scheduled times of flights. Major Dubois read a paperback book, something with a scantily dressed female and a man in a spacesuit on the cover. Bruce thought he saw the Major moving his lips when he read.

"Good morning, Major."

Dubois looked up. He blinked, but otherwise remained expressionless.

Uh-oh, thought Bruce, *I wonder if Neanderthal man speaks English.* "Hello, sir, I'm Lieutenant Steele. I've just been assigned here. Uh, I've come to sign my aircraft out."

Dubois reached under the desk and pulled out a battered green notebook. The log was dog-eared and covered with markings. "Here." He shoved it toward Bruce and turned back to his book.

Popping his gum, Bruce waited for the man to look up, say something, or just show some sign that he was alive. When nothing happened, Bruce shrugged and picked up a pen. As he copied down the information about his aircraft from the whiteboard onto the log, Catman came up and joggled his elbow. Bruce rolled his eyes toward Major Dubois, then returned to signing out his plane.

Catman wisely stayed quiet until his turn; Bruce decided not to wait for his friend and instead headed for the bus. As he walked down the hallway, he glanced at some of the murals that covered the walls. An array of fighter aircraft, starting with the old P-51 Mustang, was depicted in various shooting scenes. Bullets flew from the aircraft, usually impacting some hazily drawn enemy plane. Other scenes in the mural showed jets dropping bombs, bridges exploding, and black smoke billowing up from oil tanks.

The planes evolved into other models, finally coming to an F-4 Phantom, then at the end of the hall, the F-15E Strike Eagle. The aircraft of the 3rd Tac Fighter Wing. Bruce noted that there was no room for other planes.

The door opened into the early morning air. It was already muggy outside. Filipino weather never varied more than a few degrees, even from night to day.

On the bus, Catman crowded down the aisle after Bruce. "Sleep well tonight, boys and girls. Your Air Force is here to protect you."

Bruce threw his flight bag on the floor and flopped into the seat directly behind Charlie. "Man, oh man. What do you think Dubois uses on his head—floor wax?"

"Hey, don't make fun of older men," protested Catman. "Foggy will get a complex." He leaned over and pretended to buff the top of Charlie's head with his knuckles.

"Okay, you clowns."

Bruce found himself popping his gum. The discovery brought back memories of a few nights back—the young Filipino girl and the rush he had felt when he saw her.

He shook off the feeling. He was probably just getting excited about the flight, the first they'd had since coming in. And the girl was just an icon of his freedom. It could have been any girl, any stranger that looked his way, and he probably would have felt the same elation. It was just his subconscious clearing his mind for him.

He chewed his gum faster. *So much for self-psychoanalysis*, he thought. *Let's get down to business.*

Skipper appeared at the front of the bus; he grasped the metal railing with both hands as the bus started off. "Quick change to the radio frequencies, ladies. Listen up: Button 1 is now the squadron frequency, Button 2 is ground control, 3 tower, 4 is first departure and Button 5 is for the bomb run at Crow. That's just backwards from what we briefed. Any questions?"

"Any reason why they changed it, Skipper?"

"Not enough work for the Colonels—something's got to keep them busy."

Bruce reached into his flight bag and pulled out his knee board. Maps and a list of the radio frequencies were clipped to the wood. He quickly penciled the change.

Catman and Robin chattered away. "Hey, what about that Major Dubois? Anybody know if he can talk?"

"Nope. Probably got a command lobotomy once he made field grade, so the Wing has put him out to pasture."

"All right, you clowns," cautioned Skipper. "Try to pull one over Dubois and he'll ream you. Remember he's the flight scheduler. How'd you like to be flying Christmas day?"

"Do they have Christmas over here, Skipper? I'd have thought they'd cancel it because of the heat."

The bus moved onto the taxiway and slowed. They passed by a row of C-130 transports. The low-slung lifters were the quintessential workhorse of the 1st Special Operations Squadron.

They pulled up J ramp to a line of F-15s; the bus slowed to a stop.

"Twenty minutes," reminded Skipper.

Bruce spotted his aircraft's tail number. In the distance, palm trees just off the runway added to the feeling of stifling humidity. He and Charlie approached the fighter, each quiet, each going over what was needed to prepare for the flight.

An older man approached them, dressed in battle fatigue pants and a vee-neck T-shirt. Sweat spotted most of the man's T-shirt, especially around the armpits; he looked to be in his early forties, nearly twice as old as Bruce. The man held out a hand. He nodded to Charlie but spoke to Bruce.

"Lieutenant Steele? I'm Tech Sergeant Noresteader, your crew chief. Welcome to Clark."

Bruce stopped, dropping his flight bag. "Glad to know you. Call me 'Assassin' when the brass isn't around."

The man cracked a grin as they shook hands. "My friends call me 'Mooselips.' "

"Okay, Mooselips. Captain Fargassamo goes by Foggy."

"That's some call sign, Captain."

"It's not for the name, it's—"

Bruce interrupted Charlie's explanation. "We call him Foggy because no one can understand what the hell he's talking about." Bruce tapped his head with a finger. "Professor type. We'd call him 'Prof,' but call signs have to be at least two syllables."

"I think I'm going to enjoy working with you, Captain."

"Foggy," corrected Charlie.

"You got the 781?" interrupted Bruce.

"Yeah." Mooselips wiped a sweaty hand on his fatigues and handed Bruce the maintenance log for the fighter.

Bruce took the notebook and nodded to the waiting craft. "All right. Let's rock and roll. We've got seventeen minutes."

Charlie picked up his flight bag and headed for the fighter. Once up the stairs, he placed is gear into the cockpit and climbed in. After stowing his flight bag, he began to go over the instruments.

Bruce turned his attention to the maintenance log. He flipped through the pages. "Trouble, or anything I need to be aware of?"

"No, sir." Mooselips hesitated at Bruce's raised eyebrows. "Sorry, Assassin." Bruce went back to reading the log. "I mean, *no*. There was some preventive maintenance done on the avionics, and engine two leaked some oil during the pressure check, but I've been on top of things."

"Great." Bruce shut the book and picked up his flight bag. Mooselips took off for the auxiliary power unit while Bruce stowed his gear. Switches checked, he made his way back down the ladder and around the craft, tugging on an aileron, checking fluid levels for himself, before he finally settled into the cockpit for good.

Mooselips hovered over him, clucking like a mother

hen, as the enlisted man strapped him in. "That ought to do you, Assassin. Have fun up there for me."

Bruce pulled on his helmet. "That's a rog. Catch you in two hours."

Mooselips scrambled down the ladder. Bruce flexed his gloved hands and pulled back a Nomex sleeve, exposing his watch. One minute to check in. He clicked on intercom and went "hot-mike."

"How's it going, Foggy?"

"INS up. All screens go." The Inertial Navigation System needed at least five minutes to warm up, but once up, the laser ring gyros could bring them to their destination in a two-hour flight with less than a twenty-foot error.

Bruce clicked his mike twice, informing Charlie that he understood. He quickly surveyed the instruments. All lights glowed a soft green, visible even in the direct sunlight. Directly in front of him at eye level rose a plexiglass screen, the heads-up display, or HUD. Once on, the HUD would display critical flight and targeting information directly in front of his field of view, allowing Bruce to keep his head up.

"Okay, Foggy." This time Charlie clicked his mike twice.

Bruce listened over the radio, waiting, popping his gum. He glanced at his watch. Ten seconds.

Just as the seconds clicked to zero, Skipper's voice came over the radio.

"Maddog check."

"Two."

"Three." Catman.

Bruce said, "Four."

"Button one."

Bruce switched to the preassigned squadron frequency. The rest of the flight was already checking in.

"Check two."

"Three."

"Four."

"Start 'em up."

On Skipper's command, Bruce pointed out of the cockpit at Mooselips. Now wearing a set of headphones to muffle the sound, Mooselips punched the auxiliary power unit; black smoke rolled from the unit.

When Mooselips pointed back at him, Bruce kicked on the right engine. A growing white noise rolled in from the back of the craft. Bruce worked overtime on his gum.

Once both engines caught, Bruce checked over the instruments. Oil pressure, fuel, hydraulics, idle RPM—everything looked good.

When Skipper's command came to pull out, Bruce nodded at Mooselips and gave him a thumbs-up. With their canopies still up, the flight of four F-15Es—eight young officers strapped to their howling metal machines—crept down the taxiway.

And as much as he despised military bullshit, Bruce felt a thrill as Mooselips popped to attention and threw him a salute.

Kadena AFB, Okinawa

The flight times were all classified.

No more than twenty people knew about the keying material, the destination, fight plan, or even time of day that the Lockheed SR-71 "Blackbird" flew its mission. Even the pilots were kept in the dark, notified at the last possible minute so that they could work out their flight plans, coordinate their refueling, and keep their destination secret. The spy plane had supposedly been retired years ago, a victim of budget cuts; its very existence was a closely guarded secret.

Which was why no one could figure out how Taco Charlie, a local Japanese restaurant owner, had succeeded in setting up a portable taco stand at the end of the runway, just outside of the Kadena Air Force Base fence, a half hour before the flight was due to take off. The stand was stocked with food for tourists, complete with a crudely lettered sign in English:

AMERICAN SPY PLANE
NEXT HABU FLIGHT: 7:25 AM

It drove the Air Force Office of Special Investigation batty, but there seemed to be no harm done, and it was the standard joke that Taco Charlie was better informed than half of the intelligence services.

What went unnoticed was the presence of Taco Charlie's nine-year-old great grandson, Oniksuki. The young boy woke hours before dawn every day to pedal furiously onto the sprawling American base. Once on base, he took off for the military air terminal. There, Oniksuki waited for the morning flight from Japan. Thousands of newspapers—the *Pacific Stars and Stripes*—were delivered from Japan as the "official" newspaper of the American forces.

Haggling with the local deliverers, Oniksuki could make off with five to ten papers from each person, soon resulting in a cache of fifty to a hundred of the papers. A ten-minute bike ride up a sloping hill put the overburdened boy at the Kadena Officers' Club, where he would sit and wait in the dark to sell his papers to the American officers.

Despite all the secrecy, the one unchanging requirement that the American doctors forced upon the SR-71 pilots was a high-protein, low-fat meal immediately before a flight. Quite often the arduous missions dictated that the crew overfly "targets" thousands of miles away; the steak-and-egg meals so popular with the astronauts were ideal for the SR-71 pilots, and the Kadena Officers' Club was the perfect place to prepare the meal. Thus, anyone trying to watch the official in-flight kitchen would immediately be suspicious if they saw an order for steak and eggs come in.

Meanwhile, Oniksuki patiently sold his papers all day long, no one questioning his presence. He knew the SR-71 pilots by sight. For when the pilots turned left instead of right upon entering the Offficers' Club, and headed for the private dining room, then it was time for Oniksuki to put his papers down and pedal to his great grandfather's—the Habu was about to take off.

Exactly an hour and a half later, a diesel tractor pulled a long black plane out of the hangar. Airmen scrambled out of the way, splashing in puddles of warm water that dotted the runway. Fuel leaked out of the SR-71 Blackbird's fuselage, but no one paid the phenomenon much attention; the high-flying airplane expanded by as much as ten inches in flight because of airframe heating. The SR-71 became fuel tight once it was up to speed.

Once out of the hangar, an auxiliary power unit started the Blackbird's engines. The APU coughed on, filing the air with heavy black smoke and high-pitched whining. Soon after, the white noise of the Blackbird's engines overshadowed the whining. One airman disconnected the APU from the Blackbird while another waved two orange-covered flashlights over her head, pointing the way for the plane to follow. Once the plane started to leave, the airman snapped to attention and threw the pilots a salute.

Inside the SR-71 Major Kathy Yulok raised a silver-gloved hand and returned the honorific. She clicked her mike. "Ground control, Stella two-niner up and ready. Request permission to taxi."

"Roger, Stella two-niner. You are cleared to taxi and take off. Skies are clear, you have a window of five minutes."

"Thank you, ground control."

Kathy barely increased the throttles, making the engines climb in response. The SR-71 seemed to jump forward with even the small amount of pressure she applied. The flight had been cleared an hour ago, coordinated through the highest channels. As a result the SR-71 flight was given a priority billing as far as taxi pads, runway, and even air space. Timing was of the essence, and every routine that Kathy had accomplished, up to starting her preflight meal an hour and a half ago, was orchestrated down to the smallest detail.

There was something sexual about it. Kathy felt the anticipation, the rush that accompanied flying the fastest plane in the world. Growing up an Air Force brat, Kathy had been raised in a fighter pilot home, her father a "Smokin' Rhino" driver—the nickname for the F-4.

She clicked her mike, toggling the switch to broadcast on the intercom. "Ready, Eddie?"

Her navigator, Major Ed Prsybalwyki, came over the intercom. "That's a rog. Let's get up and get tanked."

She clicked her mike twice, affirming Ed's comment, then switched over to the tower frequency.

"Tower, this is Stella two-niner. Request permission to take off."

"Permission granted, Stella two-niner. You are cleared, your heading."

Kathy eased the throttles forward. The SR-71 started shaking. Built a good thirty years before, the 1960s vintage craft still felt state-of-the-art. Some of the SR-71s had clandestinely survived an attempt by the Air Force to scuttle the aircraft. Congressionally mandated budget cuts had dictated that the vintage spy planes be replaced by other, "national technical means" of verification. But after the Gulf War, the Air Force had squirreled away five of the craft.

Kathy glanced over the instruments one last time. The bubble of the high-altitude helmet cut back on her vision, but she forced her eyes to jump from dial to dial.

"Engines, a hundred and four; fuel, ten thousand pounds; oil, pressure looks good." She clicked her mike. "Let's do it."

Without waiting for a reply, Kathy released the

brakes and simultaneously punched the afterburners. Two Pratt & Whitney turbojets, each producing thirty-four thousand pounds of thrust, kicked in. The SR-71 takeoff roll was short, and as soon as they rotated Kathy started searching for the KC-10A Extender—the tanker aircraft that would fill them with enough fuel to reach their first checkpoint.

Kathy pulled a map from the clipboard. The Indian border was going to make this trip a long one.

Seoul, South Korea

"Hey, Roger—you got a minute?"

"Sure. What's up?"

Soloette Arquine motioned with her eyes to the ceiling. "The cage?"

"Yeah." Roger Epstein rocked forward in his chair. He placed the message he had been reading in a small safe behind him and closed the inner drawer. Shutting the safe's door, he twirled the knob and yanked the handle. The safe was the standard Government Services Agency issue, with one additional feature: if a combination was not dialed into the safe before opening the inner drawer, a pool of hydrochloric acid was released onto the papers left inside.

It was a feature Roger Epstein had had nightmares about when he first entered the Agency, but now, as Agency Station Chief, the dual-protection mechanism was second nature to him.

Roger followed Soloette Arquine up the stairs to the third floor. Decorated in Far East decor, the hallway did not reveal the embedded fine copper mesh just under the dry wall. The mesh acted as the first line of defense against electromagnetic emanations that might leak from the building.

A Marine sat behind a desk at the top of the stairs. The young man checked the identification badges of both Roger and Soloette—even though they were only two of ten operatives who had access to the floor.

Ever since the Moscow debacle, when the United States Marine Corps had compromised its integrity and security with an alleged "sex scandal," the Marines had played their detail by the book. Roger thought that there probably wasn't a cockroach here that hadn't passed Marine scrutiny.

The "Penthouse"—smaller than the lower two floors and basement by a factor of three—housed Agency operations. Communications equipment, crypto gear, computerized files, and a weapons cache dominated most of the Penthouse. The Penthouse was windowless; steel walls as thick as a battleship hull ensured that information would not be compromised. Not even a terrorist bazooka would disrupt activities.

Sitting in one corner of the room, the main feature in the Penthouse was known simply as "the Cage." Designed by the renowned antiterrorist specialist Jack Ryan, the Cage had been constructed of a hemispherical weave of copper mesh and sonic absorbers. The copper acted as a Faraday cage, isolating the inside against any electromagnetic probes.

The sonic absorbers prevented the Cage from vibrating with the small but detectable sonic vibrations set up by even a whisper. It was the only absolutely secure place in the entire complex. There had been rumors of sexual tête-à-têtes inside the cage before Roger arrived as Station Chief—the rumors had stopped, but Roger didn't know whether it was because of his presence or because they had only been rumors.

Once inside, Soloette handed Roger a folder marked EYES ONLY. Roger tore open the envelope. It was a digitized image of two people. The image looked hazy, as if taken from some distance.

Roger looked up. "Yan Kawnleno."

"Surprised?"

"Very." Roger plopped down on a chair. The man in the picture looked like any ordinary man, like the person on a crowded bus going downtown. It was in fact the same man who had successfully eluded the most sophisticated surveillance devices in the world. "He hasn't surfaced since the assassination attempt. How recently was this taken?"

"Last week." She paused. "Bangkok airport."

"*Bangkok?* Oh, oh, oh." Roger rocked back.

Soloette looked puzzled. "What's up?"

Roger studied the picture as he spoke. "Before you got here . . . Kawnleno was involved in an assassination attempt on the Thai President." It was Soloette's turn to look surprised. "We kept it quiet, trying to draw Kawnleno out, but he didn't take the bait. Turned tail and ran back up to the north." He tossed Soloette the picture. "As far as we can tell he's been running a terrorist camp, just inside the North Korean border. Brings in men and women and brainwashes them, turns them into fanatics."

Roger walked around to where Soloette studied the picture. Even after computer reconstruction, the man's identity defied doubt. The technique was simple enough: Most "friendly" air terminals had an array of clandestine video cameras positioned at the international departure points—London, Hong Kong, Tokyo, Bangkok, Rome. . . . The camera images were digitized, then transmitted via satellite to a huge stable of Cray supercomputers. The Crays laboriously compared the digitized images with the images of known terrorists and "politically sensitive" individuals, enabling the Agency to track them.

Roger took the picture back. "So Kawnleno was in Bangkok."

"We assume he took a flight to North Korean."

"Any idea who the other guy is?"

She shook her head. "Langley is still working on a positive ID. The Kawnleno ID just came in."

Roger thought for a moment, then headed for the door. "Keep me informed. Let's hope whoever that guy is, he's not Kawnleno's student."

"You got it."

CHAPTER 5

Monday, 4 June

Headquarters, Thirteenth Air Force

A moat dragon guarded the anteroom outside of Major General Simone's office.

Juanita Sanchez, General Simone's secretary, efficiently ensured that the general was never disturbed.

Major Steve Hendhold emerged from Simone's office.

"Colonel Bolte, General Simone is ready to see you."

"Thanks, Steve."

Colonel William F. Bolte pushed past Major Hendhold as he strode into the inner sanctum. He'd never really been chewed out by Simone before. Entering the general's office normally didn't bother him—he was here at least twice a week for status briefings. But then again, he'd never had one of his pilots pull an inverted roll on a final approach.

Thank God the general had had the weekend to mull it over. He knew that if Simone had really been upset, he'd have dragged him here Friday night after receiving the note. Still, Bolte steeled himself for the worst. He was here a good half hour before the weekly Monday morning briefings.

Bolte rapped lightly on the door. "General?"

"Come on in, Lightning."

Bolte kept his face expressionless. When Simone

used call signs to address people it usually meant he was in a good mood. Bolte didn't salute when he approached. He demanded it of his own people when they entered his office, but Simone had growled at him more than once for being so formal.

"What's up, General?"

"Sit down, Lightning." The General waved him to a chair. Simone picked up a sheet of paper. The office was decorated with plaques, pictures of fighter aircraft, and a picture of the Air Force Academy chapel; the chapel picture was covered with signatures. Wood paneling and thick, royal-blue carpet gave the room a cozy feel.

Simone rocked back in his chair. "How's Michele?"

"Fine, sir. She took Nanette down to Thousand Islands with the Officers' Wives' Club over the weekend. Bought more stuff then she had money for."

"How much longer will Nanette be here?"

"Stanford starts up next month—we'll get her off in three weeks."

This was one of the last summers that Bolte would have the family back together—when Nanette graduated next summer, there was no telling where she would wind up.

Simone rocked forward. "Great. Glad to hear everything is going well. So you had to batch it over the weekend?"

"I survived, sir. Only one incident downtown, and that wasn't even a late one."

Simone pushed a sheet of paper across the desk to Bolte. "How's your new flight working out?"

Bolte glanced down at the paper—a copy of the memo he had sent Simone on Friday.

"As I noted, the last F-15Es were delivered; we're back up to full strength," Bolte said. Ever since the fighters had been pulled out of Clark because of the treaty modifications, a "temporary" crew would fly in-country for only a six-month stay.

"That's not what I asked. Are they in McConnell's squadron?"

"Yes, sir. Lieutenant Colonel McConnell has his hands full; he's the last squadron to get up to full strength, so it will take a while to shake the bugs out. But Maddog Flight is coming along fine. In fact," he glanced at his watch, "they should be over Crow Valley just about now for their familiarization flight."

Simone drummed his fingers on the desk. "This Steele character. Is he as good as his record shows?"

"We'll find out real soon, sir. They start Jungle Survival School on Wednesday. As soon as they're finished, we'll put them through the wringer—run them up against the Aggressors." He made a mental note to give a heads-up to the Aggressor Squadron. Assigned to the 3rd Tactical Fighter Wing to keep the Wing on their toes, the pilots comprising the 26th Aggressor Squadron flew F-5s—a version of the USAF supersonic training jet T-38—and acted as the "enemy" against the F-15E Strike Eagles.

"Keep a reign on these boys, Lightning. I don't want them killing themselves. But don't get too tight—I don't want to stifle them, either."

"Yes, sir. Anything else, General?"

"That's it. You've got fifteen minutes before the stand-up briefing."

Crow Valley

Maddog Flight leveled off at ten thousand feet as they flew out west, over the ocean. Bruce followed two thousand feet behind Catman and Robin, who were flying in the third ship. Flying lead, Skipper brought the formation around in a loose bank, heading back east. Rhino and Digger—Captain Harley Rheinquist and First Lieutenant Lucius Brown—had the number-two spot.

Socially, Skipper, Cougar, Rhino, and Digger were

as close as Catman, Robin, Bruce, and Charlie. Although the eight made up a tight flight, they tended to run together in the two different groups. Which was a good thing, because although the four married guys could join the bachelors and have a good time, you could tell when their kitchen passes had expired and they had to return to reality. Their families were due to arrive at Clark after Jungle Survival School, and then the social chasm would only deepen.

Bruce kept a loose hand on the stick. Skipper came over the radio.

"Tuck it in to echelon right. We'll fly over Crow Valley for a look-see and a spacer pass. Two miles to feet dry."

Bruce brought the throttles up minutely, accelerating the fighter. At first, it didn't seem that he was getting any closer to Maddog Two and Three because they were accelerating as well. When Catman's craft was closer, Bruce eased off on his throttles. They were well over land now; Bruce thought that he could spot Clark in the distance.

Skipper broke in. "Maddog, button five."

Bruce punched to the preassigned frequency for the bombing range.

"Crow Valley, Maddog. Ten miles for a spacer pass, then dry work on target two."

Charlie clicked the mike. "Down and to the right, Assassin. That's the path we'll be coming in on during our low-level sorties. What used to be rice paddies all slope down into the valley. We're coming up on the gunnery range now."

Bruce clicked his mike twice.

"Maddog, bring it down to five hundred."

They flew across the valley, taking in placements and locations of various targets. Old beat-up tanks, shot-up trucks, and burned cars littered the area. Over a thousand tons of bullets, bombs, and external tanks had been dropped in the valley. In contrast to the lush greenery of the rest of the Island, the place looked like a hellhole.

Bruce knew it was his imagination kicking in, filling in devastation where there was relatively little growth, and yet the place did seem unusually sparse. Tiny patches of bare earth dotted the landscape; he was low enough to see trees fallen over on the ground, chewed up and disheveled by millions of rounds of bullets.

Once past the valley, Skipper clicked back over the radio. "Bring it back up to five thousand. We'll go in for a strafing run—keep above two-fifty feet when you bottom out."

Charlie clicked back over the radio as Bruce pulled back on the stick. "I thought this was only going to be a look-see."

Bruce switched over to intercom. "Skipper's getting nervous. He knows we aren't going to get any flying in the next two weeks, and wants us to practice."

They reached five thousand feet and circled Crow Valley in a broad, loitering pattern. There was a hint of clouds forming over the mountains, and off to the west Bruce could barely make out a line of wispy features, delineating a front. Skipper confirmed that they were still cleared for the airspace.

Skipper's voice came over the radio. "One's in dry."

The range officer came back, "Clear dry, one."

Bruce craned his neck to the left and made out Skipper's bomb run. The F-15 tore down toward the ground, breaking from the loose formation. Dropping from nearly a mile above the ground, Skipper's jet grew smaller and smaller, making it difficult to pick out in the surrounding jungle. Even the F-15's paint scheme didn't give that much contrast against the mottled greenery.

Seconds later Skipper's voice came again. "One's off, to the right."

"Two's in, dry."

"Clear dry, two."

Rhino's fighter broke from formation and followed suit. Bruce continued to follow Catman in a sweeping turn.

"Maddog, rejoin straight ahead, altitude five thousand."

"Two's off, to the right."

"Three's in, dry," said Catman.

"Clear dry, three."

"You got that, Assassin?" Charlie was looking after them again.

"Roger that. Just point me in the right direction after we pull out, Foggy." He grew excited with anticipation. Even though the strafing run was "dry"—without ammunition—screaming down nearly a mile toward the ground kicked Bruce's metabolism into high gear. It was like preparing for a game, right before he ran out of the locker room and onto the field. The crowd cheering, slapping a teammate's shoulder pads, butting heads against another defensive back—the excitement fed on itself.

This is why he had joined the Air Force . . . to fly and get that roller coaster-like thrill that came with an adrenaline rush: It was as if he were part of the aircraft, strapped onto a thirty-one-thousand-pound bronco that outperformed anything else in the world.

"Three's off, to the right."

Bruce clicked his mike. "Four's in, dry."

The range officer came on in a clipped tone, "Clear dry, four."

Bruce slammed the stick forward, as far as it would go to the right. The F-15 rolled instantly to the right and pitched its nose down. The horizon circled crazily around the cockpit. They accelerated down, still spinning. Bruce pulled the stick back to the middle after three rolls and concentrated on a blasted tank that sat in a clearing. His vision seemed to tunnel in onto the vehicle, wiping out any other sight as they descended.

"Passing three thousand." Charlie's voice came coolly over the intercom.

Numbers rolled past his vision, projected on the heads-up display. Flipping the protective cover off the button for the machine gun, Bruce's thumb lightly tapped the red button. A crosshair appeared on the heads-up display, indicating that the machine gun, although devoid of bullets, was armed.

The triangle jumped around the screen, following the projected path of the bullets.

"Two thousand."

They were traveling at a fifteen-degree angle. The seconds seemed to stretch into minutes. His mind raced ahead, thinking at unbelievable speeds. He flicked is eyes down to his instruments, rapidly checking for red lights. Back up to the heads-up display . . .

"One thousand."

His finger caressed the trigger. *To lay down hot killing metal.*

Bruce pulled the trigger. A red blinking light on the heads-up display showed that he was out of bullets, but he kept the cross hair fixed on the tank.

"Five hundred, approaching altitude. Pull up!"

Bruce pulled back on the stick. The fighter responded instantly, pulling its nose up. He immediately felt the gee-forces grow.

"Two-fifty feet. Bottom out."

"Four's off, to the right," said Bruce. As they clawed back up, the gee-forces mounted. The gee-indicator quickly rose past five, then slowed as it hit six.

Six times the force of gravity squashed him deep into his seat. It felt as if he were being covered by a load of cement. His vision grew hazy, like he was looking down a long tunnel. He grunted loudly as the gee-suit constricted, preventing blood from pooling in the lower parts of his body.

Bruce forced his head to the side and looked out the cockpit window. The tank was far below; he imagined it smoking from the hit and decided not to climb up to altitude yet.

He pushed forward on the stick, bringing the fighter's nose down and cutting back on the gee-forces. At two thousand feet he leveled off. He clicked the mike, keeping it on intercom. He couldn't find the Flight.

"Four's off blind."

"Heading two-seven. I've got them on screen," said Charlie, referring to his color radar. "At this rate, we'll have an hour to kill before that appointment at the housing office."

Lead came over the radio. "We're at your right, three o'clock, four. Five miles." He sounded pissed that Assassin had lost Maddog Flight.

"Four."

The rest of the Flight was still too far off for him to see. Below them the valley fanned out to a patchwork of level rice paddies, broken up by dense clumps of jungle. He really needed another strafing run—the adrenaline still pounded through his veins, making him feel as if he had to burn off energy. He went to intercom only.

"Foggy, any traffic around?"

Charlie sounded skeptical. "You're clear, Assassin. What you up to?"

"Let's get in a little sightseeing, then hit the blower to catch up." Bruce nosed the F-15 back down. They descended, moving down in altitude until they approached two hundred feet. The ground below them whizzed past as Bruce kept the throttles steady at five hundred knots.

He nosed the craft down until they were just at one hundred fifty feet. The tree tops looked like solid ground at this speed. Bruce hit the speed brakes and pulled back on the throttles, slowing the craft. They broke over the clearing; the next patch was at least three miles away. Bruce forced the fighter even lower until they were a mere twenty-five feet above the ground.

"Yeowwww!" A song roared through his mind: "I Go To Extremes."

"Fantail, Assassin. You've got a nice one."

Bruce looked over his shoulder. Dirt swirled in two "fantails" as the F-15's exhaust hit the ground. He turned back to the front. Flying so close to the ground was as exhilarating as diving toward it. They had about another mile until the jungle—time to pull up.

That's when he spotted the people on the ground.

Two hundred yards in front of him three people, all wearing coolie hats, looked up at the oncoming jet. They must have been working in the field; one of them carrying a bucket pointed at the fighter.

"Holy shit!" Bruce slammed the stick back; as the nose lifted, the aircraft was moving slow enough that it felt like they were going to stall. An alarm shrieked throughout the craft, warning of an excessively high angle of attack.

"Stall, stall!" screamed Charlie.

Bruce shoved the throttles forward, hitting his afterburners. The fighter seemed to vault forward as they accelerated straight up. He swiveled his head around. Through the dust, he saw hats and buckets flying everywhere; there was no sign of the people. He must have pulled the fighter up right over the poor sons of bitches.

He punched off the afterburners and arched the craft over in a loop, flying back over the field but at a thousand feet higher than before.

Charlie came over the intercom quietly. "What the hell was that, Assassin? You trying to kill us?"

Bruce banked the F-15 toward the rendezvous point. He could barely make out three people down below, shaking their fists at the fighter.

"Just seeing what this baby can do," answered Bruce, trying to sound flippant. Inside he felt like crap.

And that was before the debrief, where he *knew* he was going to eat shit.

Clark AB

Located on the north side of the base, the Officers' Club sat between the senior and junior officer's housing. Dyess Highway looped around the north side, past the Officers' Club and down to the flight line. More than once, flight crews dining at the "O'Club" had to sprint up from their tables when an alert broke out.

Young and old alike used the club extensively. The younger, and mostly unmarried, pilots frequented the Rathskeller; the married groups tended to congregate in the formal bar and dining rooms.

The pool was a middle ground for both, and as such was a "demilitarized zone" between stuffy formality and wild parties.

Captain Charlie Fargassamo relaxed in the sun. A thick book lay open on his chest. His eyes were closed, and the water from a plunge into the pool some minutes before had evaporated from his body. As he drifted in and out of sleep, for the first time since arriving in the P.I. he felt that he was in paradise.

The early afternoon sun purged this morning's flight from his mind. He normally had the utmost confidence in Bruce's flying ability. The guy was good; his problem was that he knew it.

Charlie dismissed the observation—there he was, letting his interest in psychology take over and analyze his friends for him. Bruce *was* good. It was just that sudden pull-up, and Charlie screaming about the stall, that had hit Charlie hard.

That moment he had realized that Bruce was human, not invincible, and prone to the same mistakes and errors that everyone made. But when Bruce made a mistake, it wasn't just him that was affected—Charlie's butt was on the line, too. Through the pleasant folds of heat and drowsiness, he heard a familiar voice.

"Foooggggggyyy!"

Charlie barely lifted his head and opened his eyes. Bruce, Catman, and Robin stood just outside of the pool area at the opposite side of the complex. They raised their beer bottles in a toast to him. Still decked out in flight suits—the ubiquitous "green bags" that distinguished the rated, or flying officers, from the rest of the Air Force—the three seemed to be having trouble standing up.

Charlie threw them a halfhearted wave.

"Foooggggggyyy!"

Bruce and Robin were holding Catman as they would a log. They pantomimed tossing him into the pool. Catman started squealing like a hog.

On the other side of the fenced-in pool area, not twenty feet from the three officers, two women, who certainly weighed six hundred pounds between them, bathed. The officer's squeals were meant for the two overweight women. Some people turned to stare at the men. Uproarious laughing drifted across the pool area as they left, staggering back down the steps to the Rathskeller.

Charlie sighed. He'd have to commandeer another taxi for them tonight. A shadow passed over him, then went away; probably a cloud. It was time to jump back into the pool. Opening his eyes, he sat up.

A woman laid her towel on the chair right next to him. Charlie drew in a breath. She had an ageless look, flawless; he couldn't tell if she was eighteen or forty.

A slight tan accented a white two-piece swim suit; long blond hair was set off by dark eyebrows. She was slender, but not skinny.

He realized that he had been holding his breath when his chest started hurting.

She swung her hair around, glanced his way, and showed a quick flash of teeth. She settled into her chair, then rummaged through her purse before hauling out a book. A pair of sunglasses with white frames came on before she started to read.

Charlie blinked. It was if a goddess had descended from the heavens.

Flawless.

He had leaned on one elbow to watch her, when she turned to him. She wore a slight frown. "Excuse me. I'm sorry for not asking, but is this seat taken?"

He couldn't see her eyes, but that made her more exotic. "Uh, no, it's not." He waved an arm. "Feel free to stay." *Oh, please God, stay!* He started to settle back down into his chair. He pulled his book up to him.

She lifted her sunglasses and squinted across the pool. She motioned toward the Rathskeller with her eyes. "You're sure your, ah, friends, weren't planning on using them?"

"Friends? Those guys? Are you kidding? They wouldn't be caught dead in here—drinks aren't served out by the pool. Besides, they're having too much fun to come swimming."

Dryly: "I noticed." She swung her hair behind her head and put her feet up on the lounge chair.

Charlie watched her for a moment before settling back in his seat. He brought his book up and tried to read. His hands felt wet, and if he had to speak with her again he wasn't quite sure he could be coherent. He felt ashamed at himself—he was acting like he'd never seen a beautiful girl before.

When he was in college, Louisiana Tech had had some of the best-looking girls around—absolute dynamite, and their good looks almost made up for the Southern Belle act and the sticky-sweet talk. Every location in which he had been stationed—Phoenix, Fort Walton Beach—had always had more than their share of head-turners. As a college professor's son Charlie had been around coeds all his life. For him it was easy to find a good-looking woman, but one with a head on her shoulders, instead of air—that was another matter.

But this woman carried herself with poise. Her tan meant she had free time during the day; and the bag she carried resembled those carried by flight crews.

She had to be a stewardess, then. They sometimes frequented the O'Club pool, but were usually driven away either by the families or the hordes of pilots. He stole a glance—no ring. She couldn't be a high school student, she was much too mature; and he couldn't believe that an unmarried teacher for the Department of Defense schools would have lasted this long, unless she was new.

Which led him back to his original conjecture of a stewardess.

He suddenly realized that he hadn't read his book at all since picking it up. It was as if his eyes had been flash-burned by the sight of her.

He put down his book and headed for the pool. Not looking back, he dove in and stroked for the far side. He pushed off the side and glided the width of the pool underwater. The movement relaxed him, took away some of the tenseness that had been putting his muscles into rigor mortis.

Charlie lifted out of the pool, water dripping, and headed back to his seat. He could just make out the title of her book.

Reaching for his towel, he tried to sound relaxed. "What's an airline stewardess doing reading a book called *Alive*? Doesn't that make your passengers uneasy?"

She looked up. "I'm not a stewardess."

Charlie's mind yammered at him, but he was in too far to back out. "You're not? I'm sorry—it was meant to be a compliment. But how do you like the book?"

She put down her book. "It's all right. A little gory."

"Canibalism usually is. But at least those guys had a conscience about it."

"You've read it?"

"Oh, yeah. Years ago, but it sticks with you."

She brushed back her hair. "What do you mean 'at least they had a conscience'?"

Charlie finished wiping himself off. He sat on the side of his chair. "Ever hear of Alfred Packard? There's a cafeteria named after him at the University of Colorado."

"No." She drew her legs up, but seemed interested.

"Talk about macabre. Packard was a guide in the Rockies, took a group up in the fall and got caught in a snowstorm. That spring, he was the only one who made it back from the mountains." Charlie paused. "They later discovered he had murdered, then eaten, everyone in his party to stay alive. At least those soccer players in your book knew that what they were doing was morally repugnant when they were forced to resort to cannibalism. Packard didn't hesitate to commit murder, much less eat the people."

She shivered. "So what's a pilot doing reading stuff like that? Ever afraid you'll make your friends uneasy?"

Charlie grinned. "I'm not a pilot."

She lifted an eyebrow. "Oh?"

"Really. And by the way, I'm Charlie."

"Nanette."

When he shook her hand, it took all his strength to let go.

CHAPTER 6

Monday, 4 June

Clark AB

A monkey-wood sign hung over the Officers' Club main entrance. The sign pointed to PIZZA at the left and RATHSKELLER to the right; muffled yelling and whistles came from the right. Bruce, Catman, and Robin turned toward the Rathskeller.

As they approached the door, Bruce heard methodic banging and thuds coming from inside. He cautiously opened the door . . .

. . . and pulled back as a beer bottled whizzed past his head. A female laughed, then shrieked as two men plopped her on top of a table. Music blared from speakers set throughout the room, not new music, but old, solid rock classics, the type of songs that had been popular when Bruce was in high school: Van Halen, 38 Special, Rush, Boston. It marked a fighter pilot hangout, keeping with the hard-driving songs.

They eased themselves into the room and made sure the door was closed behind them. There was little cigarette smoke in the air. In front of them a group of fighter pilots gulped "afterburners"—flaming concoctions of Wild Turkey and crème-de-menthe, ignited with a match.

Besides the girl on the table, two scantily clad females gyrated at the front of the room on a small stage. They wore cowboy attire—chaps, a frilly shoulder throw, and cowboy hats—but that's where the resemblance to cowgirls stopped. Black bikinis made up the rest of the Western outfit.

A long bar ran across the opposite wall, with four bartenders keeping busy filling pitchers of beer and mixing "afterburners."

Catman shouted into Bruce's ear over the music, "I feel right at home! We could still be at Luke, if I didn't know better!"

Bruce nodded tightly as he surveyed the place. *Yeah*, he thought, *back at Luke.* The sudden memory of Ashley raced through his head. She was behind the bar, her golden hair flying as she poured the drinks; her job as a bartender pulled in that extra money so they could jet off to Aruba, Mazatlan, or some other exotic place for an extended weekend. Bruce's hours were always changing, and at first her job had given them a chance to be together during the days when he didn't have to fly.

It had seemed perfect back then, and it was a real kick to watch the face of a senior officer's wife when she learned that Mrs. Bruce Steele not only didn't belong to the Officers' Wives' Club but was a bartender as well.

Robin waved them over to a table. Commandeering a waiter, he shouted over the noise, "San Miguel?"

"You got it." Bruce and Catman elbowed their way through the crowd.

Catman stacked another beer bottle on top of the pyramid growing in the center of the table. Bruce sipped his beer. The alcohol gave him back that nice warm glow. He knew that tomorrow morning his head would ache, his breath would smell, and he'd be passing gas like crazy, but at least he felt good now. He looked at Charlie.

"Seems there's never enough time for the simple things in life, anymore. Things are moving too fast, changing all the time." He looked wistful. "Even finding a girl who believes in relaxing—you know, stuff like holding hands, going for walks. Simple things, just spending time together."

Charlie stared into his drink.

Bruce took another pull on his beer. "I remember when Ashley and I were first married—just out of the Academy, roaring through Texas to Del Rio for pilot training. We didn't have much money then. She didn't have a job and man, were we stretching the paycheck. Even buying a malt was a big decision. We used pillowcases stuffed with laundry until we could scrape enough money together to buy a pillow." Bruce glanced at Charlie. His backseater still had his head down.

"Hey, you s'all right?" Bruce gave his backseater a playful push. *Damn, Charlie was a nice guy.*

Charlie looked up and smiled slightly. "I'm fine," he whispered.

Bruce nodded. "Great. You know, sometimes I wished there'd be more simple things like that in life to enjoy. After leaving Del Rio, Ashley and I never had the time—maybe that's why things didn't work out." He gripped his bottle tightly and blinked. The events of the day seemed to be catching up with him, welling up his emotions. . . .

Charlie said quietly, "Does she still mean something to you?"

Bruce shook his head, scared to say anything, afraid that his voice would crack. *Oh, God, how can losing your wife not affect you?* If it had been anything he had done, something that he could have changed to make her stay . . . but it had been totally out of his control. And what she had done . . .

Bruce wiped his eye with the back of his hand. He spoke in a low voice. "She would never go for a walk. She was always into keeping busy, buying the fastest car, eating the most expensive food. I guess I never thought that her working as a bartender would hurt—you know, bringing in the extra money and all. It . . .

it probably doesn't explain what she did. . . ." His voice trailed off.

Charlie leaned against the bar. "What about your Dad? Does he still mean something to you?"

Bruce finished his beer without answering. Things were starting to get hazy. He'd had plenty to drink, and if he didn't get a handle on things he'd be crying in his beer all night.

Charlie persisted. "Well, are you going to see him?"

"Someday. Sure, why not. Hell, he's stationed at Subic. We were only five minutes away when we were flying this morning, Charlie. Maybe I'll get down there after Survival School."

A voice interrupted him. "Excuse me."

Two men in flight suits slid in next to the bar. One came very close to pushing Bruce out of his seat; the other plopped down on a free stool.

Bruce opened his mouth to retort when he saw the patch on on the men's shoulders. "Rotorheads! You guys in Rescue?"

"That's a rog."

Bruce leaned over to shake their hands. "How ya'll doing? I'm Bruce Steele, and this chucklehead is Charlie Fargassamo. Assassin and Foggy." The helicopter pilots returned the handshakes.

"Richard Head."

"Bob Gould."

Bruce stood, wavered slightly, then offered Head his stool. "Go ahead. I've been sitting all night. You guys want a drink?"

"Sure."

Bruce motioned with his hands to the bartender. "Hey, include these gentlemen with the round." The presence of the chopper pilots brightened Bruce's mood, pulling him out of his funk. "So how long have you been here?"

Gould leaned back against the bar. "Oh, about fifteen minutes."

"What the Captain meant to say," interrupted

Head, "is that he just arrived here on Clark. I've been here two years and have two left."

"Your family is with you?" asked Charlie.

"Locked up safe and tight up on Thirty-First Place." At Charlie's puzzled look, Head explained, "You guys must be brand-new too. That's on-base officer's housing. You'll be staying off-base at one of the American compounds. And if you're bachelors, you'll probably be there your entire tour. That's one nice thing about coming to Clark without a family—you'll rotate back to the States faster."

At a nudge, Bruce looked up. Catman and Robin had crowded in next to him.

The beers arrived; the first two went to the helicopter pilots.

Bruce drew on his, finishing half the bottle. He smacked his lips and pointed to the two chopper pilots. "Gentlemen, meet Richard Head and Bob Gould—Rotorheads, Esquire."

"Well, I'll shit a brick. Howdy, guys. I'm Catman."

"Robin."

The four fighter jocks surrounded the chopper pilots, buying them drinks, laughing at their jokes, and in general doing everything they could to make them feel welcome. They all knew that their lives might one day depend on the helicopters that these men flew.

Angeles City, P.I.

Ceravant stood across the street from the Skyline Hotel and pulled on his cigarette. He watched a long van drive up to the front and stop. Men and women spilled out of the van, laughing, all dressed in uniforms. He tensed when he first spotted the people, but as they came into view he recognized the uniforms of commercial airline employees.

The flight crew was spending the night in the hotel while their plane was serviced. The planes were contract carriers, on lease by the United States government to ferry the military personnel from the States to the P.I. The military owned vast fleets of its own airplanes, the giant C-5s and smaller C-141s that dotted the tarmac on Clark, yet in Ceravant's eyes the Americans flaunted their superiority, thinking that their people were too good to be transported on those war machines. It was just another itch that made the entire American presence unbearable.

A human sea washed around Ceravant as he waited for Pompano Sicat. It was getting dark, and in a few moments he would be unable to distinguish one face from another. Most of the Filipino men were dressed in identical white shorts and dark pants. In their school days, the school's uniform-of-the-day was the unchanging white on black.

Ceravant had dressed the same way, in order to blend into the crowd. His avant-garde friends at the University of the Philippines would be dumbfounded if they saw him now. But then again, they'd be amazed that *anyone* would actually do something and take action against the Americans; they were long on talk, but pretty damned short on changing things.

He threw down his cigarette, then glanced at his watch. Pompano was late. Not by much, but it still irritated Ceravant. Kawnleno would never put up with this: Time was much too valuable. Finally a jeepney pulled up to the curve. A crowd of people rushed off the vehicle.

Ceravant saw Pompano slowly step down from the corrugated metal floor onto the street. The man looked around, spotted Ceravant, then started walking down the street. Ceravant stepped in behind him, then moved abreast of him. People pushed past them, but they were close enough to speak without being overheard. Pompano spoke first.

"So, my friend. What is it that you bring?"

"A plan." Ceravant touched Pompano's arm, pointing to a dark street plunging away from the main avenue. When they turned the corner they found themselves walking along a row of quiet houses. The city's roar was still discernible in the background, but the abodes seemed like a quiet oasis amid the fast-paced downtown life. There were many such pockets scattered throughout Angeles, further enforcing Ceravant's perception that the city was a two-dimensional facade, set up mostly for the benefit of the Americans. It lacked the depth, the rich history of other Filipino cities.

They walked next to walls covered with broken glass to prevent burglars and vandals from entering. Pompano reached in his pocket and pulled out a pack of cigarettes. He offered one to Ceravant.

Ceravant noticed the official blue-seal emblem that covered a portion of the top of the pack. He shook his head and pulled out one of his own.

"Ceravant, you university types take this much too seriously. You want to cut yourself completely off from the Americans? Bah, it will never happen. Everyone is in bed with everyone else, no matter how well you clean house."

"Supporting their black market only builds up the American presence. The claws are reaching deeper every day, even as they retreat from Clark."

Pompano nodded. "That may be true, my friend. Yes, I pay twice as much for these American cigarettes as that fine Filipino brand you are smoking; and yes, the American housewife that brings me a hundred cartons she received from her friends is spending my money on their base, and not in the Angeles economy." He blew a deep breath of smoke out. "But, ah! These cigarettes are from God's own garden." He crossed himself as he spoke. "Yes, I want to hasten the Americans out, but if I do not sell our countrymen these blue-seals then someone else will."

Ceravant scowled. "I did not come to debate how much better those American cigarettes are than ours.

It does not matter. Our cigarettes could taste like cari-
bou shit—"

"And some do."

"But the point is," said Ceravant, carefully ignoring
Pompano's interruption, "every American item we
buy, we sell, we push, or we use is dividing our country and forcing us farther and farther away from complete independence. The people are reluctant to have
the Americans leave, and it grows more so every
day."

Pompano stopped and puffed for a minute. He
spoke quietly. "My friend, you are missing *my* point.
I despise the Americans as much as you." He narrowed his eyes at Ceravant. "And probably even more
so, for what they did to me, did to my family. That I
can never forgive. But I must face reality. Not as an
idealistic student such as yourself, but as a business-
man. As a father who must care for his daughter."

"Yolanda is old enough to take care of herself—"

"Leave Yolanda out of this!" The rebuke came
swiftly, strongly. Ceravant took an involuntary step
backward at the harsh tone. Pompano continued, but
lightly.

"The reality I must face is greater than a simple
black-and-white decision: If a young person comes
into my sari-sari store, I do not question him if the
San Miguel he is buying is for himself, for if I do then
he will go to another store, who will probably not only
sell him the beer but set him up with a prostitute as
well. It is survival, and a economic necessity. I cannot
boycott American goods, just as I cannot boycott Japanese goods." Pompano spit at the word. "I believe
in a separate P.I., but there is reality to deal with."

Ceravant felt himself warming to the debate, but
knew that he could not persuade the old man with
words. There was a limit to what the tongue could
accomplish, and Ceravant felt that the line was close.
But he had to say one last thing.

"You must remember, Pompano. This is a war we

are fighting. Our victories are not measured in battles won. Our measure of success is the day-to-day gain that we Filipinos get from seeing the American presence diminish; from seeing them go up against frustrating odds. And that is what we need to talk about."

Ceravant took Pompano gently by the elbow and led him down the dark street.

"The raid we accomplished—we performed very well."

"Of course. Ammunition, rifles."

"Yes, that and more." Ceravant lowered his voice. "The PC convoy had a new weapon—a high-power microwave device."

"Microwave?" Pompano snorted. "What do you propose we do with this American microwave? Cook all the meat on their base?"

"A *high-power* microwave. I have read the manual. And I have looked up the implication of this weapon. It is astounding what you can glean from the American press.

"The microwave device is not an end in itself. If we use it, we should be able to force them out quicker."

"Not an end in itself. Now you are speaking foolishly, Ceravant. Of what use is a weapon that will merely frustrate? The ammunition and supplies you have recovered should enable our people to accomplish great things."

Ceravant waved a hand. His cigarette had burned down almost to the filter. He took one last drag before flicking it away. "You do not understand. A small group, a tiny fraction of our manpower, can use this high-power microwave device to disrupt American flight activities. If we can get close enough, the microwaves will disrupt circuitry, cause the flight controls on their aircraft to mess up, and they will not even know what is happening!

"Put yourself in the Americans' position: They are now negotiating with our country a plan to stay at Clark. If we can frustrate the Americans in their day-to-day activities, make them know that the Filipinos do not want them here, they will be more likely to leave the P.I. The high-power microwave weapon is one aspect of our campaign to harass them; it will bug the hell out of them!

"We will be far enough away from Clark to avoid complete burnout of their electronics, but we will still succeed in disrupting their equipment."

"Why don't we simply get a missile and fire it at them, if that is what you want?"

"Because that would give the Americans a target, something tangible to rally around—and maybe force them to stay. And they will eventually ferret us out. But this high-power microwave weapon . . . it is just the device that could help make them leave."

He paused.

"We will acquire a new base camp—a safe house to which we can flee. We are leaving tomorrow. I am in need of another driver. Can I count on your joining us?"

"How long will we be gone?"

"No longer than a week."

"That is short notice."

"Invitations are not sent out for revolutions."

Pompano was silent for a moment. "I will join you."

Clark AB

Charlie pulled Catman aside. At the bar, Bruce swept up his hands in a fighter pilot's rendition of an inverted roll. His newfound friends watched in amusement.

Charlie leaned into Catman's ear, holding him upright.

"What do you guys have planned for tomorrow?"

Catman bleared back at him; his eyes looked nearly as red as his hair. "Recover."

"We don't have to report to the Jungle Survival

School until the day after tomorrow. I thought we'd be able to take in some of the sights."

Catman closed one eye. Now Charlie *knew* he was drunk. Catman didn't resort to that maneuver unless he started seeing double.

"Okay, Foggy—what's up?" The words slurred together. "Going alone has never stopped you before."

Charlie hesitated. Bruce's sudden divorce had seemed to bowl his friend over. Whatever had happened between Ashley and him was top-secret material. There had to be something the guys could do to pop the building pressure.

"Okay, swear you never heard this from me— Bruce's dad is stationed at Subic."

Catman lifted his eyebrows; his closed eye popped open. "I thought he lived in Texas."

"He did—with Bruce's mom. You know that he's in the Navy?" Catman nodded. "But he was transferred to Subic three months ago; went remote so he could get back home faster, wouldn't have to have the family move again."

"Why didn't Assassin tell anyone?"

Charlie looked pained. "Three months ago?"

Catman frowned, then slowly nodded as the memory of Bruce's quick divorce hit him. "Oh, yeah. . . ."

Charlie wet his lips. "Don't you think it would be a good idea to get Bruce down to Subic tomorrow to see his dad? Before we go through Survival School?"

Catman smiled.

CHAPTER 7

Tuesday, 5 June

Ten miles outside of Subic Bay Naval Station, P.I.

Bruce's eyes flew open. It seemed as if he had suddenly been transported into another world. His mouth felt dry, cottony; his tongue was caked with something vile.

Somewhere in front of him a radio softly played a song; people spoke in low tones.

Bruce tried to sit up. He was slumped against a window in a high-backed seat.

A bus. He looked around. A sharp pain jolted down his body from his head to his shoulder. He winced and brought up a hand to massage his neck.

No one sat next to him. The two seats on the opposite side of the aisle were empty as well. *What the hell is going on?* he thought.

He wore loose-fitting white trousers, sandals, and a colorful shirt. A hazy memory of Charlie goading him out of his flight suit came back to him. He remembered the Officers' Club, something about a fight. . . . He touched his mouth, but felt no pain, no injuries.

The image of a helicopter flitted near the corner of his mind, but he couldn't put anything together.

He struggled to his feet. The movement caused a wave of nausea to wash over him. He placed a hand on the top of the seat and edged into the aisle.

The bus was filled with women, at least thirty ladies between the ages of twenty-five and fifty.

He swayed in the aisle, grasping the seat backs to keep steady. At the back of the bus were four kids, guitar cases and a drum set packed in with them. A hand-stenciled sign on the bass drum read THE OTHER END; they sure the hell looked like it. They shared a cigarette and glanced his way, but otherwise ignored him.

He leaned over. A middle-aged woman, dressed in a long sarong, blinked back at him.

"Excuse me." Bruce's voice sounded hoarse; he cleared his throat and spoke quietly. "Uh, ma'am. I'm sorry to—"

The woman looked away. He started to say something to the lady next to her, but she also turned her head.

He turned to the front. The laughter quieted to a low murmuring. He tapped the sleeve of the woman sitting in the seat in front of him. "Ma'am . . . Excuse me, but could you tell me where we're going? I guess I fell asleep and sort of forgot. . . ." he finished lamely.

The woman ran her eyes up and down his body. She crinkled her nose. "Subic." She turned to look out the window.

"Subic?!" Bruce was stunned. "What in the world—"

No one listened to him. *Stepford Wives*, he thought. *This has got to be a bus to hell, and it's straight out of The Stepford Wives*.

He flopped back down in his seat and stared out the window. The radio in front of the bus blared music. It brought back memories, something that he had heard before. His head started to throb; he winced, but was unable to do anything about the headache.

Then he remembered—that sari-sari store he had visited. The girl there was singing along to the same songs. This was a step back in time, back to the age when this music was popular.

The music had that same sickly sweet, freshly

scrubbed innocence, and thus sharply contrasted with the rest of the seamy Filipino culture.

He looked down and saw a huge yellow stain on his shirt. *I must have puked all over myself*. A closer inspection of the seat confirmed his suspicion. *No wonder no one is sitting near me!*

But how did he get here? Out of a flight suit and into these clothes—Charlie had something to do with it. But on a bus to Subic?

Then he remembered the conversations with Charlie about his dad. The boys didn't know about it, but that wouldn't stop Charlie—or would it? But whatever their motivation, this was Charlie's way of forcing him to meet his dad. His breathing quickened, his nostrils widened at the thought.

All he had to do was get a taxi back to Clark. . . .

He felt his back pocket—and panicked. His wallet was missing! He patted his other pockets. Feeling around the seat, he could not find his wallet. He fumbled in his shirt pocket and pulled out a piece of paper. Unfolding it, he read:

> Assassin: This was the only way, dude.
> Your wallet and $$$ are safe with us, so don't
> worry about getting rolled. Say hi to your
> Dad for us.
>
> Catman

The only way.

The boys had him figured out to a tee. He slumped back and looked out the window, trying to figure out how the hell he was going to make it back to Clark. Without seeing his dad.

His instructors at the Academy had labeled him an overachiever. Top stick at Undergraduate Pilot Training, winning the Risner Trophy . . . he was a true role model, a hero to anyone.

Except to his father.

No matter how hard Bruce tried, Joe Steele displayed no emotion, gave no encouragement.

The memories of the constant putdowns still gave him pain. Long ago Bruce had tried to understand his father's feelings: Bruce had been born while his father was at sea—the family had a long, proud history of serving as enlisted sailors. Joe Steele had not seen his son until the boy was nearly a year old, and then the first flare of jealousy arose when the young boy garnered more attention than his world-traveling father.

Bruce's lack of interest in the sea threw up a wall between the two. Bruce had gravitated toward athletics, and looked forward to attending college. Instead of encouraging the young man to pursue these interests, Joe Steele had heaped scorn and ridicule upon Bruce. "You think you're too fucking good for this family? None of your relatives have gone to college, and we've turned out fine. Look at all you've got, all you've had. Are you ashamed of us?"

The appointment to the United States Air Force Academy had been Bruce's only way out of the situation, something that he could do on his own. But the appointment only threw fuel on the fire, intensified the one-sided competition. Bruce's letters home went unanswered, and his efforts to make his father proud of him elicited no response.

When his younger brother Fred had enlisted in the Navy, the parties and hoopla surrounding the occasion quickly outstripped any show of pride that had been bestowed upon Bruce.

Then, when Joe Steele refused to show up at Bruce's graduation from pilot training, it was the final straw.

He intended to look up his father, but he wanted to do it on his own time scale. Bruce tried to settle back in his seat, but he was too worked up to relax.

The nipa huts and roadside shacks turned to row after row of corrugated aluminum-topped shanties.

Dogs yipped as the bus roared past; unclothed children, some playing in mud in front of the huts and others sitting dully on wooden stoops, all watched the bus.

The traffic increased; jeepneys darted in and out of their path. The bus slowed as it started over a long bridge. Bruce saw a brown river below them. Long canoes were being poled by men wearing Saipan-style hats. Women on the bank dumped baskets of clothes into the water, then washed them out. Upstream, an old man urinated into the water.

The bus whined, then came the crunch of grinding gears. Minutes later it slowed to a stop before a large gate.

U.S. and Filipino military men shared the building. Guards wore khaki uniforms, holstered side arms, and silver helmets. Their hair was cut buzz-short and they all stood erect, even when they walked. Marines. By the gate a sign read:

SUBIC BAY NAVAL STATION
UNITED STATES NAVY
WARNING!
PERSONNEL ON THIS FACILITY
CONSENT TO SEARCH AT ANY TIME
BY ORDER OF THE COMMANDER

The Marines guarding Subic took no nonsense, and probably wouldn't give him the time of day. No ID card, smelling to high heaven—bets were they'd just as soon lock him in the brig as try to check out his story.

You're a fighter pilot?

Yeah, *right*.

The driver opened the bus door. A marine, wearing his helmet, stepped inside and looked down the aisle. Bruce slid down in his seat and looked out the window, trying to be nonchalant, invisible.

After signing a chit held out by the driver, the guard turned to go.

They started onto the base, passing seamen and local workers. A turn gave him a view of the bay—seven large ships were moored at various locations. He picked out two frigates and a destroyer. The unmistakable conning tower and lines of an aircraft carrier were visible at the opposite end of the bay. The fleet must be in town. And so would his dad.

The Filipino driver spoke over a microphone. "Welcome to Subic. We are parked at the main exchange complex. The bus will come back here at 1530 hours and will leave at 1600. Do not leave any valuables on the bus. *Salamat po.*"

Bruce sat low in his seat and waited until the bus cleared. When the kids from the back started hauling out their rock gear, Bruce moved slowly to the front. The driver spotted him; the grin on the driver's face melted to a scowl. The Filipino leaned over and spat into a can that he kept at the front of the bus. He shooed Bruce out.

"Off. Okay, you. Get off."

"Wait. Can I get a ride back to Clark . . . ?"

"Off, you get. Hurry, ziggy now."

Bruce stepped backward off the bus. The heat hit him like a sledgehammer as he left the air-conditioned coolness of the bus. "Hey, wait a minute!" He balled his fists.

Standing on the step of the bus, the driver towered over him. The Filipino dug in his pocket and waved a dingy sheet of paper. "You see this? *Aih?* This my rules, you must obey. It signed by base commander." He pointed to a paragraph. "If G.I. disorderly I stop bus, throw him out."

"I wasn't disorderly!"

The driver stopped and spat. He looked Bruce up and down. "You get sick twenty miles outside Angeles—dirty all over. You very lucky, Joe. I want to throw you off bus, the ladies make me change my mind. I could have done it—they no let me." He spat again.

Everyone he approached ignored him. Bruce couldn't decide if it was the smell or the sight that turned them away.

He ducked into the men's bathroom outside the Base Exchange. He groaned at his image in the mirror. He quickly debated the best way to clean up, then decided to hell with it—he couldn't make himself look much worse than he already did. He stripped off his shirt and used wet paper towels to scrub himself clean. A quick rinse in the sink cleaned his shirt. Within ten minutes he looked as though he had stood in a shower with his clothes on, but at least he smelled halfway decent.

Bruce ignored the sideways looks that people gave him as he left the bathroom.

A map was posted outside of the building, protected from the weather by a plastic case. Bruce ran his fingers down the listing of facilities. His finger stopped at the notation CHAPEL. He wet his lips. The last time he'd been in church was at the Academy; he and Ashley had been married there, only hours after he had graduated. It couldn't hurt to try.

The donuts and sugary coffee that the chapel staff fixed for him gave him a sugar high. Three aspirins, and a chance to step into a quick shower, almost made him feel human again.

Chaplain White warmly shook his hand as an old, red Geo turned around the corner. The Chaplain searched Bruce's eyes. "Feel free to come back and talk, Bruce—especially if things don't work out with your father."

"Eh?" Bruce glanced at the aging Commander. "I didn't know it showed."

White smiled. "Sometimes a child has to tell his parents to go to hell before he can completely sever ties with the past." He held up a hand. "I don't mean you should do the same—that was more for shock effect than anything else."

The Geo pulled to a stop and a man stepped out. Bruce recognized the beer gut and tattoos immediately.

Andrews AFB, Maryland

The Boeing 747-200B sat at the end of the runway. The oversized cockpit looked like a graceful serpent's head, rising out of the sleek airliner's nose. To the untrained eye, and from a distance, the 747 looked like any jet transport. But the white-and-blue paint scheme, bearing the words UNITED STATES OF AMERICA, gave away the fact that the plane was an official aircraft.

The military designation "VC-25A" was assigned to the plane, a specially equipped airframe that sported a Bendix Aerospace EFIS-10 electronic flight instrument system and state-of-the-art communications gear. The jet was crammed with defensive gear, navigation aids, and electronic countermeasures. The public knew the plane as "Air Force One," although it was actually one of two aircraft; but today the plane bore the call sign "Air Force Two" in honor of the Vice-President's presence on board.

Vice-President Robert E. Adleman knew the significance of flying in the 747, rather than the old C-137Cs that were still kept as backups: President Longmire was too ill to travel, and his staff was certain that the President wouldn't need the plane.

A crew of twenty-three Air Force personnel and Navy stewards filled the plane, ranging from the pilot to the officer who carried the "football." With Longmire's illness, the woman who carried the "football" was effectively ensuring that if anything happened to the President a smooth transition of power would occur, and Adleman would have instant access to the top-secret nuclear-keying materials in the briefcase.

The presence of that young officer gave Robert Adleman a nagging sense of doubt. Lieutenant Colonel Merke was pretty enough—short-cropped red hair, striking green eyes, and a figure that wouldn't quit—but her serious nature underscored the seriousness of the trip.

A ream of papers covered the table in front of his plush seat; Dubois, one of the Secret Service men, scooped the documents up, keeping the papers in a semblance of order.

Once the table was free of clutter and Adleman could see the tabletop, the engraved Presidential seal seemed to beckon out to him. There were changes coming to his life, and he'd have to make some adjustments. Adleman leaned back and closed his eyes. *Things are going to change.*

Angeles City

It was so early that the bar girls were not in the streets. A few merchants shuffled under loads of fresh food, brought in from the countryside for the markets; cleaning crews left the all-night bowery; and a few store owners catered to the early-morning crowd. Even the jeepneys were sparse on the street.

Ceravant pulled into a parking lot at the rear of a small motel. The jeepney he drove did not seem out of place—a wild paint scheme, fuzzy balls hanging from the top. But a closer look inside the elongated jeep would have revealed several boxes lashed to the front part of the passenger compartment. If anyone tried to board the vehicle, Ceravant was prepared to politely, but firmly, turn them away.

Where were they? He had been explicit in setting the time. Then he spotted three people walking toward him. They stepped over a pile of trash and moved quietly to the jeepney. Another came around from the front, as if he had been waiting separate from the other. Ceravant made out Pompano's features as those of the lone man.

Ceravant started the vehicle and waited until the men were seated before he turned out of the parking lot. With the sparse traffic, they were leaving Angeles within minutes. The buildings grew fewer and were replaced with huts made of mud and straw. The road narrowed to two lanes; soon they passed rice paddies and saw no people at all. Ceravant slowed and half turned in his seat so that he could speak while driving.

"We will be meeting the rest of the cell shortly. From there we will travel to our new base."

Pompano leaned forward. "How long will that take?"

"Not more than a few hours. I have identified two old plantations that will serve us well—they are both isolated from the general population, yet centrally located with respect to the province. Either one will do much better than camping out in the mountains."

Ceravant glanced up at his rearview mirror; they appeared to be the only ones on the road. Soon, he knew, a steady stream of people from the outlying barrios would start their trek into the city, mostly laborers who worked on the U.S. base. By that time the Huks would be far away.

Rice paddies melted into the thickening jungle. A hand-painted sign advertising fresh fruit stood inconspicuously by the side of the road. Ceravant slowed and marked off three-tenths of a mile on the odometer. He slowed to a crawl. Just visible on the right, through the thick foliage, were the bare markings of a dirt road.

Ceravant turned onto the road and crept through the jungle for a mile. He tapped on the horn twice, then twice more before breaking into a clearing. Once he had stopped, a band of men quickly surrounded the jeepney. Ceravant made a quick head count.

"Everyone is here. Quickly now—I want us to be in place to strike before nightfall. Make sure that your weapons are well hidden, underneath the seats and covered. You two"—he pointed the men out—"drive ahead of the truck. The rest of you follow. If PCs stop us, make sure none survive. Hurry. Ziggy now." He turned to Pompano. "I want you to drive the truck, my friend. The others will ensure that you are well covered."

Pompano walked with Ceravant toward the jungle. As they drew close, the outline of a two-and-a-half-ton truck appeared. Pompano narrowed his eyes at Ceravant.

"You wanted me to come with you simply to drive this truck?"

Ceravant placed a hand on the older man's shoulder. "If you are stopped by the PC, they will hesitate before bothering you. That hesitation will give us the edge to attack and destroy them—a younger man would only draw their attention to him. Or would you rather ride with the others and have to do the killing?"

Pompano breathed through his nose and stared at the ground. Ceravant knew that he had struck a nerve. The older man had always shown a dislike for violence, while actively supporting the Huk's goals.

Pompano spoke in a low voice. "We are wasting time. I will drive."

Clark AB

"First Lieutenant Edward Holstrom?"

"Call me 'Catman'—my call sign. I haven't gone by 'Ed' for a long time." Catman plopped down in the chair offered him and looked around the office. Robin was waiting outside, ready to head downtown. Catman glanced at his watch, feeling his time was being wasted.

He sat in a typical government office—barf-brown paint on the walls, broken up by lime-green lines used for decorations. He never could understand why the non-rated pukes—non-pilots—would go to such lengths to exhibit their poor taste.

The man sitting across the table from Catman pushed his glasses up on his nose. He withdrew a wallet and flashed an official looking identification card that read DEFENSE INVESTIGATION SERVICE and had the man's picture on the side.

"Lieutenant Holstrom . . ."

"Catman."

The man pressed his lips together. "All right. *Catman*. I'm conducting interviews to upgrade the security clearance for First Lieutenant Bruce Steele. You have been listed as a reference on his information sheet. Do you know him?"

"Sure."

"Very well, how long have you known Lieutenant Steele?"

Catman stole another glance at his watch. "Assassin? Two years."

"Assassin?" The man hesitated.

"Yeah."

The investigator scribbled on his sheet.

"Now, Catman, have you ever known Lieutenant Steele to drink to excess?"

Catman thought for a moment. "No." As the man started to write, Catman continued, "I've always passed out before he got drunk."

The investigator's mouth dropped open. Catman smiled.

Subic Bay Naval Base

Chief Bosun's Mate Joe Steele stood waiting by the car. Bruce felt as if his feet were embedded in cement, incapable of movement. Bruce had not spoken to his father for the last two years. Until half an hour ago in the Chaplain's office.

And now, not ten feet away, the man waited.

There was nothing he could do to avoid the confrontation. Years ago he had sworn that he would never display the same self-centered habits, never drink himself senseless almost every night of the year like his father. Bruce glanced down at his shirt and grimaced—the faint yellow stains of vomit still decorated his clothes. *The sins of the father* . . . The very things he had abhorred had gotten him in this trouble. His face grew red; so much for learning a lesson.

Bruce swallowed and walked straight ahead to the car.

Joe Steele stuck out a hand and said gruffly, "Son."

Bruce shook his hand. "Thanks for coming."

His father looked him over. "Some party."

"Yeah." Bruce was clearly ready to get going.

"So what happened?"

Bruce shrugged. "I got a little wild. Woke up this morning on a bus—didn't know where I was, no wallet. Kind of a nightmare."

"Was the party worth it?"

Bruce had a dim memory of the night before, but his father expected another answer. Bruce felt himself slipping back to the past.

"It was okay."

His father roared and slapped Bruce on the back. "I knew those Air Force pilots had balls. That's my boy." He jerked his head to the car. "Come on. I was going to drop you off at the bus station and lend you a couple of bucks. If you have time, I'll take you by my place and show you around before you go."

"Sure." Bruce climbed into the Geo. Even though the car was old, it was immaculate inside. Another memory rolled over Bruce, that of being jerked out of his bed as a teenager every Saturday morning to fulfill his father's fetish of cleaning everything in sight—the car, the yard.

They remained quiet for much of the drive. Bruce looked out the window and spotted the fleet of ships out by Cubi Point, anchored away from the main part of Subic. They took a turn away from the base's main road. Bruce frowned—they were headed off base. He spoke for the first time since entering the car.

"Where do you live?"

"The barrio."

"I thought you had to live in the barracks."

Joe hung his elbow out the window and drove with one hand. "Not enough room. That's one of the perks of moving up in rank. Your old man is doing pretty good for himself, if you haven't noticed." He was quiet for a moment. "Have you heard from your mom lately?"

"Not since getting here."

"When was that?"

"Last week. She's looking forward to having you get home next year—eighteen months of remote duty is hard on her, but at least she knows it's the last time."

His father grunted. As they drove off base, they seemed to enter another world. The same seamy sights greeted Bruce, but along with the visual impact came a nauseating smell and incoherent sounds that had been masked by the air-conditioned bus.

His father waved a hand at the river below them. "That's called the Shit River. The Beaks use it as a sewer."

"Beaks?"

His father laughed. "You *are* new, aren't you? Beaks, flips, Filipinos. Just another name."

Just another name, thought Bruce. *Black, colored, nigger. Like it doesn't made a difference. He hadn't changed a bit.*

As they drove slowly down the street, scantily dressed girls walked up and tried to reach into the car. The girls laughed and waved as they drove on. Strange odors of burnt chicken and meat wafted through the window; loud music erupted, then diffused away as they drove past bars.

"Armpit of the world, son," said Joe, grinning. "But that's the beauty of it—you can pick and choose

whatever your taste. Like that—look at those tits!"
He pointed out a buxom black woman.

Soon their surroundings grew more tranquil. They
turned off the main drag and wove a path to a row of
low-slung buildings. The streets were still paved, but
potholes and pools of standing water dominated the
black asphalt. Bruce's father pulled up in front of one
of the apartments.

"You said you need to get back to Clark by late
afternoon?" Bruce responded with a nod. "The one
o'clock bus will get you there by three—give you
plenty of lead time. Come on in."

The apartment was typical of his father—neat,
though cluttered with tacky junk: miniature anchors,
nautical rope, dozens of model boats, wispy ostrich
feathers. His father seemed preoccupied, standing by
the kitchen door.

"Bruce, ah . . ." Joe scowled and held a hand up
to his bulging chin. Maybe that was another reason
his father had never been able to acknowledge his
athletic prowess; Bruce had been in tiptop physical
shape since high school, never even a hint of a spare
tire.

"What's up, Dad?"

"Ah, shit. Sit down, son." He waved a hand at a
wicker chair. "Beer?"

Bruce remembered last night, then answered slowly.
"Sure."

A minute later Bruce was sipping on a San Miguel
while his father downed his own can. "You know, this
really is going to be my last tour, son. Too many times
I've left your mother sitting back at home, all alone.
You and Fred were the best things to happen to her.
She loves you like crazy."

They grew quiet at the mention of Fred's name.
Bruce didn't know his younger brother well. He had
been too involved in football to have spent much time
with him . . . which made the pangs of guilt dig even
deeper. Frail as a youth, Fred eventually filled out

and took after his older brother by the time he was a senior in high school.

Fred differed from Bruce as much as Bruce differed from his father. But the younger brother had had a penchant to please, to be subservient to his father's wishes. So much so that Fred had volunteered for the Navy fresh out of high school in the centuries-old Steele family tradition. As a junior at the Academy Bruce had tried to talk his younger brother out of enlisting, but he'd been met with cold silence.

And the nail was firmly hammered in place during Fred's going-away party, when their father had drunkenly presented Fred an ornately engraved plaque inscribed: IF YOU AIN'T A SAILOR, YOU AIN'T SHIT. Joe Steele had slurred through a speech that hinted that Bruce had been destined for the plaque, made twenty years before, but that it had taken a man like his youngest son to finally fulfill a father's wish.

Fred's death last year—washed overboard when a ninety-foot wave hit the U.S.S. Bella Wood—hit the family hard.

After Fred's death, Joe Steele volunteered for a remote assignment—one without his family—at Subic, his last naval station.

Thirty-two years in the navy. One son dead, a martyr. The other seeming to do everything in his power to piss his dad off. A wife whose only purpose in life was to attend the noncommissioned officers' wives' bazaar.

His father stumbled over the words. "Now, you know I'd never do anything to hurt your mother. She and I've been married, nearly twenty-six years now." He hesitated. "Well, I've got someone to introduce to you. . . ."

Bruce didn't bat an eye when Joe introduced him to his Filipino girlfriend.

CHAPTER 8

Tuesday, 5 June

The Barrio, Subic Bay

His father's girlfriend looked pretty. Or maybe Bruce's mind was *forcing* her to be pretty, seeking a reason for his father's behavior toward his Mom.

Bruce knew the answer—the practice was openly condoned overseas. It kept the men out of the bars and out of trouble, and put some sort of routine back into their lives.

No one had ever taken UCMJ action against those who did it, even though the Uniformed Code of Military Justice specifically prohibited the behavior. Very few of the men took their girlfriends back to the States.

The woman extended her hand and smiled. "I am Tanla."

"Hi." Bruce quickly shook her hand and looked around for his seat, not wishing to show his embarrassment.

"She has to go to work," said his father, gruffly. He, too, seemed embarrassed.

Tanla nodded and slipped from the room. Bruce remained quiet; he stared at one of the anchors holding up a flower pot. Tanla appeared a minute later, smiled at Bruce, then said to his father, "You stop by later?"

"Sure." Joe Steele dismissed the woman, who left through the front door.

Bruce's father lounged back in his chair and took a pull on his beer. He hesitated before speaking.

"It's the only way to keep from going crazy, son."

"Don't make apologies on my account," interrupted Bruce. "You never have."

His father put down his drink. "Now don't start that up again." A moment passed, then, "Okay . . . okay. Bruce, I want you to listen to me."

"I am."

"I love your mother very much. If I didn't have Tanla here, I'd probably have killed myself. She keeps me honest, sober enough to go to work, and we have sex much less frequently than you'd think."

"Then why does she shack up with you?"

Joe answered softly. "Security, son. It's her way of ensuring she's always fed, always has a roof over her head. She's lived with men like me for probably ten years now . . . and as long as there are crusty ole Bosun's mates out there, she'll always have a place." He scooted to the front of his chair and placed his elbows on his knees. "She doesn't mean a thing to me, son—I'll be gone next year, and someone else will take my place. It's purely for convenience."

Bruce continued to stare, away from his father. He felt confused.

"I'm not asking you to approve, Bruce. Just accept what I'm doing."

Funny, thought Bruce. *You never accepted what I was doing*. It seemed so absurd to Bruce: The times that his father had been at home when he was younger, it had been all putdown and competition. And now, when things were upside-down, he felt closer to his father than he ever had.

Bruce whispered, "I'll try to come back after things settle down."

His father simply nodded and leaned back in his chair.

The ride back to Clark was a fog of memories, contradictions, and reminiscences. It would take time to sort out, to put the pieces together so that it all made sense.

A lifetime of beatings can't be healed overnight.

The trip took a little longer than two hours. They were stopped once by a roadblock. Men wearing colorful barongs and wide smiles waved them down and boarded the bus. The Filipino driver interpreted the rapidfire Tagalog that the men spat at him: They were collecting for the barrio fiesta and wanted to know if anyone on the bus would care to donate.

A look outside the window revealed that the bus was surrounded by men carrying rifles and semiautomatic weapons. They didn't aim the guns at the bus, yet they made no effort to conceal them.

Everyone on the bus donated at least a dollar.

The man backed off the bus, bowing and smiling while all the time repeating 'Salamat po.'

As the bus drove along the two-lane road, the rice paddies became dotted with activity. Houses began to appear, and before long they entered Angeles City. The traffic grew thick, and soon the background noise seemed to consist of one long melee of honking.

Bruce watched out the window, still sorting things out in his mind. Suddenly, he spotted a sign outside the bus: FIRE EMPIRE, the strip place he had left . . . *Friday night*? Only four days ago.

He remembered the girl he had met that night. . . . Was it really that she had been so beautiful, or had he still been on that adrenaline high from arriving at Clark, starting a new life?

"Driver!" Bruce moved to the front of the bus. "Can you let me out here?"

The driver looked puzzled. "Traffic no move."

Bruce shook his head. "I don't care—can you let me out?"

The driver shrugged, then started to open the door. He spotted the Fire Empire, then grinned widely. "Okay, have fun."

"Right."

Once off the bus the heat hit him full in the face; the sky looked like it was going to rain. Bruce darted around the jeepneys and cars, finally reaching the front of the striptease club.

"Hey, Joe—special show! Good seats for you!" A burly man waved him in.

Bruce ignored the hawker and strode up to a row of jeepneys waiting just outside the door. He tried to remember the driver and the paint scheme of the vehicle that had taken him and Charlie around. No two jeepneys were alike, but he still couldn't tell one from another.

One of the drivers gave his cigarette to his friend and called out to Bruce. "Hey, Joe—go to Clark?"

"No, the market."

"Market?" The driver grinned and threw a sideways glance at his friend. The other driver had finished off the cigarette down to the butt. "Which one?"

"Uh, one that's part indoor and outdoor. It spills into the street, high buildings all around?"

"Oh, yes—I know." The driver hopped into his jeepney and patted the seat. "Get in, Joe—I take you."

Bruce approached warily. "How much?"

The driver eyed Bruce and started to name a price. One of the men jabbered at him in Tagalog, and the driver stopped and seemed to think things over. "You been there before, Joe?"

Bruce hesitated. He wondered if the guys were about to fleece him, or if they figured that if Bruce had been there before then he would have a good notion of what the fare was. Bruce answered, "Sure."

"Okay, twenty-five peso."

Bruce climbed in back to show his approval.

Just as Bruce suspected, the man took off down one of the side streets. They wove a complicated path through the city, never quite stopping at the myriad stop signs but not racing through them either. Shortly, the high buildings that marked where the market had been appeared. The driver slowed to a stop. Bruce paid, then stepped out. Here he was back at the sari-sari store. Three children, all dressed in white shirts and dark pants, sat giggling around a table outside the tiny store. He was too far away to make out the sounds, but he could see that they all drank Pepsi. *I've still got the eagle eyes*, he thought.

As he approached, the store was less exotic in the daytime. It looked like an old county store—the type that would sell anything from individual nails to a piece of fried chicken. The long, low counter stretched completely across the back. And as before, a soprano voice trilled along with a popular song playing over the radio. The girl entered the room.

Bruce blinked and drew in a breath. She *was* beautiful.

She didn't have the features, or the relative short height, that were typical of the Filipino. If Bruce had seen her back in the States he would have been mystified as to her background. The long black hair and deep brown eyes combined with her soft, full features to give her an exotic air. . . .

She lowered her eyes. "May I help you?"

"Uh, yeah. I was here the other night—Friday?" No response. "I got some gum, and well, I guess I ran out," he finished lamely.

She turned to the shelf behind her and spoke with her back to him. "The same type?"

"Sure."

She turned and pushed two packs across the counter, brushing back a strand of hair. "Two peso."

Bruce dug out two bills. "Thanks."

"You are welcome." She flicked her eyes up at him, then lowered them, but this time shyly.

Bruce opened the pack and held it out to her. "Care for a piece?"

Silence. Then, "Thank you."

They chewed in silence for a moment. He tried to

make conversation. "Do you get much business, next to the market?"

"Some."

"Many Americans?"

"No."

"I guess this is pretty much out of the way for most of them."

"Yes."

This is crazy, thought Bruce. *The women here either try to drag you into bed or they won't talk to you.* He ran a hand through the back of his hair. She seemed willing to talk, but things just weren't going anywhere. And he desperately wanted for her to raise her head so he could see her face.

Bruce leaned against the counter. "I arrived in the Philippines last week."

"Oh?"

"Yeah. Flew in right over Angeles. It took most of two straight days to get here."

"How do you like my country?"

"It's beautiful."

"Oh? How did you find out so quickly?"

"My father lives at Subic—I, ah, visited him today, and drove through the countryside."

She brightened. "Did you get a chance to stop in any of the barrios?"

Burce remembered the roadblocks and the men asking for "donations." "Yeah, but not for long."

"The barrios can be so beautiful. My father says they used to be better. Where do you come from in America?"

Bruce was surprised to find himself droning on, expounding on the various places he had lived as a Navy brat—Virginia, San Diego—and all the bases he had lived on after entering the Air Force. She seemed fascinated by his knowledge of geography, and never once raised the issue of what he did now.

When customers entered the store she ignored

Bruce until they left, then resumed the conversation quickly.

He tried to peg an age on her and kept coming up with twenty—more mature than a teenager, but without the cynicism of someone older.

Bruce finished his beer. "I'm sorry—I never introduced myself. I'm Bruce Steele."

"Yolanda Sicat." She didn't offer her hand, but half bowed her head. Bruce followed suit.

He rubbed a hand across his face. The thickness of his five-o'clock shadow surprised him. "Say, Yolanda—I really need to get back to the base. I have to attend a survival course during the next two weeks." He softened his voice. "Is there anyway I could interest you in having dinner tonight?"

She smiled. "I'm sorry. I must stay and watch the store." Bruce must have looked crestfallen, for she said quickly, "Maybe after you return, Bruce Steele."

Bruce smiled wanly. "You won't forget?"

She laughed. "The gum-buying American? Oh, no."

He said gently, "Two weeks, Yolanda Sicat—I shall return," and turned to leave.

Tarlac, Philippine Islands

The sky drizzled a light rain, never quite breaking to a heavy downpour. The weather was well worth the trouble—certainly it would have been harder to obtain the weapons, ammunition, and that high-power microwave weapon if the day had been clear and dry; in bad weather people tended to think of themselves, and to move away from external irritations.

Today, Ceravant hoped that the trouble of getting drenched would yield them yet another prize.

They stood at the edge of a clearing in the jungle. Ceravant had directed the men to abandon the jeepneys and truck, hiding the vehicles in the dense foliage a full two miles from the clearing; unnatural sounds travel far in the jungle.

Two and a half hours of travel through the undergrowth had brought the cadre of Huks to the clearing.

Unlike the ambush of the Philippine Constabulary convoy, where the Huks had to get away as fast as they could, Ceravant fully meant to stay and use the remote plantation as a base. He had reconnoitered the location in detail, but he still didn't have a clean picture of the house's defenses.

The large, airy house sat a quarter mile away in the center of the clearing. They were almost directly behind the house, a hundred and eighty degrees from where the road came out of the jungle. Elevated off the ground by several pillars of thick red bricks, the plantation house had plenty of room for air to circulate underneath. It reminded Ceravant of a barn.

Several nipa huts sat around the house, all showing few signs of use. A children's playground sat next to the house. Clotheslines crossed the play area, and a large dirt region the size of a soccer field ran out to the jungle. To Ceravant it looked like it had once served as a holding area for crops.

Ceravant motioned to the man beside him, making a large circle with his hand. The man nodded, then crept off through the jungle to the front of the house. The minutes passed. No one came out of the house, but Ceravant saw shadows sweeping by windows and heard random sounds.

The sky grew dark. Ceravant began to feel impatient; he knew that it would be a lot easier to take the house during the day. The drizzle kept up, soaking the already waterlogged men.

Ceravant caught a glimpse of movement from the other side of the house. The Huks had reached the front. Ceravant knew that the rest of the men would be watching his position, waiting for his cue. He didn't use an animal call to notify them. Instead, he moved to the perimeter of the clearing. Nothing came from the house.

Ceravant fumbled in his pocket and pulled out a revolver; he pushed the gun firmly under his belt, crouched, and sprinted toward the nearest storage hut. He crossed the wet grass without effort, carrying his rifle in one hand. Still nothing from the house.

He waved his men to follow. Six Huks ran from the jungle, appearing from nowhere in the late afternoon drizzle. The other two-thirds remained in the jungle, covering their movement and allowing a path for escape in case something went wrong. The tactics had been gleaned from Kawnleno's teachings, but retailored for the jungle instead of the brown North Korean hills. Ceravant caught the smell of hot food wafting from the house.

He crept forward in a crouch and shifted the rifle so that he held it in both hands, the safety off and ready to fire.

A loud snap caused him to twirl. One of the Huks moved off to the left and pointed to a branch on the ground. Ceravant angrily motioned for the man to keep it quiet, then sped to the corner of the house, keeping clear of the windows. Moments later his men joined him, breathing quietly through their noses. Ceravant quickly checked them over—he made sure their safeties were off, their spare ammunition ready.

He pointed to Barguyo, the youngest of the Huks. Tasked with detonating the explosives during the convoy raid, Barguyo had been part of the New People's Army since he was fourteen. He had been recruited easily enough: as a youngster in a government-run orphanage, Barguyo had been raised by a wealthy family, the dream of every waif.

But years of sexual abuse by the rich merchant had instilled a deep hatred for those with extravagant material possessions. Ceravant had recruited the boy off the streets when the youngster had attempted to go underground, accused of murdering his foster parents. He had turned out to be the most dependable of the recruits, as one motivated by vengeance rather than ideals—which caused Ceravant to post Barguyo for the most dangerous assignments, yet keep an eye on the boy in case he should get out of hand.

Back at the University of the Philippines, the economic analogy was high risk, high yield.

Ceravant instructed Barguyo to circle the house and storm the opposite end. Barguyo nodded and slipped off with two of his compatriots. Ceravant knelt and followed his progress from underneath the house. He saw the boy's legs move swiftly around the corner. When Barguyo was in position, Ceravant nodded for the rest of the men to follow him. He pulled out the revolver and slung the rifle around his front—he didn't want to be slowed in close quarters. Ceravant swung up around the corner and lifted himself onto the porch. He didn't wait for the others as he moved quietly toward the door.

Two, three steps brought him to the screen—Barguyo mirrored his movements at the opposite end of the sprawling porch. Ceravant swept open the door and bolted inside. Nothing. He spotted a piano, wicker chairs, and a rug covering a waxed wooden floor. Ceravant peeled off to the left, his men covering the right.

They moved as if they were still in the jungle—stealthily, stepping carefully. Ceravant raced through a side bedroom and into the back kitchen. A toddler in a high chair banged on a plate; his older sister shrilled. The children's mother dropped a pot of water, splashing it over the floor. A scream. The woman knelt to pick up her child while keeping her eyes glued on Ceravant.

Someone bellowed outside the room; a single shot silenced the commotion.

Barguyo huffed into the kitchen from the opposite side of the house.

"Only one man."

The woman stood, screaming, "Noooooooo!"

"Silence!" shouted Ceravant. He wanted time to think, tried to remember how much traffic he had observed coming up the long stretch of road into the jungle. At this time of of year, plantations were dormant. More people were therefore not to be expected.

The woman gathered her two children around her, sobbing.

What to do with her? he thought. She was young enough to keep the men occupied.

Ceravant swung around and took in the men's faces; already some were smiling in anticipation. It might be wise to have a little entertainment . . . but one woman in a pack of men would soon start to sow dissension, plant the seeds of distrust and doubt, cause the formation of cliques and eventually turn the men against one another.

They had much more important work to attend to—to set in motion the wheels that would eventually save the Filipino people. He turned. The woman narrowed her eyes at him and drew her young children close.

Too bad that a few had to suffer in the interim.

Ceravant drew up his pistol and pumped two bullets into the woman's head. She sprawled backward from the momentum of the bullets; both children started screaming.

Barguyo put down his rifle and smiled at the girl. He looked quizically up at Ceravant. The look was forlorn, detached.

Ceravant didn't hesitate—they had much more important work to attend to.

Two bullets took care of the children.

Clark AB

It seemed crazy to Charlie, waiting in front of a football stadium to go to a movie. The sign over the entrance read BAMBOO BOWL, but the stadium wasn't made of bamboo nor was it shaped like a bowl—but it was the only stadium on base, so he waited.

Charlie glanced at his watch: eight-thirty. The sun was just setting and the clouds were bathed in a soft red glow. It looked like it was raining in the mountains. In the distance the roar of a jet taking off washed over the base. A string of people shuffled into the stadium. Charlie looked out over the crowd and wondered if Nanette would really show.

When they had departed from the pool yesterday afternoon, the "date" had come about because of an impromptu comment. Nanette had remarked that the classic movie *2001: A Space Odyssey* was playing tonight at the Bamboo Bowl, leaving it tentatively open that they would meet.

Darkness quickly fell. People were still walking in from the parking lot. Charlie had just begun to think that she wasn't going to show when he heard his name being called. He turned and saw her. She was wearing jeans, tennis shoes, and a long-sleeved shirt with the sleeves rolled up. Even in the dusk Nanette's face looked radiant, freshly scrubbed. She huffed up, carrying a blanket and a paper sack with two long pieces of bread sticking from it.

"I couldn't get free from the Nipa Hut." At his puzzled look she laughed and tossed her golden hair over her shoulder. "You *are* new here, aren't you? That's the duty-free shop."

Charlie nodded and took the blanket from her. "No problem. I wasn't sure I'd be able to make it." *Over my dead body!* he thought. He looked around. "So how does this work?"

"Come on." She took his arm and led him to the entrance; she just came up to his shoulder.

At the ticket booth Nanette insisted on paying her own way. They walked through the main corridor, passing by locker rooms labeled HOME and VISITOR and into a long tunnel. The tunnel opened up into the stadium. They were a third of the way up the stairs, looking out onto a football field. In the center of the field a metal scaffolding held up a large screen four stories high. Wheels were positioned on either side of the support structure and a long, worn path in the playing field grass showed where the screen was moved when the field was in use.

"Want to sit in the grass?"

"Sure."

They positioned the blanket away from the other people, mostly couples their age. Nanette rummaged through her paper bag and pulled out the two thin loaves of French bread, an immense hunk of cheese, and two bottles of sparkling water. Charlie's eyes widened.

"I could have picked something up. . . ."

Nanette handed him a loaf and tore off a piece of bread. "We had some leftovers. It's no big deal."

Charlie opened his bottle of water. He didn't miss the reference to *we*—which made Nanette seem even more mysterious.

He chewed off a piece of the bread; it was hard, almost crusty, unlike the large loaves of French bread he was used to eating. "You're lucky I didn't have *my* leftovers—otherwise we'd be eating cold chicken and bean dip."

She made a face. "Bean dip?"

"Sure. It's one of the seven basic food groups: bean dip, nachos, brownies, ice cream . . ." She was laughing before he'd finished the list. Charlie chewed on the bread for a moment. "So, tell me about yourself."

Nanette sliced off a hunk of cheese and lounged back on the blanket. She propped a knee up and leaned toward him. "What do you want to know?"

"Who you are, what you do. Why you met me here."

"That's not hard. To answer your last question first, I guess you seemed more intelligent than the usual guys I run into. There's something to be said for not trying to impress a girl with fighter talk and guzzling beer."

"I still don't know who you are."

"Does it matter?"

"No." Charlie hesitated. "Unless you're married."

She sputtered. "No, no, no!"

"Okay, then. Tell me something about yourself. Uh, where you went to school."

"I'm a senior at Stanford. My major is history, with a minor in music. I'm visiting my parents while on summer break, and I work part time at the Nipa Import Hut. I'm half-French, and I love the outdoors." She stopped and popped a piece of bread into her mouth. "That's it. Your turn."

So that explains it, thought Charlie. "Well, I majored in history, too, but that was some time ago. My father was a college professor, so I've always hung around that type of crowd. Like I said yesterday, I'm not a pilot—I'm a weapons systems officer in an F-15 and have been at Clark since Friday."

"That's pretty succinct."

Charlie grinned. "Oui, mademoiselle."

"So what's a guy like you staying around in the Air Force for? I thought they had a hard time keeping WSO's around, especially good ones."

"They do." From the way she used the Weapons Systems Officer abbreviation, Charlie knew that someone in her family had to be knowledgeable as to what WSOs do.

"Don't you want to go to pilot training?"

Charlie was quiet for a moment. "I did once. But when I joined the Air Force they were restricting the number of pilot slots. I was told that if I became a WSO, I'd have a chance to go to pilot training."

"So what happened?"

"If you're good, people are reluctant to move you. One day, when I'd finally had enough and tried to force the Air Force's hand, I was told I was too old to go to pilot training."

Nanette lifted an eyebrow. "You? Too old?"

"Twenty-eight is the limit—and I turn the big three-oh this December. Does it shock you, now that you know I'm an old man?"

"Thirty's not old."

"You know, I've never caught your whole name." She smiled slyly. "Too much information can burn you out—sensory overload."

"If I want to give you a call?"

"Nanette at the Nipa Hut will do."

"Then Charlie at the 3rd TFW for me."

The stadium lights went off just as a low rumble was emitted from the speakers—the opening strains to "The Star-Spangled Banner." As they stood, Charlie could have sworn that Nanette's lips had drawn tight at the mention of the 3rd Tactical Fighter Wing.

CHAPTER 9

Wednesday, 6 June

Clark AB, Jungle Survival School

Bruce popped a piece of gum into his mouth. The sergeant standing in front of him reminded him of his vision of Air Force Academy upperclassmen on his first day: large, intimidating, and illiterate.

Sixteen men sat in a two-layered semicircle around the sergeant. The eight officers of Maddog Flight were in the back and eight enlisted troops were in the front. The briefing room was small, and curtains muffled any sounds. Other than the chairs they sat on, an exit sign above the door on the front right was the only fixture in the room.

Dressed in a white T-shirt, "BDUs"—camouflaged Battle Dress Uniforms—spit-shined boots and a baseball cap, the sergeant strode up and down in front of the men. White hair stuck out from beneath the cap, a deep tan covered his arms, and there was no sign of fat on his belly.

He didn't look happy.

"Alls right, listen up. I'm Chief Master Sergeant Grune. This is *my* survival school. I've been running it for the past fifteen years and we haven't lost anybody yet. So if you *gentlemen* out there"—he nodded to the officers sitting in the back row—"will kindly pay attention along with the enlisted men, we'll get down to business.

"This course is designed to familiarize you with the fine art of surviving in the jungle." He paused. "Has anyone here *not* attended Fairchild or the Academy?" The references were to the Air Force survival school at Fairchild AFB, Washington, and the Air Force Academy's school. No raised hands.

"Good. Every once in a while those bozos in personnel send me some young virgin who's never been out in the woods. Since all of you are experts in eating bugs and surviving in the cold, let me tell you that the coldest it gets in the jungle is seventy-five degrees— if you're lucky. You're going to forget what you've learned and *relearn* new techniques. If you pay attention and demonstrate proficiency at your skills, the process will be easy. If you don't," he grinned wickedly, "We'll give you some extra instruction.

"I will now introduce you to the backbone of our course and our head instructor. You *will* do what this man says." He added softly, "And General Simone has assured me that our officers will comply also."

Chief Master Sergeant Grune whirled and motioned to the exit. A body pushed through the curtains. Bruce envisioned some sort of Filipino Paul Bunyan, a real woodsman—leathery, large features, and not one to put up with any shit.

Out stepped a barefoot black man, not five feet tall. He carried a long stick with feathers on one end that was almost as tall as he was. In his other hand he carried a cloth bag, which apparently contained a live creature. The front of his chest was decorated with some sort of white markings—soot?—and he appeared to have tiny stitches running up his side. It looked as though sequins had been laced into his body.

Thick, black, wooly hair stood out from his head. His eyes looked sad, and he stood quietly. The room seemed to be in shock.

"Gentlemen, this is Abuj Qyantrolo. He is a member of the Negrito tribe, and an expert in jungle sur-

vival. For the next two weeks you will do as he says."
Chief Grune looked thoughtful. "If there are any
questions, I will be available during your break—
sometime after your lunch, which Abuj is holding in
his bag. Good day, gentlemen." Grune strode from
the room.

Catman leaned over and whispered, "I bet we're
going to wish we had bugs and grubs to eat."

The Negrito blinked at the men. The room was
dead quiet. Bruce could hear Charlie breathing next
to him. Finally Abuj spoke.

"How do you do? Today, we learn the most important lesson in jungle: Always drink water." He
paused. "Second most important lesson is always eat."
He rummaged in his bag. "First I show you, then you
try."

"Arrgg." Robin screwed up his face. "I hate snakes."

Bruce reached over and patted the bags of sugar he
had sewed into his flight suit lining. It was going to
be a long week.

Tarlac

Pompano stepped back and observed the television
and the two radios set up outside the plantation house.
An electrical wire ran from the equipment to the back
of the house where the diesel generators were located.
The Huks stood around the high-power microwave
weapon in a semicircle. Ceravant had insisted on testing the device, even before burying the bodies.

Pompano called to Barguyo: "Start the diesel engine." He told the others to step back. The Huks
shuffled behind the HPM device, slinging their rifles
over their shoulders. A loud noise and a puff of smoke
came from behind the house when Barguyo started
the generator. Music warbled from the radios.

When all men had cleared the area, Pompano
turned to Ceravant and called, "I am ready."

Ceravant nodded.

Pompano and Barguyo joined the men, away from the house. Pompano boosted himself into the operator's seat and waved Barguyo up to join him, so that the young man could learn how to operate the weapon. He could barely hear the music coming from the radio. The three-meter-diameter dish was pointed directly at the electrical equipment, a hundred meters away.

Pompano switched on the HPM's generator. He watched the dials as the weapon's capacitors charged full of energy. After a half minute he turned to Barguyo. "It is very simple. After starting the generator, make sure the antenna is aimed at the target. Then push this button."

Barguyo flipped open the cover and jabbed at the button. *Pop!* Pompano jerked his head up and squinted at the plantation house. Smoke curled up from the TV and radios.

Pompano glanced at Ceravant. The Huk leader nodded quietly to himself.

Clark AB

The sixteen men gathered around the small Negrito. Dressed in only a loincloth, Abuj looked like he was the only comfortable person in the jungle.

The thick foliage formed a canopy around them. If Bruce hadn't known that they were just outside the fence of Clark, he would have thought they were a thousand miles from civilization. He couldn't see more than ten feet through the surrounding jungle.

The ground was covered with a bouncy mat of mulch. To their right a path led from the clearing. The open area was at least twenty yards across, and from the worn spots on the ground it looked as though the place had been used many times before.

A small calf bellowed at them, its tether short enough that it could not reach any of the plants to munch on. Abuj stood by the calf, which came up to his shoulder. It reminded Bruce of the "Little Britches," rodeo when the kids would try to bulldog a calf.

Abuj spoke quietly, and the others listened intently.

"In jungle, you eat anything. It simple choice: You die or something else die. I already show you how to eat bugs and snakes. Now, you learn big."

He grasped the calf's chin and held it up high, so that the throat was exposed. "Like your enemy, you must strike fast, hard. You do this for the animal, as yourself."

He nodded at Catman, who was standing just behind Bruce. "Here. You hold."

Catman wiped his hands on his flight suit and moved forward. The half circle of men widened to allow him to pass. The Negrito held the calf's neck up. Catman moved in behind the man and took the calf's chin in his hand. The animal tried to get away, and Catman had to struggle to keep it still. His face grew as red as the shock of hair on top of his head. A drool of saliva dribbled down his hand.

Abuj removed a machete from his belt. The blade looked coarse, not like the shiny, mass-produced instrument Bruce had seen displayed in stores. Abuj ran the edge along his finger. He spoke to the men.

"You must respect the animal. To kill it and not respect it is very bad." He shivered alightly. "The animal will thank you for making its death come quickly. It will help you, nourish you." He turned and looked upon the men. They had all participated in similar training either at Fairchild AFB or at the Air Force Academy during their survival course, but it had always been in groups of up to a hundred, and sometimes as many as four hundred. This was much more personal, something they couldn't watch from afar.

Abuj nodded to Charlie. He held out the blade. "I feel . . . you can know the animal."

Charlie barely hesitated. He avoided looking at anyone and stepped up to take the blade. He turned it over and ran his finger lightly along the edge. He flipped the machete back over, satisfied he had found the sharpest edge.

The calf snorted; Catman tightened his grip. "Come on, Foggy—I don't have all day."

Charlie stepped up to the opposite side of the calf and brought the blade near.

"Quick," whispered Abuj.

Charlie set his mouth. In a sudden swipe he sliced the calf's throat and brought the machete up high, nearly severing the head.

The calf bucked, straining against the tether, and Catman yelped, "Crap!" The calf ceased moving.

Catman and Charlie laid the animal down. Blood spurted from the wound, covering the ground in a bright red liquid. Abuj moved close. He placed his ear on the calf's body, listened for a moment, then moved over to the spot where the blood still flowed. He put his mouth to the wound and drank.

Bruce watched, his eyes open wide. Abuj stood and spoke, blood dripping in a tiny rivulet from his mouth. "What was once the animal is now yours. Nourishment is full of vitamin, protein. Drink . . . but respect." He turned and walked to the side. He sat cross-legged and watched the men.

No one spoke. Bruce breathed through his nose, unsure of what the hell was happening.

A sudden movement.

Charlie knelt by the dead calf and placed a hand where the blood came from the animal. The flow had slowed to a fast ooze. He scooped up a handful of blood, brought it to his lips . . . and drank.

Once finished, he sat beside the Negrito.

Catman snickered and moved back to where Bruce stood. He spoke in a stage whisper. "Hey, man—this is too weird. Reminds me of *The Night of the Living Dead*. Next thing you know we'll be going after Skipper, cutting him open and drinking his blood."

Skipper turned and glared.

One of the enlisted men knelt beside the calf and followed Charlie's lead. One by one the men lined up; the officers in Maddog slowly joined them until Robin, Catman, and Bruce stood by themselves.

Catman chattered nervously. "What the hell is going on? What do they think this is, some sort of initiation rite?" He started to sound angry.

Robin nudged him. "Come on."

Bruce set his mouth and looked over at Charlie. His backseater stared straight ahead, ignoring his inquisitive look. Bruce muttered, "I'm going to drink it just to snap those guys out of it." He strode to the calf and knelt. Bruce put his hand down. The blood still came, but Bruce needed to push against the carcass to cause enough to fill his cupped hand.

He brought the blood quickly to his mouth and pulled some in. It tasted salty and warm, thick. He quickly swallowed before he gagged. Bruce joined the others.

Catman argued with Robin at the opposite end of the clearing. They were the only two who had not partaken in the "ceremony." And the argument was one-sided—Robin was halfway to the calf while Catman admonished him to return.

"Come *on*! For crying out loud, what the hell do you think this is—voodoo land? Some superstitious munchkin mumbling a bunch of mumbo jumbo. If I ever have to drink it to survive, then I'll do it. You're crazy if you think that cow is going to help you. I can see it now—terror of darkness, the Cow From Hell! No matter where you are, it's going to hunt you down and hose you with its deadly milk."

Robin knelt and drank.

Catman had backed up to the edge of the clearing. He waved a hand at his backseater. "Well, what the hell. Do you feel better now? Are you going to save us because you are now one with the cow? Give me a break, give me a fuckin' break."

Robin stood slowly and made his way to where the men sat. His face was expressionless.

Bruce narrowed his eyes. The experience had not been a revelation, but more one of bonding with the men in the course. His mouth still tasted bitter, and certainly no religious experience had occurred. He was sure that the other men felt the same way. Yet there was something about Robin's face as he approached. . . . When he was ten feet from the men, he suddenly stopped.

Catman called from across the clearing; he sounded alarmed. "Hey, what's going on? Robin, are you all right?"

Robin lifted a hand.

"Robin?!"

Robin's fingers slowly spread out into a modified vee—and then it hit Bruce that it was the Vulcan greeting sign, from the *Star Trek* series. "Live long and prosper," said Robin in a low, deadpan voice.

Bruce sputtered, then lost control. The men rolled on the ground, laughing.

"What the hell is going on?" Catman ran for the crowd.

As he wiped a tear from his eye, Bruce realized that Catman would never understand.

Clark AB

"How ya doin', son?" Major General Peter Simone slapped the squadron duty desk as he walked by.

It took Major Brad Dubois three seconds to realize that the Commander of the Thirteenth Air Force had just walked into the squadron area.

"Squadron, atten' *hut!*"

"Down, sit down, son." Simone gazed around the room.

Major Dubois wavered slightly as he stood. "Uh, how do you do, sir, I mean general sir."

"Down, dammit. I said sit down, son." Simone waved the bald-headed man down. The general glanced at the desk: the major had a paperback book open, but other than that the long desk was absolutely uncluttered. Simone frowned. He had always believed that an empty desk denoted an empty mind. Either the man had too little to do or he was kissing things off.

Simone's aide walked briskly into the room. "There you are, sir."

Simone pointed at the whiteboard behind Dubois's head. "Okay, where's our firecracker, Steve? When's the next time he's going to rocket?"

Major Steve Hendhold squinted up at the board. Dubois started to open his mouth to say something, but seemed to think better of it and clamped it shut instead. Hendhold read slowly.

"Maddog Four, sir. The next sortie is scheduled for a week from tomorrow."

"That long? Has Bolte got them out house-hunting or something?"

"Survival School, sir. Wing policy changed to have the men go through it the first week they're on station—it acclimates them faster, and prepares them if they have to punch out when they first arrive."

"I don't know if I agree with that, but it's Bolte's Wing, not mine." Simone placed an elbow on Major Dubois's desk. "Can you arrange my flight, son?"

"Sir?"

"What the hell do you think I came down here for, a party? Any problem with that?"

"No problem, sir!" Dubois didn't have the faintest clue what he was to do.

"Good." Simone slapped the desk. "I'm about to go stir-crazy cooped up at that desk. If I don't get a flight in soon I'm going to pop."

"Yes, sir."

"I'll see Lieutenant Steele next week, then. Glad to meet you, major. Catch you on the rebound."

Tarlac, P.I.

Ceravant watched through a screen window as a last shovelful of dirt was thrown on the grave. Pompano had insisted that the graves be a full six feet deep and as far away from the house as possible.

Pompano was turning out to be very useful. Although he had not participated in the raid, the old man had not turned from lugging his share of the weapons and ammunition into the plantation. Besides directing the grave-digging, Pompano was proving to be very efficient in setting up a schedule for the work.

At first Ceravant had been taken back by the older man's efficiency, the attention to detail with which Pompano ran the encampment, but it was precisely that deed that brought Ceravant to a sudden realization: The military maneuvers were completely distinct from the homemaking. Ceravant was unequaled in the guerrilla warfare, yet he knew nothing of setting up schedules and the practical matter that it took to run a house—Pompano could draw on his many years of practical experience running a store.

So Ceravant had appointed the old man to take charge of the basing aspects, which left him even more time to prepare the other raids.

Ceravant inhaled the smoke from his cigarette. The men, having finished their work on the graves, walked back to the house, laughing and wiping their hands on their pants. The days were much cooler in the mountains. And although it rained more up here than down in the central valley, the humidity was more bearable.

He turned to a set of plans that Pompano had drawn up. Demonstrating his efficiency once again, the old man had taken a yardstick to every room in the plantation and put the measurements down on paper. The house measured over seven thousand square feet. The items Pompano had found in the bedrooms and throughout the house indicated that the people they had just buried were long-term inhabitants.

Pompano had uncovered a Christmas potpourri, along with some family heirlooms: old baby furniture and photo albums. The find had satisfied Ceravant—he did not have to worry about the owners coming and taking the Huks by surprise. Whoever the people had been, they had intended to be here permanently.

The dirt road leading to the plantation wound over ten miles off the main highway from Tarlac. The road narrowed to one lane for most of the journey. Thick jungle started to encroach onto the compressed dirt, and a canopy of foliage covered the middle section.

Ceravant discovered that the plantation had once been a small staging area for the harvest of the sugar cane crop that stretched up through the Tarlac region. Unlike the sprawling company-owned abodes that dotted the island of Luzon, this house had been privately owned and, it appeared, recently sold to the young couple.

Scores of young couples had moved out from the cities, out to the simpler lifestyle of the country. These people may well have been one of those. It was just unfortunate that they had chosen this particular spot, which had been too centrally located to pass up. But it would have been too easy for them to go to the authorities if they had been allowed to live.

The main matter was that Ceravant's Huk cell now had a permanent staging area, a base from which to operate. No longer would they have to ferry their weapons from one safe house to another. This base could very well become the dominant spot on this part of the Island. With this revelation, Ceravant decided to take advantage of Pompano's common-sense approach. He met the men and singled out Pompano.

"I want to ensure that the road to the house is well protected."

Pompano allowed the men to move on before answering. His clothes smelled of damp dirt.

"What do you mean well protected?"

"I want to be able to stop an ambush—or if that is

not practical, to give us enough warning that we will have time to escape."

Pompano leaned against his shovel. "So, you already have doubts about your assault-proof hiding place?"

Ceravant narrowed his eyes.

"I do not have doubts—I am being practical. Even with a house full of supplies and no reason to leave, we will still have to send men out to get us food. If there is only one way into the plantation, then for a high enough fee one of our freedom fighters might decide to sell out to the highest bidder."

"You do not trust your own men?" Pompano seemed to be mocking him.

"*No one* can afford to trust anyone completely." Ceravant stared hard.

Pompano spoke softly. "There has to come a time when even you must depend on someone, my friend."

"Until we bring about the new order, there can never be a time." Ceravant suddenly laughed. He reached down to his sock and pulled out a pack of cigarettes. He offered one to Pompano and the two lit up. "I am starting to sound like the PC—a threat behind every bush, so they must lock up all the people."

Pompano was silent for a long while. "Do you want the men to know about all the warning devices?"

Ceravant looked up, struck by Pompano's observation. "No. The men should be aware of some of them, whether explosives or some sort of sensor we can obtain. But no one is to know all of them. . . ."

Pompano blew smoke at Ceravant. "You do not trust me? Even though I do not complain about the lack of Blue Seal cigarettes?"

Ceravant smiled. "Especially because of that."

For half a mile the road out of the plantation was wide enough for two vehicles to pass, then it narrowed and turned sharply to the right.

An army of flowers covered the path, blooming at the start of the rainy season. A parabolic mirror was nestled high above the ground, so a car coming from either direction could see around the corner.

Ceravant motioned for Pompano to stop the truck. He hopped down and inspected the curve. "This will be a good place for a trip wire. Whoever is coming down the road will be more concerned with the upcoming curve and will not notice the wire."

"The men will remember?"

Ceravant pondered the question. He could not babysit the men all of the time, otherwise he would do nothing but ferry them from the plantation to the highway.

"They should all know." Ceravant nodded. "It is imperative that we obtain sensors. The location of the sensors will remain hidden"—he glanced up at Pompano—"and that will be my insurance policy."

"The black market in Angeles can come up with the sensors. I go back, get what I can, and return."

Ceravant remembered the cases of Blue Seal cigarettes in the old man's sari-sari store, stolen from Clark Air Base. "Do you think you can get what I want?"

Pompano shrugged. "I do not see why not. For a price, anything can be obtained at the base."

"Good. Then we will use the American sensors to warn us, and we will use their microwaves to drive them away." Ceravant nodded to himself. He knew that once the Americans had left, the New People's Army would have no real obstacle in spreading their presence. For it was mainly the American anti-Communist paranoia that had kept the fires fueled against the Huks in the first place.

For the first time in a long time, Ceravant felt good.

Seoul, South Korea

"We have a lead on Kawnleno's John Doe."

Roger Epstein lifted his brows. If it was true, it

would be the best news he had heard in over a month. It would even make the heat bearable.

Soloette Arquine pushed a folder across the Agency station chief's desk. Epstein caught it and withdrew a photograph.

The picture was digitally reconstructed, shaded in false colors to highlight the man's features. Behind the photo was the one taken last week of Kawnleno and the "John Doe."

Epstein rocked back in his chair and held the two up. The Kawnleno picture was coarse, tiny blocks of digitized elements standing out and giving the unknown man a blocklike appearance.

But comparing the pictures, there was no doubt in Roger Epstein's mind that the two men were one man. He tossed the picture on the desk and wiped his forehead of perspiration.

"Where'd you get it?"

"Manila. Sunday night."

"Philippines? And hanging around with Kawnleno? That doesn't make sense." Soloette merely shrugged at the observation. "Any idea who he is?"

"No. That's what took so long for the ID. We asked Langley to run a comparison of the original picture on all international ports. Without a name or an alias to go by, every international passenger was. tagged once we got their picture. Three lookalikes popped out of the computer scan, and I was able to throw two of those out."

"What about his destination? Did he stay in Manila?"

"I don't know. If he didn't then he bypassed the cameras, which is unlikely. Unless he left the country by boat, I guess he's probably still there."

Epstein drummed his fingers on the table. "You've checked the passenger manifests." The question came as a statement.

"We have seventeen flights to choose from, over a

twenty-four-hour period—about four thousand names. None of them have any terrorist connections, but—"

"That doesn't mean anything," Epstein finished for her. He picked up the lone picture. The man had a serious, no-joking look. There were few details other than the facial features: pockmarked skin, the hint of a half-grown mustache.

Soloette spoke quietly. "Well, what do you think? Was it a random meeting with Kawnleno, or is there something to this guy?"

"Nothing Kawnleno does is random. Whoever this John Doe is he's working in Manila, or somewhere in the Philippines." He thought quickly; he didn't like to pass the buck, but until this character surfaced in South Korea, someone else might have a better chance at him.

"Contact the Manila office and send them what we've got. Have them ship this guy's picture to the military bases there—Clark, Subic, and whatever else there is—no telling what he's up to. But if he's connected to Kawnleno, then its got to be sour."

CHAPTER 10

Monday, 18 June

Clark AB

It began to rain on Bruce and Charlie.

Of course, it had never really *stopped* raining on the two during the last two days—the P.I. were in the beginning of their Monsoon season. Seconds ago the fine mist had turned into a downpour.

They had lost track of Catman and Robin earlier in the day. Since yesterday the four had been out in the jungle practicing Escape and Evasion tactics—E & E. The Negrito Abuj Qyantrolo had purportedly been tracking them, but Bruce had seen no sign of the little black man.

And in addition to the E & E, they were also practicing other survival aspects as well: no food, or rather no food except for what they found they could eat. They had two days to go before this part of the training was done.

"Find anything?" Charlie looked up hopefully.

"No." He squatted down by Charlie and stuck a long piece of grass in his mouth. Water plopped around them. Bruce chewed slowly on the stem. "Have you figured out where we are?"

Charlie pointed to a green plastic map of the area; water beaded on the surface. "The next checkpoint should be right over this hill."

"Hill?" Bruce glanced up at the slope just visible

through the foliage and rain. "That looks like Mount Everest."

Charlie ignored his comment. "If Catman and Robin catch up with us, it will be at this checkpoint."

Bruce snorted. "The 'Woods' brothers? They've probably been captured and are back in the O'Club bar, laughing at us right now."

Bruce stood and surveyed their position. It didn't matter where they were in the jungle—none of the trees shielded them from the downpour. The leaves were saturated with water and just dumped the rainfall down on them.

Bruce motioned for Charlie to follow him underneath a towering tree. As they approached, Bruce was overwhelmed with the smell of perfume. He looked around and spotted an array of red flowers. They looked out of place among the dark green plants. "Hey, it's not so bad here." He stepped up to the tree and stood on a twisted root. "Come on, this is partially sheltered."

The two kept quiet for some time, listening to the rain hit the ground. The plip-plopping sound still came from all around, but now it lulled them into a mellow mood. The place looked serene. If the situation had been any different, Bruce might even have enjoyed himself. He thought he would have to make an effort to return to the jungle one of these days.

Charlie broke the silence. "I met this girl the other day."

"What?"

"A girl. I met this girl."

Bruce wiggled back against the bark. "The one at the pool?"

Charlie leaned up and frowned. "I thought you guys were too drunk to notice."

Bruce looked astonished. "Not notice a looker like that?" He leaned his head back and recited, "Blond, a little over five feet tall, probably, oh, an even hundred pounds . . . Age . . . ?" He turned his head. "How old *is* she?"

"About twenty. A college student."

"Jail bait. Watch out, Foggy. That means her old man is here on Clark and will be gunning for you—you dirty old man. What's her name?"

"Nanette."

"Does she have a last name?"

Charlie shrugged; his face grew red. "She didn't tell me." At Bruce's stare, he amended himself. "Okay, okay. She *wouldn't* tell me. Why, I don't know. Maybe she just wants to play coy."

"I don't know. You sure she's single?"

"What the heck do you—"

"All right, just asking." It was one thing to razz a guy about robbing the cradle, but to accuse Charlie of adultery . . .

Bruce mused for a moment. *That's neat*, he thought. *It's about time Charlie found something other than those damned books to stick his nose into. He's been moping too long about not getting into pilot training.*

"Hey, Charlie."

"Yeah."

"I . . . Well, hell, I met a girl too."

Charlie turned to him. "You're bagging me."

"No, really. That night we went to the Fire Empire . . ."

Charlie rolled his eyes. "Don't tell me—you fell in love with the girl in the floor show."

"No, honest." Bruce's voice grew quiet. He remembered the narrow street, the crowds of people. . . . "We toured the city—remember that jeepney ride? I stopped for some gum."

"Yeah?"

"Well, there was this girl in that sari-sari store." He drew in a breath. *God, she was beautiful*, he thought.

Charlie frowned. "I didn't see any Americans around there."

"She's not American." Bruce turned to his friend. "Yolanda Sicat. She's a Filipino."

Charlie looked at Bruce hard. "You're not joking."

"No. Why would I?"

Charlie relaxed back. "I can think of several reasons."

Bruce chewed on his lip and caught himself; it had actually started to taste good. "Hey, uh, what do you say we get together, go out on a double date—you know, something nice for the girls, where they don't have to worry about us putting the moves on them."

"Us?"

Bruce set his mouth. He felt that Charlie's insinuations were starting to get a little out of hand. *Sure, I might have a rep as a hell-raiser, but give me a break, I'm only human!* "Come on!"

Charlie held up his hands. "Sorry. Uh, sure—let's make a double date when we get back."

Something whistled past Bruce's ear. Two more sounds cracked through the air.

Bruce and Charlie threw themselves down and sprawled on the ground. Bruce's face was smeared with leaves and mud. A pungent odor of decaying plants filled his nose.

Silence. Bruce looked up cautiously. Nothing.

He swung his eyes to the tree that he had sat under—buried into the bark, four feet above the ground in a tight symmetric pattern, quivered three long darts. Steel, needle-thin tips came out of each dart's head.

Bruce nudged Charlie. "Look behind you."

Charlie's eyes widened at the sight of the darts. He whispered, "Where did they come from?"

"Guess." Bruce turned back and squinted into the jungle. He thought he saw something, but couldn't make out the form in the dense growth. Dark green blended with brown, black.

And then he could see as if it were clear as day.

Abuj stood just outside the clearing. The Negrito had a batch of colored sticks stuck in his thick, woolly hair; his body was painted a ripple of green and brown. He held a long, thin pole—a blowgun. He held Bruce's gaze.

Bruce slowly nudged Charlie. They watched the Negrito for what seemed to be minutes, no one speaking.

Then just as suddenly as he had appeared, Abuj was gone.

"Wow." Charlie let out his breath.

Bruce scrambled to his feet and turned for the darts. One by one he pulled them out of the tree. He turned them over in his hand. A foot long and as thin as a pencil, each had tiny feathers in the back and a sharp steel needle in the front. "Take a look at this."

Bruce turned and surveyed the jungle. He had not heard Abuj approach or leave. He had just been . . . *there*. Bruce shivered. "That guy's like a ghost. If he had wanted to hit us, we wouldn't be talking right now."

"What do you think he's doing?"

Bruce touched the tip of the dart, then jammed all three back into the tree. "He's trying to teach us something—or warn us. If he can get that close without us hearing him, he's one guy I'd like to have on our side."

"That's a rog."

Bruce recalled the Negrito's stare, as if he had been telegraphing him something—maybe about his responsibilities. And if that were so, then it started with his carrying his weight and helping Charlie out. He reached for the plastic topographical map, shook water from it, and located the next checkpoint. "I'll navigate this time."

"Okay." Charlie handed over the compass with a sigh. "Ten to one we'll wind up in Rangoon."

Angeles City

Pompano entered the sari-sari store. He nodded at the two boys sitting outside. One of them drank a Pepsi, the other sipped on a San Miguel.

The one trying to drink the beer looked slightly green around the jowls; Pompano repressed a laugh. Everyone needed a chance to grow up, experience life. Better that the boys be experimenting at his store than trying it while hawking one of their sisters to the Americans.

The Americans. If it weren't for them, he would never have had his store.

The grant monies had poured in from the American base nearly seventeen years ago, the last result of blackmail by the Marcos regime. The base had tried to win over the hearts and minds of the local people by giving out grants to needy families. Pressured by the Marcos government, the Americans had participated in the flow of money.

Only when it was found that most of the money had been diverted into the wrong hands had the grants stopped. But not before Pompano Sicat, single father of a young daughter whose mother had died giving birth, had gotten enough seed money to start his store.

Yes, Pompano, he thought. *How ironic that the very Americans you hate so much should be the ones responsible for your success.*

And here he was again, searching for American goods. Looking to the black market for the sensors that would help protect the Huk encampment.

Yolanda came from behind the counter. "Father! You are back!"

"Little one!" Pompano laughed and gave his daughter a squeeze. She towered over him by a good five inches. "How are the sales?"

"Very good. Fireworks are starting to move fast with the Fourth of July coming up."

"Good, good." He started to duck under the counter, but a sharp pain ran through his back.

"Are you all right?"

"Yes. Just my back acting up. Too much lifting for an old man."

Yolanda raised the counter for him. Pompano pushed through.

"Are you finished with your memorial, father?"

Pompano entered the back of the store. A mattress and bed spring sat along one side of the wall, out of view from the front of the store. A small stove, a half refrigerator, and a cupboard made of scrap wood filled another wall.

Off to the side were a toilet and shower. A curtain drawn across one end of the room demarcated Yolanda's side from his.

Yolanda had grown up in this small one-room building, done her homework while sitting on the bed, watched after the store when Pompano had been sick. . . . Pompano bit his lip. There must be a better life for his daughter.

But his frugality had paid off. When classes started in the fall down at the University of the Philippines in Quezon City, Yolanda would be there. It was quite fortuitous that she was able to help watch the store this summer while he was up in the mountains— "building a memorial" for the supporters of Aquino. At least she hadn't questioned the lie. Pompano smiled at his daughter.

"No, little one. I have some more material to pick up, and must go back to the mountains."

"When will you return?" There was a look of concern on her face.

"Soon. But do not worry—this will be the last time for a while that I will be away. But tell me what has happened. You said the sales were good—do I need to reorder before I return?"

Yolanda screwed up her face as if in thought. "Probably only on the fireworks. Oh, and gum."

"Gum? I thought we just reordered!"

She grew red. "Someone came in and bought it all."

Pompano smiled to himself: he knew the habit of Filipinos to buy only what they needed, one item at a time. To have someone come in and completely wipe out his stock—that meant only one thing.

"Was this a young man, little one?"

"Yes, father." She looked down, avoiding his eyes.

"What is he like?"

"I do not know him very well."

Pompano reached out and stroked his daughter's hair. Long and black, it had natural body.

How beautiful his daughter was. She had her mother's hair, and her mother's eyes.

A pain stabbed through him—

For that was all the features from Lucila that she carried, as beautiful as she was.

Her angular features, her tallness . . . even the crook of her fingers, long and dexterous. Pompano tried to keep in the rage, subdue the feelings that had nearly consumed him some nineteen years earlier.

Lucila and he were newly married, just starting out in life when they had strolled the streets of Angeles. The gang of American youths, perhaps G.I.s . . . The gang rape had been fast, brutal. Pompano had been forced to watch it, all the time swearing at the attackers. The devastating blow had been Lucila's death on giving birth, birth to a baby whose father was half a world away. Pompano had nearly taken his life at that time, but had somehow managed to pull himself through.

His involvement with the Huks, and with this New People's Army faction, had sustained him through the years. Striking back at the Americans while smiling and accepting their money. It was a way to get at the heart of the problem.

And now with this Huk encampment, his dreams would finally be realized.

Pompano looked up at his daughter and placed a hand on her shoulder. "Whoever this young man may be, I am sure he will be good to you. I must go back to the mountains in the next few days. When will I get a chance to meet him?"

Yolanda looked up. "After you return, father. I will invite him over."

Charlie plus twenty-five thousand, over Taiwan

"Charlie" translated as sixty thousand feet.

The SR-71 Blackbird pilots used the "Charlie plus" designation to identify a "base" altitude when they didn't want their real altitude broadcast to the world, especially when were speaking over unsecured channels.

At this altitude—eighty-five thousand feet—the Blackbird was over twice as high as a normal plane might fly. And traveling over three times as fast.

Major Kathy Yulok managed to relax back in her seat, even through the layers of fabric and webbing that held her pressure suit together. Now, with the mission almost over, with the data collected and transmitted, flying the SR-71 back to Kadena seemed a breeze.

In forty-five minutes she would make a low-altitude pass over the runway at Kadena and drop a small canister. The National Security Agency already had access to the information she had collected, transmitted via satellite to a classified operating location. So the low-altitude flyby was pure "war-ready"—merely an exercise for war—but it gave her an excuse to fly the bird down low and slow for a change. The film and data tapes would have been picked up and processed by the time she "hangered the bird," or put the aircraft in the hanger.

The mission had been a milk run, not overflying any unfriendly territory but instead skirting as close to the international border as possible without sending up a missile.

Not that a missile would worry her—she had been shot at before, but the rockets had always flown too slow and were too far away to do any harm.

And as it turned out, flying *next* to another country's border was practically as good as being directly overhead. With the advanced side-looking diagnostics, over a hundred thousand square miles of territory could be covered in over an hour.

So, heading back from the South China Sea, Kathy was ready to bring her in and get some rest. Everything looked good; she couldn't have asked for a better mission.

That's when she spotted the red lights.

She clicked her mike. "Eddie, you copy?"

Major Ed Prsybalwyki answered from the back seat. "That's a rog. Engine flameout on one and two."

"That's what I've got." *Great*, she thought. *Both engines are out.* She reached down and toggled a switch, trying to kick the turbojets back on. No luck. She stretched to look out the window. There was still land below them, but the coastline was heading up fast.

"Eddie, you have a fix on our position?"

"Just leaving Taiwan. What do you think?"

She pondered it for a moment. Even though the SR-71 had been in commission for over thirty years, some of the technology on the plane was still classified. Landing in a foreign country without copious prior preparation was frowned upon. Even when the nation was friendly to the U.S.

Kathy gnawed on her lip. They hadn't lost much altitude yet, but they were definitely going down. "I'll keep trying to turn over the engines. They may not catch until we get some thicker air."

"So do we circle, cry for help, or what?"

She made up her mind. "Head on home. We'll be able to take her in if we don't hit any downdrafts."

Ed was silent for a moment. "You're the boss."

Kathy keyed her mike, switching from intercom to outside radio. With the change in altitude, she had to notify the international air control.

"Ah, control, this is Stella Two-Niner at Charlie

plus twenty-five thousand. We've flamed out and are descending."

The radio came back instantly; the young man sounded like he was in a panic. "Stella Two-Niner, Taiwan center. Taipei International has a runway over ten thousand feet. Are you declaring an emergency?"

Kathy's eyebrows rose. *Declare an emergency?*

Then she remembered—Charlie plus twenty-five.

She tried to hold back a chuckle as she clicked the mike; the poor guy thought that she was sixty-thousand feet lower than she was. "Ah, negative, Control. We're heading for Kadena and will try to kick our engines over en route."

Silence. For a *long* time. Then, "Roger, Stella two-niner. You are cleared for Kadena, altitude your choice. . . . Ah, please report at intervals."

"Rog, Control." Kathy clicked off her mike.

"Ho, ho, ho," came Eddie, dryly.

"No problem. If you didn't want excitement in your life, you should have joined the Navy."

"Very funny. Just keep us out of the water."

A half hour later they glided safely onto Kadena.

Yokota AFB, Japan

Vice-President Adleman pressed his lips together. He bowed slightly at the waist and nodded to the Japanese trade minister, who was still across the room.

He really shouldn't feel slighted—having the trade minister receive him was very well within the protocol demanded by a Vice-Head of State, especially with the dominance of the Japanese economy and the overwhelming debt that the United States seemed to be unable to shake.

But Vice-President Adleman still felt slighted. He had always admired the Japanese culture and felt no animosity over its aggressive fiscal behavior—he only wished the U.S. had the foresight to put some of the practices in use for itself. But Adleman knew that the

U.S. could never shake the "Harvard MBA bottom line": throwing out long-term investments for short-term profits.

The minister's entourage surrounded the Vice-President, smiling, bowing and nodding.

A "garden" just outside the receiving room was made up of thousands of rocks, all groomed and set in flowing designs. A slight smell of incense burned in the background; Adleman was impressed by the facilities, especially considering the fact that it was on an American Air Force base.

He accepted a warm cup of sake and put it to his lips.

"Mr. Vice-President?" The trade minister steered him away from the crowd without touching his arm. They were left alone.

"Mr. Ieyasu, it is very kind of you to receive me."

Ieyasu bowed at the waist, but kept eye contact with Adleman; the Vice-President followed the minister's lead.

"Mr. Vice-President, I am sorry that we do not have very much time together. There are certain, uh, *obligations*, that I must fulfill before the day is out."

Adleman raised his cup of sake. "I understand, Mr. Minister. My agenda is quite full, I assure you. In the next two days I am scheduled to participate in more functions that I normally do in a week in the United States."

"It is not often that we are graced with such a distinguished presence."

"This visit is distinguished only by my hosts."

Ieyasu bowed slightly.

"If I may speak frankly?"

"By all means."

"Mr. Vice-President, it is no secret that this visit is not the important aspect of your trip."

So, he's interested in the Philippine agreement, thought Adleman. *But I'll play this out, to make sure*

I know what he really wants. 'An astute observation, Mr. Minister." Nice, neutral response. Your turn.

"The question of Philippine leases is a touchy one, and I want to assure you that our country will stand by the decision reached by your country." He leaned forward and seemed to listen intently.

"I appreciate your concern," said Adleman. "And I also appreciate your support—I will elicit your advice if there ever should be any to give. The United States has learned, sometimes the hard way, that we do not have a corner on common sense. Or making the right decisions." Adleman smiled and drank the rest of his sake.

Ieyasu's eyes widened. "And I, too, appreciate your candor. It is a true mark of maturity, intelligence; and I must compliment you." He nodded to the rock gardener, tending to the trove of stones. "That seasoned old gardener loves his job so much that he would gladly accept a word of advice on how to improve his art, the way his rocks pour out their message. I am happy to hear that you, too, will not be offended."

"Not at all. So if I may beg your opinion . . . ?" Adleman left the question hanging, placing the ball in Ieyasu's court. The man would now not be offended by his request for help.

A change seemed to come over the minister. He spoke in a low voice. "The Philippines represent more of an economic power to us than a military buffer, Mr. Vice-President. With glasnost and the changing winds of politics blowing across Asia, the loss of American bases does not concern us for the old reasons—there are plenty of other areas that you may stage your defensive forces from."

"We are aware of that. It is the sunk costs that concern us. There is a lot of money wrapped up in the Filipino infrastructure."

"Sunk costs should never be considered when making an economic decision, Mr. Vice-President." The trade minister smiled up at him. "Demming, one of your management specialists, made that axiom very clear to us."

Adleman forced a smile. "Please continue."

Ieyasu half bowed. "I repeat, it is not the military implications that disturb us. It is the economic impact that would send shock waves out from Manila. Today, the Philippine economy is kept at bay, supplying the needs of your military bases, ministering to the need of their own poor countrymen. We are concerned that without an American presence, the Philippines might go the way of an unbridled Korea—a mass dumping of cheap labor onto the world economy. The profits that would be obtained by even a modest effort could only free up more labor.

"This would be disastrous. It would be disastrous for those Filipinos who would not benefit from this unbridled growth, and it would undercut the economy of the Pacific Basin."

Adleman played with his sake glass. "It is very generous of you to take such interest in another country's economic welfare, Mr. Minister."

Ieyasu bowed stiffly, not missing the jab at Japan's cool concern over the U.S. economy. "It is in *our* interest, Mr. Vice-President. Both your country and mine."

"Then I do appreciate your advice."

Ieyasu nodded and bowed deeply. "And I thank you for your time. Please, the next time you come to Tokyo, we must plan some time together."

"I look forward to it."

An aide appeared at the trade minister's elbow. Seconds later, after much bowing and nodding, Adleman was once again surrounded by his own staff.

Even though Adleman had been met "only" by the trade minister, he suddenly realized the soaring importance of the event. Adleman might be tapped as President at any moment, depending on what happened to Longmire, and the man responsible for the economic condition of what was now the wealthiest nation on earth had recognized this, as well as the far-reaching implications of his trip.

The gardener looked much more important now than he had an hour earlier.

CHAPTER 11

Wednesday, 20 June

Clark AB

The row of MH-60G Pave Hawk helicopters looked out of place across the ramp from the row of F-15E fighters. The Air Force had acquired the long, low, and sleek Army Black Hawk helicopters after urgings from a particularly cognizant Colonel who had come up through the ranks flying choppers—a feat unusual in itself. The HH-3E Jolly Green Giants, the Air Force's prime rescue helicopters, were growing old and falling apart. The new procurement for the ATH—the Advanced Technology Helicopter—was still years behind schedule.

The MH-60s had only been meant as stopgap, a bridge to the ATH, but as so often happens, they had become the mainstay of the 31st Aerospace Rescue and Recovery Squadron on Clark.

The sky showed the typical June on-off, on-off rain pattern that characterized the island during the monsoon season. As the crew bus approached the flight line, pungent smells of JP-4, the highly flammable jet fuel, washed into the bus. Captain Richard Head grumbled to his copilot, Captain Bob Gould, about the weather as they stepped from the crew bus.

Gould had other things on his mind. "What I don't understand is that when I decided to go for choppers, all I caught was crap from everybody I knew. I felt like flying helicopters had made me a second-class citizen. People wouldn't treat me like a 'real' pilot. But now I haven't had to buy a drink since I've been here. I'm walking on water, and everyone wants to be my best friend. I know that fixed-wingers view helicopters different from themselves, but I've been here a week and I feel like the most popular guy in town."

Head turned and looked his copilot up and down. He shook his head. "I keep forgetting this is your first helicopter assignment. You've spent too many years in Air Training Command."

"American Toy Company," corrected Gould. "That's for all the chicken shit we had to put up with."

Head muttered, "Okay. You're new here, so I'll explain it once." He nodded to the row of F-15 fighters across the tarmac that made up the two squadrons of the 3rd TFW. "Helicopters are what keeps those dudes alive. If it wasn't for us, these hotshot fighter jocks wouldn't try half the stuff they do. Strapping themselves in a few tons of metal, hurtling toward the ground near Mach 1—and in a real war, there will be people shooting back at them. The chances of them pranging it in are pretty high, so what do you think is the only visible way out, a hope that someday if they're shot down they might survive? Us, bucko. We did it in 'Nam, then the Gulf. You see, we're the cavalry, coming to the rescue to pull these guys out of trouble. Without us those hotshots are not going to get out of there, and they are grateful as hell. So what's wrong with accepting their drinks?"

Gould nodded. "That's what I thought."

"Let's just get the hell out of here," interrupted Head. "Those girls won't keep waiting all morning."

Bruce Steele crouched at the edge of the clearing. The hole in the jungle canopy wasn't more than fifty feet across, but it gave him an unobstructed view of the sky above.

The rain had stopped last night, and for the first

time in nearly a week the sun looked like it was trying to break through. Bruce listened intently for the sound of the rescue helicopter.

Charlie stayed back in the jungle, scouting the area for Abuj or any of the "bad guys" that might have been assigned to the E & E team.

Bruce knelt and fumbled in his flight suit. He pulled out a small radio. He switched it on, then back off; a faint hissing came from the speakers. The radio was waterproof, so they would be able to broadcast their position.

He checked his watch; they should be hearing from the rescue chopper any time now. He drew out the antenna and flicked the radio on—nothing but static came out of the speaker.

He knew that they were being watched. They had found few clearings, and the E & E staff probably had all the areas reconnoitered. All the dull green foliage, as well as the absence of real food, had started to get on Bruce's nerves.

A voice crackled from the radio speaker. "Maddog, Cobra five. I am running a linear search. Please notify when you hear me."

Bruce hastily turned down the volume, then brought the radio to his lips. "Cobra five, Maddog four. We'll call when we hear you."

Bruce melted back into the jungle and waited for the sound of the helicopter. He knew that the Pave Hawk wouldn't stop crisscrossing the jungle area until Bruce called him. Bruce would then vector the helicopter in on sound alone—the louder the helicopter got, the closer they would be.

He didn't have to wait long before a faint sound caught his attention.

Bruce strained to hear. As he leaned forward, his boots made a squishing sound. It felt as if his feet were covered with fungus. He had taken off his boots last night to dry off his feet, but had had nothing dry to wipe them with. He'd settled for just airing them out, and ignoring both the smell and the way they looked.

The sound grew louder. Bruce spoke into the radio. "Cobra five, I hear you, and you are getting closer."

"Rog, Maddog. I will remain on this heading. Notify when sound decreases."

Bruce didn't answer, keeping radio contact to a minimum. Charlie brushed up against his shoulder.

"I think we're still alone."

"Not for long."

Charlie listened and nodded. "It's about time."

The helicopter made a distinct "whop-whop" sound that grew louder every second.

"Sounds like they're heading straight for us," said Bruce. "But then again, how many times have they plucked guys like us out of the jungle?" The sound seemed to be right on top of them, then it lost intensity. "Cobra five, you are getting away. Come back the way you came—we're in a clearing about fifty feet across."

"Rog Maddog four, I have three possible areas in view."

Bruce nudged Charlie. "Let's get ready." They ducked low and sprinted from the edge of the jungle to the center of the clearing. Bruce felt like he was naked without any trees around him.

Seconds passed. Then the dark body of the Pave Hawk flashed over the clearing.

"Cobra five, we just saw you. Can you back up?"

"Rog. Prepare for hoist."

The helicopter came back overhead. Even though the craft was well over a hundred feet above the clearing, Bruce could still feel the strong downdraft of the rotor. Moldy leaves flew up in the turbulent air.

Someone's head poked out from the side of the helicopter. The person quickly moved an arm up and down. A second later, the penetrator, a long rod with a weight on one end and a seat with straps on the other end, came hurtling down from the Cobra. Bruce and Charlie scrambled to get out of the way.

The penetrator bored for the ground, and just before it hit, slowed to a stop. It settled gently onto the jungle floor.

Bruce turned to Charlie. "Go ahead."

"You first. I outrank you."

"And I'm the AC." Bruce shoved Charlie forward, letting his backseater know that the Aircraft Commander still had the last word.

Charlie ran to the seat and quickly strapped in. Once fastened, Bruce spoke into the radio. "Maddog's ready, Cobra Five."

Charlie shot up through the air, then disappeared into the helicopter.

Bruce scanned the clearing—it was still empty. If this had been a real pickup, the helicopter probably wouldn't have found them so quickly. In addition, running out into a clearing was a pretty stupid thing to do, especially with unfriendlies around. But in a peacetime training environment, safety rules supreme, no matter how it affects realism.

The penetrator came back down from the helicopter; Bruce ran out and strapped in. He waved to the people above him—they brought him up like an elevator going all out.

As the clearing drew away below him, a small dark figure stepped from the jungle and watched him go up. *Abuj!*

The tiny Negrito had probably had them in his sights all along.

Well, no use worrying about it now—they'll find out how they did during the out brief tomorrow morning. But before then, he was looking forward to a shower and a belly full of food. And not necessarily in that order.

As he drew close to the helicopter, a hand reached out and pulled him in. A Staff Sergeant helped him unstrap once the penetrator was secured to the craft. "Welcome back, Lieutenant."

"Thanks."

Charlie sat in the back, covered with a blanket and drinking a cup of steaming liquid. The sergeant flipped Bruce an orange.

"Here ya go, sir. Coffee and hot chocolate in the back if you want it."

"Thanks." Bruce hesitated, then pushed for the front. He stuck his head into the cockpit. The pilot and copilot both wore shaded visors on their helmets. The helicopter was not more than a three hundred feet over the tops of the trees. Bruce called out over the roar. "Hey, guys, thanks."

The copilot turned around. Seeing Bruce, he elbowed the pilot. "Look who's here."

The pilot craned his neck around. "Well, well— Assassin, isn't it?"

Bruce grinned. "Beers on me tonight."

Head turned back to the front. "As it should be."

Tarlac, P.I.

Ceravant nodded as Pompano handed him the box. It was surprisingly light. Ceravant held his cigarette in his lips as he set the box on the table.

Light shone from a single oil lamp set in the middle of the table, its flickering glow sending shadows dancing throughout the room. This was one of the drawbacks of living away from power lines, and Ceravant had not wanted to start the diesel engines outside the house, to keep from drawing attention to the plantation. It was still light outside, but Ceravant had the curtains closed.

He pried open the box with a knife. Ashes fell from his cigarette. Reaching into the box, he picked up a long cylinder that was as fat as a sausage on one end and narrowed to a thin point on the other end. All along the top tiny sensors studded the cylinder. Ceravant lightly bounced the object in his hand. It weighed less than a kilogram and was just under a third of a meter long.

"Nice." Ceravant brought the object closer and turned it around. He took a drag from his cigarette. "Where did you get it?"

Pompano shrugged. "The market."

Ceravant replaced the device. "I mean, where did they get them?"

"The detectors are planted all along the interior of Clark. The Americans constantly replace them. Some stop working, some are run over by their jeeps or horses, some are just missing."

"How many did you get?"

"Twelve. There has not been a market for the detectors—no one besides the Americans really wants them, or even knows about them. It is my guess that the person I bought them from collected them more out of curiosity than for profit."

Ceravant nodded. He pulled on his smoke. "Who do you get them from?"

Pompano smiled and lightly wagged a finger at Ceravant. "Ah, yes. We all have our little secrets, don't we? What do you say I keep this one to myself, so that the source is not compromised?"

Ceravant smiled tightly. "Of course." The old man had started to put some distance between them, setting up an "insurance policy" so that he would be the only one who had some key information.

It was a smart move—one that Ceravant would have made himself. Pompano was proving to be more shrewd than Ceravant had initially thought. He made a mental note to withhold some of the sensor locations from Pompano.

Ceravant placed the lid back on the top of the box. "What about the receiver? How do these detectors transmit information?"

Pompano moved to a chair and sat. "That was harder to obtain. The devices detect sound to a very low level, and transmit the sounds as soon as they are heard. My, ah, *source,* he learned that the radio signals transmitted by the detectors are coded. A computerized station can unscramble the codes and tell you which detectors are transmitting."

"And where is the station?"

"I said it was harder to obtain." Pompano paused. "So I decided not to get it and use a simpler method instead."

Pompano nodded to the box of sonic detectors. "The detectors can be modified to transmit along a wire. I have brought several kilometers of wire that we can lay from each sensor to our plantation. It is a crude way to hook up the detectors, but it works."

Ceravant nodded, remembering the old radios and televisions in the old man's sari-sari store. Fixing electronic equipment was another talent the old man had to offer. "Crude, but effective. You have come up with a good plan, my friend. How long will it take to modify the sensors?"

A shrug. "Two, three hours. The wire is in the truck. I can start right away."

Ceravant took a final drag from his cigarette. Pompano was beginning to outshine all of the other Huks. As a measure of his respect, Ceravant decided then and there that Pompano would *definitely* not learn the locations of all of the sensors.

Ceravant ground out his cigarette and stood. He clasped Pompano's shoulder. "We must move quickly. As soon as you can modify the sensors I will plant them, and we will move to a location outside of the Clark Air Base to start disrupting their flights. The faster we move, the better."

Pompano frowned. "So fast? We are not rushed for this."

Ceravant breathed deeply through his nostrils. "We have a lot more at stake than what you might think. This new treaty about the American bases . . . it is a critical time. If we can disrupt their operations, put a thorn in their side during the negotiations so that it is known that not everyone supports this stupid treaty, we will succeed."

The old man nodded to himself, as if he were debating the process.

Ceravant reached down and squeezed his shoulder. "Anything, any person you need, I will get you. Once the sensors are in place, we will prepare to go to the American base tomorrow morning, early to avoid detection."

Clark AB

The phone rang twice.

"Bolte."

Charlie froze. "Uh, may I speak to Nanette, please."

"Hold on."

A moment passed. Charlie's pulse quickened. He started thinking to himself, started putting the pieces all together. Bolte—the Wing Commander. Charlie had known that he had children, but Nanette? *She wouldn't tell me who she was, acted like it was a game,* he thought. *What the heck is going on?* Meeting a blond beauty doesn't happen every day, especially one who has the poise, background, and savvy as Nanette. Charlie grew flustered. . . .

"Nanette?"

A second passed. "Charlie?"

"Hi."

She paused. "How did you get my home number?"

"Nipa Hut. I looked sad enough for them to pity me when I showed up and you weren't there."

She laughed. It sounded like music. "I'll bet. I'm glad that you got a hold of me. So, what's up?"

"Well, my roommate and I are thinking of heading down to Subic tomorrow afternoon. He's bringing a date, and I thought you might like to go along."

"Subic?"

"Bruce's father is stationed there. We'll go down, meet him, and make an afternoon of it. What do you think?"

She was silent for a moment. "Sounds like fun. Can I call you back if I can't get a replacement at work?"

"Sure." He gave her his number. "Pick you up around eleven? We can stop for lunch somewhere."

"Yeah. And your roommate—was he one of the guys out by the pool that day we met?"

"That's him."

She sighed. "I think this is going to be an interesting day."

Angeles City

Yolanda Sicat sang along with the radio, lightly adding a harmony part to the melody. The music helped get her through the day. Her father had been away from home lately, and the music kept her company.

The early years were hard, when she had first realized that she was unlike the others—the time when girlhood giggles and sly smiles had turned to boastings of what their mothers could do, and Yolanda had no mother of which to boast. She was four when she realized what it meant not to have a mother, a mommy, like the rest of them. The tears that had come were tempered by her father. He took her in his arms and assured her that she would never be alone, that she would always have a friend in music.

He had taught her more than the simple childhood melodies. Pompano had opened an entire new world, a pastiche of melodies through the radio. In all of his workings with electronics, nothing delighted her more than the day when he had given her her first radio.

Regardless of the friends she gained, Yolanda always returned to the sari-sari store to help her father. She acquired a sense of responsibility by taking care of her father, especially during those early years when he would drink too much and lie weeping on his bed, crying for her mother.

It was then that he would admonish her to stay away from the Americans. When pressed he would give her no clear-cut reason, only turn to more alcohol.

Living by the market, Yolanda had never befriended an American until this Bruce Steele appeared, although she had served them. Until now they had been nothing more than curiously foreign.

Tiny bells jangled in the front. Yolanda smoothed her skirt and glided into the store. She drew in her breath—it was the American.

He wore blue jeans and a colorful T-shirt. She had always thought that this combination was for delinquents, the types that frequented the sleazy part of town. But his clothes were so clean and good-smelling. And there was something about his eyes. . . .

"Hello, Bruce Steele." Yolanda did not look down, but smiled to herself. "I have ordered some more gum for you."

He turned slightly red. He fumbled in his pocket and held out a pack to her. "Would you care for a piece?"

"No, thank you." She reached back and flipped her hair over her shoulder. "I would think you would not have any gum left after nearly two weeks."

Bruce pocketed the pack. He leaned up against the long tabletop that traversed the back of the sari-sari store. "I've been in the jungle for the past ten days. A survival school."

"Did you have fun, learn anything?"

"Fun?" His eyebrows rose. "No. It wasn't too much fun, going four days without eating." He drew silent for a moment, then said slowly, "But now that you mention it, I guess I learned a lot. About myself, I mean."

Bruce paused. "There's something I thought we could do, if you had time."

Yolanda brightened. "Oh, tonight would be a good time to have dinner."

Bruce looked squeamish. "Uh, I'm not really too hungry, but I had something else in mind."

"Oh?" She felt slightly embarrassed at having brought up the subject.

"My dad lives near Subic. My roommate, his girlfriend, and I are heading down to see him tomorrow afternoon. Would you like to come with us?"

"To Olongapo?"

"Sure. It'll only take a couple of hours."

Yolanda drew in a breath. She had closed the store before while on her own—once to go with some girlfriends to the barrio, another time to see a music festival. Both times her father had approved of her leaving the store, and she had made each decision on her own.

This did not seem too much different. Especially if she was going to meet Bruce's parents. And father had wanted to meet Bruce, too, so perhaps this *was* a good time.

Yolanda turned and placed her hands on the table. "I think it will be fun."

"Great! I'll be by right before noon to pick you up." He started to back up.

Yolanda was surprised that he would be leaving so soon. "Can I get you something to eat before you go? You said you had not eaten for four days?"

Bruce grimaced. "Thanks, but I made up for it at lunch."

As he left, Yolanda started humming to herself. *Father would certainly approve*, she thought. She had so much to look forward to the coming year—admission to the University of the Philippines, leaving the store—and the thought made her happy to be alive.

Tarlac, P.I.

Ceravant stood, wiped his hands on his pants, and stepped back. It was just getting dark, and the dirt road was barely visible two feet away through the jungle. From there, Pompano's sensor would be invisible.

This was the last of the sensors—six of them planted by Ceravant, their location unknown even to Pompano. Two hours ago he had sent the old man back to the plantation, after learning how to bury the cylindrical detectors and lay the thin wire lines. He had instructed Pompano to prepare the high-power microwave weapon, to make sure that there would be no surprises when it was transported the next morning. Ceravant nodded to himself. They were almost ready.

CHAPTER 12

Thursday, 21 June

Hotel Otani, Tokyo

"Mr. Vice-President . . . Mr. Adleman." A hand shook his shoulder.

Adleman rolled onto his side. Light streaming from the hallway shone in his eyes. He blinked; Lieutenant Colonel Merke stood patiently by the bed. An apparition—a beautiful, sultry woman just dying to climb into bed with him. . . .

"I'm awake."

Merke pursed her lips. "Sorry, Mr. Vice-President. You didn't answer the phone."

Adleman dismissed the action with a wave. "What's going on?"

"A call from the Security Council, sir."

Adleman pushed up. "Bring in a line."

"They want an encrypted link, sir."

"The Stu-3 should handle it."

Merke shook her head. "They insist on double encryption, Mr. Adleman. We'll have to get back to Air Force Two."

Adleman's eyes widened; he was awake now. The fact that the Security Council wanted to bypass the normally secure Stu-3 classified phones smacked of something big.

Adleman swung out of bed, ignoring Lieutenant Colonel Merke's presence. She was a big girl and could avert her eyes if she wanted. He pulled on his shorts and glanced at the clock: two forty-five. The thirteen-hour time difference put Washington at three forty-five the previous afternoon.

"Any indication what's up?"

"No, sir. Secretary Acht said it was urgent and insisted that he speak with you." She nodded with her head to the briefcase she carried. "I have an updated situation briefing you could read on the way to Yokota."

"Thanks." Adleman took the hint to hurry. After pulling on his shoes he grabbed a shirt and headed out the door, fully intending to finish dressing in the car.

Adleman looked out the window from the backseat. No motorcade led the way, and at the early hour the streets were nearly empty. Even though the city was settled in for the night, flashing billboards covering the tall buildings still lit up the night sky; advertisements for soft drinks, cameras, stereos, and fast food predominated. It could have been New York, had it not been for the Japanese characters adorning the billboards.

Adleman turned his attention to the situation briefing that Merke had handed him. The title page was a red-bordered sheet with TOP SECRET stamped across the top and bottom. He flipped through the pages: A CIA assessment of the Middle East led the briefing; a Soviet air show in Dayton, Ohio, followed; all the intelligence traffic looked routine—nothing 'hot' to be found.

It made Adleman feel uneasy. He settled back and flipped the briefing material shut. Lights whizzed by as they approached Yokota Air Force Base. The military driver, a young, slim black airman, kept his eyes on the road and didn't attempt to engage the Vice-President in conversation. *He's probably scared half to death,* thought Adleman. *Either that, or he's had his butt chewed one too many times by some general.*

Adleman remembered the touch of paranoia he'd always felt when in the presence of ranking officers he had served with when he was in the military. After ROTC and law school at Brown, his stint as an Army lawyer had filled the square for military service, even if he didn't go to the Gulf. It was an unstated requirement now for political office—no one was going to be caught dead without serving some real time, not after the Quayle brouhaha.

The staff car slowed and pulled up to the gate of Yokota AFB. The guard inspected the driver's credentials, then snapped to attention and threw a salute when she realized that Adleman was in the car. It took another ten minutes to reach Air Force Two.

Someone shone a flashlight into Adleman's face for the first time as he approached the 747. The light quickly disappeared.

"Sorry, Mr. Vice-President. I had to make sure it was you."

"S'all right." Adleman blinked back the blue-and-orange afterimage of the light as he entered the jumbo jet.

"This way, sir." Merke steered him to the back, toward the Presidential chambers.

Merke shut the door as she left. The room was quiet, except for the faint pulsing of the plane's electrical systems as air pumped throughout the craft. The chamber was insulated against sound and electromagnetic emissions. Rich deep-blue carpeting with the presidential seal embossed in the center of the room contrasted with the blue-and-white patterns on the walls. Two phones sat on the desk before him—one white, the other red. The red phone had no buttons.

Adleman moved around the desk and made himself comfortable before picking up the red phone. "Adleman."

"Bob?"

The voice sounded tinny. "Yes?"

"Francis here." Even through the digitally reconstructed double scrambling, the Secretary of State's voice sounded tired. "We've got a little problem."

Adleman tightened his stomach. "Okay. How do I play in this?"

"The President is being taken to Bethesda. His situation has deteriorated. . . . It doesn't look good. We wanted to alert you before the press got wind of it. We want to keep it under wraps for another forty-eight hours until you're in the Philippines."

"Two days?! Can you keep the press off it that long?"

Acht tightened his voice. "The press is well aware of his condition. He sometimes doesn't make a public showing for days on end."

"But why keep it from the press? I knew all along it might come down to this. It doesn't seem necessary to pull me out of bed for a double-encrypted call—"

"The reason, Mr. Vice-President," interrupted Acht, with an edge to his voice, "for this double-encrypted call is that intelligence has spotted a terrorist who has surfaced for the first time in two years. This man is extremely dangerous. Yan Kawnleno was behind the attempted Thai assassination two years ago, and has acted as a consultant to terrorist groups throughout the world, from Libya to Columbia."

Adleman leaned forward in his chair. "How does that affect me?"

"Kawnleno has a reputation for taking promising young terrorists under his wing, turning them into protégés, all of the Khadaffi mold. CIA hasn't gotten a name yet, but they have verified that a student of Kawnleno is operating out of Manila. The publication of your flight all over the Philippines makes you a perfect target."

"Are you advising me to stay out of the Philippines? I can't let a terrorist dictate terms to the United States."

Acht came back instantly. "No, sir. I am not advocating canceling your trip," he said, emphatically. "It is just my opinion, as well as that of the intelligence community, that it would be a mistake to fly into Manila."

"Then what do you suggest?"

"Fly into *Clark*. You'll have some of the best defenses available in the world. No one will be able to get within miles of Air Force Two when it lands. And from there it's a simple helicopter ride to the treaty negotiations. It's much, much easier to defend against a helicopter than a jumbo jet, Mr. Vice-President. We can always change the meeting place at the last moment and have the helicopter take you there, but we can't change the location of Manila International Airport."

Adleman pondered the news. *Longmire is actually dying*, he thought. It was something he had known all along—but until now, he had not felt the weight of this responsibility.

Now every decision he made could become a major policy statement, every offhand comment would be dissected and analyzed by an academician trying to glean a shred of meaning.

Would flying into Clark actually work against the U.S.? Would that be interpreted as an American lack of trust in the Philippine government—give the impression that the Vice-President was not willing to become another Benigno Aquino, landing at Manila only to be slaughtered?

Or would his flying into Manila be viewed as the act of a rash, macho new President, one who probably ignored the advice of his closest associates?

Adleman finally spoke. But when he did, his voice sounded stronger than it had just minutes before. "We'll go into Clark. But don't publicly announce the change until my flight is in the air. It's been years since a Vice-President has visited the base, so I'll use that as my 'last-minute' excuse for changing plans."

Secretary of State Acht sounded relieved. "Very

well, Mr. Vice-President. We'll keep you updated on the President's condition."

"Fine. And please, unless there's any intelligence data that goes along with the call, I'd prefer a Stu-3."

Clark AB

"Howdy, son."

Bruce Steele glanced up, ready to growl at the person who had dared interrupt him as he was getting ready for The Flight. His eyes widened as he caught the gleam of two silver stars shining off the shoulders of the man standing next to him.

"Good . . . good morning, sir." Bruce drew himself up. *Oh, shit, shit, shit!*

General Simone stuck out a hand. "Peter Simone."

"First Lieutenant Bruce Steele, sir." Bruce shook the general's hand. A ream of flight maps covered the table where Bruce stood. The squadron briefing room was empty except for the two of them. A can of Pepsi and a candy bar sat next to the maps.

"Glad to meet you, Bruce."

"Thanks, sir. I've heard a lot about you."

Simone cocked an eye at the young Lieutenant. "I'll take that as a compliment. Let's see—you had already graduated from the Zoo when I was there, hadn't you?"

"That's right, general. You got there the year I left."

"Have you ever flown a general officer before, Bruce?"

Bruce hesitated. He had heard stories about Simone after he had left the Academy and gone to pilot training. "Blackman Simone" had not been the typical commandant, but rather had gotten rowdy with the cadets and thumbed his nose at red tape, paperwork, and bureaucrats. The story was that he was more concerned about his people than his own career. But that still didn't guarantee Simone was someone to get chummy with. Bruce decided to treat him as he would anyone else. "No, sir. My instructor pilot at Holloman was a major. That's as high as I've gone."

"Good—no preconceived notions then." Simone leaned against the preflight table. He looked more like the fatherly Chuck Yeager, "aw shucks" type than Commander of the entire Thirteenth Air Force. "Just remember when we're up there, you're the aircraft commander. I was flying fighters before you were born, so don't feel like you have to hold back because of me. The day I start puking or feeling that I can't handle a maneuver, I'll know it's time to leave the cockpit and do something really useful—like running the commissary service."

Bruce grinned. He was going to like this guy.

Major Dubois signed the aircraft over to Bruce without blinking. A book sat in the middle of the desk. From the lurid cover, Bruce deduced that he had changed paperbacks, which confirmed that the man could read. Or that he liked to look at covers.

Bruce kept up conversation with the general on the way out to the aircraft. Once they'd reached the flight line Bruce headed for the backseat of his F-15, while Simone threw his gear in the front.

Mooselips, Bruce's crew chief, stepped up and accompanied the two.

"Glad you made it back from the jungle, sir."

"You're not half as glad as me."

Bruce flipped through the maintenance log; nothing serious had occurred to the plane over the past two weeks while he'd been gone—with the exception of an upgrade to the avionics. They were all "fly-by-wire," electrical in nature, so it didn't concern him much. As long as it worked. He looked up and flipped the log to Mooselips. General Simone patted the airframe and walked around to the back.

Bruce lowered his voice. "Anything I should watch out for?"

Mooselips grinned. "Don't forget to bring your barf bag. From what I've heard the general likes to run his pilots through the wringer."

"Thanks." Bruce turned to follow Simone as he walked around the fighter.

Bruce approached Simone with a wry grin on his face. This could turn out to be fun. He pulled out a stick of gum and popped it in his mouth.

"How's it look, general?"

"Great. *This* is great." He drew in a deep breath. "Even the JP-4 smells good, brings back memories." He slapped the fuselage. "I'd give my left nut to be back in a wing, a line pilot again. Enjoy this while you can, son. These days are going to pass you up and you'll never get back to them."

"Sounds like you're forgetting the bad times, sir. There's a lot of rinky-dink stuff we put up with down in the trenches."

"I tell ya, it only gets worse the higher up you get. You'd think commanding an Air Force would give me a chance to change some of that Mickey Mouse bullshit, but I've got my hands tied. Sometimes it feels like being in the middle of a tree full of monkeys: When you look down you see the line pilots, grinning up at you; and looking up, it's the assholes in headquarters, crapping all over you."

They ducked under the twin tailpipes. The roar of a C-5B landing on the adjacent runway rolled over them, drowning out their conversation. The giant transport seemed to barely move; black smoke shot up from its tires as they touched the ground.

Bruce climbed in the instructor pilot position, behind and slightly above the general, where Charlie would normally sit. Tower treated them as just any other flight, replying to their transmissions with curt answers. But Bruce bet that the "Blackman 1" call sign sure as hell gained some attention.

General Simone and Bruce waited at the end of the runway. Radio calls mixed in with Simone's chatter. Bruce tried to pay polite attention to the general's patter, but he also tried to keep alert to everything happening around him. A loud whistling overhead caught his attention—a pair of F-5 aggressors landed, one after the other.

The radio cackled. "Blackman 1, you are cleared for takeoff."

Simone answered immediately. "Tower, Blackman. Request clearance to twenty thousand."

"Affirmative, Blackman. There is no traffic to twenty thousand."

"Thank you, sir." Bruce heard the click of Simone's mike, switching to intercom. "IP?"

"Ready, general," answered Bruce.

It felt like Bruce had been kicked in the butt.

Simone must have jammed the throttles to full afterburners. The fighter leaped forward, continuously accelerating as it rolled down the runway. Bruce kept his eye on the airspeed indicator. In no time they were passing a hundred knots. . . . As their velocity increased Bruce waited for Simone to announce "rotate," but nothing came over the intercom. They passed the rotate mark—Simone must be forcing the craft to the ground.

Bruce started to say something, but just as he opened his mouth Simone pulled back on the stick.

Once airborne, the fighter's attitude kept going up.

"Oh, shit," muttered Bruce. The fighter continued to accelerate, and soon they were pointed straight up— the F-15 was still accelerating, moving completely vertical. Now Bruce realized why the general had requested clearance to twenty thousand feet. At this rate, they'd be there in seconds.

"Still there, Bruce?"

"Rog, sir." Bruce grit his teeth. He wasn't going to say anything until Simone was about to kill them.

One mile south of Clark AB

Ceravant surveyed the site. The one road to the clearing was well guarded, and from all indications it had not had much use. He hopped down from the truck and went around to the back of the vehicle. Seconds later Pompano followed him, walking slowly.

Ceravant lifted the tarp covering the rear of the truck. Inside, a potpourri of boxes, cables, and equipment was stuffed into every corner, like a rat's nest of high-tech gear.

Pompano limped up. Ceravant threw him a look.

"What is the matter? Did you hurt yourself?"

"Getting old. These dirt roads are starting to get the best of me."

"You have been traveling on dirt roads all your life, old man."

"Not in a heavy truck, loaded down and hitting every bump."

Ceravant pulled the trap from the truck. A crowd of Huks congregated where the road opened up to the clearing. Ceravant shouted to them. "Barguyo, run down to the start of the road and help stand guard. The rest of you, help set up this equipment."

Pompano moved around the clearing, poking his nose into where the jungle started, overturning old cans and bottles that were strewn over the area. He called to Ceravant. "This place is used by kids—probably to come drink, or use drugs."

"Americans," confirmed Ceravant. He wiped his hands and joined the older man. "This is the best location I could find this close to the runway. We should not have any problem with children—keeping a guard back down the road will deter anyone from coming here. They do not want any attention brought to them for their drugs . . . or sex."

Pompano appeared to chew on his lip, then asked, "How far from the runway are we?"

"A little over two kilometers. At this range, the high-power microwave weapon should be able to disrupt their flight equipment. Not enough to pinpoint where we are, or even determine what we are doing, but enough to aggravate them greatly."

Pompano craned his neck and looked up; there was a tiny hole in the foliage that allowed him to view the cloudy sky. "Two kilometers?" He waved an arm around. "It can do that much damage?"

Ceravant strode to the truck and pulled a thick booklet from the back. He slapped it down on Pompano's hand. "Here. The cartoons show how far this weapon can be from the target, how to set it up, and how to use it."

Pompano leafed through the multicolored manual. He glanced at the illustrations of helmeted men setting up the device and operating it. He looked up at Ceravant. "I used this to set the weapon up." He pointed with the booklet up at the hole in the foliage. The clouds seemed like a kaleidoscope of black-and-white swirls. "My question is, what happens if a plane flies directly overhead, right above us?"

Ceravant stopped. He took the operating manual from the older man and flipped through the pages. A picture of an aircraft spinning out of control, just bare meters above the ground, adorned a page.

"If the plane is low enough, it goes down. . . ."

Ceravant stopped speaking. At that moment, a Pan Am 747 jumbo jet, probably carrying hundreds of servicemen and their children to Clark Air Base, roared not a thousand feet overhead.

Ceravant jerked his head up and got a fleeting glance of the jumbo jet before it disappeared. He looked back at Pompano.

The older man had his mouth drawn tight, and remained silent.

Ten miles off the western coast, P.I.

For the first time in his life, Bruce started to feel airsick.

In the forty-five minutes since General Simone had shot straight up from the runway at Clark, the fighter had not flown straight for more than thirty seconds. The general continuously slammed the craft through a gagging sequence of high-speed maneuvers, rolls, accelerations, and loops.

Bruce eyed the fuel-indicator through the bouncing gyrations. Simone suddenly spun the craft to the right, then straightened as they soared up through fifteen thousand feet. Bruce keyed the mike.

"Starting to get a little short on fuel, general."

The craft turned nose-down and Bruce suddenly felt weightless; they followed a neat parabolic path. "We used to run our jets through the wringer like this when they were first delivered to the squadron. Except you can't treat a Smokin' Rhino like this."

Bruce clicked twice on the mike. General Simone was referring to the F-4 fighter, which had been the mainstay of Air Force fighters during the sixties and seventies. Its trail of black smoke could be seen from miles away.

Suddenly the fighter turned up, as Simone brought her out of the parabolic path. Simone's voice came over the intercom.

"Let's get our feet wet before heading back, Assassin."

"Rog."

Simone pulled the fighter into a backward loop. Blue sky melted into black as they rotated around. Bruce felt as though he should be able to see the stars. As they continued to rotate the black sky turned into blue, until Bruce saw the boundary of water with land miles in the distance. They accelerated straight down, screaming through the Mach numbers. When they swept past ten thousand feet, Bruce started calling out the altitude. Simone gave no indication that he knew how high they were.

Seconds passed. Bruce wet his lips.

"Four thousand . . . three thousand . . . min altitude, general."

With no response, Bruce called out, "IP has the aircraft." He pulled back on the stick and the throttles, trying not to bring them out in too steep of an angle. Simone didn't say anything—Bruce expected to be blasted by the general for taking away control of the aircraft.

The gee-indicator rose, moving past six, then seven gees. Bruce grunted, anticipating brownout, but felt no indication even of tunnel vision. The gees dwindled off as he brought the aircraft up. At two hundred feet the jet leveled off. Bruce clicked his mike.

"All right, general?"

Two clicks answered him. "Your aircraft, Assassin."

Bruce clicked back. "I'll have to bring it up for "feet dry," general. Take a last gander before we bring her up to altitude."

Bruce glanced at the heads-up display, which indicated air speed was right on five hundred knots.

A speck through the cockpit caught his attention— it looked like an old rickety fishing boat, directly ahead of them on the horizon. Bruce immediately broke right and accelerated up. He wasn't about to capsize the boat.

Overturning a group in a rice paddy was one thing, but sinking a fishing boat miles from shore was an order of magnitude worse.

As they gained altitude, Simone came over the intercom. "That happened to me once years back, Assassin. Never quite forgave myself for strafing an unarmed boat."

Bruce kept quiet for a moment. Breaking through ten thousand feet, they passed over the beaches on the west side of the island. White sand quickly changed to jungle as they flew toward Clark. Bruce received the necessary clearances as they proceeded on to a landing.

Once down, Bruce removed his helmet and drew in deep breaths of humid air. Clouds covered most of the sky, and a light drizzle had just started to cover the ground.

Simone reached the bottom of the stairs before him. When Bruce climbed down, the general held out a slender ebony hand; his flight suit was soaked with perspiration. He showed evenly spaced teeth when he smiled.

"Thanks, son."

Bruce shook his hand. "Thank you, sir—you're the one who put me through the paces. That was some nice flying."

Simone picked up his helmet and started for the staff car that waited for him at the edge of the flight line. Sounds of auxiliary power units cranked up in the distance; laughter drifted from a group of airmen playing volleyball on the opposite side of squadron headquarters. Simone nodded for Bruce to follow. Bruce stepped up and kept pace with the general. Simone spoke straight ahead, as if Bruce weren't even there.

"Flying these jets is a cathartic experience for me; purging my soul of all the humdrum activity that comes with command." He paused. "Sometimes I think I might even take it too far, Bruce—try to push the limits of what I can do. Some people can't handle it when I take them up, refuse to fly with me anymore. That's how I weed out the true pilots." He stopped and lifted up his sunglasses. He looked Bruce over. "That took balls to take the plane away from me, Bruce. For all your bravado, I think there's a damn good fighter pilot in you. Stay with it, son. Don't let the bullshit get you down and you'll go far. I'll see to it."

"Thank you, sir. Ah, are you all right . . . ? I mean when I took the airplane away? Were you okay then?"

Simone dropped his sunglasses back to his face and growled. "I said it was a test, didn't I?"

Bruce watched the staff car drive away, the flag with two stars on it waving from the front.

"Well, I'll be dipped," he said to no one.

One mile south of Clark AB

Ceravant took a final drag on his cigarette before walking over to the HPM weapon. One man was struggling to unfold a dish antenna. The camouflaged parabola unfurled, until it was nearly ten feet across. A collector in the center of the dish stuck out a good three feet. The HPM weapon looked to be nothing more than a delicate dish, a gigantic flower that sat in the middle of the clearing.

As Ceravant approached, he could tell that the antenna was only a small part of the weapon. A long pipe protruded from an array of capacitor banks. The pipe was connected to the antenna through a convoluted series of fittings—"mode converters," the operating manual had called them. From what Ceravant understood, the weapon produced microwaves that were a million times more powerful than those found in microwave ovens; although the microwaves literally "fried" electronic components, the beam quickly spread out and was ineffective over long distances.

Ceravant paused before the device. "Is it complete?"

"Except for turning it on." Pompano emerged from beneath the dish. A motorized pointing and tracking unit held the giant antenna in place. He wiped his hands on already grimy pants.

"The manual does say that the setup time should take no longer than two hours. And knowing the average intelligence of the American troops, I had no fear that you should find the tasking easy."

Pompano ran a hand over the long metal piping that connected the dish to the capacitor banks. He spoke in a low voice. "Do not underestimate those people, my friend. That cartoon operating manual does not reflect their true capabilities—ask any Iraqi."

Ceravant fished a cigarette out of a pack in his sock. "Whatever. But that does not concern me now. What is important to me is using the weapon. When can we start?"

Pompano was silent for a moment. He answered slowly, "We are ready now. It is not difficult to operate—Barguyo already knows how. Basically, all that is needed is to charge up the capacitors, aim the weapon, and set it off. Once the weapon fires, the capacitors recharge so we can use it again."

Ceravant puffed away quickly. "So we can use it now?"

Pompano shrugged. "Of course."

Ceravant threw down his newly lit cigarette. The prospect of finally having this tool so close to the American base excited him. He felt like cranking the dish straight up, pointing toward the hole in the jungle above.

The distant sound of a jet only intensified the feeling.

It seemed as though the dream he had had over the past years was coming to a head, culminating, frothing to a finish. And all it required was "charging and pointing." It almost seemed too easy. . . .

And it was.

Ceravant realized that if he were to rush, hurry and set off the weapon, he might be tracked. The device would have to be used selectively—only against those targets that would produce the maximum effect.

Gaining access to a list of incoming aircraft should not prove difficult. Ceravant smiled amicably at the old man in front of him.

"Perhaps we should not rush with this device. Can your *sources* obtain a list of incoming flights to the American base? Flights that, if irradiated, would give us maximum political leverage?"

Pompano looked surprised. "I do not see why not."

"Good. Tomorrow afternoon will be a good time to return here."

Pompano held up a hand. "I do not know if I can obtain anything for you by then."

"But at least you should know if the information is forthcoming." Ceravant paused; he had allowed the man to keep his source, and now that Pompano played such an integral role the old man would be sure to come through. "Why don't we test the device, to make sure it still works after the trip?" He looked around the clearing. Besides the high-power microwave weapon, two jeepneys and one truck were in the clearing. "Aim the device at the truck; it is the most expendable."

Pompano shrugged and headed for the weapon. Ceravant waved for the men to move the two jeepneys out of the way.

Moments later Pompano called out, "Ready!"

Ceravant crossed his arms and nodded. The men were lined up behind the dish, now pointing almost horizontal, straight at the battered truck.

Pompano pushed a button. A sharp "pop" ricocheted throughout the clearing. Ceravant frowned. Unlike the last test there had been no smoke, no explosion. The truck looked unscathed.

Ceravant strode toward the truck. Looking inside, he saw nothing out of the ordinary. He pushed into the front seat and turned the ignition. Nothing. The engine didn't even crank.

Pompano pushed his face up to the window. "Well?"

"It does not turn over."

"What else did you expect?"

Ceravant's brows went up. "Is this it?"

"This is it." Pompano was silent for a moment. He nodded to Ceravant's watch. "Have you checked that?"

Ceravant glanced at his wristwatch. The electronic timepiece was completely blank. There was no sign that the liquid crystal display had ever worked.

And he had been standing *behind* the weapon.

Ceravant smiled.

Clark AB

"What?!"

Staff Sergeant Evette Whiltee pushed back her chair

in the control tower. The wheeled chair slid across the waxed floor. She had an unobstructed view of the outside—four major runways, F-15s, C-5s, C-130s, MH-60s, HH-3s, support vehicles, and almost anything else that the air base had to offer.

The control tower should have afforded her no surprises.

But the blip that appeared on her radar screen seemed to defy all those precautions.

It was as if someone had turned all the power off, then back on again within the blink of an eye.

And if that had happened—an abrupt power failure, for example—then her computerized systems would have undergone an immediate re-initialization sequence.

But whatever had happened, it wasn't a power failure.

The rest of the control tower acted as if nothing had happened. Evette glanced around—no one had noticed her yet.

She glanced at her computerized screen. Nothing unusual.

She thought hard. She'd been on the rock now for nearly eighteen months. Another six months and she'd be heading back to the States, back to Travis AFB where she had been guaranteed an assignment. Northern California had it all over the P.I.

And she didn't really want to jeopardize it by bringing up a questionable incident.

The longer she thought about it, the more it made sense. It had been her imagination.

She pushed back to her screen and donned her headphones.

CHAPTER 13

Thursday, 21 June

Clark AB

Bruce waited in the car as Charlie got out to get Nanette. Brilliant red-and-yellow flowers dotted the side of the yard, meticulously kept by the yard boy. Lush trees masked the house from direct sunlight. The house was one of thirty on "Senior Officers' Row," the private loop that housed all of Clark's senior ranking officers. A sign by the door read: COL BOLTE.

Bruce slouched in his seat and pulled his sunglasses down on his face. He scanned the house, but no one appeared. He knew it was crazy to try and hide—Colonel Bolte was most likely at Wing Headquarters—but the initial chewing out that Bruce had gotten the day they first arrived at Clark still stuck in his mind.

Charlie disappeared inside, and moments later came out with a slender blond. Her white shorts accented tanned legs. Bruce watched her out of the corner of his eye, trying not to appear interested.

He felt happy for his backseater. The poor guy had been searching for years for the right woman, never finding anyone with the right combination of looks and brains to satisfy him. Bruce made a mental note to be on his best behavior. And with Yolanda coming along, that should not prove to be difficult.

Bruce twisted around as they got into the backseat. "Hi. I'm Bruce Steele."

"Nanette," she said, firmly returning his shake.

Bruce started the engine. "Charlie tells me we've already met." He watched her through the rearview mirror.

She threw a glance at Charlie and smiled. "I'm surprised you remember."

"I don't; that's why Charlie had to tell me."

"A catcall across a swimming pool doesn't qualify as a formal introduction, so I guess we really haven't met."

Bruce dug out a pack of gum. He held it up to the backseat. "Gum?"

"No thanks."

He popped a piece in his mouth and concentrated on getting to the main gate. Traffic on base was not bad; it had been a while since he had actually driven. His car had not yet arrived on the boat from the States—a corvette, his "cadet car," that he had had at the USAF Academy. The rental car he was driving didn't have nearly the pickup that he was used to. But it beat the hell out of waiting for taxis and riding the bus, especially for a double date.

As they approached the main gate, Bruce pulled over to the side. Parking the car, he said, "Be back in a moment." He entered the base's Visitors' Center and applied for a visitor's pass, using his identification card as credentials. After the airman pushed the pass to him, Bruce strode back to the car.

"What was that all about?" asked Charlie.

Bruce held up the visitor's pass as he pulled back into traffic. "I don't want Yolanda to have to go jumping through hoops if things work out and she wants to get on base."

Once outside the main gate, he steeled himself for automotive culture shock. Jeepneys screeched precariously near, and pedestrians darted in and out of traffic. He kept one foot on the gas and the other on the brake. Blended with the traffic came a cacophony of noise and smells: honking horns, people yelling curses, odors of urine and stale beer, and the sound of music blaring from the bars outside the base. He rolled up his window.

"I'm going to air-conditioning."

Charlie and Nanette rolled up their windows, and all of a sudden they seemed to be in a different world.

Bruce directed his voice to the back without turning around, "I hate air conditioners. It's like giving in to the environment."

"It kills Bruce even to go to oxygen when we're flying," said Charlie.

"I wouldn't go that far," retorted Bruce. "After all those cold winters in Colorado, I can't get enough of warm weather. And resorting to air-conditioning seems to be the wimp's way out."

Nanette thought for a moment. "Man against Nature, the most basic conflict and the lowest rung in Maslov's hierarchy. Sounds like a good thesis topic, Charlie."

Bruce's eyes widened. Looking through the rear-view mirror, he couldn't tell if she was kidding or not. Maybe Charlie *had* found his match.

Bruce concentrated on finding the downtown open-air market and tuned Nanette and Charlie out. As far as he could tell, they were still discussing evolution in action when he turned onto Yolanda's street. He drove slowly past the market, avoiding the people that spilled out into the street. With the air conditioner on, it was if he were viewing the scene from inside a room, with pictures of the Filipino culture racing across the windows, projected in from some hidden movie camera.

He pulled up next to the sari-sari store and stopped. "Be right back." He left the engine running, air conditioner on. Stepping from the car, the heat hit him full blast. *That's another reason for not using the air conditioner*, he thought.

Chairs sat upside down on the tables, as if the store were closed. When Bruce tried the screen door, it was locked. He peered through the wire mesh. Nothing. "Yolanda? It's Bruce." Still nothing. Bruce tried the door again.

Rattling the door, he heard the sound of water running from inside. "Yolanda?"

"Bruce—wait, please."

He relaxed and let go of the door.

Yolanda backed out of the sari-sari store and drew shut the inner door behind her, locking it. The screen slammed against the door frame.

"Hello." She turned; a colorful blouse, long, dark skirt and sandals.

"Hi," said Bruce. He hesitated, then nodded to the car. "Ready?"

She brushed her hair back and smiled. "Yes." That single word embodied all the answer he was looking for, the innocence, the un-jaded anticipation of a new relationship. Bruce pushed aside his fears and smiled. He was finally ready to go, to introduce his father to his friends and start his life over again. He was ready for a fresh start.

Steamboat Springs, Colorado

The mountains were magnificent at this time of the year. Flowers sent their fragrant beauty wafting down the grassy ski slopes, hidden pockets of snow still hid from winter's last great freeze, and icy blue lakes seemed on the verge of freezing—General David Newman reveled in the mountains of his home state. Although he had always felt that summer was the best time to visit the mountains, he loved to ski, and usually brought his family back to Colorado at least once in the winter to race the downhill slopes. He put up with the crowds once a year to get his skiing fix, but it was the summers that revitalized him, gave him a new birth, and a new faith in being the Chairman of the Joint Chiefs of Staff.

The quiet and solitude that surrounded Steamboat

felt somewhat artificial, for all the beauty of soaring peaks and jutting mountains. Even that distant hawk, lazily circling on the thermals, perhaps had some sense of the technology bubbling all around it. As remote as General Newman was, he was still in near instant contact with the rest of the world. Although he tried to slow down on his "vacations," he had learned two years ago that he could never really have a true vacation.

A quietly efficient young man stepped up to the general. A wire ran from an earplug in his ear to a small radio fastened to his belt. He spoke in a low tone. "General, an urgent call on the Stu-3."

Newman nodded and made for the lodge. Swept for bugs by the Air Force Office of Investigation not an hour before he had arrived for vacation, a small command post had been established one door down from Newman's suite.

The conversation went quickly. As he hung up the classified phone, Newman closed his eyes and shook his head. *When it rains, it pours*, he thought. He had not been told the reason, but that was not unusual— political decisions are presented to military men as faits accomplis, not explained.

Vice-President Adleman's decision to change his plans and to go into Clark would require the scheduling of the entire Thirteenth Air Force's operational readiness around a single plane, but that was only a small part of the picture. The Thirteenth was "Blackman" Simone's outfit. Simone was a competent fighter pilot and could match any military man in a fight, but as far as being politically savvy . . . Simone would rather tell the Vice-President to go to hell than to have the Veep interfere with the launching of his jets. He had voiced his opinions in the past about the politicians wasting his time, and Newman was sure this scenario wouldn't be any different.

Newman decided to bypass Pacific Air Force Headquarters and go directly to the problem; he'd get back to PACAF later. He opened his eyes and said to his aide, "Get me Thirteenth Air Force on the line."

Moments later, he finished exchanging pleasantries with Major General Simone. "Blackman, I need a favor."

"Name it. Coming out here for a shopping trip?"

"I'm serious. Remember I saved your butt from that Academy investigation."

"You say it, you got it, sir."

Newman nodded to himself. "Good. This is important. I need somebody hot, one of your boys who will make a good impression and won't mess up."

"Pilot?"

"Of course."

Silence, then, "I've got just the man for you—a shit-hot stick, too. Won the Risner Trophy as a butter bar."

"Great. There's a plane he needs to escort into Clark, and after they land he needs to stick like glue to this VIP. Be an escort officer, show the VIP around."

"No problem. We normally use one of our hot young officers for this kind of duty; it impresses the hell out of VIPs to see someone that young be so sharp. What's up?"

Newman took a deep breath and settled back in his chair. "Are you sitting down?"

Five miles outside of Olongapo

Bruce had gotten lost only once on the trip down from Clark. They had intended to stop in a barrio housing some of Yolanda's distant relatives, but in the years since she had last visited them Yolanda had forgotten her directions.

Instead of visiting the barrio the foursome stopped by a roadside shack and splurged on *lumpia*, topped off with what seemed to be a gallon of pop. They groaned all the way to the outskirts of Olongapo.

Yolanda opened up and joined in the conversation. As he drove, Bruce studied her out of the corner of his eye. Her shy smiles turned to laughter, and she held her hand over her mouth as her sparkling, dark eyes took in the banter.

Bruce consulted a sheet of paper and turned down a long row of apartments. The city of Olongapo straddled the barrio, both of which surrounded Subic. The base traffic had tapered off when they turned for the barrio, and with the absence of the American military presence there seemed to be a remarkable increase in affluence and a decrease in the seediness. Bruce kept quiet about the observation, not wanting to embarrass Yolanda.

He stopped at a corner and scanned both directions.

Charlie leaned forward in his seat. "Have a problem?"

"No, I just wanted to make sure I was on the right street." The apartment complex looked vaguely familiar . . . but then again, Bruce had been emerging from a hangover when his father had taken him here.

Bruce decided he was going the right way and moved slowly down the street. He spotted a red Geo parked in one of the stalls and stopped. "This is it." Backing up, he pulled into the driveway.

Bruce knocked on the door. Yolanda, Nanette, and Charlie stood behind him. Joe Steele answered, dressed in a T-shirt, Navy bell bottoms, and bare feet. He looked surprised.

"We didn't wake you up, did we?" asked Bruce, somewhat hesitantly.

"Bruce! Hell, no! Come on in, kids." He turned and shouted, "Tanla, ziggy now—Bruce is here, and he's brought some friends!" He opened the door wide.

"The girls have to work tomorrow. This was the only day we were all able to get off," explained Bruce as they entered the small apartment. The room was covered with wood carvings and stereo equipment.

"Well, shit, have a seat. I should have known you

pilots never have to work. You kids drove all the way from Clark, you must be tired. Can I fix you a drink? Beer, any hard stuff?"

They found a place in the living room. Charlie sat on the couch in between Nanette and Yolanda; Bruce sprawled on the floor on an overstuffed pillow. "None for me. I've got to drive back."

"That hasn't stopped you before, has it, Bruce?" Joe Steele roared and winked broadly at Nanette. "They haven't been calling my boy Assassin just for the hell of it, have they? Has he told you that was for being a woman killer, or for playing football?" He guffawed.

Nanette smiled demurely. "This is a nice place you have, Mr. Steele. It seems quite cozy."

"Joe. Call me Joe. Are you sure I can't fix you something?"

"No, thank you."

Joe turned and opened a small refrigerator sitting by his easy chair. He pulled out a San Miguel. "I don't go on duty until eight tonight, so you'll just have to put up with me." He laughed. "How about lunch? Have you eaten yet?"

"We're fine, dad," said Bruce, quietly. "I just came over to introduce you to some of my friends."

Steele half bowed from his chair. "Glad to know you." He nodded to the girls, "Nanette, Yolanda."

Bruce looked around. "Did we miss Tanla? I thought she didn't leave for work until later."

Joe took a sudden drink of beer. "She'll be out," he said, stiffly.

Bruce saw Charlie raise an eyebrow, but the inflection otherwise went unnoticed.

Yolanda sat primly, her legs together and hands folded in her lap. She wore a smile, but Bruce could tell that she felt uncomfortable. Bruce nodded to Yolanda.

"Dad, Yolanda is planning to go to the University of the Philippines this fall. She wants to study music."

"PU, eh?" smirked Joe Steele.

"That is correct," said Yolanda, quietly.

"And Nanette is at Stanford," continued Bruce.

Bruce's father ignored the observation and shot out on another tangent. "Hey, did Bruce tell you that I didn't know that he was on the rock until I got a phone call from him one morning?"

"That's okay, Dad."

"Yeah, called up his old man right out of the blue. I started up the old Geo and found him down at the chaplain's office—of all places, my son in a chapel! And what a sight!"

"*Okay*, Dad," said Bruce, with an edge to his voice.

Joe took another swig of beer and wiped his mouth with the back of his hand. Bruce winced as his father's T-shirt came up over his belly, revealing a lurid tattoo.

"You know, the Steeles have a long history of serving in the Navy. My father, grandfather, and great-grandfather were all enlisted men. We're mighty proud of that line. Yep. Once in a while though you get an upstart in the family, someone who thinks he's too good for the rest of them, but I've kept that line going for years." The rest of the room was quiet. Bruce felt his ears grow warm as his father continued. "When Bruce applied for the Air Force Academy, I thought for sure he was one of those upstarts. Until I saw him at the chaplain's office."

He snickered as if it were a huge joke. "When I saw my boy covered with up chuck, not a dime to his name and having a hangover to beat it all, I *knew* he wasn't a yuppie—he was just continuing the Steele name in a slightly different manner."

Bruce smiled wanly. "Thanks, Dad."

Joe belched and reached for another beer, the sarcasm lost on him. "You know, son, we were sad to hear about Ashley."

Bruce hesitated, then whispered to Yolanda, "My first wife—it's a long story." Yolanda's eyes widened.

Joe swallowed a few gulps and nodded to the couch,

"But Nanette, I can assure you that Ashley was nowhere as good-looking as you. And that's coming from someone who's seen girls all over the world, from London to Sydney, Singapore to Rio. My boy may look like an officer, but I assure you he's an enlisted man deep to the core. He'll take care of you, Nanette. I wouldn't have believed it until two weeks ago, but he's a son a father can be proud of."

The room was shocked into silence. Joe leaned back and pulled on his beer, obviously proud of having offered such a moving testimony.

Bruce waited a minute before speaking. "Dad . . ."

"No use to thank me, son. I know it's been a long time coming, but you've deserved."

"Dad," interrupted Bruce firmly, "Nanette is Charlie's date. Yolanda is with me."

Joe Steele's eyes grew wide. He opened his mouth to say something, but Tanla suddenly entered the room. She smiled tightly. Her eyes seemed shaded, as if they were welling with tears. Heavy makeup covered several dark blue spots on her face.

Bruce studied Tanla. One of her eyes was black, and there *were bruises* on her face. She caught him staring and forced a smile. She brought up a hand to her face.

"I . . . I fell this morning."

Bruce swung his attention to his father. Joe belched and drew his chin up in the air. "Well, are you going to get high and mighty on me, son? After what I said about you?"

Bruce clamped his mouth shut. No one spoke, and the tension in the room seemed to rise.

After eliciting no comments with his query, Joe's voice rose minutely as he continued: "And let me warn you about something, while I'm at it. Be careful with these Filipinos, Bruce. Tanla knows she'll never get back to the States—I'm spoken for. But there are plenty others out there ready to hop in the sack with you, do anything to get you to marry them and take

them to America. Just remember: For every nice Filipino there's a beak—a year from now she could be
whoring around the massage parlors, outside of Eglin
Air Force Base, while you're up flying your fighter.
It's like the difference between a Negro and a nigger,
son—you can live next to 'em but you can never trust
'em."

Bruce stood, his face white. He breathed deeply
through his nose. "We're leaving."

"What's the matter?" Joe shot a glance at Yolanda;
her head was down, her eyes hidden. "Hey, wait a
minute. I wasn't talking about Yoli, here! I was just
giving you some good fatherly advice, son." He
sounded genuinely apologetic.

"And next you'll be telling me to slap her around
when she gives me grief."

"Now, wait a damned minute." Joe stood and
wavered. "That's got nothin' to do with you. That's
my private life, and I don't care who you are, you
don't have a right to tell me what to do—so keep the
hell out of my life!"

"I sure as hell will." Bruce turned to the couch.
"Charlie, let's get out of here."

Charlie led Nanette and Yolanda from the room.
Joe sat back down in the chair and pulled at his beer.
He turned his head and saw Bruce still standing there.

"Go on—get the hell out!" He turned back to the
front and muttered, "I don't care who the fuck you
think you are, what you've done—you're still not half
the man your brother ever was."

Bruce drew in a deep breath and clenched his hand,
jamming his fingernails into his skin. He started to
retort, when it hit him that no matter what he did, no
matter what he said, there would be no reaction from
his father except for rage.

Bruce turned. Tanla grasped his arm. "Bruce . . .
do not take it out on him. He treats me well."

Bruce forced a smile and patted her hand.

"Son . . ." Joe stood, his hands open in a shrug.

Bruce set his mouth and headed out to the car, where Yolanda waited with Charlie and Nanette.

Angeles City

Pompano reached the sari-sari store shortly after noon. As usual the market was crowded, and it pleased him to think that he would be getting some of the overflow. He felt grimy after setting up the high-power microwave weapon, and looked forward to cleaning up and having Yolanda fix him one of his favorite meals.

As he approached the store, he noticed the chairs sitting on top of the tables. He frowned. Maybe Yolanda was sick and could not attend to the counter.

He jiggled the door and it was locked; he didn't want to disturb his daughter if she was sick. Moving to the back of the tiny store, he found the back door locked as well. He hobbled over to a pile of bricks and wood. Pompano carefully overturned a concrete block several layers down from the top of the pile. He wiped away dirt and pulled out a small box. Inside the box were several plastic containers holding papers, deeds, old pictures. A key was at the bottom of the container. It had been two years since he had had to use this key.

Pompano unlocked the door and quietly entered. The store was empty.

He furrowed his brows. Yolanda was not one to leave the store unattended without good reason. Looking around the room, he spotted a white sheet of paper taped to his chair. He recognized Yolanda's writing:

> Father, The young man I told you about has invited me to Olongapo for the afternoon. This was the only time he could get off work, so I thought it might be best for me to go. If you get back, I will introduce you to him early this evening. Y.

He smiled to himself. His little girl was growing up faster than he had wanted.

Outskirts of Olongapo

The car was quiet. Bruce was immersed in his thoughts as he drove, mostly on "auto-pilot," as he didn't pay attention to where he was going or what he was doing—he let his reflexes do the driving.

He glanced in the rear-view mirror. Charlie had his arm around Nanette; she leaned back on his shoulder, looking outside the car. From the corner of his eye he saw Yolanda stare listlessly at her hands. Bruce set his mouth.

"I'm . . . sorry that my dad came over that way, Yolanda. He, well, he's pretty opinionated and doesn't think things through before he opens his mouth. He's got some real problems . . ." he trailed off.

Charlie spoke from the back. "You don't have to apologize. He said what he said, and you aren't responsible for any of it. I think it's best if we just forget about it."

Charlie caught his eye in the mirror; he nodded toward Yolanda. She still sat with her head down.

Bruce slid his arm over the seat and took her hand. She held onto him tightly. There was nothing to say for a long time, but she seemed to hold onto him as if he were a lifeline, a buoy. He could just imagine the shame she felt, the humiliation.

He knew she had other goals, other aspirations, and coming back to the United States with Bruce was probably something she had never even considered.

Bruce tried to put himself in her shoes. What would it have been like if he had been accused—slandered!—by *her* father?

But he knew that the comparison could never be made. She had much more at stake. And since the Filipino culture had ingrained in her that saving face was paramount, it was as if Bruce's father had stripped her in front of Bruce and his friends, publicly shocked and humiliated her.

Bruce glanced over to Yolanda. She shuddered quietly, as if sobbing to herself, but yet never allowing the others to see.

Bruce tried to control his voice and spoke quietly. "Yolanda . . . I'm . . . I'm sorry, and I know that nothing I do can change it. Maybe I can make you understand, tell you something that happened to me, something very close to me, that caused me shame—" he stopped for a moment, then prayed silently for the strength to go on. He found his voice had dropped to a whisper. "I was married until six months ago. I thought I had the perfect marriage, a girl that I had dated all through high school and college.

"How well can you know a person after seven years of dating and three years of marriage? But I guess it really didn't matter—whatever is inside is the true person, and that doesn't always show.

"Ashley and I drew apart the last few months, her job and friends demanding more of her time. Her best friend used to keep her company on those overnight trips I had to take, and I had always thought that it was a good idea." He paused, then forced himself to continue. "One night, I came home after a flight was cancelled, and I found Ashley . . . Ashley with her girlfriend and a couple of guys . . . all . . . in my bed. That was the last time I saw her. Everything else, the separation, the divorce was all conducted through lawyers. I couldn't bring myself to face her again. Or tell my friends about it.

"I guess things like being honest with each other, spending time taking walks, or just reading together . . . doesn't mean much to some people. I know I can't undo what my father did to you, but—at least you should know that you aren't the only one to experience pain."

Bruce stared straight ahead. The road was clear,

and rice paddies on either side diffused into jungle; it didn't take much to drive, and Bruce did the minimum keeping the car on the road.

Bruce felt a hand on his shoulder; Charlie squeezed tight.

Yolanda still sobbed quietly. Charlie removed his hand and settled back in his seat.

When Yolanda leaned her head over to Bruce's shoulder, he felt a peace he had not felt for what seemed years.

The White House

Secretary of State Francis Acht closed his eyes and leaned back in his chair. The first-floor room was down the hall and two doors down from the President's study. Normally reserved for the President's National Security Advisor, Acht was using the room as a temporary situation room.

He didn't want to draw undue attention to the President's absence, but he knew that the effort was almost useless. Sooner or later someone on the White House staff would speak to the press—a "highly placed anonymous source," getting in brownie points with the reporters and thus raising his stature in the press's eyes.

Acht opened his eyes and glanced at the note just handed him: The President was still in surgery, and the prognosis was bad.

Adleman was due to arrive in the Philippine Islands in less than twelve hours and, with any luck, should be able to wrap up the treaty by Sunday. Most of the details had been hammered out by a team handpicked by Acht. Adleman's presence would assure Philippine President Rizular that the U.S. was not treating the Philippines as a whore.

Acht blinked his eyes. The room's hand-rubbed wood finish, dark blue decor, and soft lighting had been designed to soothe the tensions that might affect decisions.

The Secretary of State stood and shuffled to the curtains. Drawing the thick fabric aside, he looked out onto the White House lawn. Few cars passed by the barriers erected alongside the yard's perimeter. He could barely make out people as they walked along the street in the warm Washington night. Sometimes it felt as if all the security precautions were designed to keep him in, rather than keep the masses out.

A sharp rap came at the door. "Come in."

The National Security Advisor stood at the doorway. "No change. Things aren't looking good."

Acht threw one last look outside and sighed. Things were moving too fast. And it was no time for secrecy. "Let's go ahead with the press release."

"Should we have Adleman return, then?"

Acht shook his head. "The treaty is too important. If we pull him back, we might give the wrong message to Rizular. There's too much riding on this."

"So you think it's the right thing to do, telling the press?"

"Absolutely. We've got the contingency plans ready. Adleman is flying from one American base to another. I think all of our ducks are in line. Just leave out how critical the President really is. We don't want to start a panic."

"And if Longmire dies?"

Acht shrugged. "We've done everything we can. We can't put the government on hold, waiting for the worst. Business goes on. Mr. Adleman has been apprised of the situation and we've taken all the security precautions we can." He paused. "This treaty is just too damned important. Let's just pray that Longmire holds on until we can get Adleman back here," he glanced at the calender, "in something more than seventy-two hours."

CHAPTER 14

Thursday, 21 June

Clark AB

Major General Simone paced up and down his richly decorated office, scowling. For the first time since he had stopped smoking some ten years before, he literally ached for a cigarette. He didn't crave any booze—which was a good thing, for he would have stopped drinking years ago if he had. But he would have killed for a good hit of nicotine.

He shouldn't have gotten upset. He'd met politicians before, wined and dined them, but that had been when he was Commandant of Cadets, never when he was in an operational unit. *Why can't they just leave me the hell alone?* he thought.

The Thirteenth Air Force had an established routine for dealing with political VIPs—usually congressmen, whose wives and staffers accompanied the politicians on their "fact-finding junkets." More often than not the trips turned out to be nothing more than Air Force-funded spending sprees, underwritten by the taxpayers.

Simone had a staff whose job it was to accompany the groups, showing them where the best buys were and the places to avoid. Simone usually made a star appearance at the beginning and again at the end of each trip, profusely thanking the delegation for showing up—but making damned sure that his operation was not affected by the junket.

But this trip by the *Vice-President*, of all the useless people! The place would be crawling with Secret Service, NSA, DIA, OSI, and probably XYZ agents. Flying would stop, then be staged to provide a "demonstration" for the Veep. He'd have lunch with the troops in their cafeteria, tour the base—meaning the whole base would come to a standstill as everyone picked up trash and painted old buildings. The nightmare would go on and on.

He stopped in the center of the room and bit his lip. *Okay*, he thought, *pissing time is over. Time to get down to business.* Much as he hated swallowing frogs, his philosophy was that if he had to swallow, then swallow the biggest frog first.

He walked over to the intercom on his desk and slapped at it.

"Steve, get a hold of First Lieutenant Bruce Steele. Tell him"—he paused, then slowly grinned to himself—"tell him he and his backseater are to fly escort for a VIP coming into Clark tomorrow morning."

Angeles City

As Pompano settled back in his chair, he spotted a red four-door car approach from the market. Pompano narrowed his eyes. Rich Filipinos did not make a habit of coming to the market themselves.

He spotted the American license plates.

A cold chill came over him, and a sudden vision of people taking him away, accusing him of stealing their HPM weapon, swept through his mind. But then it hit him that they would be coming in some sort of government car, a dark blue color so as not to draw attention.

The front door opened and a man stepped out. . . .

Yolanda got out of the other side. Pompano's breath quickened; his face grew warm. *Yolanda? What have they done with her?!*

Yolanda looked surprised when she saw him.

"Father!" Pompano remained silent. "You read my note?"

"*Aih.*"

She smiled, as if she had dismissed his obvious anger, and instead turned to the American. As tall as Yolanda was, he still towered a good six inches over her. Yolanda said proudly, "Father, I would like you to meet Bruce Steele."

Pompano stiffly waved a hand. He glared at the young man and ignored his daughter. He spoke in Tagalog. *"He is not welcome on my property. He will leave."*

Yolanda looked puzzled. "Father?"

"Did you not hear me?" He still avoided looking at Yolanda and bore his eyes into the man. The American shifted his weight from one foot to another: he looked puzzled.

"Yolanda, I had probably better leave. . . ."

"Father?!"

Pompano made a cutting motion with his hand and still spoke in Tagalog. *"No. He is not welcome. Leave this store now, or I will call the P.C."*

"But father, I must explain. This is the—"

"Yolanda, I'd better go." The young man nodded slightly to Pompano's daughter and turned to leave. "Please don't take it out on your daughter, sir. It is entirely my fault. I can assure you—"

"Out!!" Pompano commanded in English.

The American shrugged and left, the screen door slamming behind him.

"Father!"

Pompano turned for the back room. "Shut the door, Yolanda; we will talk."

"Yes, father."

Yolanda joined him moments later in the back. Pompano waited for her, sitting quietly in a chair. He waited until she sat. "Yolanda . . ."

"Father, Bruce Steele is a gentleman. You caused me to lose face, and you shamed him—"

"Quiet!" His daughter stopped talking and dropped her head. She folded her hands.

Pompano drew in a breath, trying to calm his pulse. It was the first time in a *long* time that he had had a run in with an American. He ignored the ones he passed on the streets. The few who entered his store were politely refused service. But now, one . . . *accosting* his daughter!

Pompano strained to stop the shaking. "Yolanda, you must stay away from the Americans. I have told you many times."

She looked up, her eyes red and brimming with tears. "But why? What is so bad about going somewhere with a gentleman?"

"I *told* you."

Yolanda stopped and dropped her head again.

Pompano started to continue, but stopped. He let out a breath, suddenly tired. "Yolanda . . . my little girl."

"I am not little anymore, father."

"Yolanda, you must listen very carefully to me. There is a good reason why I do not want you near the Americans. We are proud to be Filipinos, and there are many things out of our control. We must stay together. The Americans will treat you as their little brown sister if you give in to their wishes."

"Bruce is not like that, father!"

Pompano raised his voice slightly. "They are *all* like that. You must understand. These are lonely men, away from their homeland. And young, lonely men turn to the only thing that consoles them—women. It does not matter what these women look like, who they are. It is only the fact that the women give them company. . . . And when they bring these women back to their country, then they quickly see that the Filipino women are not like their own."

"But this is different! Bruce Steele and I have never spoken of going to America. This is not the same!"

"It always is, little one." Pompano squeezed the

back of Yolanda's neck, then moved to his chair and sat heavily. "You still do not understand, do you?" Yolanda looked up at him and shook her tear-streaked face. "And I cannot explain it to you any clearer?" Again, she shook her head.

Pompano sighed and slumped back in his chair. "I did not know when to tell you this, but this seems to be the time." He smiled to himself, then grew serious. He knew he would not be able to keep it from her forever.

"This liberty battalion, the group of Filipinos I associate with to build memorials for our war heroes? The Aquino memorial?"

"Yes?"

Pompano leaned forward and took his daughter's hand. He looked down at the floor and spoke forcefully. "The Liberty Battalion does not exist. I have been involved with a faction of the Huks, the New People's Army." Pompano looked up, and Yolanda's eyes were wide. "To strike back at the Americans. Nothing more—I do not believe in what most of the Huks want, I do not think that they will be able to change our government. It is my only way to get back at the Americans, to make them pay in some way for what they have done."

"But, father . . . why?"

Pompano hesitated. "You must understand, little one. I do not condone the killing, I do not participate in any of the Huk raids. I only provide my services, my talent, when it means that the Americans will be affected." He breathed deeply. *If there was any way to spare her feelings, but I cannot,* he thought.

Yolanda looked at him intently. "How can you say that? If this is true, do you not accept some of the responsibility for the killing? What would make you strike out at the Americans this way?"

Pompano stroked her hand; his voice grew quiet. "I loved your mother very much, Yolanda. She was everything to me."

Yolanda brushed back her hair. "You have told me that, father."

Pompano closed his eyes. "But what I have not told you is that nineteen years ago, before you were born, your mother was raped, brutalized by a gang of Americans. She never regained consciousness, and you were born nine months later." He opened his eyes. Yolanda's mouth was agape, her eyes wide.

Pompano nodded. "Yes, you are my daughter, little one, but only because I was married to your mother. I do not know who your father is—he was sent back to the United States, taken away before our judicial system could ever indict him."

Yolanda put a hand to her mouth and stood. She knocked her chair over, but Pompano let it lie. She started sobbing, then turned for her small room.

Pompano struggled to his feet and he called after her, "The Huks were the only way I could strike back at them! I love you so much, Yolanda. . . . You are my only reason for living." He hobbled over to her room. A red curtain separated her tiny cubicle from the rest of the back room. Pompano leaned up against the wall and spoke softly to his daughter, over the crying.

"Now you understand why I demand that you stay away from the Americans. To do otherwise would be to spit on your mother's grave, no matter if you believe what I say will happen to you or not." Pompano suddenly felt tired. His joints ached and he felt like giving up.

He placed a hand on the door frame and called out quietly. "Yolanda . . . Yolanda?" The sobbing sounds grew quiet. Pompano tightened his grip on the frame. "I . . . I was planning to sell this store and go to Manila when you went to school. Quezon City is not far, and you could have a place to come when things get too hectic for you. My work with the Huks here is finished.

"Instead of waiting until your school starts this fall,

I will sell the store now. Move to Manila . . . this month." He ran a hand up and down the wood frame. Pompano glanced around the little room, the place where he had raised his daughter for the past eighteen years. He remembered the laughter, the tears that this room had seen—her little friends visiting, her finishing homework in the small corner in a chair. . . . It would be hard to leave, for the memories it held could never be replaced.

But he knew those same memories would now hold nightmares for his daughter, and she would wake up in the middle of the night realizing that she didn't have any blood family alive. Yet this was the only way it could be.

Pompano called out quietly, "What do you think, little one—would that make you happy? We could leave for Manila as soon as I sell the store."

It took a long time for her to answer, but when she did her voice sounded somewhat surly. "Do not call me 'little one' anymore."

Clark AB

Bruce slammed the door to the Bachelor Officers' Quarters. Catman and Robin had been waiting outside for him, but Bruce didn't feel like talking. He stomped into the room, went to the refrigerator, and pulled out a beer.

A knock came at the door. "Assassin."

"Get lost!" Bruce popped the top on the beer and took a swig.

"Assassin, come on, open up." The rapping continued.

Bruce ignored the men and slouched down on a chair in the small room. He pulled at the beer, drinking until he had finished half of it. He fumed, pissed at the world in general.

It had been bad enough for his dad to act like a

jerk, but then to get thrown out of the sari-sari store by that little Filipino. What the hell was going on?

That morning he had been on top of the world, his future looking so bright that he almost felt like wearing shades.

And now—crap.

A sound in the kitchen caused him to whirl. Catman peeked out from the door. "Hey, Assassin."

"How the hell did you get in?!"

Charlie's voice came from the kitchen, out of sight. "It's my kitchen, too, Bruce."

Bruce glared at Catman and turned away. He pulled on his beer.

Catman called out, "Assassin, I just came over to tell you that our house is ready. We can move in next Monday. Charlie has lined up a housemaid, and she's coming over tomorrow morning so we can interview her."

"Party time, dudes! This is one excellent arrangement!" Robin's voice interrupted Catman. He took one quick look in the room, saw the expression on Bruce's face, said, "Uh-oh," and backed up, out of sight.

Catman waited a moment before continuing. "'So what's happening?" The phone started to ring.

"Nothing." Bruce shot back.

Charlie pulled the two officers back into his section of the BOQ complex. Bruce heard quiet whispering, then a "No shit!" Silence, then, "Hey, Assassin, uh, we're sorry, man. We'll check back with you later."

The phone kept ringing, but Bruce ignored it. Catman and Robin left.

Charlie called out, "Gonna answer that?" When Bruce didn't reply, Charlie slipped into Bruce's room and picked up the phone.

"Hello? No, sir—but I'll put him on." Charlie held the phone up. "Major Hendhold."

"What else could happen now—ship me out to Greenland?" Bruce took a last swig of beer and grabbed at the phone. Charlie backed out of the room. "Lieutenant Steele."

"Bruce, Major Steve Hendhold. General Simone has a flight for you and your backseater tomorrow morning—you're to escort a VIP into Clark."

"Yes, sir." *Wouldn't you know it*, Bruce thought. *Probably the worst day in my life, and I can't even get tanked to blow off steam.* And so it goes.

Washington, D.C.

"Ladies and gentlemen, I want to clear up some of the rumors floating around, so if you will refrain from asking questions I'll read the official press release."

Juan Salaguiz, the White House press secretary, set his mouth and surveyed the crowd of reporters. It was four-fifteen in the morning, but he had a good turnout. Most of the press were red-eyed, still sleepy from being pulled from their beds forty-five minutes ago, but they were all attentive.

Three years ago Juan could never have imagined himself in front of the national press corps. His gas station in East L.A. had never brought in much money, but Juan had involved himself in local politics ever since graduating from the College of the Canyons, a community college up north. Getting involved in the fight for water rights, then in national issues, Juan soon found himself leading the election efforts of the Hispanic community for President Longmire.

News of good work travels fast. Once Longmire had been elected into office, and the deciding factor was revealed to have been the Hispanic swing vote, Juan was offered the highly visible job of press secretary for the new administration.

Juan took the job seriously and never withheld information. If something broke, Juan took it upon himself to accurately broadcast the information to the press. It was his job to be the intermediary, and he let his supervisors worry about what news they would give him.

So when Juan Salaguiz had sleepily answered the call from Secretary of State Acht an hour ago, he arranged the press briefing within fifteen minutes of the call.

"At two-nineteen yesterday morning, President Longmire was admitted into Bethesda Naval Hospital for a type of surgery known as a thoracotomy. The president has been suffering from acute adenocarcinoma, lung cancer, and has been undergoing chemotherapy for the past six months. The public will be informed as soon as a prognosis is made."

Juan looked up. "I have time for just a few questions. Patti?" He pointed to an older woman dressed in a bright red dress.

"Juan, is the Vice-President planning to cut short his trip to the Far East?"

Juan shook his head. "The final negotiations with the Philippine government will continue. The treaty should be signed on Saturday, and Vice-President Adleman is scheduled to deliver it to the Senate Monday morning."

"A follow-up, Juan . . ."

"Go ahead."

The woman shifted her weight, as if she found it difficult to stand. "Thank you. What are the contigency plans, in the event that something should happen to the President? If the worst should happen, will Mr. Adleman be called back in spite of the treaty's delicate nature?"

Juan cleared his throat. He had always been one to say a glass was half-full instead of half-empty. "Vice-President Adleman is aware of the President's condition, and is also aware of his constitutional obligations. That is all I can say for now." Juan set his mouth and looked around the room for the next question. "George?"

A young man dressed in a smart suit stood and read

from a notebook. "If the President was admitted to Bethesda yesterday, why wasn't the press notified? Is this an attempt at a cover-up, and who has been running the government during President Longmire's incapacitation?"

Juan rolled his eyes. *Mother Maria*, he prayed to himself, *please help me get through this without punching anyone out!*

CHAPTER 15

Friday, 22 June

Yokota AFB, Japan

"Mr. Vice-President, we're on a tight schedule. . . ." Lieutenant Colonel Merke quietly urged Adleman up the stairs while keeping a smile on her face.

Adleman continued to shake hands with the enlisted men and officers who had gathered around the stairs to Air Force Two.

Merke tapped Adleman's elbow and kept her voice low. "Sir, thunderstorms are forecast for the Clark area. We need to go."

Adleman nodded while continuing to talk. "The President and I cannot say enough about the importance of the job you are doing—underpaid, overworked, and putting your life on the line for your country. We are working on these compensation problems, but for those of you who are giving the best years of your life serving our country, America salutes you!"

Adleman straightened and threw the crowd a full-handed salute, bringing back memories of Reagan at his best, playing up to the cameras. The men and women went wild.

As Adleman entered the plane he turned to Merke, flushed. "*That's* the way to leave them—cheering for more." He rubbed his hands together and made his way back to the suite. "Any word from Washington?"

"No, sir. The President is still in critical condition, and there's been no change."

"How about repercussions from Rizular? Has word gotten back on how he feels about landing at Clark instead of Manila?"

"Nothing out of the ordinary." As they reached the back of the plane, Lieutenant Colonel Merke handed Adleman a sheaf of papers. "Here's the latest situation briefing . . . and here"—she handed him another bundle—"are some memos to sign. Flight time is approximately two and a half hours; we're expecting to encounter some weather."

Adleman grunted and glanced over the papers. He entered the suite and said, "Make sure I'm awake a half hour out of Clark. If reading this doesn't put me to sleep, I'm going to try and catch a nap before we land."

"Yes, sir."

As he shut the door Adleman felt uneasy, as if he were forgetting something. Maybe he was starting to take this job more seriously.

Clark AB

Yolanda stood outside the main gate. The morning rush hour was over, and only a few people were straggling onto the base.

Signs in English and Tagalog warned her that only personnel on official business were allowed on the base. A contractor's entrance was visible twenty-five yards away. Filipino and American soldiers manned both gates.

A half hour before she had told her father she was going to the market, to walk around and clear her mind. Pompano had smiled at her and encouraged her to get up and around—she thought that he was happy that she wasn't moping, rebelling.

She didn't know what he would do to her if he learned her true destination.

Someone jostled her elbow. She looked around. "Excuse me." The man who had bumped into her was already walking through the gate.

As she approached the gate she felt a light drizzle begin. She looked to the sky; the clouds seemed to have come closer to the ground. She hurried her stride to the gate.

A uniformed Filipino stepped from the concrete guard shack as she approached, took one look at Yolanda, and waved her through.

She clutched the yellow pass and moved quickly through the fence. The Filipinos entering the base streamed toward a row of buses, but they first approached a brown-shirted man, who seemed to give out directions and point them to specific buses. Yolanda was heading for the man when she heard a voice behind her.

"Hey, wait a minute!"

Yolanda turned, feeling suddenly cold. The drizzle had increased to heavier drops.

"Hold up." A uniformed American ran toward her. He wore a blue beret, a gun holstered at his side, and camouflaged fatigues. The American kept one hand on his beret and the other hand on his holster. He huffed up to her.

"Excuse me, could I see an ID?"

Yolanda looked puzzled. "He said I could enter."

"Yeah, and he didn't check your ID either. Dependent or not, it's a rule, miss." He smiled amicably.

"Excuse, please?"

He started to say something, then looked at her closely. He frowned. "Say . . . you *are* a dependent, aren't you?" Yolanda thrust out the yellow sheet of paper. The military policeman's eyes widened. He took the sheet and scanned it. "Well I'll be dipped. . . ." He squinted at Yolanda, then down at the sheet. "Yolanda Sicat?"

"Yes?"

"You're not a dependent?"

Yolanda answered slowly. "I do not think so."

He looked her up and down, then slowly handed the sheet back to her. His voice suddenly sounded gruff. "I'm sorry. Uh, I could have sworn you were a dependent. I mean, you look like an American." He stopped, embarrassed and unsure of what to say next.

Yolanda took back the visitor's pass. She lowered her eyes and stood there. The rain continued to increase in intensity. The policeman backed up.

"Sorry . . . Go on, then." He turned and jogged back to his post.

Yolanda turned and headed for the man shepherding people onto the buses. She took her place at the end of the line, under an awning. The intensity of the rain had increased, so that it was difficult to see the main gate from where she stood.

When Yolanda's turn came, the man whirled to her. She stood at least a head above him. She shoved the yellow visitor's pass at him.

"I wish to visit Lieutenant Steele."

"Lieutenant Steele?" The man lifted a brow and studied the paper. "Do you know where he lives?"

"No."

The man set his mouth. "Not married?" Yolanda looked surprised, but shook her head. The man brightened. "Okay, Bachelor Officers' Quarters. Blue line, that bus over there. Look for many two-story buildings with a sign out front: BOQ." He nodded to the third bus in line.

"*Salamat po,*" said Yolanda, but the bus dispatcher was already helping the next person in line.

She paid the one peso fare and settled back near the rear of the bus, which soon filled with Filipino workers and American youths.

Yolanda looked out the window as the bus rounded the long runway. Although the giant American base was not more than five miles from where she lived, she felt as though she were on a totally different world. Everywhere the grass was cropped close to the ground—a shame, she thought, for this would have provided a huge grazing area for water buffalo.

The buildings were all well kept and painted, yet no one worked outside them. It was all puzzling to her.

But whatever the difference between the two worlds, she knew that she must not let it affect her meeting with Bruce. He seemed to be an honest, decent man . . . nice-looking, and he treated her well. But her father's wishes must come first.

She closed her eyes. *My father's wishes*, she thought. *But he is not even my real father!*

The thought left her cold, unsure of what was happening. Things had seemed to be so secure in her life: the knowledge that someday she would attend the University of the Philippines, thinking that it was *her* father that had raised and protected her.

She opened her eyes, but couldn't see through her tears. Discovering that she really was an outsider tore her apart. The lie she had lived through the years only intensified her feelings—telling her childhood friends that she had never known her mother, when it was her *father* she had never really known.

What kind of man would rape her mother? Knock her senseless, so that she would never regain consciousness?

No wonder that Pompano—yes, he *was* her father!— was driven to get back at the Americans.

She too felt the anger, the blind white rage.

It was the only thing she could do, to save face and to ensure that her girlhood dreams were not dashed . . . to meet with Bruce and explain, however hard it was, that they could not go on seeing each other.

Ceravant let the phone ring twenty times, then slammed the receiver down. *"Booto!"*

He glanced at his watch. *Pompano should have gotten the flight times by now*, he thought. *If I am to start the harrassment, I cannot afford to wait for the old man.*

He lit up a cigarette, the last one in the pack. He crumpled the container and threw it across the room. Sucking on his cigarette, he thought through his options. He could not allow the HPM weapon to just sit in the jungle. It worked and was ready for use. But without the incoming flight information Pompano would provide, the HPM would be a mere random operation. He knew that was what he had originally wanted, but the vision of the 747 flying overhead had sparked his imagination. *Bringing down an entire plane!*

He glanced at the phone. The sooner he had the flight schedule in hand, the sooner they could start the operations. Ceravant finished his cigarette.

By this afternoon he would be back in action, operating the HPM weapon.

Catman had the boom box cranked up to the max, playing vintage Toto.

The rock group played the type of technorock that Catman couldn't get enough of. He'd seen them once, playing a concert in Phoenix, and the live concert hadn't differed at all from his CD. They were that exact, that . . . *perfect.* Like executing a belly roll, a pilot turning a supersonic fighter around in the opposite direction from where he was looking, checking a blind spot. At over one thousand miles an hour. A technically correct, technically *perfect* maneuver in the hands of a shit-hot fighter pilot. The best.

Catman had just pushed out of the bed and begun to flip through his CD collection when a curt knock came at the door.

He ambled to the door and swung it open, wide.

She stood no more than six inches away, just under the overhang.

"Uh . . ." It was all he could manage to get out. Behind him came the erotic beat of Toto's "Rosanna."

The girl held out a wet sheet of paper to him. "Excuse, please. I am looking for Bruce Steele."

"Bruce, uh?" Catman gathered his wits about him and tried not to stammer. *Of course*, he thought, *the house girl. There is a God in heaven*. He swore to himself that he'd attend Sunday School for the next twenty years. "Come on in and get dry. Sure, you're looking for Bruce—uh, I'm his roommate."

She hesitated before entering. "You are not Charlie."

"Charlie? No, no. I'm Catman, Ed Holstrom. Call me whatever you like. Bruce, Charlie, and I are all getting a house—I'm really his roommate." He stopped talking and just grinned. *Thank you, Charlie, for picking out this woman. Thank you, thank you, thank you!*

The girl stood at the door, uncertain whether to enter. Catman just watched her, drowning in her large brown eyes, slipping along on her long, black hair. It was time to make his move. And to think he had almost turned down this assignment to Clark! He grinned like a goofy puppy . . . until he realized that he was at a Mexican standoff. He tried to make her feel at ease by sticking out his hand.

"I didn't catch your name. If you want to come in, I'll let you know the kind of food I eat, how much we'll be paying you, and that sort of thing." Catman stood aside to allow her to enter.

She frowned and ran a nervous hand through her wet hair. "Excuse, please. I do not understand why you will be paying me."

"For doing the house. You know, making the beds, cooking the meals, cleaning up . . ."

The girl slowly shook her head and took a step backward, into the downpour.

"Hey, wait. . . ." Catman felt suddenly foolish. "You're not coming here to interview as a house girl?" His voice trailed off.

"No."

"Aw, crap. I mean, I'm sorry. Really. Look, come on in, before you drown out there." Once inside, she shook her hair, allowing the long, dark strands to fall at her side. Water dripped onto the carpet.

"Why are you looking for Bruce?"

She tightly grasped the yellow sheet of paper. "It is very important. I must see Bruce Steele right away. He gave me this to come onto Clark Air Base if ever I needed to see him."

"He's not here. Bruce was selected to escort the Vice-President of the United States into your country. The Vice-President, you know, the number two guy for all America? Bruce is just too busy right now."

Yolanda's eyes widened. "Then . . . he will not have time for me?"

"Not for a while, I'm afraid."

"Then you must bring me to him. Now."

Catman chewed on his lip. "You can't wait?"

She shook her head.

Catman stared back. He couldn't tell her age, but she couldn't be more than a few years younger than he. With infinitely more innocence, and a boatful of persuasion to boot.

Catman had always been a sucker for good looks.

He squinted at the rain still pounding down outside. Visibility had been reduced to a quarter mile, and the clouds seemed to be descending to around five hundred feet. If anything, they'd delay Bruce's flight just to see if the weather would turn around. If he called a taxi and they hurried, they just might be able to make the squadron briefing room. . . .

Catman turned for the phone. "Stand by one minute."

Thirty seconds later he was assured that a taxi would pick them up in less than five minutes. He briefly thought about changing clothes and getting an umbrella, but quickly shoved the idea. Umbrellas were for wimps. He knew that was the *real* reason why pilots in flight suits didn't use them: preservation of the species.

Kadena AFB, Okinawa

Major Kathy Yulok hated her dark green Nomex flight suit. Within her she knew it didn't *really* matter, but that wasn't the point.

As an SR-71 pilot she was authorized to wear the bright orange flight suit that marked her as something special, that seemed to proclaim: Here is a person a cut above everyone else, with quicker reactions or steadier hands. It was the most explicit ego-stroking device she had ever seen in her operational career.

But it was something she didn't take lightly. Her thoughts drifted to her dad, his Wing carousing around in their "green bags," special people because they flew fighters. She remembered seeing a poster with the caption "I dreamed I was the hit of the ball in my Nomex flight suit." In the same way she knew she didn't have to prove herself, explain to someone that no, she was not just a tanker pilot, when she wore her orange flight suit.

It wasn't a big deal, but it was what she had earned.

And now, being forced to wear a green bag just so no one would know that she was a SR-71 pilot didn't make her any happier.

But it was a simple matter of "need-to-know." No one but the SR-71 pilots had a need-to-know about the time of their next classified flights, or even that the plane was still being flown; so here she was, slumming.

She stepped out of the crew van and briskly climbed the stairs to the Kadena Officers' Club. Her flight wasn't for another few hours and she had slept in, so this really wouldn't be breakfast. But the dietician always insisted on a high-protein, low-fat meal just before the flight. Just in case.

"Paper, ma'am?"

Kathy smiled down at the voice. A thin, brown-skinned youngster held up a copy of *Stars and Stripes*. The boy was here every morning without fail, hawking copies of the American printed paper. Kathy suspected that what he earned might be the only money the boy's family saw. She dug in her knee pocket and fished out two quarters. "Keep the change."

The boy bowed as he sat when she flipped him the money. "Thank you, ma'am."

She started reading the front page while walking into the club. Finding an article on Indonesia, she almost missed the door to the special dining room for SR-71 pilots—a left turn, instead of a right, once inside the main entrance.

Clark AB

Yolanda followed Ed Holstrom through dark hallways; some of the ceiling lights were not working. She could just make out paintings on the walls—murals, like those on the sides of buildings in Angeles City, except that these pictures were of planes, flying high over the countryside. The murals mixed in with an unusual smell—food and some sort of fuel; this place seemed so strange to her.

They turned a corner and entered a bright room. A group of men, all dressed in the same baggy green jumpsuits, were clustered around a table. Large pieces of paper covered the table, and one of the men was taking notes.

Ed Holstrom called out, "Yo, Assassin."

Yolanda spotted Bruce—he had looked up, startled. "Catman." Then when he spotted Yolanda, his eyes widened. He said, "Just a minute," over his shoulder as he moved toward her.

She saw Charlie at the table. He waved and flashed a grin at her, then went back to studying the maps on the table.

Bruce set both hands on her shoulders.

"How did you get here?"

"Ed Holstrom. And this." She folded the yellow visitor's pass in her hands.

"What's up? Are you all right?" Yolanda kept quiet; she looked up at him. Bruce glanced around the room as if he were searching for something. He nodded with his head. "Over here—we can talk." He led her to a row of telephones, set apart from the rest of the room. Plaques and emblems of all sorts of strange things—sleek planes with tiger heads, large planes with impossibly large bellies—covered the walls.

Bruce leaned up against a counter holding the row of black telephones. He moved his head close and said softly, "How's your dad? Has he cooled down any?"

Yolanda shook her head. "Father is still very upset with you—and me."

"That figures." Bruce drummed his fingers against the wooden counter. Someone yelled from another room; the men by the table all laughed, and Yolanda felt her cheeks grow warm.

Bruce drew in a breath. "Well, how long do you think it will take for him to cool down? I don't mind meeting you away from the sari-sari store, but I'd really prefer to have your father's blessing on this." He lifted a finger and ran it lightly down her arm. "I don't want you running around behind his back—not on account of me."

She slowly shook her head. "Bruce . . ."

A voice interrupted them. "Assassin, get the lead out. Wheels up in thirty minutes."

Bruce rubbed his hand against her arm and smiled. Yolanda drew in a breath. *He doesn't even know me*, she thought. *What my dreams are, what my future holds.*

She lowered her eyes. "Bruce, you are a very nice man. We have not spent much time together, but from what I have seen, you have a, what you say"—she stumbled for the word—"good future ahead of you." Yolanda started to talk fast. Frightened that her words might well up into tears, she tried to put the other people in the room out of her mind. She stared at the zipper on Bruce's green jumpsuit.

"My father and I have had plans for many years for me to attend the University in Quezon City. This is very important to me. My father is selling the sari-sari store so we can go down to Manila and get another store set up before school starts. I will have a chance to spend time with him." She looked up and set her mouth. "This is something that I want very much. I cannot turn my back on my father, go against his wishes."

Bruce spoke for the first time. "*His* wishes?"

"Yes. And mine."

He was silent. "Yours . . . ?"

"And mine," said Yolanda firmly.

"Are you sure about this? Is this what you really want?" Yolanda nodded stiffly. Bruce grasped her lightly by the shoulders. "Yolanda, look at me—tell me this is what you want."

She hesitated. "This is what I want."

"And us?"

"With us, it cannot be."

Bruce dropped his eyes and smiled bleakly. He rubbed her shoulders, halfheartedly it seemed. "If you're sure that's what you want. I just can't believe that you would change your mind so fast. And . . . what about your father forcing you? He seemed so hostile, it's hard for me to believe this decision is what *you* want."

Yolanda bit her lip. Bruce was right, but she knew it was her decision—she could go against her father if she wished, but there were too many dreams, too much time invested in what she really wanted.

For if she went against her lifelong desires and kept on with Bruce, would she not, as Bruce's father had implied, be following Bruce only to get back to the United States?

"Hey, Assassin!"

"Just a minute!" Bruce returned hotly. Then to her, "I've got to get going." He sounded defeated.

Yolanda spoke softly. "My . . . my father is not

angry at you, Bruce Steele. He does not even know you." She was at a loss for words. "My father is a member of an, an anti-American group, the Huks, an organization of . . . patriots. It is not important why this is so." She closed her eyes, remembering Pompano's hushed voice as he told about her mother's being brutally raped. "But his anger is against all Americans, not you in particular. You are a fine man, Bruce Steele, and I do not want to hurt you.

"Your friend, Ed Holstrom, thinks very highly of you. He told me that you were personally chosen to escort the Vice-President of your country. You have many such friends. And what I have seen, and from what you have told me about your way of life, it truly is amazing . . . but, it is not for me."

Bruce stood silent, his mouth set.

A voice came from outside the room. "*Assassin*— get your ass out here!"

Yolanda put a hand on Bruce's chest. "I wish you the best, Bruce Steele."

Bruce smiled tightly. When he spoke, his voice just about cracked. "Time to kick the tires and light the fires, then." He reached out and lightly touched her cheek. "Thanks. I guess." He strode away.

Yolanda turned and watched him move to the table in the center of the room.

A bald, bullet-headed man stuck his head into the room. He growled at Bruce. "It's about time, Romeo. Charlie's out there keeping the van warm for you. Let's get a move on."

Bruce lifted a dark brown bag and swung it over his shoulder. When he reached the door he hesitated, then walked quickly out of sight without looking back.

CHAPTER 16

Friday, 22 June

East China Sea

"Mr. Vice-President, we're a little more than an hour and a half from Clark. Just to let you know, there's severe weather at the base. Visibility is down to less than a quarter mile, and the cloud ceiling has descended to less than three hundred feet."

Robert Adleman leaned forward to the intercom on his desk. He was rarely interrupted for a weather report in-flight, unless conditions were really bad. From what Colonel Wingate, the pilot of the modified 747, was saying, it didn't sound good.

Adleman spoke into the intercom. "You're the expert, James. What's your call—divert?"

"No, sir. Clark's got the best all-weather capability, as well as micro-burst diagnostics. From what tower says, it's just a heavy rainfall with extremely low visibility. If we're heading for the Philippines, Clark is where we want to go."

"You don't sound convinced."

Colonel Wingate came right back. "The weather is right at the edge of our allowable limits. It'll be rough going in, but I just thought I'd let you know what you'd be landing in."

Adleman drummed on the desk. Spread out in front of him were the latest agreements and negotiation points on the P.I. Treaty, faxed to Air Force Two not fifteen minutes before. From what Adleman had deciphered, a treaty for all the American bases was imminent. The only holdup was a Filipino request to immediately release back to the Filipinos John Hay Air Station, a "resort" base high in the Philippine mountains. The base was innocuous, nothing to be lost if it were decommissioned—but it would be a huge public relations benefit if it were turned over. Still, the American team was insisting that it was part of the entire base structure.

Adleman didn't see anything wrong with the Filipinos' request. This was what President Longmire had wanted him to do—break the stalemate, complete the treaty, show that he was capable of international politicking.

Adleman lounged back in his chair. "How soon before the weather breaks?"

Colonel Wingate said, "Can't say. At least twenty-four hours."

Twenty four hours I can't afford, thought Adleman. *Not with Longmire's condition the way it is.* "Okay, let's get to Clark. I've ridden in thunderstorms before."

"Yes, sir, Mr. Vice-President."

Adleman studied the papers strewn out on the desk in front of him. *Just what Longmire wanted to happen,* he thought. A sudden thought hit him—what if this stalemate had been dreamed up by Secretary of State Acht, a preprogrammed path Acht was leading him down to ensure a smooth transition by the public? It smacked of something artificial, and Adleman didn't like the behind-the-scenes implications.

Adleman brushed the thought aside. No matter, for if push came to shove that's one nice prerogative of any President—he decides who his cabinet members will be.

Clark AB

Bruce was livid on the way out to the flight line. Charlie kept quiet, not speaking—and it was a good thing. Bruce just might have torn off Charlie's head.

The weather looked about as bright as his life right now. Which gave him even more of an incentive to rise above the clouds, high above the earth, where the sun would lighten things up. Skipper and Cougar kept to themselves.

A figure came into view, sloughing through the water. The man wore an olive-green pancho and looked like a creature that had crawled from a swamp. He stomped up to the van and poked his head inside.

"Assassin?"

Mooselips looked like an entirely different person without his white T-shirt.

"Yeah."

"She's ready to go. Had a small problem with the avionics, but we got that replaced an hour ago. Anytime you gentlemen are ready, we're standing by for you to crank up the auxiliary power units."

"Let's do it." Bruce grabbed his flight bag. Skipper stood. Bruce said to the driver of the van, "Any way to get us closer to the aircraft?"

The Filipino driver slapped his knee and grinned. "Sorry—you know rules."

"Yeah," muttered Charlie, "written by a bunch of staff weenies who never had to fly in weather."

Bruce clicked the mike. "Ready?"

"Check complete."

"Crank it." Bruce pointed at Mooselips, just visible through the rain. The crew chief cupped his hands and yelled something to the man kneeling by the plane. Seconds later, a whine came through the canopy.

"Pressure, good. Fuel, good. Inertial navigation system?"

"Up," said Charlie.

"Let's get out of here." Bruce waved at Mooselips. He and the other enlisted man scrambled around to the front of the F-15E and removed the wheel blocks. When Mooselips appeared at the front of the craft, he snapped to attention and threw Bruce a salute. Bruce returned it and pushed forward on the throttles. Skipper's fighter followed at his wing.

Ground control cleared them directly for the runway. Although Air Force Two wasn't due into Clark for another hour, the place was already closing out flight windows and giving the Vice-President's plane "clear skies."

Bruce clicked his mike. "Tower, Escort One. Request permission to take off."

"Permission granted, Escort One. Skies are clear to thirty thousand."

"Rog. Got that Skipper?"

Two clicks affirmed that Skipper was primed.

Bruce didn't ask Charlie if he was ready—he simply slammed the throttles to full forward. The F-15 Strike Eagle seemed to leap forward as the afterburners lit—over fifty thousand pounds of thrust generated by the Pratt & Whitney engines.

They rolled down the slick runway, gaining speed every second.

Bruce watched the airspeed indicator, counting to himself as they passed through one hundred knots, one twenty-five, one fifty. The plane felt like it wanted to reach up and claw into the sky. Bruce kept the nose down.

Charlie's voice came over the intercom. "Ah, rotate, Assassin."

Bruce still kept the stick forward. As Charlie started to speak again, Bruce yanked back on the stick.

The F-15 slipped into the air. Bruce kept the nose rotating back until they were pointed straight up. *If Blackman can get away with it, there's nothing stopping me,* thought Bruce.

"Yowwee!" Charlie zinged out. "It's going to be one of those days, Assassin."

They quickly disappeared into the clouds. Bruce kept his eyes glued to the attitude indicator, ensuring that they kept climbing. Charlie reported the altitude in clipped tones.

As they continued to climb, the sky grew brighter.

Within seconds they broke through the heavy cloud layer. Bruce eased the nose over. The clouds extended to the horizon, fluffy, thick, and pure white. Bruce craned his neck around the cockpit. Seconds later Skipper popped up behind him. Bruce clicked his mike.

"Loose trail, two."

"Rog."

Bruce flipped down the shades on his helmet so that the polarized lens cut out most of the glare. They continued to climb, but at a more gradual rate.

The two fighters were alone, nothing around for a hundred miles.

Bruce clicked his mike. "Got me a heading for intercept?"

Charlie came back immediately. "Air Traffic Control confirms heading three-two, five hundred miles out."

"Let's meet the Veep."

"Rog."

Bruce slammed a quick roll to the right, rotating the F-15 quickly around its axis. *Now* he was starting to feel human again.

Angeles City

Ceravant threw a half-smoked cigarette at the floor. "Booto! At least give me the name of your black market contact!"

It took a full minute for Pompano to slowly scribble a name on a sheet of paper.

Ceravant ground out the cigarette and grabbed at the paper. "This is the phone number?"

"Yes."

Ceravant pocketed the paper and paced up and down the length of the sari-sari store. Moments before he had locked the door, shielding them from any potential customers.

Ceravant tried to hold in his rage, but did not succeed. Even Pompano's gesture of supplying him with the black market contact did nothing to defuse his anger.

To control his emotions, direct his anger, and thus bridle his energy, was a basic axiom of Kawnleno's. But the wrath that Ceravant felt could not be contained. Not when this, this . . . *old man* sitting across the counter could be so blasé, so indifferent about quitting.

Ceravant turned to Pompano. Maybe he could reason with the fool. "When do you plan to leave?"

"I have already put the sari-sari store up for sale. Today we are packing. On Monday, we will drive to Manila and find a place to stay."

"What if you do not sell the store?"

Pompano shrugged. "Someone will buy it, if not as a store, then for the space."

Ceravant stopped pacing. He leaned against the counter and stared at Pompano. "But *why* are you quitting? We have done so much—the plantation is a secure base, the high-power microwave weapon is working . . . we are just beginning to do all that we planned. Why pull out now?"

Pompano sighed and slowly rose from his stool. He shuffled over to a shelf and picked up a pack of cigarettes. He pulled one out and offered it to Ceravant; the Huk refused. "I told you, I am old, tired. You just said that you have succeeded in doing everything you set out to do."

"Except drive out the Americans, start a new beginning!"

"Yes, yes." Pompano waved smoke away from his face and sat down stiffly.

"I cannot believe this! There must be another reason." Ceravant thought for a moment. "What has your daughter done to make this happen so fast?"

Pompano looked puzzled. "What?"

"Your daughter. Everything you do revolves around

her—and you tell me that because you are *tired* you want to move? What about *your* dreams?"

"Those are for the young men, Ceravant, not for me." Pompano drew on his cigarette and was silent for a moment. "I have accomplished all I set out to do by laying the foundation for harassing the Americans. But now my daughter has reached a new plateau in her life, and I must move to help her." He stopped at a noise from the back room.

"Father?"

Ceravant scowled. He threw out a arm. "Your little one is calling, old man. Run to her." He crossed his arms.

"Father, why is the front door locked?" Yolanda appeared in the doorway. She drew a hand up to her mouth at the sight of Ceravant. "Oh." She lowered her eyes. "I am sorry." She turned to leave, but Ceravant called out.

"Wait, little one," he said sarcastically.

"Father?" Yolanda glanced at Pompano, then narrowed her eyes at Ceravant.

"Go to the back," said Pompano.

"No, wait." Ceravant slammed a hand on the counter. Pompano set his mouth. Ceravant lowered his voice. "Yolanda, your father wants to sell the sari-sari store. What do you know about this?"

"I . . . I . . ." she glanced at her father. Pompano nodded stiffly. Yolanda continued. "We are moving to Manila. We will get a very good price for this store. That is all. Why do you want to know?"

Ceravant's brows went up. The girl seemed forward, impudent. Ceravant forced a smile. He relaxed and spoke soothingly. "This move seems so sudden. I want to know why your father made such a hasty decision."

Pompano interrupted. "You do not have to answer, Yolanda. Quickly, go back and—"

Ceravant held up a hand. "No. Wait."

Yolanda looked at her father, then drew herself up.

"I know about your organization, Ceravant. My father explained it all to me. I know about the Huks."

Ceravant looked alarmed. "You told her?!"

Pompano answered wearily. "Let her finish."

Yolanda's chin jutted out defiantly. "If my father chose to help the Huks, then he has to answer to no one. But that is not the reason why we are leaving." She turned to the old man. Her face was flushed, as if she was proud of what she was about to say. "Father, this morning I told Bruce Steele that we are leaving. He is now out of my life. I will never see him again."

Ceravant narrowed his eyes; he spoke slowly. "Who is this Bruce Steele—an American?"

"Yes. A pilot, and a very important man. He was picked to escort the Vice-President of the United States onto the base this morning."

Ceravant's eyes grew wide. "The Vice-President? The news said that he was flying into Manila."

"I was there myself when Bruce Steele flew out to meet him. He said that within two hours the Vice-President's plane will land. But that is no matter to me. We are through, father."

Ceravant grew excited. This information was much more valuable than anything he had ever dreamed of obtaining from Pompano. *The old man had come through after all!* This was a chance to disrupt the Vice-President's plane! Or if they were lucky, maybe even cause the plane to crash!

He looked to Pompano; the old man's head was down. Yolanda noticed her father's condition and moved to him. She put an arm around his shoulder.

Pompano whispered, "You took a chance going out to the American base, little one. Did the young man get angry at you?"

Ceravant gently interrupted; he had to garner some more information from the girl before he left.

"Yolanda . . . did this Bruce Steele say anything more about the Vice-President?"

She shook her head, then turned to her father. "I explained why I had to leave, Father. I . . . I ensured him that it was not him, that there were many factors—my school, selling the sari-sari store, you and the Huks. . . ."

"What?!" Ceravant took deep breaths. *What had the girl said?* He said tightly, "You . . . told . . . this . . . *American* that your father was connected with the Huks?"

Yolanda looked puzzled. "Everyone knows they only operate in the mountains. Father even said so himself."

Ceravant slammed a hand on the counter. The "smack" reverberated throughout the tiny store. His breath quickened as he narrowed his eyes at Pompano. "Do you know that the Americans can now connect me with you, old man? If they know the Huks are in Angeles and that you are their point of contact, then it is simply a matter of time before their intelligence service makes the connection. This . . . this could very well be the end of the Huks, the New People's Army!"

Pompano waved a feeble hand. "Go on, Ceravant. The damage is done. But leave me out of it. Leave *us* out of it." Pompano's shoulder's drooped. "I am through with you. By the time you are back up in the mountains, I will be in Manila, lost in the crowds."

Ceravant's breathing seemed out of control. He could not believe the stupidity of the old man. The rage took a hold of him, blinding him and focusing his energy on the arrogance of Pompano.

Ceravant slipped underneath the counter. Yolanda grasped her father by the shoulders and tried to draw back.

Ceravant reached down and pulled the girl away from her father. She careened off the floor and skidded to the wall, striking her head. Ceravant lifted Pompano up, but could not pull him off the ground.

Pompano outweighed Ceravant by at least thirty pounds.

"You will not hurt us again." Ceravant slammed Pompano against the wall. Pompano slid down to the floor, letting out a barely audible, "Ooof."

Ceravant drew a leg back and kicked at Pompano. The old man grunted and held up a hand, trying to fend off the blows. Again and again the kicks came, until Pompano began to bleed. When the old man did not move, Ceravant tapped him with a toe; Pompano moaned. Ceravant drew back his foot and aimed his next kick at Pompano's temple, but he held it there as he at last gained control of his emotions.

Ceravant breathed deeply, feeling the adrenaline racing through his veins. An excitement filled his blood, making him feel flush with power.

The Vice-President of the United States!

A sudden noise made him turn. Yolanda was lying on the floor, holding her hands to her mouth and sobbing. Ceravant could not see her face as she cried, only her long black hair.

He smiled to himself and felt something stir deep inside him. If there was ever a way to completely get back at Pompano, Yolanda was the key. But there was something else, something about the Vice-President's plane.

If the HPM weapon caused the plane to crash, then the Vice-President's death would only heighten the American frustration. But suppose the Vice-President survived! People sometimes live through plane crashes. . . . Then there was a chance of capturing the Vice-President.

The thought caused Ceravant to breathe deeply. His face felt flush. The Vice-President! The man would make a perfect bargaining chip . . . but how to find him, after the plane crashes?

A thought struck him: With her father dead, Yolanda would have complete ownership of the sari-sari store. It would be a good way of getting more manpower.

He glanced at Pompano. *No, better to have the old man live. Pompano's black market contacts would be useful. And with the girl as a hostage, Pompano would do as he was told.* A plan began to form in Ceravant's mind.

He tied Pompano up, lashing him to a chair; a rag in the old man's mouth ensured that he would not be heard. Ceravant then slipped into the back room and dialed the number on the paper that Pompano had given him. A man answered. A few minutes of dickering convinced the man that Ceravant was sincere.

"That is right. Pompano and his daughter are ready to sell their store, and I am serving as their agent. You know how much merchandise moves through here, how important it is to the Huks. Now, they offer the sari-sari store in exchange for your immediate help."

"Where is Pompano?"

"Does it matter? I have the documents."

The man was impressed. "The store could bring a large sum of money. What kind of help do you need?"

Ceravant watched the girl and smiled. "A plane could crash in the next hour, somewhere near the American base. There is a very important occupant inside that plane. If you can deliver him here, a simple trade will take place—that person for the store."

Hesitation. "That will take a lot of men."

"Whatever you think the store is worth."

"Just a minute." The man came back a minute later. "The store includes exclusive rights to deal with the Huks?"

"Of course."

Another pause. "You will have him."

Ceravant hung up, filled with anticipation. One thing remained to be done. But when you're working with fate on your side, it's something you don't have to worry about.

The girl followed him outside, unresisting but still in tears. He moved out the back door to Pompano's truck. Rain splashed around him, cutting visibility.

Even with traffic, it would take him less than half an hour to get to the high-power microwave weapon. Plenty of time before the Vice-President's plane arrived.

Bethesda Naval Hospital, Maryland

Ensign Clounch watched the monitors. It never occurred to her that the triple backup systems could almost always be counted on to work.

When President Longmire started gagging, Julia Clounch hit the "Stat" button and, at the same moment, a computerized alarm went off throughout the hospital. Within seconds, the President's hospital room was full of doctors and medical personnel.

When a quick attempt to clear Longmire's throat failed, a tracheotomy was performed.

Julia Clounch continued to keep track of the diagnostics, even though her job was over. She hadn't noticed Captain (Doctor) Barnett, Commander of the Hospital, enter the room. Barnett cleared his throat.

"Nurse?"

Julia jumped in her chair. "Yes, sir?"

Barnett squinted at the diagnostic monitors, still showing the President's vitals. After studying the monitors, Barnett set his mouth. His voice sounded tired. "I'll need that open line to the White House."

East China Sea

"Assassin . . . ah, got a little problem here."

"Go ahead, Skipper."

"I'm losing oil. Pressure's dropping."

Bruce glanced at his heads-up display. They were still fifteen minutes from meeting the Vice-President's plane. He clicked his mike. "Can you hold on to intercept?"

"Negatory. But if we turn back now I'll be okay."

Bruce started to abort the mission, call back to Clark and inform them that Air Force Two would have to make it "in-country" without an escort. Single-ship formations were frowned upon; all missions demanded a two-plane minimum. It wasn't a rule to screw with.

But he remembered Simone's comments about using his judgement . . . and escorting the Vice-President seemed a hell of a lot more important than holding Skipper's hand.

"Skipper."

"Rog."

"Break for Clark. We're going on."

Silence. Then, "You sure, Assassin?"

"That's a rog. Now get back."

Bruce almost thought he could hear Skipper shrug. "It's your flight."

Bruce tensed up. Skipper's fighter broke off to the right; Bruce lost sight of him as he left. *Damn*, thought Bruce. He hoped he hadn't stepped on it. This wasn't the time to make the wrong decision, but it *was* up to him. . . .

Skipper's voice came over the radio. "Good call, Assassin. See you on deck."

"We're starting the descent, Mr. Vice-President."

Adleman sat with his head in his hands. He had just hung up the phone with Acht. *Any time now*, he had said. *We're going to need an immediate, overt transition*. And the plane could immediately head back to Washington once they'd refueled.

"Mr. Vice-President, we're starting to descend through the cloud layer, and we'll need you buckled in, just in case there's any turbulence."

He didn't want to think about it, being sworn in as President, waiting for the final call informing him of Longmire's death. But the plane was committed now, so they'd have to make the transition on the ground. He glanced at his watch. Twenty minutes.

* * *

Bruce paced the giant 747 as it lumbered across the sky. He kept the F-15 a hundred yards away, a *long* way since he was used to flying wing tip to wing tip.

That was probably the reason General Simone had chosen him in the first place. The general would have known that Bruce was sensitized to safety, especially after flying with the Thirteenth Air Force Commander. Besides, Bruce knew he was the best.

When the 747 began its descent into Clark, Bruce moved a mile behind it. The jumbo jet seemed to move slowly against the backdrop of clouds. The 747's cruising speed was actually not that much less than the F-15's, but the transport's huge size made it appear much slower.

Bruce followed the same flight path and rate of descent. When the clouds enveloped the cockpit, blocking out the blue sky that surrounded them, Bruce fixed his eyes to the avionics.

Now, until Air Force Two and the F-15 had landed, their survival depended solely upon the intricate solid-state circuitry of the flight instruments. The two planes were packed with all the newest high-tech bells and whistles the government could buy. Even in the thick cloud layer, Bruce knew that he was a hundred times safer up here than he would be driving his car on the ground.

Bruce clicked his mike. "Keep me honest, Foggy. I don't want to step on the big one in front of the brass."

"That hasn't stopped you yet."

Bruce clicked his mike twice. "Let's make it a first."

Angeles City

The drive took less than half an hour. There was virtually no traffic in the heavy downpour. Even the jeepneys kept off the road. Once in a while Ceravant had to jam on the brakes of Pompano's truck, to avoid hitting a pedestrian scurrying across the street.

That would be all he needed—right at the moment when his wildest dream was about to come true.

Yolanda lay on the floor beside him. Gagged and tied with twine, she had stopped struggling ten minutes ago.

Ceravant couldn't allow her to tell the authorities about him. It would have been easy to finish her off—or would it? At any rate, she would prove to be an excellent hostage if something went wrong.

Ceravant slowed as he approached the road outside of Clark. No planes flew overhead, but the missing roar of jet engines had been replaced by the sound of a deluge. The turnoff was muddy, and once off the main road Ceravant stopped the truck.

A moment later, a figure wearing dark rain gear and holding a rifle appeared at the side of the road. The figure waved Ceravant on.

Ceravant nodded to himself. *At least the cell remains at its post.*

He drove the truck to the opposite side of a clearing. A person appeared at the truck's door as Ceravant stopped. The figure stuck his head up close to the window. It was the boy Barguyo.

Ceravant rolled down the window. Rain splashed in. Ceravant peered up, but could see only darkness where the hole in the trees should be.

The boy said, "Ceravant, is it time?"

"Yes." Ceravant shot a glance at the girl; she moaned slightly and moved her legs, but she was well bound. Ceravant opened the door and joined the boy, oblivious to the rain. "We need to prepare the weapon, charge it, and shoot it off when we hear planes."

"You have a flight schedule?"

"Yes. If we are lucky a plane will fly overhead. I need you to set off the weapon."

Barguyo shouldered his rife. "That is easy. Which plane do you want me to hit?"

"There will be at least two planes. Strike against both of them. Then load the weapon in the truck and meet us back at Pompano's sari-sari store. Do you know where it is?"

"I can find it." Barguyo thought for a moment, rain streaming down his young face. "The weapon is not much longer than the back of your truck. Why can't we load it on the truck now, set the weapon off, and simply drive away when we are done? We should save much time that way."

Ceravant looked astonished, then proud. Barguyo would surely play an important part in the future of the New People's Army. He clasped the boy's shoulder. "Very well. Instruct the men. After the weapon is on the truck, pick two men to stay with you. The others will come with me."

Barguyo responded by grinning. He turned and headed for the weapon. Ceravant heard a shrill whistle, then, "Quickly—it is time!"

A group of men appeared from the jungle, where they had been waiting underneath a shelter. Ceravant stepped back into the truck. Water ran off his clothes onto the seat. The rain swept a fresh smell into the truck—*an omen, a fresh start,* he thought.

Everything was in place.

The problem, after they had downed the Vice-President's plane, would be to reach it before the Americans. The highest priority would be to mobilize the Huks throughout the countryside to spread out and find the plane.

CHAPTER 17

Friday, 22 June

One mile outside of Clark AB

Once they had loaded the high-power microwave weapon onto the truck, Barguyo jogged over to Ceravant. The Huk leader stayed in one of the jeepneys, off to the side. A girl lay in the back of the jeepney, bound and gagged—Barguyo paid her no attention. If Ceravant had wanted him to know about the girl, he would have said something.

"Everything is ready."

Ceravant glanced at his watch. "Any time now." Ceravant smiled at Barguyo—the boy looked back with pride.

Ceravant said, "Remember, there will be at least two planes. You must keep firing the weapon."

"Will the planes really crash?"

Ceravant shook his head. "I am not sure. The Americans always think their weapons are so powerful. We will give them a taste of their own medicine." The Huk leader pulled at his jaw. "I will need you to hurry to Pompano's store. And make sure you bring this weapon back with you, no matter what else happens."

"Aih." Barguyo waited until it was clear that Ceravant was finished before he left. As he walked through the rain back to the high-power microwave weapon, Barguyo was thankful for everything he had, everything that had happened to him.

The greatest lesson he had learned from Ceravant was to soak up everything he could and take advantage of it. The very position he was in now, serving with the New People's Army to institute a new order, was the greatest example of that lesson. If it had not been for Ceravant, Barguyo would still be a waif, wandering the streets of Manila begging for money.

But in the Huks, each person worked according to his ability, doing what he could to contribute to the cause. That was what Barguyo liked the most—he was given responsibilities based on how well he had performed, not on his age. Anywhere else he would have been a mere go-fer, but here he held positions of importance. He was good at what he did.

No one questioned Ceravant's orders. *Perhaps,* thought Barguyo, *they are remembering Ceravant's slaughter of the woman and her children at the plantation.* That would deter anyone from disobeying his directions.

The convoy of jeepneys left the clearing, leaving Barguyo and the two other men alone. Barguyo moved to the back of the truck and manned the high-power microwave weapon himself. Stretched out in the back of the truck, a generator supplied power to a box labeled MAXWELL LABORATORIES: HIGH-ENERGY DENSITY CAPACITOR SYSTEM. From there, an array of thick pipes and other cables wound around to a three-meter dish that pointed straight up. The system was crammed in the back of the two-and-a-half-ton truck, but as Pompano had pointed out, it was made to be transportable.

Barguyo waited. The diesel generators chugged away. He knew that when he set the weapon off he would hear a sharp crack, but he also knew that if he stayed away from the front of the antenna he would not be harmed.

It was nearing ten in the morning, but it seemed like dusk. The clouds gave the clearing an ominous appearance, and in the low light things farther away than ten yards lost form. Over the splashing of rain, Barguyo picked up the faint whine of jet engines.

Fifteen miles northeast of Clark AB

A few miles away from the relative flatlands surrounding Clark, the jungle gradually sloped up to a mountain. A muddy road wound through the foliage, allowing access to the mountainside.

Emil Oloner sat on his motorcycle on the muddy road and peered across the land toward Clark. Emil sat a good twenty feet below the cloud layer. Above him, cottony wisps swirled by, almost close enough to touch.

It normally took Emil ten minutes to reach the mountain, and another five to race his motorcycle to the top. He lived for the weekend motorcycle races. But with the rain and mud Emil now cursed the weather, for the muddy journey had taken nearly a half an hour.

He bent over his small Honda and pulled out a radio. Flipping the side switch, a burst of static came from the speaker. He pressed the "Send" button and spoke in Tagalog. "This is Emil."

A moment passed. "Where are you?"

"In place."

"Contact us as soon as you see it."

Emil simply clicked off the radio. *Of course I will contact you,* he thought. *Why else would I leave my job to come up here and watch for a plane to crash?* The hundred American dollars that had been promised him would come in handy, but he would get the prize only if he spotted the plane first.

Ten miles outside of Clark AB

Instrument flying was one of Bruce's strong points. It was all too easy to get mixed up in the clouds, have a gut feeling that the plane was flying in a wrong attitude, try to fix the problem, and end up pranging it into the ground. Only by trusting the cockpit instruments—even when you thought they "felt" dead wrong—could a good flyer remain a live flyer.

The clouds were thick. Bruce couldn't see the front of the F-15E. The altimeter read five thousand feet, and their airspeed had slowed to two-fifty knots. Charlie read the checklist.

"Gear down."

Bruce let the lever down, lowering the landing gear. "Check."

A vibration filled the cockpit as air rushed around the gear. The drag from the landing gear slowed the F-15E down. Bruce couldn't see the flaps, but moments before he had extended them to full. It seemed like he was hanging everything but the kitchen sink out there on the wing, trying to extend the camber, provide the Strike Eagle with more lift as the fighter slowed down.

In his helmet Bruce could hear the tower on Clark giving final approval for Air Force Two to land. Bruce had extended the distance between himself and the jumbo jet to three miles. Soon he would hear the tower directions come over his earphones.

Barguyo heard the noise grow louder. It was a much deeper roar than fighters' flying out of Clark.

As the jet grew closer, Barguyo prepared himself. On the rugged control panel, all the instruments were labeled with English words. There were digital controls, lights and dials. But the only things that concerned Barguyo were the green light that indicated weapon readiness and a red button he needed to depress.

The jet's engines increased in volume, rolling white noise throughout the jungle. Barguyo looked straight up and could not see anything—still the noise increased. He caressed the red button with his thumb, ready to instantly push it.

On and on it came . . . and just when it seemed

that the noise had peaked, Barguyo caught a glimpse of the white bottom of a huge jumbo jet.

Barguyo punched at the button, again and again. Each time he depressed the firing mechanism, the high-power microwave weapon seemed to jump. It made a sharp "crack" sound, but was otherwise unimpressive.

The jet engines suddenly sounded different—they took on a strange, multi-frequencied pitch.

Whatever the HPM weapon had done, it seemed to have affected the huge jet. Barguyo glanced at the control panel—it still glowed a bright green. He sat back in the truck and made himself comfortable, but in the distance he heard the roar of another jet. It was much higher in pitch than the first one, more like one of the fighters.

Setting his mouth, sixteen-year-old Barguyo prepared to strike again.

POP!

Bruce's earphones seemed to rattle with reverberations.

"What the hell was *that*?" Bruce scanned the heads-up display. He could have sworn the instruments had jumped, but everything seemed normal.

Pop! Pop! Pop! Pop! Pop!

"I've got scrambled readings, Assassin," said Charlie.

A voice broke over his headphone. "Air Force Two, we have you diverging from flight path. You are too low and heading away from Clark. I say again—"

Bruce flipped to "Intercom" only. "See anything?"

"You kidding?"

"On radar."

"Negatory." Silence. Then, "I'm getting ghost blips all over the place. It looks like we were hit by some sort of jammer. I'm flipping up my visor to get a better look."

Bruce flipped back to the tower frequency. "Tower, Escort One."

"Break away, Escort One. Air Force Two is not responding.

"Air Force Two, come in. Do you read? You are *too* low and heading away from Clark. Answer, Air Force Two."

Bruce hesitated before breaking away from the flight path. Was there anything he could do? Probably not, if Charlie couldn't pick out the Vice-President's plane. The smart thing would be to get above the clouds and wait for directions. *Some escort I'm turning out to be,* he thought.

Bruce clicked his mike. "Escort One heading up to twenty thousand." He flipped over to intercom. "Where are we, Foggy?"

"One mile from the runway—"

POP POP POP POP POP POP POP . . .

A staccato of bursts exploded over Bruce's headphones. Tempered plexiglass from the heads-up display blew up, then sagged back in crushed plastic. Screams came over the intercom.

"Foggy!"

"I can't get it off—oh God, it doesn't come off!"

Bruce scanned the instruments; nothing was working. Needle dials were pegged, and none of the digital instruments was on. He tried to pull back on the stick; the F-15E moved sluggishly—he still had hydraulics. Wind seemed to roar in the back, as if a hole had been punched over Charlie's part of the cockpit. Still the screaming continued.

"Charlie, are you okay?"

The screams broke to spastic sobs. "Oh, God, Bruce—it hurts! I can't see! I can't get it off!"

"What? Can't get what off?"

"Oh, God! The helmet! Help me . . . something . . . I can't stand it." Bruce could imagine him clawing at the helmet, trying to get it off.

What had happened? Had they been hit by a missile—antiaircraft fire? Was Charlie's helmet punctured?

"Do something, Bruce—I can't last much longer!"

Bruce flipped to Guard, the emergency frequency. "Mayday, mayday! This is Escort One, I have an emergency. Instruments out . . . I'm going to need some help."

Nothing came over the radio, not even static. Bruce flipped through the frequencies. "Mayday, mayday! Can anyone hear me?" Still nothing.

Bruce pulled back on the stick to gain altitude. His instruments were out. He didn't know how high he was, where he was going, or how much fuel he had.

"Please, God, help me!" Charlie's voice broke into a crying fit.

Bruce felt short of breath. He was afraid he was going to die.

Clark AB

"Holy Mother Mary," muttered Staff Sergeant Whiltee. "Why me? And why now?" She quickly cleared her radar screen and initialized the search sequence. There it was again.

She keyed her microphone and got a direct line to her supervisor, Chief Master Sergeant Figarno. "Chief, I've lost Air Force Two." She tried to keep her voice steady, but the others seated around her looked up sharply.

"What?" He appeared at her side, wire from headphones trailing behind him. Ramrod-straight, with jet-black hair and penetrating eyes, Figarno was one of the youngest Chief Master Sergeants in the Air Force.

Whiltee pointed at the blinking numbers that were diverging away from the main flight path. "Air Force Two is going down and I can't get them to respond."

"What about the escort?"

"I waved Escort One off—*hey*, there it is again!" Whiltee and Figarno watched in amazement as the screen blinked. Not once, but seven or eight times in a row. When the blinking had stopped, Escort One was also veering from its designated path. Whiltee immediately started calling over the radio. "Escort One, you are too low and deviating from flight path. Come in, Escort One. Do you copy?"

They waited for a moment, but nothing came over the airways. Figarno leaned into the screen. "What's happening?"

"I don't know." Whiltee wet her lips. "They won't answer."

"What do you mean they won't answer?"

"You heard me—Air Force Two and Escort One aren't transmitting!"

Figarno's voice stayed cool. "But is it because of our equipment or theirs? When your screen blinked, did that mean that our gear was knocked out of commission, or theirs?"

"Let me try something." She typed rapidly on the keyboard next to the screen. The screen reconfigured and showed a test echo. Whiltee pointed at the blip. "That's a return signal from Wallace Air Station. It's not our gear that's broken." She switched the screen back to Air Force Two and Escort One.

Figarno straightened. "All right, keep trying to raise them."

"Yes, sergeant." Whiltee turned back to the screen and spoke into her microphone.

Chief Master Sergeant Figarno strode to a red telephone sitting on a table in the center of the room. He picked up the phone. "This is Figarno. Threatcon Delta Emergency—launch rescue helicopters and patch me into Thirteenth Air Force."

Fifteen miles northeast of Clark AB

The jumbo jet flew beneath the low cloud cover, away from Clark. If Emil had not been watching for the plane he would not have noticed it.

It appeared to be making a normal approach to a runway, decending at a slow rate with its nose elevated slightly higher than its tail. But the jumbo jet was headed toward no runway; instead, it seemed to be aiming for the old Del Playo rice field. And, even more curiously, the plane's landing gear was not extended.

Emil had sat just off-base at the end of the Clark runway many times, drinking San Miguel and watching the lumbering jets scream overhead in a landing. He would laugh with his friends, and they all hoped to someday witness a crash. What a sight that would be! But the planes always seemed to land, and all Emil had to show for his outing would be a ringing in his ears.

But today . . . this jumbo jet kept heading to the ground, unwavering in its determination to land in the rice paddy. Emil flicked on the radio.

"The Del Playo rice paddy—a jumbo jet is about to crash."

Emil heard excited voices in the background. "Are you sure? The Del Playo fields?"

"Of course. But I do not think the plane is going to make it." Emil dropped the radio to his side. Like a behemoth the jumbo jet continued to drop in altitude. It kept a constant rate of descent.

Still a good hundred feet in the air, it overflew the end of the rice paddies. The plane kept coming down, lower and lower, until the bottom of the craft just scraped the top of the jungle.

Seconds later, the plane's wings ripped from the body; they tumbled out, spewing a liquid fire from its ends and skipping across the tree tops. The jet's fuselage started to flip over, but it skidded in the trees and made a gash a quarter of a mile long. The crash seemed to take forever, and Emil reveled in it.

When the long fuselage finally stopped moving, no flames came from the wreckage. The sound of the crash reverberated over the countryside, reaching Emil a half minute after the plane first hit the tree tops. The wings exploded and burned, two hundred yards on either side of the plane.

Emil spoke into the radio. "The plane has stopped, north of the fields."

But no answer came back.

Emil stowed the radio and started his motorcycle. He felt elated. After all these years he had finally witnessed a crash. Best of all, he was going to get paid for doing it.

Clark AB

The alert siren warbled an ear-splitting shriek. There was no time to think—only react.

Captains Bob Gould and Richard Head threw down their cards and ran for the doors, knocking over the table.

Gould managed to shout, "This for real?"

Head puffed out, "I don't want to find out," as he followed right on Gould's heels.

The two ran fifty yards through the rain, across the slick asphalt helicopter pad to their MH-60 Blackhawk. The modified attack helicopter looked menacing as they approached, a crouching gargoyle ready to devour anyone who came near.

Gould swung into the helicopter just as a crew of enlisted men reached the auxiliary power units. Head waved a finger quickly around his head, indicating that the men should crank up the APUs. Seconds later, the engine caught and spat out thick smoke.

"Bringing up engine one."

Gould fumbled for his headphones. "Wait, wait—warmup!"

"Hurry up, then!"

Gould started running through a modified checklist. "Can you get Tower?"

POP POP POP!

Head fumbled with the radio equipment, muttered a curse, then tried a backup unit. "No. Radio's shot."

Gould punched on the avionics package. Something flipped, then there was a soft sigh as the lights slowly grew dim. "What in the world?" Gould stared incredulously at the panel. He toggled the power switch. "Look at this!"

Richard Head reached over and tried the switch himself. "Well, I'll be dipped." A quick run-through of the electronics modules confirmed his suspicions. He slouched back in his seat. "All the fly-by-wire stuff is out."

"*All* of it?"

Head checked a few more items. "Yeah. Everything that's run by solid-state." Head pulled off his helmet and waved to the men outside in the rain to cut the APU. "I know our stuff is soft, but this is crazy. It's like someone hit us with a bolt of lightning."

The intercom went silent as the lights went out. Vice-President Adleman grasped the sides of his chair. His breathing increased.

The 747 jerked to the right, then straightened. It *seemed* to straighten, but papers continued to slide off the desk onto the floor. A lamp crashed against the bulkhead, spraying glass.

Adleman felt helpless.

Muffled shouts came from outside the chamber.

Adleman felt the plane suddenly bump. He felt a growing wetness around his crotch; he couldn't stop from urinating. The plane bumped again, this time harder, and his stomach seemed to fly up into his throat. He closed his eyes, but nothing changed—he was still alone and in the dark, helpless.

A dozen things ran through his mind, the foremost being that he had lost the chance to become President of the United States.

Then came faint brushings underneath the plane. It started as a scrape, then quickly crescendoed to a tearing, ripping, jarring, flipping, nauseating sound that seemed to bore right through his body. It went on, slicing and burning up through his senses. Thick acrid smoke, sharp alarms, and screams penetrated his senses.

The plane seemed to be ripping away. Wetness filled the cabin, splashing him with water, leaves, and branches.

And then it stopped.

Silence.

Adleman thought that everything was quiet until he made out the soft sound of water dripping, then moans of other people.

Dim light filtered into the aircraft from holes ripped in the side of the craft. He tried to move, but found that one of his legs was jammed in between the safety chair and the desk. He pushed up with his hand and cried out "Help!" but his voice cracked.

A sharp pain shot through his arm. Adleman tipped back his head and tried to get as comfortable as the pain would let him.

Sirens on the base ran up and down the scale. Throughout Thirteenth Air Force Headquarters preparations for Search and Rescue, Site Security, Hospital Mobilization, Disaster Preparedness, and Personnel Readiness had swung into action.

Major General Simone paced up and down his office, conferring via conference calls with the different emergency site commanders. "Maintenance, one more time—what's the story on the Blackhawks?"

A voice came over the intercom. "Both MH-60 Blackhawks lost avionics as they prepared for flight, general. The specialists are dismantling the units now, and we have an open line with the contractor."

"The HH-3s?"

"We're working on getting one up, sir. They . . . ah, weren't being used because of the Blackhawks. We are cannibalizing three of the Jolly Greens in the shop."

Simone strained to keep his voice calm. "So we have no Search and Rescue support."

"Correct, general. Not at this moment."

Simone turned to Major Steve Hendhold, who stood in one corner of the room, speaking on a phone. "Steve, get me Subic. We'll have them throw everything they can to help us."

"General," interrupted the Colonel from maintenance, "there's no need to call in the Navy. We should have the Blackhawks up and flying in fifteen minutes."

"And if we don't, then that's a quarter of an hour lost. I don't care if the Boy Scouts find the Vice-President, I'm not going to let inter-service rivalry hold up this rescue."

Hendhold held up a telephone. "General, we got through to General Newman."

Bruce took no time deciding what to do. The clouds were too low to safely fly any lower, so he flipped the fighter upside down. Charlie was incoherent. Bruce hesitated, then turned off the intercom—he couldn't afford to let Charlie's pain affect what he was doing.

He slowed his airspeed and pulled back on the stick. The F-15E descended through the clouds.

Or at least Bruce *hoped* they were descending. From the blood pounding in his forehead, he could tell they were still inverted.

Bruce strained to see through the clouds. There was nothing but gray-white randomness out there.

Flying upside-down gave him two advantages: With his instruments out, his "feel" for which way was down was better this way; and more importantly, since the cloud layer was so low, if he was right side up, he might not see that the fighter had broken through until they were too close to the ground. This way, the cockpit would be the first thing below the clouds.

Bruce pulled back on the throttles, slowing his air speed. He tried not to rush his descent, but the thought of pranging into the mountains gnawed at him. *If only they're tracking me on radar*, he thought, *they're at least keeping other planes away.*

The descent seemed to take forever. *Slowly, slowly, don't rush. . . .* He imagined he heard Charlie's screams of pain, saw images of what—broken glass in his backseater's face? Suddenly he saw swirls, could make out patches of cloud. Bruce pushed the F-15 lower.

Below him now were buildings, streets. It seemed orderly enough to be Clark. He thought about flipping back over, but decided to get a fix on the runway first.

Bruce pulled the F-15 into a slow bank, lost altitude, and fought to pull the craft back up. He searched for buildings, anything that might give him a clue as to where he was. He spotted the Officers' Club.

The runway came up almost too quickly.

Bruce remembered the stunt for which Colonel Bolte had bawled him out upon his arrival at Clark. . . .

Bruce waited until he was over the road and pulled a tight turn, flipping the F-15 over just as he started to flare out.

The runway spread before him, white lights running down the two-mile stretch and disappearing into the rain at the other end. Bruce continued to descend, and when the wheels touched the ground he finally eased his grip. He shot off the drag chute, further slowing the craft. The runway was slick, but at least he was down.

It seemed strange: he was alone out there, no fire trucks, ambulances, military police. He brought the canopy up and rain started coming in. The screams had stopped from behind him, but he could still hear Charlie's sobs. "Charlie—hold on!" As he unstrapped and turned to try and see Charlie, he heard the sirens approach.

Barguyo glanced at his watch. Five minutes had passed since he had fired off the weapon for the first time.

Barguyo listened intently for sounds other than the rain and wind, but could hear nothing. Ceravant had directed that they continue to shoot at other airplanes, but he thought that it was time to show some prudence.

If there were no other planes in the area, Barguyo reasoned that the Americans might start looking for them by some other means.

And Ceravant had indicated that it was important to bring the high-power microwave weapon back.

Barguyo motioned to the Huks. "*Aih.* Quickly—let us dismantle the dish."

The State Department, Washington, D.C.

"Mr. Acht, General Newman."

The Secretary of State raised an eyebrow and took the phone. After asking some basic questions, he hung up and turned to his aide. "Get me the National Security Advisor . . . and the Speaker of the House, while you're at it." He held up a finger. "And have the President's press secretary hold off on that announcement."

The aide looked puzzled. "Any problems?"

"Just do it."

One half mile north of the Del Playo rice paddies

The rain covered their movements, hid the sound of the jeepneys. The rice paddies were easy enough to negotiate, but the jungle just north of them was another matter.

They left the jeepneys and struck out for the plane. *A half mile north.* Three men with machetes cleared the way. The men rotated the point position every few minutes to keep a fresh person in the lead. Normally, moving through the jungle was an arduous task, something that would not be attempted without much preparation. And for a very good reason.

Owning Pompano's sari-sari store was a sufficient

reason. For years Pompano had used the services of the black market network, and for years he had kept the profits a middle man accrued. Everyone knew that Pompano would soon be putting the store up for sale, but the chance to have it now was too appealing. It was more than a store, it was the entire infrastructure for black market operations.

They checked their weapons. With their firepower—"confiscated" from American military police—Adleman should present no problem.

Ceravant took the long way home, driving back to Pompano's store to await the Vice-President.

Pompano's black market contact should be scouring the countryside by now. The thought made him glow. He was the victor, no matter what happened.

If the Americans somehow found the high-power microwave weapon while it was being used, he would not be there. If the weapon worked but the Americans found their Vice-President first, he still would have succeeded in harassing the Americans, just as he had set out to do. If Pompano's contacts somehow found the Vice-President, that would be the best of all worlds. Even if the worst occurred, the minimum goals would have been accomplished.

Yolanda lay on the floor of the jeepney, covered with a blanket, invisible to outsiders. Ceravant smiled at the young girl, whose hands were tied.

Ceravant pulled out a cigarette. It took four matches to light it in the damp weather. He blew out smoke and spoke quietly to Yolanda.

"I have a proposition for you, little one." Yolanda struggled with her bonds at the use of her father's pet name, but she quickly tired and stopped. Ceravant smiled again. "I think you will find it amusing. You see, this store of your father's is destined to help the Filipino people. Whatever money it is worth, I will soon trade it for the American Vice-President." Yolanda stared back at him. "So all you have to do is to provide me with some papers," he shrugged, "a note, a deed, whatever it takes, so that I can give it in exchange for the Vice-President."

Yolanda jerked her head back and forth, signifying a "no." Ceravant chuckled.

He took another drag on his cigarette, then lightly tapped the ashes onto her face. Yolanda jerked her head away and tried to kick, but her legs just banged against the steel bottom of the jeepney.

Ceravant moved closer to her. There was no one in the small alleyway. Even the sounds of the people in the market were muffled by the patter of rain on the mud and street.

Ceravant brought his cigarette close to Yolanda's shoulder. "It would be a pity to mar this beautiful flesh, wouldn't it, little one? Your father is so proud of you, loves to show off his beautiful daughter. I wonder what he would do if his only child were covered with burn marks. . . ." He jabbed the glowing end of the cigarette into her flesh.

Yolanda's scream came from deep within her, a cathartic purging of agony from her soul. The shriek seemed to go on forever, muffled only by the sock stuffed in her mouth. Tears dripped onto her as she sobbed.

Ceravant pulled the cigarette away. He looked at it and took a thoughtful puff.

CHAPTER 18

Friday, 22 June

Kadena AFB, Okinawa

Colonel Alan Rader hated being a messenger boy.

As deputy Commander of the 313th Air Division at Kadena, he was on call to stand in for the boss. And since the order had come straight from General Newman himself, Rader didn't ask the chief why—after thirty years in the Air Force, he knew how to follow directions.

Colonel Rader knew things weren't going his way when he was refused permission to cross the runway. He grumbled to himself, but knew that even he couldn't wave off the tankers that were taking off. A KC-10A roared down the runway, lifting off and barely clearing the trees at the end of the long, reinforced asphalt. Once in the air, the tanker would circle at some predesignated spot and rendezvous with the SR-71 that was about to take off.

As he rounded the bend, Rader spotted an old man pushing up a sign outside the base:

SEE THE AMERICAN SPY PLANE
SR-71 HABU
NEXT FLIGHT TIME: *1145*

Already the tourists had started to line up, and they even had that damn taco vendor out there, selling refreshments like it was a carnival.

When Rader reached the flight line, he was waved inside the double-partitioned hangar containing the SR-71. Noxious fumes filled the hangar. A red warning light rotated at the top of the ceiling, five stories up. He grabbed his briefcase and followed a young lieutenant, dressed in fatigues but responsible for the entire SR-71 maintenance, into the SR-71 pilot ready room.

Major Kathy Yulok turned as they entered. She was dressed in the silver pressure suit worn by the Habu pilots. Thick gloves, and white hose that ran from the suit to an air-conditioning unit, completed the outfit. She held her helmet in one hand. "What's the holdup Colonel?"

"Sign this." He held out a paper.

Yulok raised an eyebrow. With her gloves on she clumsily scribbled her name on the classified receipt, and Rader handed her the briefcase in turn. "For your eyes only, Major."

She moved to the far side of the room, placed the leather briefcase on a table, and waved the support personnel to the opposite corner.

As she opened the case and scanned the message, Rader felt like a damned idiot, babysitting the briefcase for a Major. He himself wasn't "cleared-for-weird," since he didn't have the sensitive intelligence security clearances needed to read the message that Major Yulok had, but he had been instructed by the Chief to see that Yulok personally read and understood the orders.

Yulok snapped the briefcase shut. Rader took it from her. "Any questions, Major?"

She set her mouth. "No, sir. Is anyone else aware of this?"

"Just what the hell do you think?"

"I hope not. Thanks." She turned and jerked her head at the copilot, also dressed in a pressure suit. "Let's go, Eddie."

When they left, a team of support personnel followed, some carrying the air conditioner, others holding hoses out of the way so they wouldn't get snagged.

Rader watched the parade. He didn't let it show but he felt a pang of envy, a feeling that even though he was a bigwig on the totem pole, a person who commanded one hell of a lot of authority in the 313th Air Division, that woman would see all the action.

Whatever was going on, she was about to jump right in the center of all the attention.

It was a feeling that Rader knew wouldn't pass. And what was worse, when he retired from the Air Force, he knew it wouldn't get better with time.

Clark AB

They got to Charlie before helping Bruce down from the F-15. Bruce couldn't see what was going on, so all he could do was to remain out of the way. The rain had changed to a hard drizzle, but Bruce tuned it out. There were too many emotions, too much sensory input, for anything to make sense: the strong smell of JP-4, the people crowding around the craft, the incessant jabber, sirens in the background.

Charlie screamed when they tried to move him. Bruce overheard a quick conference between the medics before they decided to sedate Charlie.

By the time the drugs took effect, they had Charlie out of the fighter and into an ambulance. The siren started up, lights rotated, and the ambulance pealed off.

Colonel Bolte joined Mooselips at the top of the fighter as Bruce slid out of the tight-fitting cockpit. "Charlie will be okay, Bruce." The Colonel reached out a hand to steady him. "Can you tell me what happened?"

Bruce started for his flight bag, but suddenly felt tired. He tossed his helmet back onto the seat. "I don't know, sir. I can't figure out what the hell hit us."

"You heard Tower wave you off. Why didn't you do what they said?"

"I didn't have time."

"What do you mean, you didn't have time? There was a good sixty seconds before you got hit again—"

"I said, Colonel, I didn't have any time," interrupted Bruce. "From what I could tell, we were hit about the same time as Air Force Two. It just got them harder, and didn't come back and get us until later. . . ." He trailed off. "Hey, what the hell *did* happen to Air Force Two?" Bruce suddenly shifted gears, his scope of cognizance broadening. He looked around the runway. "Did it taxi in already?"

"It's down," said Bolte.

"Down? Where?" Bruce was still confused. A few minutes earlier, he'd been flying for his life.

"I don't know, son. We're trying to find out. That's why I want to know what hit you. What can you remember?"

"Colonel." A Major in fatigues stepped out of a staff car at the bottom of the stairs. The back doors to the car opened and two men dressed in suits emerged to stand alongside the Major. One of the men straightened his tie as he looked up at Bruce. "Colonel, we're ready for the debrief."

"Right." Bolte clasped a hand on Bruce's shoulder. "Good flying, son. I'm glad someone learned a lesson from Khe Sahn."

The rain ran down Bruce's face, but it tasted salty to him as he wet his lips. *Salty?* He realized he must have been sweating in the F-15. Then as he raised a hand to wipe his brow, he saw a smear of blood on his fingers. He touched his forehead and winced.

But what the hell was Bolte talking about? "Khe Sahn, sir?"

Bolte took off his sunglasses. He narrowed his eyes at Bruce. "You didn't study that maneuver in fighter lead-in?"

"What maneuver, Colonel?"

Bolte looked at Bruce strangely, then put his sunglasses back on. He muttered "What in the hell . . . ?" then said to Bruce, "Clouds were so low back in 'Nam that F-105s had to come in upside down, spot where their target was, then roll over to pickle them off."

Bruce shrugged. He was starting to feel worn out. "Sorry, sir. Can't say that I heard about it."

"Too bad. What you did was a ringer for that maneuver." He put an arm on Bruce's back and motioned with his head to the bottom of the stairs. "These people need to debrief you. Try and remember everything that happened."

"Who are they?"

"Secret Service and intelligence types. Just cooperate as much as you can—and remember, they're on our side."

"Thanks, sir." Bruce climbed down the aluminum stairs. The men in suits moved aside for him.

"Bruce." Colonel Bolte's voice came from the top of the stairs. Bruce turned; rain kept him from seeing the Colonel clearly. "Bruce . . . about Charlie. He'll be all right. I've got a daughter that has a stake in this too."

Bruce nodded and turned back for the car. The men in suits motioned him into the back of the dark blue staff car; they were off as soon as the doors closed.

Air Force Two

The screaming had finally stopped and low moans now filled the plane.

Vice-President Adleman tried to move and couldn't. It didn't feel like he had broken anything—at least he didn't feel any pain, the sharp twinge of bone grinding against bone.

Light diffused into the chamber from the rear of the plane. A hole must have been torn in the tail section. The sound of the dripping rain and the smell of spilt fuel overwhelmed his senses. A memory of the crash came back to him. He yelled hoarsely. "Is anybody there?"

"Mr Adleman?"

Merke! Her voice sounded weak; the sound came from just outside of the chamber.

"Merke . . . can you get in here?"

"Just a minute."

"Mr. Vice-President, are you all right?" It was McCluney, the Secret Service agent.

Adleman tried once more to push up. Something seemed to be on his leg, pinning him down. His eyes grew accustomed to the dim light. Reaching down, Adleman tried to push the object away—his desk had ripped free from its anchor in the plane's floor and tumbled across the chamber, pinning him during the crash.

Adleman grunted as he tried to move the desk. "I need some help."

Merke's voice came back. "Hold on, sir. I'll be right there." Adleman heard scraping against the chamber wall. He imagined a jumble of objects crammed up against the door, trapping him in.

Adleman fell back, relieved. They might have crashed, but now they were all right

The men stumbled upon the plane. The jumbo jet lay nestled in the thick jungle, trees pressed up against the fuselage and tiny fires flickering around the metal body. The rain seemed to have prevented the plane from bursting into flames.

Rifles at ready, they fanned out around the craft. A hole in the jet's back allowed half of the eight-man group to enter; the other four entered in the front. They didn't know how much resistance to expect, but they prepared themselves for the worst.

Adleman lay back on his couch and rested. He thought about getting out of the plane, lowering himself down to the ground, but at least inside he remained dry.

Minutes before, Merke and McCluney had freed him from the desk, and now the two were checking the rest of the plane. Adleman had urged them to go, for the sobs and cries coming from the front of the plane had begun to subside.

Merke had a long cut on her face. Adleman had wanted to join the two in their expedition to the front of the craft, but McCluney firmly pushed him to the couch. None of the emergency radios worked, so Adleman decided he would remain back here.

Longmire resurfaced in his mind. *What happens now?* Adleman felt ashamed that he should be thinking of succeeding the President, but it *had* to be on the top of his mind. That was what his position was all about.

Something moved in the back of the plane.

Adleman struggled to an elbow. It sounded like a twig had popped, as if someone had been walking just outside of the jet. But that was crazy. . . .

"Merke? McCluney?"

Gunshots came from all around. Adleman heard the sound of bullets ricocheting throughout the cabin. Screams . . .

"Merke!" Adleman sat up. A sound came from the back of the plane, where the hole in the tail section was. Adleman's breathing quickened. His mouth felt dry, cottony.

Two men appeared from the back. Adleman couldn't make out their features, but he saw that they carried rifles. Sporadic gunshots came from the front. One of the men spoke.

"Adleman?"

"Yes, that's right." Adleman started to stand up. He threw a glance to the front of the plane. "What's going on? The gunshots . . ."

Lieutenant Colonel Merke came sprawling into the

chamber, followed by McCluney. They stayed on the floor as three men stepped into view. The man who had asked Adleman his name pointed at the Vice-President and said something in a foreign language.

Adleman took an angry step forward. "What's going on here? What are you doing?"

The man lifted his rifle. Adleman drew in a breath. The man swung the rifle down to Merke and McCluney, then calmly shot a bullet through each of their foreheads. He put the rifle down and said a single word.

"Come."

He turned and disappeared in the back. Another man grabbed Adleman's elbow and shoved him roughly forward. As they moved for the hole in the back of the plane, the last thing Adleman saw them pick up was the "football," the briefcase that Lieutenant Colonel Merke had carried and which contained the authorizations for starting a nuclear war.

Clark AB

Bruce felt completely wrung out. The intelligence team in charge of debriefing had reconstructed his flight from takeoff to landing.

Angles of approach, radio frequencies, parameter settings, wing loadings . . . everything that Bruce could possibly remember was squeezed out of him during the interview.

With the interviews behind him Bruce felt at a loss as to what to do, so he wandered the halls aimlessly.

Thirteenth Air Force Headquarters served as the Command Post for rescue operations. There were so many colonels moving in and out of the Headquarters building that a bomb could have taken out ninety percent of the chain of command.

"Lieutenant Steele?"

Bruce turned wearily around, to find Major General Simone staring grimly at him.

Bruce stuttered. "Excuse, me, sir—uh, General. . . ."

"Bruce. Come over here. Come on." Simone waved him to the side, away from the flow of traffic. Bruce walked stiffly with the General until they reached a cross hall. Simone looked Bruce up and down.

"For crying out loud, man. Someone told me you were wandering around up here. Now just what the hell do you think you're doing?"

"Sir, there must be something I can do. If you wanted me to escort the—"

"Shut up, dammit!"

Simone paused a full ten seconds before speaking. "Bruce, you did one fine job. A hell of a good job getting your backseater and that plane back in one piece. It was shit-hot flying, and I seriously doubt that anyone else on this base could have done it. Including me.

"Now if that was all there was to this, if Air Force Two weren't burning out there in some field, or maybe sticking into the side of Huk hill, then I'd throw a parade down MacArthur Avenue for you. Trot out all the young filles, get good and blasted with the boys." Simone's voice grew low. "But it's not. You've done all you can, son, and as good as you are, you can't do everything. Right now you're only getting in the way.

"Why don't you get your car and head home. I'd get someone to drive you, but I've got everyone hopping. Have a beer. We'll call you when we need you."

"I don't have a car, sir."

"I tell you what." Simone dug in his pockets and fished out a pair of car keys. He tossed them to Bruce. "Here. Take my car—you can't miss it, it's in my slot."

Bruce returned the keys. "Thanks, anyway, sir."

"Go ahead. Go see your backseater, get a good dinner, get some sleep. Just don't wreck my car." Simone turned back for his office.

Angeles City

When you don't want to draw attention to yourself, be sure to conduct your business in public.

Ceravant did not always adhere to Kawnleno's axiom, but he did so now.

The rear of Pompano's sari-sari store was set against an alley. At the far end of the alley, the two-and-a-half-ton truck looked like any other truck with a tarpaulin protecting its cargo.

Ceravant sat on a chair in front of the small sari-sari store. He smoothed the bundle of papers before him and turned them over on the table.

Down the street the market was prospering even in the bad weather. All along the street, business was growing—and Ceravant could now see why Pompano's store would bring a high price. Pompano still sat tied up in the store, ready to be a scapegoat for what Ceravant had planned next.

As Ceravant flipped the bundle of papers over, his thoughts turned to Yolanda. She had fainted after the first cigarette burn, and afterward it had been easy to convince her to turn over the deed. The papers had been hidden in a steel box, buried in the back yard, underneath a pile of brick and wood scraps.

And it had been what Ceravant had suspected: Pompano had signed the property over to the girl years ago. Ceravant was sure that the date on the deed coincided with Pompano's first contact with the Huks. Insurance that if Pompano was found out, his daughter would retain the property rights.

But now Yolanda's signature on the back forfeited her ownership.

As Ceravant waited, he ran through the possibilities in his head. *Plans within plans, contingencies within contingencies—the possibilities were limitless.* He strove to keep as many doors open as he could.

A car came slowly down the street and then stopped. A man stepped out "Ceravant."

"*Aih*. Around the back." The man waited for Ceravant to lead.

Ceravant moved the deed from hand to hand. As the car pulled around to the back, Ceravant spotted a muzzle aimed at him from the backseat.

The man looked up and down the alley before nodding to the car. The driver got out and went around to the trunk, leaving one person still covering Ceravant from the rear. Opening the trunk, the driver reached in and pulled up a body. The driver grunted, then pulled the body out of the truck with a jerk. He dragged the body to where Ceravant stood and propped the man up. Blood from the back of the man's head oozed down the door. The driver returned and placed a briefcase by the unconscious man.

Ceravant squatted and peered at the man. He certainly looked familiar, but that did not mean that it was the Vice-President. He patted the man's suit coat and pants, but found nothing. Ceravant looked up. "How do I know it is him?"

"*Aih*." The first man motioned with his head to the driver of the car. The driver pulled out a wallet, flipped it open and shoved it at Ceravant. A driver's license read: ROBERT E. ADLEMAN.

Ceravant straightened. "What about the others on the plane?"

The man merely blinked at Ceravant, ignoring the question. The driver stepped back into the rain toward the car and scanned the area from side to side.

Ceravant slowly handed over the deed. "You will find all the papers in order."

The man flipped through the papers. "Pompano has signed them. It says his daughter sold it to you." He sounded surprised.

"You did not think it would be so?"

The man glanced up at Ceravant. "I have dealt with Pompano for years. This store, this location, is extremely valuable."

Ceravant shrugged. "He was anxious to sell it, and

I gave his daughter a good price." He bent down to the American captive. The Vice-President's head lolled to one side, leaving a smear of blood on the door. Ceravant put his arms around the American's chest, grunted, and lifted him. The men just watched him. Ceravant dragged Adleman through the mud and rain to the back of the jeepney.

The man who had been covering Ceravant raised his rifle and started toward the jeepney. The first man grinned and called through the rain.

"I am sorry to disappoint you, Ceravant, but we have changed our minds! You see, now that we have the store, Adleman is even more valuable to us!" He nodded to the man with the rifle. "Kill Ceravant." He turned to the sari-sari store. . . .

Suddenly, from inside the house, a volley of shots rang out, muffled in the downpour of water. The black marketers jerked in spasmodic actions, falling at crazy angles to the ground. Ceravant heard the sound of bullets shattering bone.

Barguyo stepped from inside the house, holding an M-16. Ceravant merely nodded at the boy as he picked up the briefcase. Pompano would be left with the dead bodies, but he would never talk, especially with Yolanda held hostage.

As Ceravant drove off, Barguyo and the two Huks with him dragged the bloody bodies into the house, shut the door, and walked through the summer rain to their truck.

Charlie plus five thousand over Clark AB

Major Kathy Yulok couldn't see her target, but the sensors on the instrument panel glowed a bright green. Below her, cloud cover stretched as far as she could see. From this attitude, the horizon seemed to be just over the SR-71's nose. They were flying relatively low this sortie, but it was the highest pass she was going to make.

It was really a job for the SR-71's high-flying cousin, the TR-1, but the closest plane would have taken over five hours to get to Clark.

Yulok toggled her mike and spoke directly with Thirteenth Air Force Headquarters. "Blackcave, Shakedown One. Cameras are rolling."

"Rog, Shakedown. Waiting your pictures."

The cameras on the SR-71 were a far cry from the original chemical film that the Habu used to carry, thirty years ago when the aircraft was first commissioned. Now, ultrasensitive charged coupled diodes, integrated with adaptive optics, fed their digitized pictures directly to a satellite link located in the SR-71's long flared nose. The digitized images were bounced from satellite to satellite until it was finally downlinked to an Air Force ground station—a fifty-foot satellite dish located at a classified operating location known only as Tango Whiskey Three.

A 64-processor Cray-4 supercomputer unscrambled the coded imagery and integrated the pictures with sophisticated three-dimensional algorithms, false colors, and blink technology to produce ultra-clear pictures. The resulting pictures were scrambled again and faxed to Clark.

Thirty seconds after Major Yulok had announced that cameras were rolling, Major General Simone looked over the shoulder of an intelligence officer as the young captain poured over the photograph.

"Bingo." He drew a circle around what appeared to be a long gash in a jungle of trees. "This has got to be it. If Shakedown can get a closer picture, we can confirm it."

Simone straightened. "Get a chopper out there."

"Shakedown One can get us a closeup in five minutes, general."

"And if that's Air Force Two, we'll get there five minutes faster. Move it."

He didn't have to repeat himself.

*   *   *

"Bring it in, bring it in! Hold it steady now!" Staff Sergeant Zazbrewski stood halfway out of the MH-60 helicopter hatch, leaning over the side, a hand on the crane. The line played out nearly a hundred and fifty feet before it hit the ground.

Zazbrewski saw the para-rescue specialists—PJs, in the jargon of the rescue folk—leave the harness and fan out to investigate the crash site.

"Hurry up, dammit!" Captain Richard Head turned his head and motioned impatiently for Zazbrewski to give them the sign to pull up. Holding *any* helicopter motionless was a herculean feat.

Zaz waved an arm at the helicopter pilot. "They're off."

"Thank God." Captain Head pulled the MH-60 Blackhawk up as Zazbrewski reeled in the line. They would circle the crash site until the PJs radioed for them to drop a stretcher. If one was needed.

Head surveyed the debacle as he brought the helicopter up another hundred feet, keeping a good fifty feet or so below the cloud cover. Head hated flying in this weather—he had a fear that something would suddenly swoop out of the heavy clouds and hit his helicopter.

A gash ran through the forest. The jungle hadn't burned, since rain had soaked the trees and underlying foliage, but he saw some singeing alongside the craft's silver body. The wings had torn off a good half mile away, and the fuselage looked intact. It was a wonder the thing wasn't in a million pieces.

Clark came over the radio: "Fox One, Blackcave. Have you located any survivors?"

Head keyed his mike. "Blackcave, Fox One. That's a negatory. We'll keep you posted."

The 747's fuselage was nestled down in the gash, virtually invisible unless one had watched the plane go down.

Within minutes HH-3s and CH-53s from Subic had joined Head, Gould, and Zazbrewski. After dropping their teams of Navy SEALS, the other helicopters flew in a coordinated circle, waiting for word from the rescue teams below. Head kept his Blackhawk moving in a continuous bank.

Head's radio cackled. "Fox One, PJ. We've got no survivors here."

Head wet his lips. "PJ, Fox One. Come again?"

"You heard it, Fox." The PJ's voice sounded bitter over the radio. "No survivors. *Nada.* Inform Blackcave they'd better get some OSI out here, ASAP."

The Air Force Office of Special Investigation? As soon as possible? Head keyed the mike. "Say again, PJ."

"You bastards listening up there? It ain't pretty down here. This is something the OSI needs to jump on, pronto."

"How's that?"

There was a long pause. "Everyone's dead—no survivors. Whoever didn't die in the crash has been killed—throats slit, bullets through the head. The only person we couldn't find is the Vice-President. Comprehend? Lonestar is not here."

CHAPTER 19

Friday, 22 June

On the road to Tarlac

They had left the rice paddies far behind and were on the final leg to the plantation. The road was crowned in glorious green, and everywhere Ceravant looked it seemed like he was being applauded for the ultimate coup. The rain—on the road, falling in the jungle, splashing up onto the side of the jeepney—all seemed to symbolize a washing away of the old, something never to be seen again. It was glorious. Ceravant saw it as a validation of the very things he had so dearly believed in and fought for.

Every so often he had to sneak a look to the back, to see if the figure of Robert E. Adleman, Vice-President of the United States of America, was still there, still moaning and quivering, still waiting to be used to free the Filipinos.

And from the most powerful nation on earth!

A half a mile behind, the truck trailed Ceravant, bringing the high-power microwave weapon and the girl.

At this point, Ceravant couldn't have cared less about either of them. Only about Adleman. And what the Vice-President could do for Ceravant, dead or alive.

Angeles City

Bruce rapped on the door. He couldn't understand why no one was home on the day Pompano and Yolando were to sell the store.

"Yolanda?" Bruce walked around back, trying to peek into the tiny windows set high off the ground. Broken glass, cemented into the window sill, lined the windows.

Bruce looked around the back and moved to the back door, trying to remain under the overhang. He pounded on the door before noticing a brownish-red splotch. He knelt and ran a finger across it. Bruce's heart began to palpitate.

He straightened. "Yolanda!" He fumbled with the doorknob, and it swung open. . . .

A smear of bloody tracks led into the back room. Bruce's breathing quickened. He entered the store, almost afraid that something was going to jump out at him, or that someone would come in through the back and start yelling, accusing him of—

Three bodies were stacked in the side room. Blood still oozed from wounds on their heads, their shoulders—a fetid smell filled the room. Urine and feces, body waste purged from their colons relaxing.

Bruce yelled: "Yolanda! Are you here? Yolanda?!" He peeked into the front room and he spotted Yolanda's father tied to a chair.

Bruce didn't know his name. He untied the man's gag. "Where's Yolanda?"

"*Arat aka booto!*" His face was swollen, bruised. One side of his head oozed blood. Bruce straightened and looked around. The back room. He spotted the tiny bathroom and wet some towels hanging on a towel rack. They were tiny, pink towels with hearts sewn in them—probably Yolanda's, something she had made for her father. Bruce used the towels to dab the old man's wound.

"*Ceravant . . .*" His eyes widened. "Yolanda?" He

coughed. The man made a small motion with his hands near his mouth. "Drink . . . water."

Bruce moved one of the wet towels next to the man's lips. "Here. Don't take it too fast." He squeezed water into the old man's mouth.

The man closed his eyes and asked, "Yolanda. What . . . what did you do? Where is she?" He opened his eyes.

"I don't know."

"Yolanda." He sounded firm.

"I don't know where she is. What happened? Can I get you some help?" He hesitated. "What's your name?"

The man coughed. "Pompano." Bruce tried to untie him but Pompano jerked away.

"I do not need any help. I must find Yolanda."

Bruce squatted in front of Pompano. "You're in no condition to do anything. Especially to find your daughter." He wet his lips. "Who are those men in the back room."

"What men?" Pompano coughed. Blood mixed in with the spittle.

"Back there." Bruce was growing impatient.

"My Yolanda . . . my little one. If Ceravant has taken her, I will hunt him. I will find her!"

Bruce helped Pompano to his feet. The two staggered into the back room. When Pompano saw the three men, he released his hold on Bruce's shoulder and dropped to a knee. He crossed himself. "Holy Mother Maria . . ."

"You know them?"

Pompano simply nodded. His chest started to heave. Bruce held onto the man and moved him away from the bodies. Pompano vomited in a corner.

Bruce wiped spittle from Pompano's lips. "What's going on? How is Yolanda wrapped up in this?"

Pompano waved an arm toward a chair propped against the back wall. Bruce helped him to it, easing the old man into the spartan seat.

Bruce felt his breathing quicken. The world seemed to have gone crazy: dead men in the back room, the old man tied up, and Yolanda taken . . . where? His temper started ganging up on his fear, causing his glands to rev into high gear.

Bruce started pacing, both nervous and anxious to get to the bottom of it. "Yolanda! Where is she? You know something, but what aren't you telling?"

Pompano only shook his head.

Bruce moved over to the old man. He drew back a hand, then looked at Pompano. *God, help me!* thought Bruce. He felt like he was going to pop apart. He grabbed Pompano by the collar. "Where is she?!"

"Ceravant. It was him. He must have . . . succeeded." Softly, as if he were defeated. "And he took Yolanda."

"Where is she?!"

"You cannot get there."

"The hell I can't!"

Pompano glanced at Bruce, then looked away. "And you will die, along with her." He paused. "Ceravant is clever. He has taken her to the mountains. He has taken . . . *precautions* to ensure that no one approaches his place."

Bruce knelt in front of Pompano. He saw a white-haired man with deep wrinkles and a defeated look in his eyes. "This Ceravant. You said he succeeded. In what—taking Yolanda?"

Pompano slowly shook his head. "No. That is only part of it. A very small part of it." He looked up. "If I am right, then he has your Vice-President. And if you try to go there, Yolanda and your Vice-President will die."

"But you've got to help me. Where are they?"

"You do not understand. It does not matter how you try to approach Ceravant. He will not reason with you. Ceravant has worked hard, for too long, to accomplish this."

Bruce slammed his hand against the wall.

"Dammit, Pompano. Ceravant could not have known about the Vice-President coming to Clark. *I* didn't know until this morning. Don't tell me that he's devoted his life to this."

"It does not matter that this is your Vice-President, or even my daughter. Ceravant has been waiting for an opportunity. *Any* opportunity. He has trained long and has prepared to grasp at any straw." Pompano breathed deep. "And I know how fruitless it would be to try and hunt him down, because I have helped the man."

Bruce turned at this revelation. *"You helped?"*

"Aih."

"Then you can help me. You know where he is, how to get to him!"

Pompano merely shook his head.

"You've got to!"

"I cannot take the chance. As long as I keep away, Ceravant might not harm my little one."

"*Might* not? Get real, Pompano! He's got the Vice-President of the United States there. Do you think he gives a damn about Yolanda?"

Pompano looked up coolly. "I do not care who else he has, especially if it is an American. My daughter is the only one who matters. I will not risk her life."

Bruce's breath quickened. He couldn't believe the gall of the old man—the stubbornness. It just seemed plain friggin' crazy that the guy wouldn't want to jump up and do everything he could to save Yolanda—or the Vice-President. Bruce couldn't put himself in the older man's shoes, show any empathy at all.

With a sudden movement, Bruce reached down and jerked Pompano up out of the chair. He ignored the kicking, even the bite that Pompano tried to take out of his shoulder, and carried the old man out the door and through the rain to General Simone's black Corvette.

After throwing Pompano in, Bruce held up a finger

and growled, "Try to get out and I'll tie you to the top."

He sloshed to the driver's side and started the car.

The White House

Juan Salaguiz smoothed his jacket and adjusted his tie. The mirror reflected back a gray suit, white shirt, and his "power" red tie. It also showed what appeared to be a freshly scrubbed face. The bags around his eyes had been hidden by makeup, and Visine ensured that his eyes were not bloodshot.

On the outside, Salaguiz perfectly fit the part, that of a cool, highly competent spokesman for the United States government.

Inside, he was frightened to death that the press would scratch the surface of his coiffured image, and that the ensuing revelations would generate panic.

Two more minutes and he would be stepping before the cameras of the three commercial networks and CNN. Another five minutes and he would be done.

Salaguiz studied the crib sheet in front of him. The announcement would express grave concern about the President's chances, when in reality all that was keeping the Commander-in-Chief alive was the rhythmic chugging of the life-support system.

A null reading on the Alpha wave scan had showed no brain activity for the past two hours. Technically the President was still alive—as cognizant as a vegetable perhaps, but still alive. Salaguiz was prepared to explain that no contact could be made with the Vice-President because he was out on a tour. The plan was to keep the Vice-President's crash under wraps until the Speaker of the House could be located.

Summertime on the Appalachian Trail had served too much of a temptation, and the man who was next in line for the Presidency had taken off, with little advance warning, on a hike.

An hour and a half! thought Salaguiz. *Who would*

*ever have thought that things would turn around so
fast?* Even the special arrangements for bringing
sophisticated communications gear along with the
Speaker on his yearly vacation had not covered this
unanticipated, spur-of-the-moment nature walk.

If they could just keep the press at bay until the
Speaker was found . . .

Tarlac

The road to the plantation was muddy and difficult to
negotiate. Ceravant left the jeepney twice to get the
truck out of swamps. He stood by the side of the road
in front of the truck, yelling and motioning with his
arm for Barguyo to rock the truck back and forth.

The canopy of foliage over the road protected them
from most of the rainfall. Water pooled on the road,
adding to the mud and muck that made the going so
difficult. They finally broke into the clearing where
the plantation was located. Ceravant was convinced
that no one would be able to sneak up on them. With
the sensors he had planted along with the mire on the
road, he could hold off an army. Or at least give him
enough time to bolt through the jungle.

Four men appeared in the clearing after Ceravant
drove in, stepping from their hidden positions in the
jungle. They wore ponchos and carried their automatic weapons by the barrel. Ceravant waved through
the windshield at them, then motioned back at the
truck that was just coming into view. The men moved
to help the truck back up against the house.

Once satisfied that the high-power microwave weapon
was in a position to be rapidly deployed, Ceravant
waved the men back to their posts.

As the Vice-President and the girl were taken
inside, the men whistled at Yolanda. They nudged
each other and talked among themselves, hoping that
this time Ceravant would offer them the girl.

Ceravant quelled the jocularity with a stern look.

"Whatever happens, leave the girl alone." Ceravant caught a few words about "having her all for himself," but he ignored the muttering.

He left it unsaid that Yolanda would serve as additional insurance in case they were detected. The Americans had vowed that they would not negotiate with terrorists. Ceravant knew that they stood steadfast on this policy. But he also knew about the power of graphic newscasts: They could sway even the most hardened politician. Certainly, the execution of a beautiful young girl on live television, with the promise that the Vice-President of the United States would be next, would cause even Solomon to capitulate.

Ceravant had decided to demand the immediate evacuation of all the bases. The treaty would never be signed.

He scowled at the Huks who were herding Yolanda away to the large master bedroom. A few days earlier he had met with Pompano in that bedroom and finalized the plans concerning the high-power microwave weapon.

"Once the girl is locked up, bring the Vice-President to the kitchen."

Adleman was still unconscious. Diffuse light filtered into the room; Ceravant still insisted on keeping the electric generators silent. The rain and low clouds made the kitchen appear gloomy, but it was still the best-lit place in the house.

Adleman slumped across a table, his head lolling to one side. Spittle ran from his mouth. Ceravant studied the man. Next to him was the briefcase that the black marketeers had left. Locked, it looked important.

The Vice-President wore a light-colored short-sleeve shirt that was torn in the back and splattered with mud. Black, mud-caked shoes and dress pants made up the remainder of his apparel. He seemed to be the same age as Ceravant, but Ceravant knew that the Vice-President was fifteen years older. Lying on the wooden table, Adleman looked the absolute antithesis of a respected world leader—helpless and beaten.

Ceravant ran his hands over Adleman's slacks. There was nothing more in his pockets than what Pompano's friends had given Ceravant. He pulled out Adleman's driver's license from his wallet. About half of the Huk contingent had gathered around. Barguyo stood quietly next to him.

Ceravant said to the boy, "Get me paper, something to write with."

When Barguyo brought Ceravant the requested pen and paper, Ceravant sat at the table next to Adleman and composed a letter, addressed to the President of the United States. He started to write a deadline by which the reply should be made, but he leaned back, thoughts racing through his head.

The Americans would drag their feet, no matter what the stakes, unless they had proof that the Vice-President was about to be executed. Putting pressure on the American government to respond, would increase their chances of success.

One day. They would have twenty-four hours to respond.

Ceravant finished the letter, folded the paper, and presented it to Barguyo. "The commanding officer at Clark will take this. You are to deliver it to one of the guards at their gate."

Barguyo took the message and flipped it over in his hand. He looked skeptical. "This is it? They will give up their bases because of this letter?"

Ceravant smiled. The boy continued to amaze Ceravant with his insight, his quick grasping of subtlety. Ceravant placed a hand on the boy's shoulder. "No. This letter is meaningless without some proof that we will follow through with our threat." He handed Adleman's driving license to the boy. "This is to validate that we have their Vice-President. You will give this to the gate guard with the letter. But there is something else you must give them."

Ceravant motioned with his head to one of the Huks standing by the kitchen sink. "Throw some water on the American."

They rolled the Vice-President onto his back and splashed a pot full of cold water into his face. Adleman coughed, sputtered as the water roused him.

Ceravant moved close to the Vice-President's face, smiling down at the man. "Welcome to the Philippine Islands, Mr. Vice-President. I am afraid that this treaty you seek is not a very good idea. And there is something I must do to ensure your people know that we are quite serious about it."

Adleman continued to cough. "Who . . . are . . . you?"

Ceravant nodded to four of the Huks. "Hold him."

"Hey!" Adleman moved his head from side to side.

The four Huks pinned Adleman to the table, one man on each of his arms and legs. Ceravant rummaged through the kitchen drawer and pulled out a strand of fine wire. Wrapping his hand with two potholders, Ceravant wound the wire tightly around his fists. "This will hurt more if you struggle, Mr. Vice-President. And you have to allow us time to stop the bleeding."

Ceravant barked to Barguyo. "Hold his index finger."

The boy looked puzzled, but moved around to the Vice-President's right arm. He pried open Adleman's fist.

"Oh, God—no! Wait . . . wait!"

Ceravant tuned out Adleman's voice; the Vice-President's body strained against the four Huks. "Pull the finger."

Barguyo extended the index finger and pulled as hard as he could. Adleman's knuckle popped. The finger moved away from the joint, leaving a small depression at the knuckle. Ceravant quickly wrapped the wire around the finger.

"As I said, the driver's license will validate our

claim that we have the Vice-President." Ceravant jerked on the wire, pulling it as hard as he could.

Adleman screamed. . . . The yelling, sobbing seemed to go on forever.

Ceravant picked up Adleman's bloody finger, white cartilage showing at the cut. Adleman cradled his fist in his arm; he curled up in a fetal position, moaning.

Ceravant gave the digit to Barguyo. "And this will ensure that they know we are serious."

Clark AB

The door to Simone's office flew open. Major Steve Hendhold grimly motioned with his head.

Bruce stood. Pompano remained seated.

"Lieutenant Steele—you've got five minutes."

The young major looked like he had aged years. His uniform was sharp but his eyes were red, puffy. From conversations overheard between various colonels, Bruce had caught on that Hendhold was coordinating the different search agencies.

Bruce nudged Pompano, "Let's go." When Pompano sat mute, Bruce reached down and yanked Pompano up by the elbow. "I said let's go."

Hendhold raised an eyebrow at Bruce but remained tight-lipped. Simone's secretary watched wide-eyed as they strode past.

Simone's office was plastered in royal blue and seemed to spread out to cover an acre. A podium stood at one end of the room, and a chest-high table was covered with maps, ops plans, and message sheets. General Simone did not look up when they entered, but he called out, "Come on in, Bruce. What'cha got? Juanita said it was important."

He didn't offer a chair or even a handshake. Simone held up several photographs and squinted at them, as if he were comparing a series of overhead photography. When they reached the table, Simone seemed to notice Pompano for the first time. He nodded to the older man but spoke to Bruce.

"You've found something?"

"General, this is Pompano Sicat. I think he knows where the Vice-President has been taken."

Simone narrowed his eyes at Pompano while Bruce filled the general in. When he had finished Bruce said, "I'm not certain that he does know, general. I can't get anything out of him, and didn't know who else to go to."

Simone folded his arms and looked Pompano up and down. Bruce stood silent and watched the two— in a way, they were very much alike, both physically and in terms of personality. Both were dark and squat, even with Simone standing a good six inches over Pompano. And neither of them put up with crap.

Pompano remained mute.

Simone said, "You helped bring the Vice-President's plane down?"

"No. But I set up the high-power microwave weapon."

Simone's eyes widened. "An HPM weapon? Where the hell did you get one of those?"

Pompano shrugged. "From the PC, one of your military aid shipments."

"But HPMs aren't any good unless you're a few hundred yards away from the target. What did you do, get right up to the runway?"

Pompano didn't speak.

Simone continued to stare at Pompano. He said slowly, "Bruce, you and Steve leave Mr. Sicat and me alone for a couple of minutes. I want to have a talk with him."

"Yes, sir." Bruce backed away and left the two standing there. Major Hendhold closed the door after they had left the office.

Bruce looked quizzically at Hendhold. "What's up, Major?"

Hendhold shrugged. "Beats me. Maybe the general

is going to Indian-wrestle him. Either that or shoot the poor bastard."

Bruce smiled feebly at Hendhold's attempt at humor. He thought of an irresistible force meeting an immovable object.

Both runways hummed with activity. The clouds still hung a precarious three hundred feet above the ground and the rain continued to fall. Captain Richard Head stayed inside the MH-60 Blackhawk with Bob Gould, and waited for the crew bus.

Down the ramp and around the corner from Base Operations, a fleet of six MC-130H Combat Talon II aircraft from the First Special Operations Squadron started their engines. Four Allison T56-A-15 turboprops rumbled alive on each of the airplanes; black smoke kicked out behind the MC-130s and swirled up and out of sight into the falling rain.

Specially equipped with fourth-generation terrain-following radar, precision navigation, a Fulton STAR midair recovery unit, and myriad self-protection systems, the black-snouted Combat Talons looked inherently evil to Richard Head. The MC-130s were used to flying into areas best left unmentioned, close to the deck and completely unobserved. They had so many bells and whistles hanging off the airframe that Richard Head suspected they could fly into downtown Moscow, take out all the electronics in the city, and get the hell out without ever being seen.

The Special Ops boys kept mostly to themselves. Commanded by Colonel Ben Lutler, a quiet, steely-eyed veteran of nearly thirty years, the First Special Operations Squadron told no one what they were doing.

Today, Special Ops was pulling out all the stops. Head knew that they would be combing the jungles, searching for any sign of the Vice-President.

The MC-130s rumbled past, sending out gusts of wind that swept through the drizzle. Head could feel the Blackhawk helicopter rock as the squat planes roared by.

Head turned to Gould. "Looks like we're the only ones not up in the air today."

Gould lounged back in the copilot seat with one foot up on the instrument panel. He picked at his teeth. "Give them an hour and we'll be back up. They'll want us to have Zaz hanging out the door, swooping through the trees looking for Adleman."

A voice came from the rear of the helicopter. "What? You guys bad-mouthin' me again?"

Gould pointed out the crew bus coming through the drizzle. "It's eating time. Let's get something down before they send us out."

"Rog." Head turned to the back. "Zaz—one hour. You comin' with us?"

"Naw, maintenance is bringing out some bang-bang. Bring me back a sandwich, would you?"

"Yeah."

Head lifted an eyebrow at Gould. "Bang-bang? Somebody thinks we're going to be shot at."

"They don't give us live ammo for nothing, Dick. Kind of makes you feel like ole Barney. You know, no real bullets for the deputy sheriff of Mayberry?"

"Yeah. And don't call me Dick."

Fifteen minutes. Bruce fidgeted, waiting for Major General Simone to come out with Pompano.

He called the hospital and spoke with Nanette— Charlie had stabilized, but they wouldn't know about his eyes until later. The ophthalmologist was driving down from Bagio and wasn't due back to Clark for another few hours.

Nanette assured Bruce that there was nothing more he could do. She promised to keep him informed.

A small army of colonels and their assistants waited in the foyer with Bruce.

Major Steve Hendhold entered the room and crossed into Simone's office. The young Major carried a handful of sheets, pictures, and maps. The door closed behind him.

Bruce felt acutely aware that he was by far the youngest and lowest-ranking officer in the room. And on top of that his flight suit was still dirty, smelly, and smeared with blood. Bruce didn't exactly look like the quintessential wonder boy, but there was nothing he could do. He decided to ignore the colonels and keep to himself.

A burly security policeman entered the office. His uniform was soaked with water and he looked worried. He carried a manila envelope as though it held something precious. He sought out Simone's secretary, Juanita.

"I need to speak with General Simone."

"You and every other person on the base."

"It's urgent. It has to do with the Vice-President."

Juanita pressed her lips together and picked up the telephone. She dialed a number. "Major Hendhold, someone here needs to talk with you."

The security policeman grabbed the phone, turned his back to the crowd, and spoke quietly.

"Bruce?"

"Yes, sir?" Bruce became instantly alert.

Simone stood at the door, holding on to the handle. "Come on in." Bruce walked briskly past the other officers.

Pompano sat in a chair at the far end of the office. Major Hendhold was on the phone, talking quietly with his back turned to them.

Simone looked irritable. "Let me make this quick. I've assured Mr. Sicat that no attribution will take place if he helps us locate the Vice-President. So that leaves us with one final issue to settle. And frankly, I'm not happy with it—Mr. Sicat refuses to budge."

Bruce set his mouth.

"The upshot is this: Mr. Sicat does not want any harm to come to his daughter. He refuses to allow anyone to help him rescue her. He's afraid that this

Ceravant character, or whoever the hell masterminded this act, will kill her at the first sign of a raid. Going in there to rescue his daughter and the Vice-President is non-negotiable. Am I correct?" Simone looked down at Pompano. The old man nodded stiffly.

Bruce looked puzzled. "I don't get it, sir. What do I have to do with this?"

Pompano stood. He blinked but otherwise looked impassive; he spoke in halting English. "You are responsible for Ceravant kidnapping Yolanda."

"Hey, wait one damn minute. . . ."

Simone held up a hand. "Hear him out, Lieutenant."

Pompano's nostril's flared slightly. "Yolanda would not have been taken if you had kept away from her. Ceravant has taken her to a well-hidden place. There are too many safeguards; no one can get close to it without being detected. There are . . . sensors . . . mines." Pompano shook his head. "It is too dangerous. If only you had left her alone . . ."

Simone persisted. "But if you tell us where it is, we could help you."

"No." Pompano stared back at the feisty general. Bruce almost thought that they were going to go at it, toe to toe.

Major Hendhold interrupted, his hand over the phone. "General, there's an urgent message for you."

Simone waved him away. "Later, Steve."

"General . . ."

"Dammit, Major. What the—"

"*Now*, General! Tech Sergeant Merkowitz is in the foyer. It has to do with the Vice-President." Hendhold spoke quickly into the receiver. "Send him in."

Simone growled to himself and headed for the door. Tech Sergeant Merkowitz entered and snapped a salute. Simone bore into him.

"All right. What 'cha got?"

"It's for you, general. Some Filipino kid delivered it to the gate, not ten minutes ago. I thought it was a joke . . . until I looked in the envelope."

Simone glanced at a handwritten note taped to the manila envelope. He read through it before he looked up. "Well, you've collaborated with this Ceravant character, Mr. Sicat. He claims to have the Vice-President." He handed the note back to the security policeman. He opened the envelope.

He stared hard and drew in a breath. "Oh, my God." He reached in carefully and withdrew a small plastic card.

He turned it over in his hand and read from it. "It's Adleman all right." He glanced back inside the envelope and set his mouth. "And they've got him."

Bruce took an uncertain step to Simone. "Sir, you still don't have proof."

Simone ignored him and spoke instead to Merkowitz. "Who else knows about this?"

"You're it, sir. I thought I'd better get over here right away."

"Good, man." He nodded to the door. "And keep up the good work."

"Thank you, sir. Afternoon, General." Merkowitz started to bring his hand up in a salute but seemed to think better of it, and instead just backed out of the office.

Simone walked slowly to the podium.

Bruce cleared his throat. "Sir, I was just pointing out that—"

Simone looked up and stopped Bruce with a bland stare. "Lieutenant, take a look." He shoved the envelope under Bruce's nose.

Bruce's stomach flipped at the site of a severed finger. Blood covered the bottom of the envelope. Thick, brown stains were smeared across the finger.

Simone threw the envelope on the table. The finger rolled out. "There you go, Mr. Sicat. There's your answer. Do you really think that someone who could do this to the Vice-President of the United States would hesitate to harm your daughter? And for what reason—because I don't reply fast enough to his demands?"

Simone shook the handwritten sheet of paper. "What do you think is going to happen when I get this to Washington? That they will trust some damned crazy fool hiding God-knows-where in the jungle to keep the Vice-President alive? And in exchange, move the entire American military presence out of the Philippines? In one day? Well? What the hell do you think, Mr. Sicat? Come on! Do you really think that this Ceravant bastard is going to sit by *and let your daughter live*?!"

Simone breathed deeply. He now stood a mere six inches from Pompano's face. The Filipino stood rigidly, unblinking. He seemed to take in all of Simone's ire.

As Simone continued to stare down at the old man, Pompano's eyes flickered away from the general. He lowered his gaze. Bruce watched the old man steal a glance at the table, then finally rest his sight on the severed finger.

Simone cocked an eye at Pompano. "Well?"

"The place . . . it is too well defended. And Ceravant has probably deployed the HPM."

"But you've *got* to let us try!"

Pompano shook his head. His eyes started to fill with tears. "My daughter . . ."

"She's dead if you don't help us."

"No," whispered Pompano. "I . . . can't."

Simone stared at Pompano. "Get him the hell out of here and have him interrogated. It's time to stop screwing around."

Bruce nudged Pompano. "Come on." He felt a sudden stab of sympathy for the old man. He didn't know why he felt that way but then again, he had never had a child, never been in this situation. He didn't know what he would do if it were his daughter.

As Bruce was leaving, the phone rang. Hendhold answered it. "General, it's Pacific Air Command."

Simone didn't look up from the maps. He growled, "Take a damn message."

Hendhold spoke quietly, then looked up. "Sir . . . President Longmire died at eight-twelve in the morning, Washington time. And until the Vice-President is found, they can't officially swear in a new President." Hendhold hesitated. "They want him found. Now. No more excuses."

Simone glanced up at Bruce and Pompano. His face was gaunt and drawn tight, so that his ebony features stood out. "Well?"

"Your . . . *President* . . . is *dead*?" Simone simply nodded. "And if the Vice-President is rescued . . . he would become . . ."

"Our President, Mr. Sicat. That's the way we work."

"If Ceravant found this out, he would never give up the Vice-President." Pompano wet his lips. He seemed to be thinking something over. He stepped back and glanced at Bruce. "Too many people would be noticed. Ceravant would kill both Yolanda and your Vice-President if he had any warning. Yet . . ."

Simone approached them. His interest was clearly piqued by Pompano's suddenly willingness to at least communicate. "What are you thinking?"

"I know where the sensors are located. I can get through the jungle."

"A small special operations team can accompany you—stay behind you," Simone interjected.

"No. Too many people."

"What the hell do you want?" exploded Simone. "Name it! How many—who? When?"

"One person beside myself." Pompano turned to Bruce. "You are responsible for Yolanda being there—you will come with me."

Simone held up a hand. "Wait a minute. He's a fighter pilot, not a Jungle Joe."

"Two people can slip through the jungle unseen. I can get us through to the . . . hiding place. I know how Ceravant stakes his guards, and it will be a simple matter to rescue Yolanda and your Vice-President, then move back out to the jungle.''

"If it's so damned simple, then why can't you let some *trained* people go with you? People who know what the hell they're doing?!''

Pompano shook his head. "I cannot oversee more than one person. I will not allow my daughter to die because of some American's enthusiasm when rescuing your Vice-President. And since Ceravant has the HPM weapon, you cannot fly in. I know the area.''

Bruce jumped into the foray. "Pompano is right, general. I've been through jungle survival, I can handle it. A chopper can drop us off near the hiding place. A few of the air-to-ground guys can give us air support once we rescue the Vice-President.''

Simone turned to Bruce, astonished. "What in the hell are you talking about, Lieutenant? This isn't some party you're going to! It's rescuing the President of the United States! What are you going to do, waltz in there and *ask* them for Mr. Adleman? You're not a Rambo, you don't even have combat experience!''

"It's our only chance, general,'' interrupted Bruce. He felt a sense of justification. Here was a chance to cleanse the error he had made in allowing the Vice-President's plane to have been taken down in the first place. He had been personally responsible for *escorting* the plane and had failed. He couldn't speak fast enough to get all the feelings out: that Yolanda would never have been abducted if it hadn't been for his persistence in seeing her . . . in going around Pompano's back during the last few days of their relationship. . . .

"All right!" Simone held up a hand. Bruce fell silent, words still stuck in the back of his throat. Simone studied Bruce and Pompano; his shoulders slumped. "All right, all right. Do it.'' Simone shot a glance at his aide.

"Get a Blackhawk ready to take Lieutenant Steele

and Mr. Sicat in. Scramble Bolte's wing and have them ready to lay down enough metal to sink this island once Bruce gets Mr. Adleman out." He was silent for a second. "And get Lutler from Special Ops on the line—have one of his MC-130s get the Fulton system ready."

Simone turned back to Bruce. "All right—twenty minutes. Get Mr. Sicat out to the flight line; swing by Special Ops for combat vests." He hesitated. "And Bruce."

"Yes, sir?"

"The second you get back into the jungle with Adleman—get on the radio. We're getting him the hell out of there, either with a Fulton pickup or a Blackhawk."

"Yes, sir."

Major General Simone watched the door slam. His eyes were focused on the ornate wooden door, carved out of monkey wood from the jungles outside of Mactan, at the tiny Air Force station in the southern Islands; but Simone saw nothing. Nothing but the lives of four people hanging on a thin thread of hope.

"General?"

Hendhold was standing by the phone. Hell, that was all the Major had been doing the past few hours. Standing by the phone and relaying bad news.

"What is it?"

"Admiral Greshan's office at Subic. They're pretty upset at being left out of the Search and Rescue planning."

"Stall them. Tell 'em we're trying to pull the Navy planners in on this as soon as we can."

"Yes, sir."

Simone's thoughts drifted back to Bruce and Pompano. His mind shifted into high gear. As soon as the Blackhawk let the two down into the jungle, he'd have another reconnaissance run made of the area. The Vice-President wouldn't be far away.

Once Simone had the hiding place pinpointed, he

knew he could mount his own rescue mission, a *real* mission, with troops who were trained for this type of stuff; not an old man and a fighter pilot. They'd be able to watch the place from a distance, keep an eye on Bruce's progress—even take out the HPM weapon, if it had been deployed. For if something did happen, Simone swore that he would be right on top of it.

"General? Sorry to interrupt, sir, but Subic isn't buying it. Even though Admiral Greshan is out with the Fleet, he's demanding an answer."

Simone pulled in a breath. "I'll take it." Time for Hendhold to get some rest—Simone knew that he couldn't dodge all the crap coming his way.

CHAPTER 20

Friday, 22 June

Clark AB

Thop thop thop thop. Helicopter city. Squat, heavy, big ones with camouflage green; medium-sized ones with cold, sleek features; and baby ones with tiny rotors, ones that didn't even belong to the Americans but existed solely for the Philippine Constabulary.

Everywhere helicopters. They bubbled out of the ground, growing from the black asphalt and multiplying in the rain.

Bruce checked over the pistol and M-16 that had been given to him by the Special Ops Squadron. He was not very proficient in either, knowing only that the gun was a .38-caliber with a silencer. He had shot the M-16 once at the Academy, and again during Jungle Survival School. Bruce was a fair shot, but he knew that if it ever came down to using the weapons, they were in deep trouble.

They gathered their weapons together. Bruce caught a glimpse of himself in the front mirror. Blackened face, camouflaged fatigues, and jungle boots. He had never cared for playing army.

As they walked toward the helicopter, a familiar face appeared at the hatch. "What's the matter—you like the rain? Hurry up so we can get out of here."

Bruce brightened at the sight of Captain Head. "Cripes, I couldn't have asked for a better crew."

"Come on, Steele, get your ass on board." Head stayed out of the rain and motioned for the two to hurry.

Bruce swung up into the chopper. He turned to give Pompano a helping hand, but the older man shrugged him off.

Head glanced at the old Filipino. Pompano drew himself up and stared blandly at the helicopter pilot. Head said, "It's going to be tough navigating in this weather." He made a motion with his hands. "You understand? The clouds are low, and we can't see very well. Especially if we get up into the mountains."

"I understand."

"Then can you show me where it is we're going? I'm not crazy about flying into the side of a mountain. This is definitely not VFR conditions." At Pompano's blank stare, he said, "VFR—Visual Flight Rules. You know, being able to see where we're going."

"I will tell you where to go."

Head set his mouth. "Look. I understand what you want, but we just can't do it like that—"

Bruce grabbed Captain Head by the arm and pulled him aside. "Listen, the guy's a rock. Nothing gets into his brain unless he wants it to. Simone just had a pissing contest with the guy *and lost*! So do what you can, but don't argue with him."

"Give me a break—look at the weather, for crying out loud!"

"Do you really think the military would mount a rescue mission with this old fart and *me* if they didn't have to?"

Captain Richard Head opened his mouth to speak, but closed it and snorted. He threw up his hands "Okay . . . okay." He threw a glance at Pompano. "A pissing contest with Simone?"

"Honest."

A flight-suited man swung up on board and banged on the bulkhead separating the cockpit from the rear of the helicopter. "Ready, ready. Let's crank it." Two other men joined the crew—gunners—and sat in the back.

Head settled into his seat. He waved an affirmative to the man. The man turned and cracked a smile at Bruce.

"Howdy, Lieutenant. I'm Zaz, if you need anything. Gotta have ya strap in, if ya would."

Bruce set his M-16 on the floor and strapped himself into one of the webbed seats. The seats extended down either side of the helicopter. To his right was a hatch, and an automatic weapon hung from a mooring, ready to be swung out the door. The .50-caliber machine gun could be used at either hatch.

The sound of rain was soon overcome by a high whine outside the craft. Bruce recognized the auxiliary power unit. The sound was soon followed by a vibration in the helicopter as the main rotor started up. The rain had left a fresh, washed-out smell throughout the chopper, but that too was replaced by heavy fumes of JP-4 as the craft started vibrating faster.

Bruce leaned back and watched out the side of the craft. He couldn't see through the rain across the tarmac. His senses seemed abuzz, numbed by a cottony layer. *Thop thop thop thop*. JP-4, the rain, the vibrations—the excitement seemed to catch up with him, fully hit him in the gut, as he realized that it wasn't just Yolanda that they were going after. Losing the Vice-President was one thing; hearing that he was now only an oath away from the Presidency was another.

But grasping that he was going to slip through the jungle to rescue him—with the help of an old Filipino with knee problems—made Bruce want to throw up. His stomach lurched. Bruce turned his head and frantically tried to unbuckle, but couldn't get his fingers moving fast enough. He vomited just as the chopper lifted from the ground.

Seconds later Zaz shook his head as he surveyed the mess on the helicopter floor. "Damned fighter pilots. You can dress 'em up, but you can't take 'em out."

Pulled out of a nap, Catman felt like he was still dozing. Colonel Bolte had been terse during the briefing; none of the grab-ass that usually accompanied the pre-flight briefs took place.

Dead serious.

It was the emphasis on "dead' that got Catman worried. . . .

Orbit at thirty seven thousand feet and wait for the tankers launched from Kadena. You'll be going in "hot" when the balloon goes up, and it will have to be pure IFR—Instrument Flight Rules—with the FLIR and LANTIRN. They'll be taking out the Vice-President, so if you miss the bad guys on the ground and hit any friendlies, chances are you'll be taking out the next President of the United States. Any questions? Okay, if nobody messes up then nobody dies. Nobody but the bad guys.

One more thing. You're not screwing around Crow Valley anymore, hosing down old trucks. This is it, gentlemen; the real thing. Are there any questions?

FLIR: Forward Looking Infra-Red. That and the LANTIRN navigation and targeting pods had been designed for low visibility. They weren't made for this weather, and cripes! especially not with a three-hundred-foot ceiling, pea soup for rain. . . . And they were supposed to go after an unknown target?!

They picked up their helmets and stepped out into the rain, toward their war birds.

Steamboat Springs, CO

"General, the Stu-3 is up. Washington is on the line."

"Thanks. And shut the door behind you."

General Newman waited for his aide to leave the communications room. When the news of Longmire's death broke, a helicopter had been dispatched from

Peterson AFB in Colorado Springs to pick up the Chief of Staff. Newman couldn't be in Washington for another ten hours. A hell of a way to run a war.

"This is General Newman."

"Dave—Francis Acht."

"Good afternoon, sir. I'm scheduled to get to Andrews by midnight. General Westschloe at Pacific Air Command is throwing every plane that can make it to Clark out over the Pacific; we're ferrying in over ten thousand troops from Korea and Japan to aid in the search. By the time I get to Andrews, Clark's population will have doubled."

"That's good. But it's only a start. Dave—we've located the Speaker. He's jumping at the bit to get something provisional set up."

"Provisional?"

"That's right, provisional. The Attorney General balks at doing anything rash, say swearing in the Speaker until Adleman is found—at least until she can get a ruling on this. Dammit, Dave, you guys have *got* to come up with something! The lawyers are having a field day interpreting the accession . . . and no one wants to commit to having the Speaker step in.

"We're holding back all public announcements until we get a handle on this. We need an answer, *anything* that might indicate that Adleman is still alive."

Newman interrupted. "General Simone is working the problem, Mr. Secretary. There is a strong lead that he is following, and he has his best people on it now. We're aware of the situation in Washington; there is just nothing more we can do until we actually find Mr. Adleman."

Both men avoided calling Adleman the Vice-President. At this point he was either the President or a dead man. Newman felt as frustrated as Acht, but even more under the gun. Even with the changes in Eastern Europe, the Middle East, and Korea, the cuts that the military had been seeing for the past decade had started to affect operational capability. A military surge of this magnitude was the first real test that the forces had seen since Iraq.

Acht seemed to settle somewhat. "Keep us informed. Secretary Zering isn't here right now, but he wanted me to pass along that he supports what you're doing and will meet with you tonight at Andrews."

The reference to Newman's boss, the Secretary of Defense, brought a smile to the general. The feisty little secretary was probably off slashing bureaucrats' throats. It was the first time that Newman had smiled in the past three hours.

A tap came at the door. "The helicopter is ready, General."

Newman spoke hurriedly. "Thank you, Mr. Secretary. If anything breaks, we'll keep you informed."

"Fine. Fine. And General Simone . . . this lead he's working on . . . what are the chances it will work?"

Same as a snowball in hell, thought Newman. *A damned First Lieutenant fighter pilot and a sixty-year-old-store keeper.* But it was all they had.

"I can't say, sir. Really can't say. But Simone says his best men are on the job."

Outside of Tarlac

"This way." The old man sitting behind Captain Head pointed to the right. The Blackhawk followed the road two hundred feet above the ground. It reminded Richard Head of a James Bond movie, of the helicopter swinging in behind a car carrying the British secret agent.

Flying this low had led to typical reactions from the ground: people shaking fists at them, young children jumping up and down and waving, startled chickens flapping around the farms. So far there were no unexpected hazards—Gould kept a running commentary from the flight maps, singing out whenever they were about to come up to a tower.

Head glanced down at the navigation sensors. The

TADS/PNVS—Target Acquisition Sight and Pilot Night Vision Sensor—used forward-looking infrared to assist them in the low visibility. The system was slaved to their line of sight and displayed imagery that allowed them to hug the ground.

Pompano pushed his face right next to Head. He watched a small road as it swept by below. "We are five miles away. You need to land us—quickly."

"By the road?"

"No. You need to take us over the jungle." He motioned with his arm at a point to the right.

Head squinted, but could not make out anything more than a mile away. "You want me to take you in there?"

"Yes. But stay away from the dirt road, or you might be heard."

"I got news for you, gramps," said Head. "They can probably hear us if we're three miles away. But after all these search flights, they might not pay attention to us. If that's where you want to go, I'll get you there." Head turned away from the road and banked over the trees. They were only a hundred feet above the tree line; misty shapes of hills rose up, just out of view in the cloud and rain.

"Can you find a clearing?"

"If not, we'll let you down on the crane. You'd better get on back with Bruce."

"*Aih.*" Pompano unstrapped and moved slowly to the rear of the helicopter.

Head glanced down at the navigation system. Once Pompano had left the cockpit he looked up. There was no clearing, as far as he could see—only the dense growth of trees. Head leaned to Gould. "Craziest thing I've ever heard of. It'll be a miracle if it works."

"You got it," said Gould.

At three thousand feet in the clouds, the MC-130 couldn't be heard on the ground. The dense cloud layer dissipated the sound from the plane's four engines.

The lack of visibility didn't prevent the crew from the First Special Operations Squadron from completing their mission. In fact, the cloud layer actually enhanced their ability to do their job—keeping track of the MH-60 Blackhawk flying just below the cloud layer.

Colonel Ben Lutler watched over the shoulders of the two pilots in the cockpit. Outside the cockpit window there was nothing to see—a gray mishmash of formless patterns. It looked like a black-and-white TV set after the television station has gone off the air.

But on the console, a color-enhanced display showed the MH-60 Blackhawk in astonishing detail. An elongated pod fastened to one of the MH-130's wings held the AN/AAQ-18 Adverse Weather Vision System, a microcomputer-controlled radar and infra-red surveillance device. The back of the MC-130 was crammed full of navigation, surveillance, and electronic countermeasure gear, enough high-tech weaponry to sizzle equipment for miles around.

Everything seemed to be going smoothly. Minutes earlier, the Blackhawk had turned sharply over the jungle and started to slow. When it started to hover over a part of the jungle, Lutler bit his tongue and waited for the MC-130 aircraft commander to pull the plane into a tight orbit.

The EWOs—Electronic Warfare Officers—sat in the back of the craft and kept the AN/AAQ-18 trained on the helicopter. The EWOs were specialists in the electro-optical bells and whistles hanging off the airframe. They could listen to a radio signal and tell what kind of gear was transmitting it, where it was, and what they had to do to take it out. They were known as "wizards," and were treated as such.

When the MC-130 banked into a turn, the console continued to display the chopper.

"This is it." The pilot turned to Lutler. "What do

you think, sir? We'll track Lieutenant Steele once the Blackhawk lets him off. Should we start trying to pin down their destination?"

"Yeah. But don't broadcast where they're going if we find it. There's a flight of F-15s orbiting six miles above us, just itching to roll in and take out the bad guys. We want to make damn sure the Vice President is out before we call them in."

"Rog." The pilot turned and spoke over the intercom to the rear of the craft. "EWO, pilot. Do a sweep search on buildings near the Blackhawk."

"That's a rog. We'll get you a list soonest."

Lutler settled back in his chair. The wizard had spoken. In minutes they should have a fix on the Vice-President's location. If it was close by, another few hours and they'd be ready for the pickup.

Outside of the cockpit window the two-pronged fork of the Fulton Recovery System was invisible in the clouds. The concept was simple: A person on the ground would strap into a harness and deploy a balloon; the balloon would lift up a cord for the MC-130 to snag. The person on the ground would be jerked into the air and hauled into the Combat Talon.

The only problem was they'd have to come down out of the clouds before they attempted a recovery.

It should be a piece of cake.

Right . . .

"This is it!" Zaz unbuckled and stood in the back of the Blackhawk. Bruce fumbled with the straps. He checked over his combat and survival vest for the tenth time. Two long clips of ammunition fit over his shoulder. He thought momentarily about leaving the extra bullets behind, but they did give him a sense of security.

Grabbing his M-16 he stood and joined Zaz. The two gunners remained in the back of the craft. Zaz swung a winch out from the bulkhead and positioned it near the hatch. The Blackhawk hovered a good twenty feet over the top of the trees. Zaz turned to Bruce and yelled over the *thop thop thop* of helicopter blades.

"Know how to do this?"

Bruce remembered being lifted up through the jungle at the end of survival training. The last thing he had seen was Abuj, his dark face silently watching him being hoisted away. Bruce wished that he had the small Negrito with him now.

Pompano stepped from the cockpit. Zaz led the old man up to the penetrator seat.

"This will take you through the trees and get you to the ground. Sit on this seat, and keep your arms and legs in tight. Lieutenant Steele will help you off once you get down. Are there any questions?" Pompano shook his head. Zaz turned to Steele. "Ready, sir?"

Bruce stepped up to the penetrator. Zaz helped him to climb on. The device looked like a long pole that flared out and back again. Bruce sat on the flared section and wrapped his arms and legs around the pole. The penetrator had enough weight to push through the thick jungle foliage, and still offer Bruce protection from the branches.

Zaz put his mouth next to Bruce's ear. "We'll drop the Fulton pack when you give us the signal after the rescue. You'll have that option if you can't find a clearing for us to get you out. Got your radios?" Bruce nodded and patted his survival vest. "After we let you off, Captain Head will return to base for refueling—we can't do an air-to-air in this weather. We'll be back up here in an hour. All you've got to do is call. We'll know where you are: there's an MC-130H tracking you."

"Right." Bruce swung the M-16 over his shoulder and grasped the penetrator. He took a deep breath. "Let's get it over with." He knew that they were being watched from a MC-130, but he didn't want Pompano to know just how *closely* they were being tracked.

Zaz started the wench. The penetrator swung off the floor and over to the hatch. Bruce moved out of the helicopter. The rain immediately soaked his fatigues. The wind came straight down, washed down from the rotors. Suspended in air, he swung back and forth, as if on a huge pendulum. He looked straight ahead, and could tell he was getting closer to the jungle.

Seconds later the foliage enveloped Bruce; green, wet, wood smells enveloped his senses. He couldn't see the ground. A branch flipped up and ran across his body. There were crashing sounds of tree limbs breaking—he thought everyone would hear them descend.

The bottom of the penetrator hit. The jungle was a morass of greenery, leaves, shrubs, tree trunks, branches, all jumbled together. Bruce waited a second to see which way the penetrator would fall, then he leapt out. . . .

He hit a tree, stumbled backward, and twisted his right foot. He crashed through a thicket of plants, finally coming to rest on the ground. He waited a full second before moving. He face stung where the exploding heads-up display had cut him earlier in the morning.

He pushed up off the ground, covered in mud. He tried to rock back, but putting weight on his right foot caused him to wince. He fell to the side. With a hand he pushed himself up, then sat on a large rock to examine his boot. His foot wasn't broken, but when he tried to put weight on it again, it stung like crazy— probably sprained.

The penetrator remained on the jungle floor, dormant. Bruce pushed up and wobbled over to the blunt device. He pulled twice on the line and jumped back on one leg. The line tightened, then pulled the penetrator back up. A mass of leaves rained down as the penetrator disappeared through the jungle canopy.

Bruce quickly plopped down. He rummaged through

his survival vest and pulled out a thick wind of bandage. He tightened the laces on his boots, then wrapped the bandage around his ankle on the outside of the boot.

He could barely hear the helicopter, which lifted his spirits. If he had a hard time detecting the Blackhawk, the bad guys would too.

It didn't take long for the penetrator to appear. Bruce heard the crashing noise from behind him. He favored his right foot and moved through the dense growth. He found that by zigzagging around the larger plants, he could make good time.

He spotted the penetrator right before it hit. "Jump!"

Pompano pushed off backward and landed with an "Ooof!" He immediately bounced up. Bruce hobbled up. "Are you all right?"

"Aih." Pompano narrowed his eyes and looked Bruce over, but didn't say a word.

Bruce shifted the M-16 to his left hand. "Okay—where do we go?"

Pompano pulled a compass from his pocket. It was tied to his pants. He consulted the instrument, then nodded with his head. "This way." He smoothed his vest and started off.

Bruce shrugged. How Pompano was going to navigate without any landmarks was a mystery to him. The old man had perhaps spotted something while still in the air. Be that as it may, Pompano was a good fifteen feet away by now, and would soon disappear in the jungle if Bruce didn't keep up with him.

The White House

"Mr. Salaguiz, Ed Hoi from CNN. There has been a news blackout at Clark Air Base in the Philippines. Any comment?"

Salaguiz raised his eyebrows. "News blackout? I don't follow you."

"Blackout: a clampdown. Our correspondent covering the Vice-President's arrival has not reported in, and we're unable to raise him, or anybody at Clark for that matter. In light of the President's death, would you care to comment?"

Salaguiz spread his hands. "I don't know."

"Mr. Salaguiz! NBC has the same problem!" "Los Angeles Times . . ." "ABC!" "Mr. Salaguiz!" "Salaguiz!"

Charlie minus twenty thousand over Tarlac

Major Kathy Yulok hated flying this close to the ground.

Her SR-71 was relaying intelligence data to Clark in an attempt to pinpoint the location of the high-power microwave weapon. With a three-meter dish, the weapon should be clearly visible with the equipment she carried. But if the HPM device was down there, it must be squirreled away.

Kathy checked her fuel. The gauge looked low again; she had already refueled twice. A KC-10A tanker orbited three thousand feet below her. She decided to tank up and get back to Kadena. If the HPM weapon was not deployed, there was nothing more she could do.

Tarlac

Ceravant watched Adleman, waiting until the Vice-President awoke. The plantation's front room had a long picture window that looked out over the front yard. The jungle circled around the yard, a good quarter of a mile away. Through the drizzle, Ceravant could barely see the single road that led from the plantation.

Ceravant sat in a leather chair. The Vice-President's briefcase was next to Ceravant. Adleman and Yolanda were at opposite ends of a long couch. The girl was curled up there, watching him without making a sound. Adleman's head was thrown back against the couch. He moaned slightly and moved his head from side to side. Barguyo was the only other person in the room. He had delivered the ultimatum to Clark.

Twenty-four hours! thought Ceravant. *By then either the Vice-President will be dead, or the Americans will be preparing to leave.* The thought almost made him intoxicated, cocky with power.

To think—a simple matter of bringing down a plane! *He* owned the jungle! For years the Huks had done what they wanted, always escaping the token resistance of the Philippine Constabulary.

Moving into the plantation had been a master-stroke. No one would think of searching for them here. And even if someone stumbled across the mountain hideaway, the sensors he had planted would give him ample time to escape into the jungle.

Adleman's life was truly in his hands.

Adleman stirred. His eyes fluttered open. He pulled his right hand toward him. Heavily bandaged, the hand was useless. Adleman tried to sit up, but it seemed to cause him too much pain.

Yolanda glanced at Adleman, then swung her gaze back to Ceravant. She reminded Ceravant of a trapped animal, cowering in fear of its life.

Ceravant smiled at Adleman. "Mr. Vice-President. I am glad that you are awake. I wanted to thank you for helping us get rid of the American bases."

Adleman's eyes seemed almost ready to glaze over. But he met Ceravant's gaze and stared back. "I . . . will do nothing . . . to help you." His voice was hoarse.

"No? Then what about your finger? Surely you remember what happened. That was but a small sign of what will happen to you if your President does not remove your troops."

Adleman drew in a breath. He seemed to notice the briefcase, but didn't say anything. He coughed, kept his eyes fixed on Ceravant. "You're crazy."

"We will learn shortly just how valuable your life

is to your fellow countrymen. You Americans have such a funny way of showing your allegiance to your comrades. The Romans' *Pax Romana* lasted for years because one murdered Roman citizen would lead to a hundred tortures. But you Americans . . ." Ceravant shook his head. "You will allow a hundred to be kidnapped, and yet do nothing in return. So we will see. If your President thinks we are bluffing"—he shrugged—"then we simply deliver your dead body to them."

"That's . . . insane." Adleman coughed. "What have you to gain if you kill me? You . . . lose your bargaining chip."

"Oh," smiled Ceravant. "We would first want them to consider carefully what they were about to do." He motioned with his head to Barguyo. The boy stood and walked up to the couch. He held a small camera, and took several pictures of Adleman and Yolanda, sitting back expressionless on the couch.

Ceravant spoke to Adleman, as if with an afterthought. "The girl . . . I was planning on using her to ensure our safety if we were stopped on our way here. But since no one stopped us, there is even a better use for her. If we have not heard from your people in twelve hours, these pictures of the two of you will reach Clark. Yolanda will accompany the pictures. She will be in, shall we say, not very good shape, when she arrives—if she is alive at all. Your President will have plenty of reason to believe that we will carry out our threat."

Adleman's eyes widened. He whispered hoarsely, "But . . . what will you gain . . . if I . . . die?"

"Gain? Oh, Mr. Vice-President. You do not understand. *That* is not the point. Having killed the Vice-President of the United States of America, having proved that we are capable of shooting your jets down at will, your own people will insist you get out of the Philippines. We win, no matter what happens. We are merely talking about time scales now, about when these events are going to occur. If you live, the bases will be vacated immediately. And if you die"—Ceravant shrugged—"it will take a little longer, but you will still pull out." He thought for a moment. "This is yours?" He nodded to the briefcase.

"Yes." Adleman wet his lips.

Ceravant started to have Adleman open it, but decided to wait. They would have time later. He nodded to Barguyo. "The girl has served her purpose. Take her. You and the others do with her what you want. In ten hours, she will leave for Clark with that camera."

A tight smile came across Barguyo's face. He walked toward the couch, grabbed Yolanda by the arm, and yanked her up.

"Wait!" Adleman struggled to the edge of the couch. His voice sounded gravelly. "Leave her alone. She does not—"

"You have no place in this," said Ceravant, with an edge to his voice.

"You will not . . . touch her. Or I swear I will have you."

Ceravant raised an eyebrow at Adleman. "You are in no position to threaten us, Mr. Vice-President."

"Leave . . . her . . . alone!"

"I see." He motioned with his arm. "Barguyo, take her. As for you, Mr. Adleman, you have not learned your lesson. You think that somehow you are going to walk out of here, safe and sound. Since raping the girl does not convince you who has the upper hand, we need to give you another lesson."

Barguyo held Yolanda's arm behind her back. She struggled, and even though she towered over the boy, she could not break his grip.

Ceravant stood. "Now, Mr. Vice-President, we return to the kitchen. Let us see if, once your other index finger is removed, you will finally show some civility." As he approached the couch, a Huk came running into the room.

"Ceravant—we just heard the news!"

"What?"

The Huk motioned with his eyes to Adleman. "The President of the United States has died. Once the Vice-President is sworn in, he will become their President!"

Ceravant clenched his fists in excitement. "So! Things have changed for the better!" He turned to Adleman and gave a mock bow. "Well, Mr. *President. You* are now in control; you can make the decision to leave the Philippines! I think it is time to deliver another note to Clark, telling them of your decision— with your index finger to personalize the message, of course."

CHAPTER 21

Friday, 22 June

Tarlac

Sloughing through the jungle, Bruce had no time to think about the pain. For the first few minutes his ankle had hurt. Now the tingling had gone away and all that remained was a tight feeling. If only the swelling would stay down for a few more hours. . . .

The rain had ceased to be a factor. It seemed as if he had been hiking for all his life in the wetness. Squishy shoes, chafing clothes . . . and constant rivulets of water ran down his face. It just didn't matter anymore.

Pompano trooped ahead, never looking behind him and moving through the jungle like a machine. Every once in a while he stopped to look at his compass, but there were no rest breaks or pep talks. Just straight ahead to his destination.

It had been three hours, and Bruce had lost track of how far they had gone. After the first steep climb, they had encountered no other hill. The jungle had no outstanding landmarks. They could have been traveling in circles, for all that Bruce could tell. There were about five feet between the trees; low brush filled the intervening space. Often the sight of a banana plants would break up the montony, but it was like living in an infinite world of trees and brush.

And rain.

He almost bumped into Pompano when the old man suddenly stopped. Bruce spoke in a whisper. "Are we there?"

Pompano shook his head. He consulted his watch. "Another half hour."

Bruce broke out a canteen and drank deeply. He offered it to the old man. Pompano hesitated, then took a drink.

Bruce shifted his weight; his ankle yelped at him. "Where are we going?"

Pompano blinked. He studied Bruce for a moment. "We are going to a clearing, about a half mile wide, with a house in the center. I had the helicopter place us four miles away, on the other side of a ridge."

"That was the hill we climbed about two hours ago."

Pompano looked at Bruce. "It is time to start listening for . . . the others. There are some guards, but they are concentrated by the road and just outside of the clearing. There should be one sensor not far away. I doubt whether Ceravant planted any on his own away from the road, but I cannot be sure."

Bruce wet his lips. The stop had given his legs a rest, but feeling now returned to his ankle. "What's the plan? You said we could get in without being seen."

"Once it is dark we can slip up to the house. Ceravant is a man of habit, and I think he will keep your Vice-President, and Yolanda . . ." Pompano hesitated, then spoke hurriedly, "In the side bedrooms. The house is not alarmed, and we can take our time getting them out."

Bruce shook his head. The plan didn't make him feel any more comfortable. *You just don't waltz into a place and leave unnoticed!* "I don't know. . . ."

"Ceravant has guarded the entrance to the plantation. He is sure that no one could get in without being detected."

Bruce knelt down and itched at his leg. His pistol

slapped at his side. He tightened the holster and ran his hand over the long silencer. *Just in case*, he thought. His ankle felt worse and worse. He straightened. "Let's get going."

Pompano turned, consulted his compass, and took off.

As Bruce followed, he felt inwardly relieved. It was the first civil conversation he had had with the man.

Thirty-seven thousand feet above the ground the cloud layer broke into crystal-clear sky. Maddog Flight orbited a good five hundred feet above the top of the clouds.

Catman kept in a loose trail, bringing up the rear of the three-ship formation. The F-15s were in a near constant bank. They didn't want to be far from the action when the call came.

The clouds seemed to extend forever. Twenty miles away, a KC-10A tanker pulled in and started its own orbit. If the fighters needed fuel, they had their very own gas station.

Catman flipped on the intercom. "Robin—you still awake?"

"Negatory, Catman. You woke me right in the middle of a dream."

"What do you think is going on down there?"

Silence. "Besides the rain?"

"Rog."

"Beats me. You think Assassin is having fun?"

"Get real."

Robin was silent for a minute. "Look on the bright side. He's got a hell of a lot of trees to hide behind."

"Yeah. Just like jungle survival."

Catman glanced at the LANTIRN interface on the heads-up display. The tiny pod fixed underneath the left air inlet was the key to eventual success. The infrared optics were cued by the F-15's inertial navigation system, and they granted the pilots enough precision to lay their weapons down in the crappy weather.

Just roll into the clear, following the LANTIRN, and trusting in the electronics all the way. They'd even have to pull up while still in the clouds. . . .

Catman hoped that the Special Ops boys would feed them the right data for the flight profile. He didn't want to think about what would happen if something went wrong. Three hundred feet above ground level—where the clouds broke—was not a long distance to react, even if they did go in on a shallow angle.

Captain Richard Head positioned the "1 to 50,000 map" right up to the windshield. A lime-green Dayglo line zigzagged across the map, outlining the path that they had followed into the jungle.

Minutes before, a few hundred copies of the map had been xeroxed and faxed to the ground troops searching for the Vice-President. Battlefield fax machines—durable enough to withstand being dropped into combat from the back of a C-141—were in use throughout the search areas. The entire search team was rerouted up to the area where Bruce had been dropped. They would set up roadblocks and wait.

Head squinted at the map and tried to figure out a faster way to return to the drop area. He followed the rough contours of the hills, ridge lines, and mountains that peppered the northwestern part of Luzon. A town called Tarlac seemed to be the closest seat of population. There were no other features except for a few towers and a handful of bridges.

Gould popped into the cockpit and slipped into the right-hand seat. He glanced at the map. "What do ya think—half an hour to get there?"

Head jabbed a finger at the map. "At least. You know, I'm not too crazy about going back and forth between the drop area and here, having to refuel if we're forced to loiter."

"If this is so all-fired important, then why the hell can't they swap us off with another Blackhawk?"

"Good question. But since we're the only chopper around, I guess we're it."

"Still, you'd think they'd pull some of the other guys off the search effort."

"They will. I was told to yell if we needed help, and they'll get someone out to us."

"Hell of a way to run a war. Sometimes I wonder what the commanders are thinking when they come up with things like this."

Head folded the map and leaned over to stick it in the leg pocket of his flight suit. "Hey, don't complain. That's all you pilots ever do: bitch, bitch, bitch. Let's get back up there."

"I thought you were worried about having to keep coming back to refuel?"

"I am. But if we land outside of Tarlac, we'll save fuel and be a half hour closer."

General Simone stood behind his high-backed chair in the center of the Thirteenth Air Force Command Post. An array of oversized, color liquid-crystal displays covered the walls.

He stared at a computer-enhanced display of two blobs slowly moving through the jungle. Taken from the MC-130 orbiting three thousand feet above, the images faded in and out as Bruce and Pompano stepped around trees and scrub brush. The view slowly rotated as the MC-130 kept in a continuous bank, circling the two. The signal was shot to a geosynchronous satellite 22,400 miles above the Earth, then relayed back to the command post.

The next screen had the same wobbly infrared features, but it showed the top part of what appeared to be a plantation. The airy house was located in the center of a clearing. People moved around the perimeter of the house. A closeup view showed men carrying rifles.

The details of the house were smeared—because of a huge heat source and the clouds, said a Lieutenant from Intelligence—which diffused the IR radiation getting to the sensors on board the MC-130. They couldn't tell if the HPM weapon was there or not, so to play it safe they had to keep away.

Bruce and Pompano were half a mile from the clearing. Their progress had slowed. No guards were around them.

The other screens displayed various communication links, aircraft in the air, and their locations. People walked through the command post, updating the screens and constantly feeding information into the combat-control database.

Simone studied the screens with a tight mouth. He picked up a phone on a stand at his right. "Get me General Newman."

Thirty seconds later, the Chief was on the line. "Pete. What's the status?"

Simone drew in a breath. If it hadn't been for Newman's backing, Simone would now be commanding the Army Air Force Base Exchange Service, banished from operational command by the other generals who had disliked his style. He could be frank with the Chief.

"It's going, general. Thank God the Seventh Fleet is out and not at Subic. Can you imagine Admiral Greshan trying to pull rank and heading this thing up?"

"Greshan wouldn't have fallen for that crazy stunt of sending Steele out with that old man."

"And the Vice-President would be a dead man." The adjective *Vice* was faintly stressed. "But that's not the reason I'm calling."

"Shoot."

"We're tracking Steele."

"Have you located Adleman?"

"No. He's probably inside the house, along with Pompano's daughter. It will be getting dark here in less than two hours. My guess is that Steele is going to wait until dark, then try to sneak up to the house."

"Do you think they can do it?"

"I don't know. This Pompano is good. He's had years of experience getting through the jungle. It's his territory. On the other hand, I'm worried about his allegiance."

"What about Steele?"

Simone leaned forward against the chair. He watched the ghostly image of Bruce slipping through the jungle. The Lieutenant's body stood out in the infrared, hotter than the surrounding rain-soaked foliage, even though no features could be discerned. "He's right at his peak—we couldn't have sent him to Jungle Survival School at any better time."

"Good. Good. The only thing that worries me is getting them out. Dropping a line from a helicopter seems awfully risky."

"We're using the Blackhawk to drop a Fulton Recovery System. Once the balloon is up, the Vice-President can be taken out of there in seconds, hopefully surprising the bad guys before they can use their HPM weapon. Bruce and Pompano will hide in the jungle. We're already feeding targeting information into a flight of F-15s. The Strike Eagles will give Steele the cover he needs."

Newman was silent for a long time. "I don't want to second-guess you, Pete—"

"You're not, general. If it makes you feel any better, I've had all the Blackhawks and Jolly Greens deployed out to Subic. We're loading a cadre of Navy SEALs on board—the nearest thing we've got to an assault force here. At the first sign of trouble, we're dropping the SEALs into that clearing. But if we do that, we've got to take out that HPM weapon first."

"You'll risk killing the Vice-President."

"We believe they'll kill the girl first, then use Adleman as a bargaining chip. If we're quick enough, we will succeed."

Newman remained silent for a moment. "I don't

like any of this, not one bit, Pete. It's too quick, and the odds are in their favor."

"General, there's a young man out there in the rain risking his life for the Vice-President, and another man risking his life for his daughter, and that's our best bet. I don't like *any* of the things we're doing, but it's better than rolling over and playing dead."

"Pete . . . thanks. And keep me informed."

"Thank you, sir." Simone hung up and turned back to the screen. The image of Bruce Steele wavered in and out of view. On an adjacent screen, figures showed thirty-four Air Force helicopters at Subic. Eight of them were loaded with SEALs.

The others were ready to be used as backups and to fly support personnel into the area. The one Blackhawk set aside for delivering the Fulton Recovery System was already in the air.

Bruce glanced at his watch. Water covered the clock's face, but the numbers 1853 blinked up at him. Another hour until sunset.

Pompano moved ahead of him, pushing thick jungle growth out of the way. They had slowed their pace. Bruce tried to pick out any signs of human life—threads from a shirt caught in the branches, broken leaves, or broken branches that were shoulder high.

Pompano was certain that they would soon reach the clearing. He slowed to almost a crawl and seemed even more careful where he stepped. He reminded Bruce, in the way he handled himself, of Abuj.

Suddenly Bruce froze. Pompano had stopped. Bruce strained to hear, but couldn't make out anything except the incessant dripping of water as it cascaded down the leaves.

Pompano barely turned his head to look at Bruce. He didn't speak, but Bruce could tell what he was thinking, just by his eyes.

Yolanda.

Pompano crept forward. One foot up, then slowly

down to the ground, applying weight, testing to ensure that no stray sticks were underneath his foot, ready to snap in an unnatural sound.

Bruce imitated the old man and forgot about the time. He was almost afraid to breathe, for fear that the very sound of the air coming out of his nostrils would alert the Huks.

Step, move, test. It was a pattern he recreated a thousand times. Step, move, test.

With this slow cadence, Bruce's ankle began to throb. He imagined it swelling, engorged with blood. Soon he would no longer be able to stand the pain. . . .

Pompano stopped.

Bruce squinted past the old man. Just ahead, Bruce could barely make out light—not shining at them, but rather diffusing though the heavy canopy of green. It had to be the clearing.

Bruce brought up his hand. 1921. An hour until dark.

An hour to rest, to run over the plan, mentally steel himself for what was to come. A half hour to pray that he wouldn't tie up; an hour to pool the energy he needed for the rescue.

Or the last hour he had left to live.

Ceravant frowned. It wasn't the shrieks of the girl that disturbed him. The men were just having their fun, spending time enjoying her.

No, it wasn't her cries, or even the sobs. Ceravant had decided to wait, to be one of the last to have her.

What disturbed Ceravant was something subtler. Something just out of range of his hearing. A low rumble.

He stepped outside. By the side of the house, just visible around the corner, was the back of the truck holding the high-power microwave weapon. The smells of dinner wafted out from the back of the house. The walls muffled Yolanda's voice. He wondered if he were hearing things. It resembled a giant gathering of . . . mosquitoes . . . buzzing somewhere out in the jungle.

The mosquitoes would come when the rain stopped, but he knew that they were not flying now.

Ceravant pushed back inside. The corner room held all the electronic equipment. He picked up a microphone. "Any activity?"

A voice came back seconds later. "No traffic."

Ceravant frowned. He walked over to the bank of detectors set up by Pompano. Each detector had a long line running from it. He put his ear to each speaker, but heard nothing other than the damned rain, falling from the clouds.

Still not satisfied, he stepped from the side office and went back into the front room. The girl's cries were already growing weaker. What would they be like in another seven or eight hours?

A young Huk stumbled from the back, pulling up his pants and grinning stupidly. Ceravant waved an arm toward the door. "Get the high-power microwave weapon ready."

"Are the Americans coming?" The man's voice was instantly alert.

Ceravant listened for a moment.

Nothing.

Still . . .

"Probably not. But it will be good practice for you to prepare the device." When the man did not immediately leave, Ceravant growled, "Quickly!"

Colonel Lutler watched over the shoulder of one of the Electronic Warfare Officers in the back of the MC-130. Black cloth was thrown back on top of the array of instruments. When the MC-130 was not operational, the cloth ensured that no unauthorized people would be able to look at the sophisticated electronics.

The EWO intently watched his screen. Sensors were trained on the house in the middle of the clearing, a bright blob, no detail possible with the amount of heat coming from inside.

People walking away from the house came gradually into view once they were ten or so yards away. The farther they got from the house, the better the infrared sensors worked—but the clouds still masked the detail.

Lutler straightened and started for the cockpit; the EWO was so wrapped up in his surveillance, he didn't even notice Lutler leave.

As he approached the cockpit, Lutler knew the sun would soon set, enabling even more infrared detail to be picked out. But he also knew the inside of the house would remain hidden, like a jealous mother guarding her young.

Bruce stretched his legs. His ankle was growing more painful.

He tried to forget it, and swung his M-16 around to prop his leg up. Fumbling with his holster, he pulled out his service revolver and stared at the silencer attached to the barrel. A faint smell of gun oil drifted through the drizzle. If he was going to use anything, he'd use this first. He'd save the M-16 for later—after all hell broke loose.

Pop . . .

Bruce froze.

The sound came again. Faint. It was as if . . . someone had moved just inside of the clearing, walking lightly on the grass.

Bruce held his breath.

Pompano opened his eyes. He stared at Bruce and kept still. The sound grew louder.

Something thrashed in the leaves. A branch rustled where it was moved, brushed back. . . .

Bruce grasped his revolver, moving it slowly up . . . up until it pointed at head level. The gun shook. He tried to keep it steady, but rain, sweat, and blurry vision kept him from seeing straight.

Pop. . . .

Silence.

Footsteps, and the person walked away. The noise was quickly lost in the symphony of sounds that surrounded them.

Bruce lowered the gun. The silencer made the gun feel heavy. He hadn't noticed it at the time.

He felt drained, exhausted from the wait—and they hadn't even started.

Bruce holstered the weapon, allowing the barrel to slide down into the stiff leather. His chest hurt—he realized that he had been holding his breath when the guard walked by. But he had survived. Survived the jungle, and now survived the first line of defense that surrounded their prize.

In the growing darkness, Pompano watched, unblinking. His cheek was raw, a scab not yet having formed by his temple. He spoke a single word: "Come."

"Over there." Captain Bob Gould pointed across the cockpit. Head saw a paved parking lot next to an old store.

The store looked deserted. Head craned his neck, surveying the area. No towers, telephone or power lines. "How far are we from the drop-off point?"

"Ten miles."

"Let's go for it."

As he brought the Blackhawk around, Gould got on the radio and informed Thirteenth Air Force of their position.

The sun's last rays ignited the clouds below, turning them into giant fields of pink cotton candy. Catman watched the spectacle with only half a mind. Most of his attention was focused on the giant KC-10 Extender flying thirty feet in front of him. The aerial refueling boom was pumping fifteen hundred gallons of JP-4 into the F-15. For the last six minutes, Catman's fighter had been gulping fuel.

"Break away, break away!" At the command from the boom operator, Catman banked down and off to the left. Catman clicked his mike.

"Lead, three. Break away, break—"

He was interrupted by Skipper's voice. "Three, lead. Rejoin at orbit point. Assassin's going in. I say again, Assassin's going in."

Catman set his mouth as he pulled toward the rendezvous point.

CHAPTER 22

Friday, 22 June

Tarlac

As they moved through the clearing, Bruce kept in a crouch. His M-16 was strapped to his shoulder. He fanned his service revolver back and forth as he jogged, to cover the area before him.

Pompano moved faster in the clear than he did in the jungle. The house was about a quarter mile from the jungle, right smack in the center of the clearing. A quarter mile—how many times had Bruce run that distance? He would have run ten times that in a single football game.

Out of the corner of his eye, Bruce spotted someone moving. He kept the Huk in his peripheral vision: His night vision best discerned objects when viewed from the side.

Through the rain and darkness the person appeared to be moving away from them. Bruce swung his pistol around, back and forth, as he covered their path.

Pompano slowed. He held a hand down, then motioned quickly to the left. They peeled off from their straight-in approach and swung wide to come around to the side.

The building was long in the back and airy. The windows were open, but rain was kept from coming in by a large overhang that encircled the perimeter of the house. Strong smells of food cooking caught Bruce's attention and made his stomach grumble.

Laughter mixed with faint shrill cries came from the house. Pompano slowed as he heard the noise. *Yolanda*! Bruce caught up to Pompano and silently urged him on. As he passed the old man Bruce could sense Pompano shaking, quivering with what had to be rage for his daughter's safety.

They reached the corner of the house. No sound came out of the window in front of them. Bruce and Pompano stopped to catch their breath.

Bruce breathed through his nose, trying to keep the huffing inaudible. He gritted his teeth to keep the pain out of his mind.

No one heard them. Or at least, no one indicated that they did.

The house sat on concrete blocks. The space underneath the house was too cramped for anyone other than a child to crawl through. After a quick glance, Bruce backed up against the house, certain that no one was staked out underneath.

Pompano drew up to him. "Yolanda is being held at the other end of the house. Your Vice-President is probably in the bedroom at this end."

Bruce nodded. He could still hear the screaming, the moans.

Pompano grasped the rifle barrel tightly. "I can not allow this to happen to her."

Bruce leaned over to Pompano. The motion caused him to yelp in pain. He nearly fell, but straightened himself against the house's wooden siding. Bruce forced a whisper. "We'll have to split up, try and break into the house at the same time. Can you take her to the south side of the clearing?"

Pompano nodded. A low rumble of thunder rolled through the clearing. Pompano pulled his revolver from the holster and nodded to the opposite end of the building. A sob came through the rain. "I cannot allow this to continue." He crouched down and started out.

Bruce breathed deeply. He turned toward the house.

Pompano was already a quarter of the way to Yolanda.

The overhang sheltered Bruce from the rain. He limped to the nearest window. No one was around. He couldn't see Pompano, and just prayed that the old man would succeed.

Bruce pushed up on his tiptoes. The effort almost bowled him over, but he managed a quick look inside the room.

A body was sprawled over a bed. It was tied to the bedposts, rope wrapped around the person's arms and feet. It looked like the person had been hog-tied.

A guard sat back in a chair, across the room from the Vice-President. His head nodded, then jerked back up.

Bruce wet his lips. He crouched in the mud and patted his survival vest. He pulled out the small walkie-talkie and turned the gain and volume to low. He whispered directly into the small microphone, "Blackcave, Assassin," then held the speaker to his ear.

Ten seconds passed. It seemed like ten hours to Bruce.

"Assassin, Blackcave. Go."

"I've found Lonestar, but we've got trouble. Looks like we're not going to make the jungle."

"Assassin, can you talk?"

Bruce looked hurriedly around. "Negative."

"Assassin, give us an assessment."

"Blackcave, scrub the Fulton plan. Get a chopper at the south side of the clearing ASAP. We're not, repeat *not* going to have time to get to the recovery packet. You're going to have to pull the Vice-President out of here on a chopper—we'll duck into the jungle and wait until Maddog covers us before pickup."

A minute and a half passed. Bruce wondered if he

should call up again, but a voice came over the speaker. Bruce held the instrument to his ear. "Give us the word, Assassin. The Blackhawk will be there two minutes after you holler."

"Rog."

He had started to collapse the walkie-talkie when he heard water sloshing.

Bruce fell back against the side of the house. A guard carrying a rifle, the barrel pointing down at the ground, rounded the corner of the house. He drew deeply on a cigarette, threw it out into the water, and turned toward Bruce.

"Fox One, Mother Hen. Your quarry is in sight, ready for pickup. Stand by for a two-minute bolt." The MC-130's message was short and curt.

Captain Richard Head clicked his mike twice. "Rog." He turned to Gould, who had already started running through the checklist. "Let's crank it."

Clark AB

"General, they've made their move."

Simone growled into the microphone. "I know."

"Plan B: Do you want them to launch?"

Simone thought it over. Helicopters filled with Navy SEALS waited to fly in for the assault. He didn't want to send in anyone and risk Adleman's life, not if Bruce could pull it off. But he needed the option open. . . .

"Launch, but have them orbit five miles away. We'll land them if they're needed."

Tarlac

Bruce lifted his pistol up instinctively. His fingers had squeezed off two rounds before he stopped. His hand kicked back with each shot.

The silencer surprised him. He had expected not to hear anything, but the muffled sound seemed to ricochet around the building and out into the clearing.

The man looked startled when hit; he fell back. Bruce waited for an instant, wondering if the man was faking it. He half expected the guard to get up and start firing, or at least yelling. He crouched by the window, anticipating some reaction from the guard inside.

Nothing happened.

It all seemed too easy.

Bruce turned to the window and put his hand up to the screen. The guard had started to snore. Bruce pushed, moving the protective mesh back into the room.

The Filipino suddenly opened his eyes. He spotted Bruce and scrambled for his rifle. . . .

Bruce whipped his pistol over the windowsill and slammed off three shots. The guard slumped back against the chair, then fell to the floor.

Bruce pulled up and rotated his right leg inside the house. He tried to move as fast as he could. He hoped the rain had masked the sound of the guard's fall.

Bruce scanned the room as he lowered himself down to the wooden floor. A chest of drawers, a low table, a mirror, and the bed decorated the spartan room. Outside the door he could hear muffled talking.

Adleman lay on his back, his arms roped together and tied to the top of the bed. Bruce unsheathed a surgical blade and sliced through the ropes. Adleman stirred. He moaned, then blinked.

Bruce lunged over and put a hand on the Vice-President's mouth. Bruce held a finger up to his lips, indicating silence. Adleman's eyes widened, then he nodded.

Bruce sliced the ropes by Adleman's feet, then pulled his legs around. Bruce helped him to his feet.

"Who . . . are you?"

"Later."

Adleman put an arm around Bruce's shoulder causing him to lose his balance and nearly trip over the dead guard.

The Vice-President spoke with difficulty. "Are you . . . all right?"

Bruce waved him toward the window. "Sprained ankle."

Adleman hobbled to the window. He rubbed his hands together. Bruce noticed they were heavily bandaged, but didn't say anything. Adleman peeked out. "It's clear."

The sounds in the back bedroom had quieted. Ceravant didn't notice the silence for some time.

He sauntered to the back. When he reached the door to the bedroom, he could not open it. He jiggled the door knob. "Open it—you cannot shock me!"

He chuckled to himself. The men had enthusiastically participated in the gang rape, venting their frustrations—it was not a woman Ceravant had brought them, it was a *toy*. Something to be used, thrown away.

Ceravant jiggled the doorknob harder. "It is over. Come out now."

Still nothing.

Ceravant frowned. He placed a shoulder up against the door and pushed. When it did not give, he stepped back and kicked at the doorknob. Another kick shattered the wood; the door swung open.

Two Huks lay across the bed, bullet holes in their heads. Ceravant's eyes widened. "The Vice-President!" He yelled at the top of his voice. "The Vice-President! Quickly!" And ran from the room.

Shouting erupted from the outer room. The sound of feet, thundering down the hall, grew louder and louder.

Bruce reacted immediately. He pushed Adleman out the window. Adleman yelped, then disappeared from sight, head-first. Bruce heard a muffled "Ooof" as the Vice President hit the ground.

Bruce pulled out his radio and punched the ON

switch. He whipped the M-16 off from around his back as he spoke. "Mother hen—Mayday, Mayday! Pull us out!"

He had the wits about him to stuff the walkie-talkie into his pocket. Backing toward the window, he kept the M-16 aimed at the door. He reached out with his hand and found the window sill. He managed to get his foot up to the sill when the door splintered open from someone kicking.

Bruce let go with a burst from the M-16. There was a scream, then the kicking stopped.

More yelling. Feet running and people jabbering. Bruce's nostrils filled with acrid smoke from the automatic weapon.

A round of bullets zinged into the room as Bruce fell over backward. He tried to keep from landing on his ankle and almost hit his head, but he rolled and flew out into the mud.

Adleman sat up against the house. Bruce waved and shouted. "Come on!"

Adleman winced in pain. "I think my leg is broken."

Bruce crawled forward and grabbed at the Vice-President. He grit his teeth and stood, ignoring the blinding pain that shot up from his ankle.

"Come on!" Bruce jerked Adleman up and started dragging him; they were in the rain, water covering them. "Help me, you son of a bitch!"

A volley of shots peppered the area. A zing flew past Bruce's ear. He ducked and tried to drag Adleman faster. Bruce felt as if his leg would explode any moment—his ankle had to be broken.

Lights flickered through the rain and darkness, bouncing from the house as lanterns were taken outside. Bruce squinted through the downpour; he couldn't see any sign of Yolanda or Pompano. All around came shouts and bullets, curses, the tart smell of gunpowder.

*   *   *

One of the Huks ran in front of Ceravant and kicked the door at the opposite end of the house. *"Booto!"*

A volley of shots ripped through the door.

"Back—get back!"

The man crumpled, blood running from his stomach.

Ceravant took an instant to decide what to do. He ran out the front, yelling at the top of his voice. "The Americans! They are coming!" Out in the rain, he spotted two of his men underneath the overhang by the right side of the house. They looked quizzically at him, holding cigarettes. A group of men poured from the house, rifles at ready.

Ceravant pointed to the high-power microwave weapon in the truck. "You two—start the device. Everyone else—capture the Americans!"

"Where are they?" "What? I only hear—" "Which way?"

One of the men unfolded the three-meter dish antenna.

Barguyo appeared on the porch, rifle at port arms. He looked wildly around. "Ceravant—which way do I go?"

Ceravant motioned toward the high-power microwave. "Stay here—direct the men setting it up."

Barguyo took a step out into the rain. Ceravant motioned for his rifle. Barguyo hesitated, then, grudgingly, turned the weapon over. "I . . . I must join the others."

Ceravant nodded to the HPM device. "You are needed here. Your talent is too valuable to lose."

Shouting mixed with the sounds of gunfire came from behind the house. The rain made Barguyo look like a little drenched rat, so hopeless standing there, as he was not allowed to join his comrades. Barguyo's mouth twitched as he spoke.

"But what can I do?"

"The HPM weapon can stop them."

"How? I do not hear a plane."

The shouting continued. It sounded as if the men were chasing a fox through the clearing.

Ceravant set his mouth. "They did not get here through the jungle. Someone will fly in to pull them out. The HPM weapon will stop them." He turned to join the others, leaving the boy in charge.

"Got 'em, got 'em, got 'em!"

The Electronic Warfare Officer on board the MC-130 Combat Talon looked excitedly up, for the first time all flight. His eyes weren't adjusted to the blacked-out interior, but he threw his head back and took in the darkness—for relief of eye strain, if nothing else. The Coke bottle-thick glasses he wore didn't get in his way as he clicked the mike.

"Pilot, EWO. Assassin is away from the house, carrying a captive."

"Rog, we copy the image up front. Can you make out any details?"

The EWO squinted back at the computer-enhanced infrared screen. "Negatory. The house is too bright, but—wait! A crowd has come into view. They don't look like they're bidding Assassin a fond good-bye."

A second passed. The pilot's voice was replaced by Colonel Lutler's. "Can you pinpoint the good guys from the bad?"

The EWO leaned into the screen. He played the small recessed ball on the side of the control panel. The view jumped from person to person, but he still couldn't get a good ID.

Two additional figures ran from the house at right angles from Assassin—if it *was* Assassin. The EWO swore to himself.

"I can't get a positive."

"Then scratch calling in Maddog right now. There's too much uncertainty to have them blowing the hell out of everything. Put them on standby."

"Sir, what about the Vulcans?"

"What?"

"The Vulcan cannons. It might be too tight for the F-15s down there right now, but we could use the IR to direct the Vulcans, at least to lay down a shield until the Blackhawk arrives."

"Have they deployed that HPM weapon?"

"I haven't spotted it, sir. But as long as we stay at least five hundred yards out, the HPM's intensity won't bother us."

Lutler appeared at the young officer's side. He placed a hand on the EWO. "I'll help the gunner set it up, you sing out and aim it. Have the pilot bring us into range."

"Rog." The EWO turned back to his scope. He clicked his mike. "Pilot, EWO. Lutler will fire the Vulcan."

"I know, EWO. I figured that's what he'd have us do. We're pulling into position now."

Seconds later the EWO heard the side hatch come open and the Vulcan twenty-millimeter cannon swing into place. Colonel Ben Lutler positioned the cannon as the EWO slaved it to the IR sensors.

Captain Head bypassed the standard five-minute warmup and punched the main rotor engine after a ninety-second surge. The rotor caught, causing the Blackhawk to vibrate.

Three minutes later they were in the air, a hundred feet over the top of the jungle. Gould kept in communication with Mother Hen. The MC-130 vectored them in to the south, but warned them to stay away from the house in the middle of the clearing.

Head looked over to Gould as he pulled his night goggles down. "Tell Zaz to break out the miniguns. The hoist will have to wait."

Bruce quit trying to pull Adleman along. He positioned himself under Adleman's right armpit and lifted, carrying the man.

Bullets whizzed by, zinging into the ground and sending up sharp splashes of mud. Bruce tried to keep low, but the Vice-President threw off his center of gravity.

Step, slide. Step, slide.

Bruce squinted up, out of breath.

The jungle was still a hundred yards away.

Bruce dropped Adleman to the side and swung the M-16 around. The house looked close. He hadn't gone anywhere.

He pulled back the safety and took a knee, aiming the automatic rifle towards the bobbing shapes that came toward him. . . .

Lightning. Thunder.

The sound nearly bowled him over. It came in a long, drawn-out *zzzziiipppp*, trailing red light behind it. . . .

And it came again.

Bruce fell back onto his buttocks, stunned. The sound struck again, peppering the area in front of him. Screams came from the house—around the corner and to the far left. *Zzzziiipppp*—the sound echoed throughout the clearing, rolling back and forth.

A Vulcan cannon! Someone was covering him, either from a gunship or a helicopter. The bullets rained down from above at an unthinkable rate, so fast that the ear couldn't discern an individual round going off. It sounded like one long shot, two- or three-second bursts at a time.

Bruce found himself breathing hard. He took a moment to allow his chest to slow down, then turned to Adleman.

The Vice-President lay on his side. His head rolled listlessly; mud covered most of his body. Bruce put an ear by Adleman's mouth—he was still breathing.

Bruce swung the M-16 over his shoulder, secured it, then straightened. He dragged Adleman to his knees and managed to get the Vice-President over his shoulder. Bruce took an unsteady step, then started for the jungle. He moved as quickly as he could, but now he didn't look back.

Captain Head brought the MH-60 Blackhawk around in a tight bank. Gould kept his head glued to the infrared and terrain-following radar, calling out the altitude. There were no obstacles to worry about twenty feet above the tree line. As they approached the fire zone, Gould continued to rely on the electro-optical instruments.

The clearing they were vectored to was lit up brighter than a centennial birthday party.

Gould scanned the clearing while Head lowered the craft to prevent them from being seen. They were two hundred yards away. Bolts of Vulcan cannon fire erupted from the MC-130 orbiting two hundred feet above them, inside the clouds.

Head clicked the mike. "Mother Hen, Fox One. Do you copy our location?"

"Rog, Fox One. Don't get any closer."

"Rog. Ah, the pickup, Mother Hen. Looks pretty dangerous, even with your cover. Do you want to call in a strike?"

"Negative, Fox One. We're saving Maddog—some friendlies might be in the house."

Head thought for a moment. He saw sporadic gun-fire bolt across the clearing then stop, as the MC-130 trained its cannon on the sniper.

Head clicked the mike. "Do you have a visual on Assassin?"

"Ah, we think so. They're heading for the south side of the clearing. Can you pick up?"

Head watched the firefight continue. The Combat Talon was doing a damn good job, but there were too many bullets flying. Maybe if the bad guys could be diverted . . . Out in the open the Blackhawk would go down in seconds. Assassin needed to reach the jungle.

"Negative on the pickup, Mother Hen. What about the Fulton?"

"Can you drop it?"

Head clicked over to the intercom. "Zaz—the Fulton Recovery hardware ready to drop?"

"Rog-o, Captain."

Head flipped back to the ops frequency. "Rog, Mother Hen. We'll do a quick pass and drop it on the south side."

"Do it to it."

Head clicked his mike twice, then said to Gould, "Make sure Zaz gets it right the first time. We aren't going back if he misses."

"Right." Gould spoke quietly into the microphone, talking with Zaz in the back. Head drew in a breath and wheeled the Blackhawk around. Seconds later, they were headed straight for the mouth of the beast.

Bruce dumped Adleman on the ground, then dragged him a few feet into the jungle, watching out for his leg. The Vice-President had fainted from the pain. Bruce scanned the area for Pompano and Yolanda, but didn't see them. God, he prayed that she was all right. . . .

The Vice-President was breathing, and that was all that mattered at the moment. Except for Yolanda . . .

Keeping a lookout through the brush, Bruce pulled out the walkie-talkie. "Mother Hen, Assassin."

"Good to hear from you. How's Lonestar?"

"Salubrious and copacetic. We're ready for pick up."

"That is kind of hard right now, Assassin. Can you move back to your original dropoff point?"

Bruce glanced at Adleman. *No way.*

"Negative on that idea. Can you pick us up here?"

"South side of the clearing?"

"Rog."

"Ah, a change in plans. Your friend Fulton is drop-ping in. Will Lonestar be able to ride the balloon?"

Bruce exploded. "Negative! Get a chopper down here!"

"Can't do that, Assassin. Too much activity. You'll have to go the Fulton route."

Bruce fumed. He said reluctantly, "Rog on that, Mother Hen."

"I say again, can Lonestar handle it?"

Bruce glanced at Adleman. "Rog."

"Are you near the pickup point?"

"Rog."

"Glad to hear that. You've got some friends sitting at thirty-seven thousand waiting to help you out. After they make their run, you get that balloon up so we can get Lonestar outta there, ya hear?"

"Rog."

"Have you spotted that HPM weapon they're sup-posed to have?"

Bruce shook his head. "Negative. But I can't see the front of the plantation house."

"Okay. Let us know if you find out."

Bruce waited a minute before switching the walkie-talkie off. In the distance, gunfire broke through the otherwise peaceful night. The yells had subsided as the Huks conserved their energy for the hunt.

"Ready, ready—*now*!" Captain Head yelled into the intercom. Zaz grunted, then pushed the bulky package overboard. The yellow tarp covering the device flipped over in the air as it fell the fifty feet to the ground. As soon as the package was off, the Black-hawk returned to the relative safety of the trees, away from the clearing.

He didn't find a place to duck to the ground, but a distance of a quarter mile from the plantation seemed sufficient protection.

Now it was up to Bruce.

*   *   *

The package hit the ground with a thud. It bounced once, then took a roll toward the jungle before stopping. Bruce spotted it as it fell.

He hesitated a moment, then slipped out from the cover of the jungle, dragging his right leg. The rain had slowed, increasing the visibility. He could now make out the plantation house in the center of the clearing. Bolts of minigun fire sizzled the ground, keeping the area clear. No one shot at him—he started to feel confident that things were going to work out.

Bruce tore into the package. He pulled out a carefully folded balloon, unwrapped the fabric and spread it out on the ground.

Next came the helium canister, then the harness and a long wind of thick cord. He swung the harness over his shoulder and grabbed the cord. Bruce attached the cord to the balloon and unwound it, backing up toward Adleman. Every two feet, tiny infrared sources lined the cord. The IR would make the line visible to the approaching MC-130 when the balloon was in the air.

Bruce backed up to the jungle, and then dragged Adleman by the arms into the clearing. His bandaged hands were soaked, and in the dim light Bruce could make out red stains that seeped through the material.

Bruce struggled with the harness, pulling it over Adleman's limp shoulders. He laid Adleman on the ground and straddled the Vice-President's stomach, grunting to get the harness fastened. Rolling off, he pulled out the walkie-talkie.

"Mother Hen—ready for pickup."

"Rog. Inflate when ready. We'll have to come around from the south, so you won't be covered for about a minute. Will you be able to get through the jungle for a Blackhawk pickup?"

"Yeah. Just hurry."

Two clicks came over the radio. Bruce hobbled back into the jungle and pulled out the M-16. He snapped in a fresh cartridge of bullets and made off for the balloon.

The MC-130 continued to hose down the clearing. Bruce couldn't see anything move—the gunfire from the ground had almost stopped.

The quietness should have cheered him, but instead it made his gut churn. Pompano had demonstrated his ability of getting through the jungle undetected, and if that indicated the Huks' capabilities, Bruce was in great danger.

He hopped to the helium container and quickly connected the hose to the balloon. Some gas bled away, but he managed to get the joint screw on tight.

The balloon slowly inflated. It grew first in girth, then in length. It wasn't big enough to carry Adleman, but its sole purpose was to get airborne and carry the sensor-lined cord up with it. For the second time that night Bruce swore that he would never badmouth an Air Force training course again—especially a survival one.

Bruce punched the IR emitters on and walked the cord back to Adleman. The balloon continued to rise, moving slowly up over the trees as Bruce let out the line. He couldn't tell how high the balloon had risen, having lost all sense of height up against the low clouds.

Bruce turned, spooked. He listened intently, but couldn't hear anything. Even the rain had nearly stopped.

A diesel engine ran in the distance. It sounded as if the house had started a small motor to generate electricity, but no lights came from the plantation except for the distant flickering of oil lamps. . . . Was it the HPM weapon?

Then something else seemed wrong . . .

The MC-130 was gone!

He looked wildly around and crouched, fanning the area with his M-16 at ready. Nothing.

What had Mother Hen said—it would take a minute before they'd be back? And already it felt like ten.

Which meant they'd be here any second. Bruce fumbled with the radio. "Mother Hen, Assassin. I hear a diesel engine. It could be the HPM weapon."

A voice came back over the radio. "Rog, Assassin. Keep us posted."

He grabbed Adleman by the feet and swung him around until his head pointed north, toward the plantation. When the MC-130 popped over the tree line, it would snag the line and jerk Adleman up.

"Mr. Vice President—Mr. Adleman." He slapped Adleman. *"Wake up!"*

Adleman rolled his head to one side. He coughed. "The football . . ."

"Huh?"

"The nuclear codes . . ."

"Here." Bruce reached out and wrapped Adleman's arms around the base of the line. He ignored Adleman's rambling. "Roll your head up, close to your arms. You'll be out any second now."

A deep roar rolled over the clearing; the sounds of turbo props reflected off the ground and rang around the area. It sounded like Mother Hen was about to make an appearance.

Ceravant waited until the shooting from above had stopped. Trapped by a volley of fire, he had been unable to move from the tiny depression he was in. The jungle was two hundred yards away—but every time he tried to move, a rain of death shot through the air, pinning him. He could not even get back to the plantation!

At first he thought the silence was a ploy, a trick by the Americans so that they could kill him on the run. But after a cautious try, he started moving toward the jungle. The Vice-President had to be at the south end, perhaps deep in the brush by now—why else were the American bullets keeping him trapped?

As he made for the jungle, a sudden thought hit him. *What if this is only the beginning—if they were clearing the area for more Americans to land?* He cursed Barguyo. He should not have left a boy to do a man's job, no matter how mature the boy had seemed. If Barguyo had been thinking, he could have downed the American aircraft.

He turned around and started sprinting for the plantation. The run did not take more than a minute. Sloshing through the mud, he nearly tripped over one of his dead comrades. When he arrived at the house, he sought out the high-power microwave weapon. One of the men cowered underneath the porch; the other was nowhere to be seen. The diesel engine used to charge the capacitors chugged away.

Ceravant snapped, "Where is Barguyo?"

"Here." A voice came from underneath the microwave weapon. Barguyo was smeared with grease. "The antenna—if one of the bullets had hit it, we could not use the weapon."

Ceravant flicked a glance at the device. The antenna was bundled up, hidden from stray bullets. "How fast can you start the machine?"

Barguyo answered as he pulled himself back up onto the truck. "Less than a minute."

"Then start firing as quickly as you can, and do not stop." Ceravant pointed toward the south. "Aim the weapon that way. Quickly!"

Barguyo had the antenna erected by the time Ceravant started back for the jungle. As Ceravant turned, the three-meter dish rotated around and pointed to the south.

The *pop pop pop* of capacitors cycling through their discharge started soon after.

CHAPTER 23

Friday, 22 June

Tarlac

Colonel Ben Lutler threw his head back and closed his eyes. It had seemed like he had been on the Vulcan cannon for hours—ten minutes was more realistic.

And in another forty-five seconds they'd be done. Pick up the Vice-President, pull him on board, and head on back to Clark. And after a two-hour debrief, hit the Rathskeller with one hell of a war story.

Lutler opened his eyes. The young EWO still had his head buried in the screen. Lutler made for the cockpit. He looked over the shoulder of the pilot. Both the pilot and copilot wore ANVIS-6 infrared night-vision goggles, allowing them to spot the cord deployed by Assassin on the ground. Lutler didn't want to disturb them, but dammit, he just *had* to know.

"Do you have it?"

The pilot spoke without turning. "Rog. Thirty seconds to pickup."

The MC-130 skimmed above the tree line, not twenty feet above the top of the highest branches. Lutler wouldn't be surprised if the mechanics found leaves lodged in the underbelly. . . .

Pop pop pop pop pop!

"What the hell!"

The cockpit lights blinked, dimmed, then went

completely off. The IR panel cracked, and the sound of breaking glass cascaded throughout the cockpit; smoke rolled through the air. Lutler steadied himself against the left-hand seat.

"What's going on?"

The copilot leaned forward, his head in the maze of electro-optic sensors; screams came from the back of the craft.

"What!"

"I've lost INS, all IR sensors!"

Inertial navigation system down? What was going on?!

"Ten seconds to pickup!"

"Can you see it?"

"Rog, rog—oh, *shit*! All I've got are hydraulics!" The pilot's voice sounded hysterical; he reached up and snapped an array of levers. "All electronics are down! They must have used the HPM!"

"Abort, abort!"

"NO! You've got to pick him up. Inform Blackcave they have the HPM."

"We can't even navigate, reel him in! We'll kill him—abort! Radio's out." The MC-130 tipped a wing to the right, barely missing the balloon. A crashing sound came from outside the right window as the wing swept into the tops of the trees. The pilot fought to keep the lumbering craft under control. "Keep it under the clouds—we're going VFR!"

Lutler sat unsteadily back in the jump seat, his heart racing. *VFR—visual flight rules.* Twenty feet above the trees and zero-zero visibility. Great. Make my day.

Bruce stared in horror. The MC-130 roared over the trees, its wing scraping the topmost branches as it missed the balloon. The Combat Talon looked as if it might crash, wheel around on a wing, and impact the ground, but it straightened and flew to the east.

The cord wobbled from the near miss. Adleman kept his head rolled up in his arms.

Bruce pulled out the walkie-talkie. "Mother Hen, what's your status? The pickup—are you coming around?" He wet his lips and surveyed the clearing. Still nothing. The clearing seemed eerily quiet. Except for the faint sound of a diesel engine, nothing drifted from the plantation.

Adleman peeked up at Bruce. It seemed to take an effort. "What . . ."

"Mother Hen, come in, dammit!"

Motion. Bruce caught a glimpse of something move out of the corner of his eye. "*Mother Hen!* Where the hell are you?!" He swung the M-16 up and kept the clearing covered.

Adleman relaxed his head, dropping back down to the soggy ground. He still held on to the Fulton cord, but his shoulders had slumped back, no longer ready for the pickup. Adleman whispered, "What . . . next?"

Bruce ignored him and brought the walkie-talkie to his lips, still sweeping the rifle barrel around. "Mayday, mayday! Mother Hen . . . *anybody*! Come in! Fox One—can you hear me?"

Silence.

Bruce set the M-16 down and flipped through the frequencies. Still nothing. He shook the small radio. "Come on!" Turning the gain up as high as he could, he placed the tiny speaker up to his ear. Nothing— not even a hiss. He threw the walkie-talkie aside. "So much for high tech."

"What . . . next?"

Bruce scanned the area. There was still no sight of Yolanda and Pompano. Picking up the M-16 he debated what to do. He didn't look at Adleman as he spoke. "I don't know. If anyone's still alive out there, we're sitting ducks if we stay here. But if the '130 comes back, this is the only way to get you out of here."

"The . . . radio?" Adleman coughed.

Bruce placed a hand on the Vice-President's chest.

He continued his surveillance. "It stopped working. Water probably got to it." *Come on,* he thought, *think*! What would the Combat Talon do—come back? But why did they break away in the first place? Did they see something on the ground?

It had been at least a couple of minutes since the MC-130 had departed. Bruce strained to hear a noise—anything—that might give him a clue as to what was going on. But all he heard was the faint chugging of the engine, and the muted dripping of water in the jungle behind them. In the distance the diesel engine coughed, then abruptly stopped. The clearing grew even quieter.

What next? He set his mouth—staying here was out of the question. Everyone on Clark probably knew where he was by now—they'd send somebody after them. But right now the highest priority was to get out of sight.

Bruce shifted the M-16 to his left hand. Favoring his ankle, he used his right hand to fumble with Adleman's harness. "We're going to get back into the jungle—wait things out."

"The plane . . . is it coming back?"

"Someone will." He unfastened the harness and threw it back, pulling the vest off of Adleman. He squatted and placed an arm underneath Adleman's arm. "Can you walk?"

"I don't think so."

Bruce pulled up Adleman's pant leg and drew in a breath. The Vice-President's leg bent at a crazy angle. Bruce debated if he should try to set the bone back in place but dismissed the thought. Their first priority was survival.

Barguyo scrambled down from the operator's seat on the high-power microwave weapon. He squeezed past the dish antenna and climbed to the rear of the truck. Faint light from the house illuminated the generator, sitting dormant. Barguyo ran a hand over the generator. Nothing appeared wrong. . . . He unscrewed the top gasket. *Maybe the fuel?*

He turned and found a canister lashed to the side of the truck. Heaving the five-gallon can up, he re-fueled the generator and tried to restart it. Nothing. He suddenly remembered the cartoon-like operator's manual that came with the weapon.

Barguyo lowered himself to the ground and climbed into the truck cab, rummaged through the glove box, and pulled out the manual. Flipping through pages, he came to a cartoon of a soldier refueling the genera-tor. He mouthed the words written in large English letters: WAIT TEN MINUTES FOR ENGINE TO COOL BEFORE RESTARTING.

He closed the manual and smiled to himself. And he never thought that learning English back in the barrio would come to any use.

Captain Head pulled the Blackhawk up from the tree-tops. "Did you catch that?"

Gould scanned the instruments. "Yeah. It was just like what happened back at the runway, right before our electronics crapped out."

"Think it's that HPM stuff?"

"Beats the hell out of me." Gould flipped various switches back and forth. "Whatever it was, we were far enough away not to get zapped." He shuddered. "Imagine going down in the jungle?"

Head didn't answer. He flipped on the mike. "Mother Hen, Fox One." No answer. "Mother Hen—come in. Have you picked up Lonestar? Mother Hen, Fox One." He waited some seconds before throwing a glance at Gould. "I don't like it."

"What do you say we take a look?"

"We did it once. What if Mother Hen is keeping radio silence?"

"What the hell for? What if she got zapped by the HPM?"

"Look, Dick—I don't care if they've got phasers.

What if they got the '130? They could have brought the plane down."

"If they got them, they could get us."

"Or anybody. Let's take a look."

Head ran over the rationale. It didn't take much to convince him that if *they* didn't go in, nobody would.

"You got the '15's number?"

"Rog." Gould leaned forward and punched the frequency into the radio.

He clicked the mike. "Maddog, Fox One."

"Fox One, Maddog One."

"Maddog, we've lost contact with Mother Hen."

A moment passed. "That's a rog. We've lost them too."

"We're going in to take a look. Ah, looks like the bad guys have that HPM weapon—electronic warfare and all that. It's probably housed in that plantation house. It will only affect you within a five-hundred-yard range. If you don't hear from us after a while, sure would be nice if you didn't forget us."

"Fox One, Maddog. You've got five minutes and we're strafing the house, unless you say the word. Sound all right?"

"Rog." Head clicked the mike twice, then reached down to reset the tilt of the rotor. "Keep an eye on that clock. If we're still there, I don't want any fighter jocks hosing us down." Head paused. "Any trouble with the IR?"

"No."

"Okay, you cover the sensor and I'll look for them with the night-vision goggles. We'll come in low over the south side of the clearing." As he spoke, Head flipped down his ANVIS-6 night-vision goggles. "If they're not there, we'll get the hell out of Dodge. And never call me Dick!"

Ceravant moved as quickly as he could. He slipped through the jungle, just outside of the clearing where the brush and foliage had not yet thickened. The south end of the clearing was not far away. He carried his M-16 with one hand and used the other to push branches aside.

Moments earlier he had seen the American aircraft divert its route. *The HPM weapon!* He smiled at Barguyo's effort.

If the Americans were still interested in the clearing, then the Vice-President was still here.

Five more yards. Another fifteen feet—half the distance for a first down. One-twentieth the length of a football field. Something that Bruce was used to running in less than a second.

Now the distance seemed insurmountable.

Bruce held Adleman up while leaning against the Vice-President. Like two dominoes, ready to collapse, they painfully made their way to the jungle, to cover.

Bruce pushed with all his strength . . . until he heard the unmistakable sound of a helicopter rotor.

Seconds later a dark object thundered overhead. Once over the clearing, it dropped below the top of the trees. *The Blackhawk!* Bruce's heart yammered in excitement. He quickly scanned the clearing, but still couldn't see Yolanda.

He turned and started limping for the helicopter, pulling Adleman along with him. The Blackhawk shot down to the ground in a combat landing.

Bruce skipped with his left leg while barely touching the ground with his right. Vice-President Adleman understood what was happening; he helped with a limping lope, and didn't cry out.

The helicopter whipped up a gust of wind, sending water flying. The sound of the engine filled the clearing. Someone scrambled out from the helicopter, crouching and running low to the ground. As he approached, Bruce could see the man's night-vision goggles.

Bruce recognized the approaching man Zaz. Zaz

took the Vice-President over his shoulder and yelled, "Let's move it!"

Bruce started after him, but without Adleman's support, he couldn't walk upright.

Zaz turned. "Come on!"

"I . . . can't." Bruce waved him on. "Get Adleman on board . . . I'll make it."

Bruce crawled toward the Blackhawk, pushing the M-16 ahead of him. He tried to stand, wobbled, then started skipping on one leg. He lightly touched down with his right foot, and had to hold back a yelp.

He tripped and fell forward.

Looking up, Bruce saw that Zaz had reached the Blackhawk and was pushing the Vice-President into the helicopter. Zaz turned and sprinted back for Bruce.

From the noise, Ceravant thought that a plane had landed in the clearing. He moved cautiously to the jungle's edge.

There, just visible against the black jungle, was a helicopter! Fifty yards away! The audacity of the Americans, to hide like vermin and then bring in a helicopter to spirit the Vice-President away!

The helicopter looked evil, like a huge bug that had zoomed out of the night to squat in the clearing. A side panel opened and someone sprinted from the craft.

Ceravant moved quickly to the south, remaining at the edge of the jungle. The Americans would be too concerned with their Vice-President to notice him. . . .

He brought up his rifle, took aim, and cracked off a shot.

Bruce had pushed up and started to straighten when Zaz suddenly went sprawling. "Hey!" The action surprised Bruce. Zaz wasn't more then ten yards away. Bruce crawled over to him. He was just about there when he heard a *zing* whiz past his ear. *Someone's shooting!*

Bruce flung himself out, then rolled to the right. A volley of bullets zippered the ground around him. Bruce swung the M-16 up and started firing into the jungle.

The Blackhawk's engines suddenly whined, rising in pitch. The wind increased as the helicopter rose from the ground.

Bruce waved the Blackhawk away. "Go on! Get him out of here!"

The Blackhawk rose to twenty feet, then slowly rotated. Bruce squinted; the side of the helicopter came into view. Sticking out of the side was a long-nosed minigun. A burst of flames came from the weapon.

The jungle erupted in a crash of sound as the twenty-millimeter rounds ripped through the foliage, again and again sweeping through the jungle.

Bruce crawled with his elbows over to Zaz. The young enlisted man bled from the mouth. His face was slack.

Bruce ran a hand over Zaz's body. He couldn't find the bullet wound. Nothing indicated where Zaz had been shot.

Bruce slapped the man to see if he was still alive. If the Blackhawk hurried, there would be time to get Zaz back to Clark, fly him straight to the hospital. . . .

The minigun stopped firing and Bruce jerked his head up. The Blackhawk's engine coughed as the helicopter listed suddenly to the left, over-corrected, then wobbled to the right. The Blackhawk just slipped from the sky.

It twisted until it was nearly sideways. The rotor hit the ground and the craft suddenly whipped around, thrown by the rotor's angular momentum.

The Blackhawk tumbled once, twice on the ground, bounced and started to fall apart. It didn't explode, but tiny flames flared up all around it. Some of the fires died immediately, but flickering flames cast shadows out on the ground.

Screams. A shriek, then moaning came from the Blackhawk.

Bruce crawled to the site, only fifty yards away. If the Blackhawk had rotated any more, it might have crashed right on top of him.

Bruce clawed at the ground.

The clearing fell silent. Bruce could hear the flames even from fifty yards away—and the sound of the diesel generator coming from the plantation once again.

He pushed everything out of his mind and concentrated on just one thing: reaching the Blackhawk.

He suddenly froze. Someone was moving, not too far away.

A figure crept out of the jungle and moved toward the crash. Rifle at ready, the person moved twenty yards to Bruce's left. Bruce tried to make himself flat against the ground. In the glow from the helicopter's fire, Bruce couldn't make out who it was.

Bruce pulled the M-16 carefully around. He brought the figure into his sight, then slowly squeezed the trigger. . . .

Nothing. Bruce silently cursed. The cartridge was empty.

He rolled over and fumbled in his vest, pulling out a cartridge. He tried to slip the extra bullets into the automatic rifle without being heard; when the mechanism *clicked* he stopped, holding his breath, but the person continued to creep forward.

Bruce brought the rifle around. When he had the person back in his sights, he slowly squeezed. . . .

Ceravant stopped. Moments before he had spotted the remnants of a bright yellow tarpaulin lying at the edge of the clearing. *Were all the Americans on the helicopter? Had they all been killed in the crash, or were more hiding? And if they were hiding, then why weren't they helping at the crash site?*

It didn't make sense to remain, to stay in the clearing—not with a rescue vehicle ready to whisk them away. Ceravant convinced himself that there were no others.

He walked toward the helicopter.

"Fox One, Fox One—are you there? Come in Fox One."

Catman tried to stretch out his body in the F-15 cockpit, tried to relive the stiffness. The moon lit up the clouds below them.

Skipper had failed to raise the helicopter. Contact had been abruptly broken when the Blackhawk landed for the pickup.

Vice-President Adleman was still down there, and Assassin had to be with him.

"Maddog, check coordinates loaded into the LANT-IRN. Come in from the south, and GIBs." Skipper was referring to the "Guys-in-the-Back" seat: "Sing out those checkpoints. It'll be tricky, but if you stay on the coordinates, you'll do fine. I don't want us splashed out on some mountaintop. I'll try to take out the HPM weapons on the first pass. Check in."

"Two."

Catman clicked his mike. "Three."

"All right. One's in hot. Off to the right."

Catman looked out the cockpit canopy. A mile in front of him, Skipper's F-15E banked to the right and disappeared into the clouds. Another minute and Catman would be doing the same—screaming in from thirty-seven thousand feet, popping out of the cloud layer at three hundred feet, and taking out a target he had never seen.

And the whole time, relying on Robin to keep him from pranging it into the ground.

All for the team.

Now he realized why he could never quit the Air Force and fly for the airlines, even at twice the pay.

Ceravant moved slowly through the jungle. Soon . . . soon!

Bruce squeezed the trigger. Was it Ceravant, that madman about whom Pompano had spoken so bitterly?

The shrieks of pain coming from the burning helicopter turned to sobs. There was only one voice. And whoever was moving toward the helicopter had to be going to finish off the survivor. As the person got closer to the helicopter, Bruce noticed the figure walking with a limp. Stocky, squat features . . . it reminded Bruce of . . . *Pompano*!

Bruce struggled to a sitting position. "Pompano— *Pompano*! It's me—Bruce!"

Pompano swung around, bringing his rifle barrel around with him.

"Bruce?" A faint voice came from behind him. Bruce turned—Yolanda stepped uncertainly from the jungle. "Bruce—you were not on the helicopter?"

"Yolanda—no!" Pompano waved her back into the foliage.

"Bruce!"

"Yolanda!" Pompano crouched and started toward the jungle; he looked around. "It is too dangerous!"

"Father . . ." She spoke to Pompano, but looked at Bruce.

Pompano hissed, "Yolanda!"

A shot rang out. Pompano whirled and dropped his rifle. He clutched at his arm. "Yolanda, get down!" He fell to his knees. Another shot . . .

Bruce swung his M-16 up and fired into the jungle. Yolanda threw herself onto the ground. Bruce fired over her.

Bullets peppered the area around Bruce.

Bruce shot off a few more rounds, fanning the jungle. Popping another cartridge into the M-16, he waited. The sniper was still out there.

Another moan from the helicopter. Bruce wasn't more than twenty yards away, but the sniper would surely try to stop him. He wet his lips. "Yolanda." His voice was hoarse. "Yolanda, don't answer. Stay where you are—I'm going to help your father."

Bruce crawled backward. He aimed the M-16 at the jungle, keeping cover on the sniper.

He gritted his teeth from the pain. Sweat trickled into his eyes, mixing with the grime and mud, causing him to blink. He wiped a hand across his face.

As he approached Pompano, the sobbing from the helicopter grew louder.

Bruce had to hurry. The sniper could take potshots at Bruce all day long unless Bruce drew him out of the jungle. That was the only way he would have a chance of stopping him.

Sweat ran down Barguyo's face. Moments earlier, bullets, hurled from unseen gargoyles in the clouds, had peppered the area around him. The bullets had spat up globs of mud as they struck the ground. He heard screams from his fellow Huks as they were hit from the burning metal raining from the sky.

But now the clearing was still from bullets, quiet. Except for a growing whine of jet noise, descending from the clouds.

Barguyo pressed his thumb against the HPM firing button. He pushed his head against the throbbing metal capacitor bank and wished that the invisible electromagnetic waves would take out the rest of the American force.

How well it had worked! Bringing down the Vice-President's plane, that helicopter in the field . . . If only the HPM weapon would hold out for this final onslaught of American attackers . . .

Barguyo drew in a breath and strained to keep the firing button depressed. The sound of an American fighter jet grew louder and louder. It must be making a run toward the plantation. Barguyo pushed up from the control panel and tried to look through the clouds. Nothing. The sound increased. He wet his lips.

Ceravant was nowhere to be seen. No other Huks were in sight. Had they deserted him? Had the remainder of the New People's Army left the plantation to escape through the jungle? The thought sent a surge of fear though his body. Was he all alone, left here with the injured?

The memory of Ceravant befriending him as a youngster raced through his mind. He had been all alone then, and Ceravant had taken him in. Could he now stay here to repay the debt he owed him? Certainly *Ceravant* was still around . . . ?

A high-pitched whine caused Barguyo to jerk his head up. He tried to cry out, but his larynx couldn't react fast enough to what he saw: A long, tubular missile was breaking through the clouds and racing straight for the HPM antenna. He couldn't make out any of the missile's features in the scant milliseconds left in his life. His final thoughts exploded in a mishmash of white light as the HPM weapon died with him.

Skipper watched the heads-up display, paying no attention to the swirling clouds outside the cockpit. As they drew closer, a popping sound grew in his earphones. The LANTIRN projected a rectangular target onto the display. The rectangle blinked furiously. Cougar yammered in the backseat, "Pull up, pull up! We're being jammed!"

Skipper kept on, oblivious of the warning. He focused on taking out the HPM weapon. He jabbed the bomb switch. "Maddog One, bombs away. Off to the right!"

A voice came instantly over the radio. "Maddog Two, in hot."

Pop pop pop pop! As Skipper pulled back on the

stick, the high-definition TV in the middle of the console exploded, sending glass flying into the heads-up display.

"Mayday, mayday!" Skipper still had hydraulics, but he couldn't tell where he was going. *Keep it cool, don't panic!* "Cougar—what do you read?" No answer. "Cougar? Cougar?!" He flipped to the Guard frequency and fought to keep the fighter level, although without any instruments he couldn't tell up from down. "Mayday, Mayday! Maddog One . . ."

A noise caught Bruce's attention—a piercing whine that started to rocket up through the frequencies. Then a flash—and the plantation exploding in a fireball. A burst of flames rolled over the house, igniting the wood frame. The sound of a jet thundering overhead caused him to turn, but he couldn't see anything in the clouds.

Seconds later there came the dull thud of something *huge* hitting the ground, ripping through the jungle—and the subsequent shock of an explosion. Bruce didn't wait to guess what had happened, who in Maddog had just bought the farm.

He slowly positioned his body, then rolled to the helicopter. He tried to keep the plantation in view as a reference point as he rolled, around and round. . . .

Shots hit the mud around him. Bruce stopped rolling and swung his M-16 up.

The sniper stood at the edge of the clearing, aiming at Bruce.

Ceravant brought up his rifle. *Pompano, or the American*? He knew that Pompano had the stamina to survive, but this American needed to be taken care of. He pulled off a round of shots.

Bruce squeezed the trigger as hard as he could, trying to coax more energy into the bullets. He fanned the area, spraying metal into the jungle.

A second bomb hit the plantation, shooting debris and burning wood high into the air. Bruce allowed the brilliant flames from the explosion to guide him as he covered the jungle with round after round of bullets. When his weapon ran out of ammunition, he quickly inserted another cartridge.

He brought the M-16 up. . . .

The first bullet ripped through Ceravant, stunning him. *It did not even hurt!* He *was* a god, indestructible, able to accomplish anything he pleased. . . .

Seven other bullets spun him around, causing him to fling out his rifle. His vision blurred; vomit crawled up his throat. The last thing he saw was Yolanda's body, her silhouette against the burning plantation house. . . .

By the light of the fire Bruce could make out a figure sprawled facedown in the mud, just inside the clearing. A rifle lay by his side.

The sound of moaning caught Bruce's attention. He dragged his M-16, but as he approached the helicopter set the rifle down. "Mr. Adleman? Gould . . . Head?"

No answer. He had to get in.

Bruce pushed up and tried to straighten. Flames still flickered inside the Blackhawk. He could use the helicopter's structure to support himself when he entered. He had started to hop in when Pompano's voice stopped him.

"Bruce."

Bruce turned. Pompano's face was bloodied and his left arm hung limp by his side. But in his right hand he held the pistol given to him by the First Special Operations Squadron—the thirty-eight with a silencer.

Pompano motioned with the gun. "Bruce . . . leave the Vice-President alone."

"What?"

"Move away."

Bruce reached out and placed a hand on the Black-hawk's fuselage. It was not hot to the touch, so he supported himself. "Pompano . . . we're through. . . ."

The roar of a jet rolled over the clearing. A volley of bullets from the strafing fighter's cannon tore into the house and jungle, taking out the rest of the vehicles that had been untouched. The jet engines echoed throughout the area, finally dying with deep reverberations.

Bruce glanced at the chopper. "Pompano—the helicopter could explode! We've got to get him out of here!" Pompano simply clicked back the trigger. "Pompano! For God's sake, why? After all this . . . *why*?!"

The Filipino spoke softly. "I only went with you to save my daughter. She is safe."

"But the Vice-President!"

"No—he is your *President* now. And what do you think your Chief Executive will do about the Philippines when he takes office? Be kind to them and pull your bases out, because he was mistreated?" Pompano shook his head. "I assure you, if Adleman lives, the bases will stay. This whole event will only convince him of the necessity of keeping an American presence."

"What the hell are you talking about? Why did you help rescue him?"

"I have already told you—to save my daughter." Pompano's eyes grew misty.

"But to let Adleman die . . ."

". . . would surely convince most Americans, your *public*, that the Philippines are not worth their while, not worth the billions they are spending here. For if your President is not safe here, then no other American would be safe."

Bruce stared. He drew in a breath. "I can't allow you—"

"Move away from the helicopter."

Yolanda's voice interrupted them. "Father."

Pompano kept the pistol trained on Bruce. "Yolanda—get back."

"No, father." Bruce swung his eyes to where she stood. She held a rifle, the one the sniper had used, and it was pointed at Pompano. Her father. "Father—don't make me use this."

"Yolanda—you do not know what you are doing!"

"Yes I do. Leave Bruce alone."

Pompano hesitated. "Little one . . . Think of the future of your land, your people."

"I *am*, father. This . . . this is a different world now. We cannot go back to the old ways. I have seen this Vice-President suffer. He tried to make them stop *using* me. *My* people raped me . . . not the Americans."

Pompano took a step backward. "Yolanda, little one. You don't know what this will do to us. The chance this gives us . . ."

"Put down the gun, Father."

"I cannot. . . . This is my life."

Yolanda's voice wavered. "Father?"

They stared at each other. Bruce tested his leg. If he'd been in better shape he'd have leapt at the old man, tried to take away the gun.

Pompano whispered. "I can't, Yolanda." He turned back to Bruce and raised the gun slightly.

Yolanda screamed. "No!" Her rifle wavered.

Bruce leaned to the left, onto his good leg. . . .

He fell to the ground and rolled to the side, away from the helicopter. Three shots rang out. A bullet tore into Bruce's arm. It felt like someone had taken a hot needle and jabbed it straight through his flesh. Another bullet whizzed by his head, spraying mud.

He grabbed his arm and rolled over, expecting to be finished off.

Nothing.

Bruce peered up. Yolanda stood with her hands over her mouth. Pompano grimaced. Bent over, he gripped his leg where Yolanda had shot him.

Bruce started to push up. *Yow!* Between the arm and his right ankle, he was falling apart.

He hobbled into the helicopter, stepping over the bottom edge of the hatch.

Peering around the edge of the cockpit, he saw Gould and Head strapped into their seats, night-vision goggles in place. A line of blood ran from Head's mouth.

A moan came from the back.

Bruce tried pulling himself into the craft, but couldn't make it with one arm. He hopped around to the back and looked in. . . .

Crumpled up against the corner, one of the gunners and Vice-President Adleman were pushed under the troop seat that ran down the length of the back. Bruce reached in and grabbed Adleman's arm. The Vice-President groaned.

It took Yolanda's help, but ten minutes later, Gould and Adleman were lying at the edge of the jungle. Bruce pulled Pompano away from the others. All three were still alive.

They left the other bodies by the helicopter.

Bruce held Yolanda with his left arm. They sat, quietly watching the Blackhawk burn. They had sat for only a few moments before the helicopter exploded, sending a thick fireball rolling up into the air.

A minute later, a fleet of eight HH-3 Jolly Green Giants swooped down into the clearing. A cadre of Navy SEALS thundered out of the helicopters and fanned out into the clearing.

They found Bruce and Yolanda sitting mute, and holding hands.

POSTLUDE

0225 Monday, 3 December

Enroute to Travis AFB, CA

Zero-dark early.

It was the middle of the night, but Bruce was wide awake. The giant C-5 aircraft felt motionless as it flew over the Pacific Ocean. The lights in the passenger chamber were down low, and most of the people around him slept.

He pulled out the telegram for the hundredth time and read over the twixt, an electronically transmitted message:

CAPTAIN BRUCE STEELE
3rd TFS/3rd TFW/13th AF
CLARK AFB PI

1. SUBJECT APPOINTED SPECIAL ASSIS-
TANT TO THE AIR ATTACHÉ, REPUB-
LIC OF THE PHILIPPINES. PERMANENT
CHANGE OF STATION TO QUEZON
CITY, P. I. AUTHORIZED.

2. IMMEDIATE ASSIGNMENT AUTHOR-
IZED WITH ONE (1) MONTH LEAVE EN
ROUTE BEFORE REPORT DATE OF NOT-
LATER-THAN 1 JANUARY.

MILITARY PERSONNEL COMMAND

Quezon City! Yolanda had written several times since she had left for school, some three months before. She had said her father was still bitter, but improving. Now he would be in the same city. . . .

It had taken her months to gain the courage to speak to him again. She had sought professional help, and Bruce hadn't wanted to push the relationship, to force her to move too fast. They both had a lot to sort out, but things were definitely looking up.

Bruce wasn't naive enough to think the assignment was purely out of Military Personnel Command's benevolent nature; he saw President Adleman's hand in his assignment. A phone call three weeks before from the President had ended with the statement: "You can have any assignment you want."

The political-social circle would call for some adjustment—dinners, formal uniforms, hob-knobbing with the elite.

No more throwing beer bottles, that's for sure.

Catman had had a fit, thinking Bruce could get the whole Flight assigned to the new Advanced Tactical Fighter undergoing testing at Edwards; all of them but Skipper and Cougar, that is.

Bruce drew in a breath. *Skipper, Cougar, Head, Zaz, and the two helicopter gunners.* The Americans were lucky to get off with only six casualties. No telling how many more would have died if Skipper hadn't taken out the HPM weapon.

Bruce tried to push those memories from his mind.

One month leave. Charlie and Nanette were picking him up at Travis AFB in northern California. Palo Alto was only a three-hour drive. He looked forward to catching up with Charlie. Too bad he'd had to take that medical discharge, but Nanette's letters indicated that his condition was improving. More importantly, he loved Stanford, even if he only had fifteen percent of his vision back.

And then on to Texas, one last trip to see his mom. And Dad.

His father had come by the hospital on Clark right after he was pulled out of the jungle. Bruce didn't remember much of the meeting. He was too doped up at the time.

A letter from his mother six weeks later informed him that his father was retiring, too shook up to remain in the Navy. The loss of one son had been bad enough, she had written—almost losing another had made his father want to settle down.

Bruce didn't look forward to the visit, but he promised himself that he would at least try to be civil.

One month.

He looked forward to recharging, getting some rest.

He folded the twixt and shoved it in his top pocket.

It was the first time in, what—*years?*—that he hadn't worn the old green bag. He'd been through a lot in that suit.

It was going to take some getting used to.

But, above all, he would miss the flying. Taking off with Simone in the front seat, blasting away with afterburners, straight up.

Or screaming down from five thousand feet and laying hot, killing metal onto targets; pulling back up, grunting to keep conscious as the gee-suit kicked in.

Or just flying at night above the clouds in his Strike Eagle, watching the moonlight reflect off the water through a hole in the cloud layer. . . .

The road not taken.

The Air Attaché job was too important to turn down; it opened too many doors for him to walk away from them. And with Yolanda there, it could only make things better.

But he always knew what he would come back to . . . what he was the very best at doing . . . the best in the world.

And what he loved more than anything else on earth.

About the Author

DOUG BEASON is a Major in the United States Air Force and has lived in such places as California, Canada, Okinawa and the Philippine Islands. A graduate of the United States Air Force Academy, he holds a Ph.D. in Physics and is currently the Deputy Director of Advanced Weapons and Survivability at the Phillips Laboratory, Kirtland AFB, New Mexico. He recently served on a Presidential Commission directing NASA on how to get back to the Moon and explore Mars. He is also an accomplished short-story author in addition to his several novels.

Author's Note

This book is based on current research, as well as my memories while I was in the Philippines as a high school student (1968—1970) . . . selectively updated to reflect *some* of the changes that have occurred. Places such as the old Officer's Club and Rathskeller may have changed—but certainly not the men and women who make up the Philippine experience.

There's an epidemic with 27 million victims. And no visible symptoms.

It's an epidemic of people who can't read.

Believe it or not, 27 million Americans are functionally illiterate, about one adult in five.

The solution to this problem is you... when you join the fight against illiteracy. So call the Coalition for Literacy at toll-free **1-800-228-8813** and volunteer.

Volunteer Against Illiteracy. The only degree you need is a degree of caring.